Runeheart

ᚱ

By Gino C. R. Marchetti, II

The author welcomes your thoughts and comments:
runeheartnovel@gmail.com

The cover artist may be contacted at the following:
danart.artstation.com

eBook ISBN-13: 979-8-9868927-0-2
Paperback ISBN-13: 979-8-9868927-1-9
Hardcover ISBN-13: 979-8-9868927-2-6
Hardcover with Jacket ISBN-13: 979-8-9868927-3-3

Dedication

R

For everyone who longs to be free.

R

οὐ γὰρ ὃ θέλω ποιῶ ἀγαθόν, ἀλλὰ ὃ οὐ θέλω κακὸν τοῦτο πράσσω. ... Εὑρίσκω ἄρα τὸν νόμον τῷ θέλοντι ἐμοὶ ποιεῖν τὸ καλὸν ὅτι ἐμοὶ τὸ κακὸν παράκειται· ... ταλαίπωρος ἐγὼ ἄνθρωπος· τίς με ῥύσεται ἐκ τοῦ σώματος τοῦ θανάτου τούτου;

R

Maximum negotium tecum habes; tu tibi molestus es. Quid velis nescis; melius probas honesta quam sequeris; vides, ubi sit posita felicitas, sed ad illam pervenire non audes.

RRR

Special Thanks

R

I owe my thanks to many.

First, to my early readers for their hands-on work with this novel: Dad, James, and Kelsey. Your feedback helped to make the story better, and your interest helped to encourage me in the (often arduous and tedious) process of editing.

Of course, I must also thank my family, especially my parents, Linda and Gino, and my friends for their encouragement, support, and bearing with my ramblings about writing—I love you guys.

Thanks are also due to my undergraduate writing instructor and *paisan*, Angelo Volpe, who taught me that, though "life is short, and writing, long," it is worth the struggle. Volpe, I owe you a Snickers ...

Finally, I must also thank you, dear reader, for taking the time to read my debut novel. I hope you enjoy *Runeheart*.

RRR

Chapter I

Purify me, O Kinsmen Redeemers, O Holy Two!
Purge me of my hidden fault, for ye alone have
plumbed my depths and know how deeply my
iniquities run. Heal the mortal wounds which ye
have inflicted in righteousness, and bear ye away
my disgraces. I pray ye, teach me wisdom in the
secret heart, where once only darkness dwelt, that
all may see and rejoice in you unto the ages of ages.
— From *Carmina Diva, Pars LI*

R

I knelt at the teakwood prie-dieu, which stood before the east-facing altar in the corner of my sitting room, and clasped my tremulous hands in prayer. Two candles—one was brown and decorated with a golden, majuscule *A*, and the other white with a similar majuscule *L*—stood at the horns of the altar. Both burned in their candlesticks, wax rivulets dripping onto the altar's wooden mensa.

Between the candles, two gilded icons scattered dancing candlelight upon my darkened face. I squinted, for my eyes had grown accustomed to darkness, but despite their blinding resplendence, I forced my teary eyes to gaze upon the icons of the Two Holies. The first bore the radiant image of a wolf, Holy Luváli, whose fur gleamed silver and whose eyes were golden suns. Under his chin and leaning against his forepaws was an illuminated tome decorated with malachite vines and leaves. Though I made my eyes hold the divine wolf's gaze, his eyes burned into my soul and set my heart ablaze with fear—fear of his fiery wrath against what I was and what my flesh longed for.

As the wolf's wrath pierced me, I shifted my gaze to the second icon. This one was of a man, Blessed Andar, dressed in radiant silver, who held his own tome. Upon it, a white-gold dove held a malachite olive branch in its beak, yet I gazed upon Andar's face instead. I flitted between his brazen eyes—one narrowed to bear witness against sin, the other full of sorrow for what surely awaited me—but I found no rest there.

Unable to bear the gazes of the Two, I looked to the censer between these icons. From its vented top, wisps of fragrant smoke curled, dancing as they floated into my lofted study and the ceiling's shadowy vault. Those nebulous trails of smoke were my prayers vanishing into Oblivion.

I inhaled the spicy incense, closing my eyes to block out the reflected light of the Two. That scent, this entire ritual, had once been a balm for my troubled mind. Now it did nothing to soothe me, and I poured forth tears in sorrow.

I ceased mouthing the "Prayer of the Penitent" and turned the pages of the leather-bound penitential, which the vicar at Melbù had ordered me to recite, with trembling hands. An enormous scarlet *T* overshadowed every other handwritten word below. It spelled *Temptation*. A coal-black, impish figure, with no nose and embers for eyes, clung to the letter's stem and clawed his way toward the top. Another devilish figure, astride a flaming hellhound, prowled atop the letter, and the hound howled at a bloody moon and unholy black star, which shed its dark light upon the debaucheries below.

In the bottom margin of the page were lurid images of men, women, he-wolves, and she-wolves engaged in a demonic orgy. They poured goblets of wine into each other's mouths, the wolves lapping up what spilled onto the ground. All danced around a fire that threw off brownish-red flames, and dark, smoky phantoms flew into the darkness and hovered over the drunken revelers.

Everywhere, women had collapsed with their breasts and legs exposed. He-wolves and men drew nigh, eyes burning with unnatural lust. Between the fallen women, drunken she-wolves wobbled and presented themselves to the debauched he-wolves and naked men.

On the facing page, women and she-wolves, with distended bellies, tore their hair, clawed their faces, and howled. The men and he-wolves, eyes filled with unsatiated lust, gazed on the women whom they had impregnated. Elsewhere, women and she-wolves gave birth as blood poured and monsters emerged from between their legs. The men and he-wolves, seeing what they begot, slew themselves and their concubines with sword and claw. At the top of the page, the devilish rider and his demonic lupine steed spied the sight below and cackled.

I pried my eyes from the horrid scene and read, *"Temptation: All must avoid stirring up temptation within themselves, for to stir up such is to walk willfully into sin. To sin through willfulness and to entertain temptation is to put one's soul at risk of eternal fire. Yea, one must hate sin entirely, but especially those sins which are most shameful: idolatry, sorcery, divination, fornication, and lusts for alien flesh."*

My eyes flitted everywhere—the illuminated manuscript, the altar, the icons of the Dead Gods—but they found no place of rest. But, why should a wicked man expect to rest among the holy? No, but I rested my eyes upon my trembling hands, which lay palms up on my thighs as I knelt in unholy terror.

I clenched my eyes and fists shut. My heart raced. I dug my nails into the callused flesh of my palms. Blood flowed. A groan escaped my clenched lips. The blood was hot, but it could not expel the bone-deep chill from my limbs.

Sweat beaded on my forehead, nose, and bearded upper lip, and great drops fell onto my upturned palms. They stung my wounds.

I rocked forward on the prie-dieu, running my nails across the clawed-out furrows in the otherwise immaculate kneeler's boards. I leaned over the altar, my bloody hands folded once more. The blood—my blood—dripped upon it. A profane offering, but an offering, nonetheless. Perhaps they would hear me now ...

The prie-dieu shook in time with my body. The candles, too, shook.

I bowed my head against my bloody hands. I prayed, but the fire in my soul grew hotter while I grew all the colder.

My blood dripped.

Still, the Two were silent.

R

"Ma," the boy called, "we're at the road's end. Now's the fork they said to look for." The wind howled, and the boy pulled the fur-lined hood of his cloak tighter around his face. "Ma?"

A woman called from the rear wagon, "Do you see a signpost, Aros?"

"Maybe … With this snow flyin', I canna say for sure." He pulled back on the reins, and the horses stopped. "Arve, go see if there's a sign."

The younger boy on his right grunted, mumbling about the cold.

"C'mon, Arve; Da is countin' on us to—"

Arve huffed and jumped down. His boots sank into the ever-rising snow with a crunch, the frozen crust breaking under his weight. The boy trudged on, patting the horses as he passed. His outline blurred in the whirling snow.

"Aros?" his mother called.

"Arve's lookin', Ma."

An eternity passed while the biting wind stung him. He licked his lips and hissed as they cracked. Metallic-tasting blood filled his mouth, and though he sucked his lips, the pain did not die. He cleared his throat rhythmically and rubbed a gloved hand against his thigh.

"Oh, Andar, please let us be close to somewhere … anywhere. Please …" He lifted his gloved hand and made the Sign of the Two—an inverted V that touched from the inner corner of one brow to the other, from the vertex of which a vertical line ascended—upon his forehead to seal his prayers. He put his hand back to the reins as snow crunched nearby.

For not but a moment, he thought it was Arve, but the sound had come from his own side of the cart.

One of the horses nickered and stamped its hooves. The panic was infectious as a second horse stamped at the snow, pulling on the reins, followed by a third.

"Whoa. Easy now. 'Tis nothin'. Just a deer ..."

A flash of gray shot by on his left.

"Must be the snow and wind." He heard a soft *crack* on his right. "Arve?" He peered forward to see if it was him.

Another crack sounded on his right, and then on his left again. He shot his hand to the belt knife laid across his lap. With his numb, gloved fingers, he fumbled with the handle, unable to draw the blade.

All the horses danced now. He pulled back harder on the reins.

"Brother? Hurry, brother. I—"

Wolves howled in the woods nearby. Aros froze.

The horses reared and jerked, Aros fighting to rein them in.

The sound of crushing snow returned. Boots? Paws? Whatever it was, it drew nearer.

"Arve?" He saw a form huddled low to the ground in front of the cart. A man? A wolf?

"Aros, there's ... Out there, there's ..." Arve leapt aboard and grew silent. Great puffs of steam poured from his mouth and nose. "Wolves."

"Was there a sign? What did it say? C'mon, Arve; I want to get out of here."

The younger brother looked at the elder, fear plain in his eyes. "Uh, 'tis—"

The wolves howled again.

"Arve!"

"'Tis, uh ... 'Tis a lodge in a mile, to the left. To the right, in ten miles, a-a town. Melbù or somethin'."

Aros snapped the reins and steered left. "Ma, there's a lodge only a mile away. We'll ne'er make the trip if we head to the town, no with Da as he is. The horses'll no be able to go much farther neither."

His mother did not respond, but he made out the distinct crack of reins. *Oh, Andar, let there be room ...*

R

A scratch at the door brought my prayers to an end. Dazed, I glanced over my shoulder, my brow smeared in blood. I raised my eyes to the heavens. Was this the way the Two would deliver me? Had they received my sacrifice? Or, would I fall away once more?

For now, this shall be my escape.

I unlatched the front door, and morning sunlight, diffused by the storm clouds, illumined my darkness. Along with the light, four great beasts rushed past. The snow and chill also rushed in but could not cool the burning within my breast.

Raynor perked his ears and stared at me with his single, glowing yellow eye—he had lost the other as a pup when he had stuck his snout in a badger's den. He greeted me with a bark from near the stone hearth, which jutted out into the sitting area, and he stretched his lithe body while letting out a high-pitched yawn as he curled up in his usual place on the bearskin rug. Two of the other wolves, Ragnar and Ada, each had a hunk of meat from some unidentifiable animal in their maws as they sat by the larder door. Ever obedient, they entered with their prizes only after I acknowledged them. The final wolf, after she had made her obeisance at the altar, sat at my side.

"Freya." I scented a wolf's greeting as I spoke. Her tail beat the floor as she gazed up at me, her tongue hanging out as she panted. I caressed her head and scratched behind her ears, but I also coated her fur with my blood. The bloody gouges in my palms sullied everything I touched.

Freya nudged my left leg and looked at me with large, gold-brown eyes. She followed at my heels while I searched for a cloth with which to bind my hands, and only after did I scratch her ears again.

Her tail bounced, and she scented contentment with both the attention I showed her and with the pack's hunt. She circled my legs and wedged her head between them so I would scratch her whole body. Her tail beat my legs as she stood under me, and I scented my contentment to have the pack with me. She barked and licked my hands and wrists, unbothered by the blood upon them. The warmth of her body, so natural in comparison to the hellish warmth of mine, comforted me.

When she settled down, I rekindled the fire and set a kettle of water, which hung from a peg on the wooden mantlepiece, to boil. I reached for one of the many pipes arrayed on the pipe rack upon the mantle, but my bandaged hand hovered over it. With my head hung low, I stared at the bandage and leaned my elbows against the mantle. I gripped the braid of hair at the nape of my neck with both hands.

A penitent ought not indulge in pleasures, but I could not give even this little thing up. I hated myself for this simple thing, these little pleasures, which I could not give up for my soul's salvation.

You're weak ...

Freya sidled up by my side. I placed my hand upon her head, letting my own continue to hang.

"I'm in a bad way, friend."

She whined, her sympathetic eyes shining, but I refused to engage her. Rather, I snatched up my pipe, threw myself into one of the three chairs before the blazing fire, and smoked furiously, ignoring the pipe's bite.

Freya set her exceptionally gray head on my knee—her custom when I was troubled—but I still paid her no mind. Instead, I gazed upon the swirling, intertwined vines carved into the mantle. I traced them with my eyes, never coming to an end or a beginning, and though they were beautiful, they unsettled my mind, which would not gaze upon the vines as a whole, but only in part.

I slid forward in the chair and stretched out my long legs before the fire. I closed my eyes and sighed, but my mind's eye continued to wander ceaselessly over the images of tangled vines.

As I contemplated the maze of vines, Freya pushed her face toward mine. She breathed upon my face, and I looked down to find her staring at me. I rolled my eyes before scratching her chin with my free hand, while I held my pipe to my lips with the other. I puffed on the pipe, and a great cloud enveloped me as I stared into the inferno before me.

"I'm so tired, Freya."

The she-wolf wedged her head under my free hand, but I pulled away. Disappointed, she sprung up, her front paws landing on my inner thigh. I grunted and instinctively shot out both my hands to guard that singular part of me my otherwise loving pack cared little to protect.

Burning tobacco fell from my pipe onto my hands. I leapt from the chair, and Freya jumped, also, shaking tobacco and dottle from her fur. I stamped the smoldering tobacco and cursed, "Damn dog."

Freya hung her head, ears flat, and she backed away with a whine. She scented sadness and, more bothersome to my conscience, fear.

Sitting back in my chair, I covered my face with my bandaged hand. "I'm sorry, Freya. I shouldn't have called you that." I set the pipe down and gestured for her to come.

Though reluctant, she approached with her tail tucked and her body low to the ground.

"I avoid one sin only to commit another, and that against the ones I love." I knelt upon the hardwood floor and nuzzled her head. "Forgive me."

She licked me and barked. As if a war-horn had sounded, the other wolves charged. They yanked on my heavy linen pants and linen tunic sleeves with their teeth, careful not to tear them, and pulled me to the ground. Though I stifled my laughter—I had allowed myself too much luxury already—I let them pull me down. When a sloppy tongue found its way into my ear, however, my resolve broke.

The wolves nipped at my thick, well-oiled beard and pulled on my bound hair. The dark-brown braids, which were streaked with patches of the lightest gray, flowed across my temples to the loose knot behind my head. This came undone, and my hair spread wildly about me while I lay on the floor.

I rolled onto my back in submission, and one of my packmates claimed his victory by pouncing on my gut. I gasped and covered my eyes with my forearm, trying in vain to stop the flurry of slobbering tongues that lapped at me. Thus we played until the kettle whistled louder than our barking, growling, and laughter. Only then did they stop long enough for me to free myself.

Fending off Raynor's last attempts to pull me down, I took the pot, filled a cup with loose tea, and poured the boiling water. Tea in hand, I relit my pipe and puffed away between sips. From my chair, I smiled at my pack huddled before the fire. "Thank you, friends."

A noise somewhere between a growl and a bark rumbled in Raynor's throat. He blinked once at me, scenting contentedness—the earthy smell of a warm den filled with packmates. He then fell asleep.

I took another sip of tea, one more toke on my pipe, and set both down. I shut my eyes and fell asleep, scenting contentedness, too.

RRR

Chapter II

*Look mercifully upon the sojourner and wanderer,
for such are ye in this world.*
— *Evangelium Andaris, Caput XXIII*

R

I woke to the sound of Ragnar growling at the door, and he bared his teeth with his ears and tail straight back. Had anyone entered, he would have torn them apart.

Behind him, Ada and Raynor waited, ready to fight, though not growling like their leader. Only matronly Freya, who nudged my slouching frame with her nose, remained unperturbed.

"I'm up, Freya." I stretched and yawned. "What has you so on edge?" I sniffed the air but smelled only smoke from the fire and the musky scent of fearsome anger held at bay.

Ragnar scented back a burst of garbled scent-images, *"Outside. Invaders. Strangers. Noises—horses, people. Danger."* The last scent-image was neither fearful nor trusting, but a statement of fact.

Unsure what he meant, I took the wood axe that was ever by the door. It had been a long time since I had wielded any tool as a weapon, and though I hated to admit it, having the axe in hand comforted me.

I ran my thumb across the cold, smooth wood, and a sudden wave of nausea and—anxiety? adrenaline? ecstasy … aye, timeless yet particular ecstasy—overtook me.

The cries of men and clashing blades resounded. Horses screamed, struck by arrows, and grown men shouted and cried. I was on a battlefield once more. My vision ran red. My heart raced. My mind was on bloodshed.

I stared down a man in full plate armor. I bore no weapons, but he trembled before me. I was on top of him. Someone screamed, but I knew not who. And blood. A fountain of blood shot forth as I ripped his throat out with my teeth. I turned my face to the sky—

A pounding on the door brought me back. The wolves backed away, knowing what kind of berserker I could become.

I inhaled the smoky, dry air of my home to ground myself further. At the threshold, I gripped the axe with white knuckles and instinctively traced the faded red tattoo on my right wrist with my other hand. *No, it has nothing to do with that. Those days are long behind me.*

The pounding continued. "M'lord, m'lord, have mercy. Let your servants in, or we shall die." The woman's voice was thick with the clipped, tonal ring of a westerner.

At the sound of the woman's voice, Raynor bounded forward. He bowed on his forepaws to invite a chase, and his tail quivered. *"People. Many. Small and large. Horses."* He cocked his head, and his tail ceased to wag. He whined, *"Fearful ... dying."*

What are the Two placing before me?

I narrowed my eyes and tilted my head as I listened to Raynor, but the one-eyed wolf added nothing else. Still unsure, I leaned toward the door.

"Dear woman, do you come as a friend?"

"Aye, m'lord, we mean you and yours well, but we come to you as less than friends. I, m'lord, am your servant, as are my own. Please, we are desperate to find shelter, e'en if only in your stable, so we can weather this storm, which grows worse by the minute. But if you do no receive us, m'lord, my children shall perish, as will my husband, who is ill."

I recalled what Raynor had scented—little ones and great ones, death and fear. I knew she told the truth, yet I pressed her, "What proof do you have of what you say? It's dangerous to take in strangers."

"Aye, m'lord, but do you no hear the cry of my wee daughter?"

A baby, who had been silent a moment before, wailed.

A pang of guilt overcame me—I had sinned to ask for such a proof—and duty prevailed. "Dear woman, I will let you and yours in."

Though the wolves relaxed when they heard the voices of the people, I scented for them to stay back in utter silence. "*Men. Hatred. Wolves.*" These three images coalesced into one of chaos, one which the wolves knew well.

When I looked at the wolves, I also spotted the penitential lying open upon the altar. Its gruesome illuminations shimmered in the firelight, and I immediately regretted my hospitality.

The woman called again, "M'lord, are you there?"

"Give me but a moment." I rushed to close the book and hid it among the other prayer books stacked under the altar. Nobody could know the truth about me. Even I could barely face it.

As I opened the door, violent winds pelted my face and arms with snow. My eyes watered, and I let my unexpected guests pass. First, two little boys tramped in, holding the hands of a young woman, whose blonde hair slipped from under her hooded cloak and over her shoulders in two long braids. The two boys stamped their feet with exaggerated force and shook off the snow covering them. Their hoods bounced back to reveal they were identical towheaded twins, not more than four years old.

Two more boys—slightly older by the look of them—held the hands of yet another young woman. Her hair—auburn, unlike the other's—also flowed from under her cloak's hood and over one shoulder in a long braid. She struggled to hold the boys' hands as they fought to break free and run to the fireside. These boys flung their hoods back as they broke away, revealing heads of gold and flame.

After these, another young child followed. Judging by size alone, this one was undoubtedly the oldest of the five little children, and in this child's arms was a doll held close to her chest. What I first imagined was a doll began to wail, however, and the girl—it was clear she was a girl, for no boy would care so tenderly for a baby—cooed and rocked the babe in her arms. She, too, proceeded to the fire and settled in among her siblings.

After so many children, three men entered, though only two were on their feet. The younger two men dragged the limp body of the third between them, his arms draped over their shoulders, and they lay him near the fire on the bearskin rug where I had played with my pack. At his side, the young men sat huddled together with the others.

Seeing so many, I regretted my pity anew.

A woman, nearly as tall as I, lowered her head as she crossed the threshold and shut the door behind herself. She pulled her hood back, and curly, unbraided locks of gold fell freely about her shoulders. She fell to her knees at my feet. With both arms, she embraced my knees, and I nearly fell backward.

"M'lord, Andar and Luváli bless thee. We pray thee, receive us as thy servants." She touched her forehead to my calfskin slippers. All the while, she kept her arms wrapped around my knees, her body contorted in supplication. "Send thy servants no away, but grant us those things needful, for we here place our lives, our own and those of our kin, before thee. Have mercy, O lord."

I looked upon this suppliant stranger who had placed her family's future into my hands with this invocation. How deep a desperation she must have known to have invoked this rite.

My gut twisted. There could be no rejecting them now. If I did, I truly would be damned—to reject a suppliant was to reject the Two. Aye, the Suppliant's Plea ... the Writings warned it was no trifle. Wasn't it just like the Two, though, to warn about trifling with this plea while they sent their beloved suppliants to the door of a monster like me?

But, for all my misgivings, I could not close my heart to this woman. Her persistence in hanging upon me, though my answer was too long in coming, shamed me. It convicted me of my faithlessness and repented me, too.

I sighed and raised my eyes toward the shadowy vault where the incense of my prayers had ascended. *Fine ...*

I placed my hands upon her head and spoke the sacred reply, "Arise, dear woman, I receive thee." Yet, to the oath, I added, "But not as servants do I receive thee and thine, dear woman. Ye are guests and friends, if ye mean me and mine no harm. I am Rune Corinsson, who shall from this time on be a host and friend to thee and thine, and my posterity and thine alike shall share in this inviolable bond until Andar and Luváli, The Sacred Two, consummate the age."

She looked up at me with pleading, bloodshot eyes and refused to release my legs. My heart ached and burned within me.

"Oh, Lord Corinsson, we owe you our lives." She touched her forehead to my feet once more.

"You shall call me Rune—I am no lord."

She inclined her head, rising at last.

"Now, as for your horses, send—"

"Lor—Master Rune"—the woman's deep blue eyes widened—"how did you know we had horses?"

I cursed myself for my carelessness and said, "How else could you have come here? You could not have come on foot, not with children and your sick man."

"Of course, Master Rune, I suppose to one such as yourself 'twould be obvious."

I grunted and shrugged. "Whatever the case, have your young men stable the horses around the back. There are plenty of stalls."

"Aye, Master—"

"And one more point. I am neither lord *nor* master; only Rune."

The woman bowed at the waist, her hair nearly sweeping the floor. "Aye, sir. Howe'er, I must be beggin' your pardon. Though you welcome us as guests, and e'en friends—which is beyond what we may have hoped—'twould be a sin for us to call you less."

I frowned. "Is your conscience truly so bound?"

" 'Tis, Master Rune." She bowed again, even more deeply than before.

I waved my hand, and the woman rose, back straight but eyes lowered.

"Then let it be. Only have your sons fetch those poor horses from that icy hell."

She nodded. "Aros, Arve."

The two young men, who had dragged their father inside, stared into a nothingness far beyond their mother.

"Our host wants you to fetch the horses. He's a stable for them."

The boys drifted toward us like wraiths, devoid of life and hope.

"Ma," one said, "how'll we know where to brin' 'em?" The young man, his eyes unfocused, scarcely noticed me. His face, though partly shadowed by his hood, was clearly frostbitten and raw.

Something was wrong with the lad … It wasn't his poor complexion, nor did he share my nature—none of them did—but he was full of something that made me … uneasy. It was not fear, nor disgust, nor anything like what I felt toward him. It was something else …

His mother's voice brought me back to reality. "Master Rune'll tell you, Aros." She gestured at me with an open hand. "He is"—she bowed yet again—"our host and has graciously welcomed us."

Aros torpidly imitated his mother's bow. His darkened, sunken face, poor posture, and slight frame made him look almost like my former fellow slaves. But no, that wasn't what drew my attention to him either. Besides, that was something

I scarcely wished to think about, anyway. That had all been a long time ago …

I stiffened when I realized I, too, stared into nothingness like him.

I blinked the confusion away and nodded curtly. "You can find the stable behind the house. Even in this blizzard, you'll make it out."

The other boy, Arve, who also appeared exhausted, though slightly less distant, spoke, "But what if we"—the boy's voice cracked, betraying his youth—"still canna find it?"

"Well, lad—Arve—I'll send Raynor with you." Just behind Arve sat the four wolves.

Raynor's ears perked and swiveled toward me. His tail beat the floor.

"He'll lead you safely."

Arve narrowed his green eyes. "Who's Raynor? Your so—"

The boy had no chance to finish before Raynor jaunted over.

"This"—I pointed—"is Raynor."

The one-eyed wolf, whose head came to the boy's hip, sauntered up behind Arve and stuck his head between the young man's legs in an unorthodox greeting.

The boy stared into Raynor's golden eye. The little of Arve's face I could see under his hood blanched. "Wo-wol—"

A flash of motion in the corner of my eye caught my attention as Aros shot a hand under his cloak and drew a knife from the sheath hanging horizontally across his waist. Before even I could react, Ragnar leapt between Raynor and Aros. He bared his fangs and flattened his ears. His tail was straight, and he growled low enough to rattle bones.

I, too, snapped into a fighting stance, arms uncrossing, feet spreading, toes curling to grip the floor. Time itself slowed, and I stood outside myself, caught up in the familiar ecstasy of battle. Unconsciously, my right hand shot forth and grabbed Aros' knife-wielding hand by the wrist. I scented calm to Ragnar, but he refused to back down.

"Put the knife away, lad. My pack won't harm you."

The lad gasped and pulled away, and I loosened my unduly tight grip. He glared at me. His wide yet fiery green-gray eyes were like those of a greenhorn soldier facing his first enemy. I had once had eyes like those, too …

His eyes revealed no recognition of my words, and so I guided his tremulous hand from above his head where it was poised to strike. "It's all right, lad." When the boy's knife was at his side, I tentatively let go of his wrist. "Now, put that away." The blade rattled against the metal lip of its sheath.

Aros' eyes, and the terror they held, aroused a sense of pity within me. It compelled me to open his cloak and guide his hand to sheathe the knife. Only then did Ragnar cease to growl.

I glanced around the room for other signs of danger, but all I saw were looks of fear. The young women had gathered all the children behind themselves, and the children all clung to their protectors. Arve was pale and trembling, and Raynor had slipped back out from under him, tail between his legs. Aros trembled where he stood, rubbing his gloved hands together, and he made a rhythmic clicking noise in his throat. Their mother covered her gaping mouth with both hands.

Part of me hoped they would choose to leave of their own will, now that they'd seen how I lived, but I kept that desire of mine quiet.

"Is everyone all right now?"

I received no reply.

"You've nothing to fear from my pack."

"But they're wolves," Arve managed to say. "Wolves ... They—"

"They're monsters," Aros finished. "Killers. Beasts." He flexed his hand, as if to grab his knife again.

Raynor, who kept backing away, yelped as if wounded, and Ragnar growled.

I scented for both to be still.

"Lad, my wolves aren't like that."

The others all stared at me.

"Let me prove my pack, my wolves, are not like what stories say. They're anything but brutes or monsters. They're Luváli's folk, or have you forgotten that one of the Two was a wolf?"

All were silent, and the scent of fear slowly died away in all but Aros. This was the power of faith—to banish the terror of a monstrous form with the assurance that a god had once borne it, too. It had been a long time since I had seen that kind of faith.

I beckoned Freya with my hand. "Look."

Everyone darted their eyes between the wolf and me as Freya walked between the two young men, her head held high, and sat at my right.

"Arve, this is Freya, my dearest companion. Please, lad, come and say *hello*."

He shook his head.

"No? Well, will anyone greet my family? I swear they'll do you no harm. If I thought they might, I'd never have allowed them to remain when I welcomed you."

The stomping of tiny, booted feet on the wood-planked floor broke the silence. The youngest pair of boys bolted from behind their sisters, who shouted in unison, "Troy, Eirik, no." Heedless of their sisters' cries, the boys threw themselves at Freya, arms outstretched to embrace her. "By the Two Holies, no!"

The boys hung upon Freya by fists full of her gray winter coat. "Doggy!"

Ragnar became indignant at hearing his mother called "dog" for the second time that day.

I looked askance at him. *"Only pups. You were one. I remember ..."*

The hot indignation faded and turned into the same annoyance he felt when Raynor stole the last bit of meat from a kill.

Freya, unlike her alpha son, exuded joy. *"Pups. New life. Energy. Hope."* Her scented thoughts were a jumble, which I doubted even her kin could comprehend. She licked the boys, rolling over on her back, her tail bouncing. She let out a high-pitched whine and a short howl.

The boys climbed upon their new friend. They pulled, tugged, and giggled as they played. "Nice doggy," one said, while the other pretended to bark and howl.

Freya licked the boys and rolled about, never complaining at their roughness.

I barked a laugh. "Do you believe me now, dear guests?" Oh, to be a child again with the confidence—or, was it foolishness?—to play with monsters because some stranger said they wouldn't bite …

Raynor sidled up to Arve again, tail still tucked between his legs. The wolf nudged Arve's leg with his nose, and Arve started. Raynor stepped back, lowering his stance to avoid a blow that never came.

Each stared at the other, neither moving nor speaking. They refused even to breathe. Arve held out his hand, and Raynor sniffed, touching the tip of his muzzle to it. When the encounter did not end in disaster, Raynor licked the tips of the stranger's fingers. Arve laughed, and Raynor licked the boy's hand all over. Soon, the two were face to face. Raynor licked Arve's ears, and Arve scratched Raynor's. The earlier fear had vanished.

Ada, Ragnar's mate, made her own timid approach toward those who remained by the fire. Though uncertainty tinged all their actions, curiosity overcame fear as the two sides united. The three younger children petted Ada, though the young women ensured they did so with great care, and the she-wolf licked their fingers and nudged their hands in return.

The children's mother also drew near to Freya, who welcomed the new, gentler hands. With their mother near, the boys grew gentler, too, and Freya rose. She doled out sloppy kisses to the boys and nuzzled their mother's hand.

Only Aros and Ragnar refused to meet. They glared at one another with the same animosity as before.

I turned to the lad. "Aros."

The boy gave no reply.

"Ragnar."

I received only the vaguest of scented replies.

"*Young. New alpha. Protecting pack. True alpha wounded.*"

"*Dangerous. Threatened pack.*"

"*Young. Impulsive. Confused.*" I waited for those scent-images to settle, but the alpha's fiery anger remained.

"*Threatened pack,*" the wolf replied.

"*Make peace. Welcome him.*"

Silence.

"*Ragnar, Alpha of Four. Rune, Alpha of Five. Make peace. Offer protection. Enlarge pack.*"

Ragnar narrowed his eyes and scented the image of a wolf rolling before his alpha. The wolf broke his gaze with Aros, softened his stance, and approached his rival.

Aros tensed, flexing his hand. He made that same rhythmic huffing sound deep in his throat.

"Aros"—I stepped beside him—"Ragnar will make peace if you allow him. He's the alpha of his pack and, for the time, you are the alpha of yours, at least as he perceives you. He only wanted to protect his pack, and that's something you can appreciate, I think. Make peace, and he will consider you as his own, protect you as his own."

Aros glared at me from under his hood. "He'd have killed me. He—"

"Lad, you drew a knife on his brother. What was he to do? What would you have done if someone pulled a knife on yours?"

"The other one snuck up on Arve; what was I to think?"

"You can see no harm was meant." I pointed to Raynor and Arve, who wrestled with one another a few paces away.

Ragnar stopped just outside Aros' reach.

"See? Ragnar will make peace if you will. Do what's best for your family and meet him."

The young man's steely eyes softened. "Are you sure he will no—"

"Ragnar will consider you as his own. He would give his life for you. That's what he means by coming to meet you."

Aros sighed and nodded but did not move.

I gave him a push—a leap of faith is often a precipitous, forced freefall at first—and he knelt before Ragnar, holding out his upturned hand. Ragnar lowered his nose and sniffed. Aros flinched but put his hand back out, and Ragnar placed a paw upon it.

When all had made their greetings and amends, I clapped my hands. "All right. Now, let's get your poor horses out of this blizzard. Raynor, Arve."

Raynor and Arve both leapt up.

"Aros."

He rose and turned his back to his former enemy.

"Go fetch your horses, lads. Raynor will guide you."

Arve looked at Raynor then at me. "He'll scare the horses, no?"

Raynor cocked his head at the young man and whined.

"He'll stay far enough away and downwind. The horses will never know he's there."

Arve nodded, and he and his brother wrapped their cloaks around themselves. Raynor leapt out the door and into the storm, barking at his charges to follow.

"Give them as much food and water as they need. If they need blankets, you can find those in the stable, too."

Both boys nodded and departed.

I turned to their mother, who had taken the twins to her side. "Now, let me take a look at your husband."

RRR

Chapter III

To care for the bodies of the ill and dying, to bear their shame, is the highest art after the cura animarum, *for care of bodies is analogous to the work of the Two. Yea, he who practices this art with diligence earns for himself a place of honor in the age to come.*

— From *Enchiridion Artium*
Hypocrathekeris

ℝ

The unconscious man, Harvald, lay on the bearskin rug before the fire, his body covered with the cloaks of his family. With every rasping breath he took, he shuddered. The eldest daughters knelt at his side and wiped his sweaty brow with the cloths and handkerchiefs they had scrounged together.

The children all watched me with sorrowful eyes as I knelt at their father's side. I stripped the cloaks away and slipped an arm behind his shoulders and under his knees, the damp fur of the bearskin brushing against my bare forearms.

With him in my arms, I strode across the once-polished hardwood floor, which was now scuffed and claw-marked, to the bedroom. Every step elicited an agonized moan from Harvald, and I tried shifting his weight about in my arms to reduce his pain, but no matter how I tried, he was in constant pain. Every muscle in his body was in rigor—his fingers had curled into tight fists, and the tendons of his wrists and neck jumped out. His sweat bled through his clothes and coated my arms, fever-heat radiating from his skin.

The bedroom, which many lords and ladies had once occupied back when I rented my home as a summer getaway, was cool and dim. The room was full of opulent furnishings—a heavy wardrobe, vanity, and silvered glass, bedside tables, and a carpet of the softest dyed Sviari dromedary wool—but the darkness obscured much. Indeed, apart from a layer of dust that covered everything, there was no better place to lay the man.

Calling for the top, dust-covered linens to be stripped, I laid Harvald in the oversized, four-poster bed, its curtains wide open. His wife, who had freely revealed her name—the laws of hospitality forbade a host to make such inquiries before a meal was served—was Gale, had acted before I finished speaking.

I wiped my sweat-coated hands upon my pant legs and spoke, "Forgive me, ma'am, but for your husband's sake, I must ask you some pointed questions. I will make them as few as necessary." Before she could reply, I continued, "Did someone send you to seek help from me?"

Gale blinked uncomprehendingly. "No, Master Rune. We come from the far west, 'cross the mountains—you can tell we've traveled far, no doubt. We were—are goin' to Ebria, but this storm came up, and we could go no farther. When we came to the crossroads and saw this lodge was closer than the town ..."

I wanted to ask why they had chosen a location as far as Ebria—it was nearly a thousand miles from my home to Ebria, and another nine-hundred or so from here to the nearest mountain pass in the west—but I focused on the matter at hand.

"I understand. Now, I can treat your husband, if you'll suffer it."

"Master Rune, are you—"

"I've been many things, Gale. But, aye, I'm a hypocratheker."

Her mouth hung open ever so slightly, and she squinted.

"You'd call me a barber-surgeon."

She put a hand to her mouth. "Then, Master Rune, 'tis Holy Andar who brought us to you. Praise him."

I wished I could have denied her words. Instead, I affirmed them, "Amen. So it seems. Still, I must have your answer. May I—"

"Aye, do whate'er you believe necessary. I place his life in your hands." She bowed, and I inclined my head.

I stripped Harvald of his outwear. He, like all his family, wore heavy woolen clothes—a kaftan and belt, a woolen, outer tunic and under tunic of linen that both tied at the breast, sturdy pants, winingas, and calf-high, turn-down leather boots—all colored with the soft pastoral colors favored in the west—the greens and yellows of the pasture lands in the foothills, and the pale blue of the open sky—and hemmed with colorful geometric embroidery.

I discarded Harvald's kaftan, and Gale snatched and folded it at once, setting it and every other piece of clothing I cast aside upon the dresser opposite the bed.

"When did he fall ill?" I asked as I unlaced his tunics. "What were his symptoms?"

"He fell ill—well, ill as he is now—four days back. He had a fever, sweats, shakes, and his whole body was stiff as 'tis now. He'd groan through the lon' hours of the night, shakin' like he was caught up in a ground-shaker."

I squinted as I tried to understand her accent, which I had not heard in decades.

"Any problems breathing? Or vomiting, seizures, di—"

Her eyes were uncomprehending. I would need to use simpler terms.

"Fits, the flux, or the like?"

She blushed and stammered.

"I'm sorry. I know this—"

She straightened her back, brushed out her skirt, and cleared her throat as the blush faded. "No, Master Rune, you must know—you're no our host alone now."

As she spoke, I tried unsuccessfully to remove my patient's tunic painlessly, but as I lifted his back off the bed, he groaned pitifully.

Gale gasped as if she herself had been hurt—how could anyone doubt a husband and wife were one?—but she recomposed herself.

"Aye, all these, but no the fits. His arms and legs shake lightly and become stiff, like ropes pulled fast, though."

"I see." I removed Harvald's outer tunic. "I'll need towels from the kitchen and washroom. It's the door left of the fireplace. Have one of your children fetch—"

Gale bowed and rushed out mid-sentence.

Harvald moaned again as I crooked his undertunic over his head. The foul scent of his long-unwashed, filthy body poured off him, and I tossed his tunic into the growing pile of clothes with a grimace. Even in the dim firelight that entered from the living room, Harvald's skin was pale—no, ashen—and not just in comparison with my darker olive-brown complexion. Even compared to a westerner's fair skin, he was pallid.

I poked and prodded as I was trained to do. I spotted a few bed sores—undoubtedly from lying in the bed of a wagon for so long—on his shoulders and hips. When I palpated his abdomen, the muscles of which were drawn tight to reveal Harvald's well-muscled frame, I still found no cause of his illness. Thus, I slid my hands up toward his neck and noted the few great purple and black welts from bruised ribs—I would have to ask Gale about those—and some minor scrapes, which were healing nicely.

Then, though it disgusted me, I set my ear to his hairy, clammy chest. His breathing was shallow and labored, and his heart beat too speedily for a man at rest, but this also revealed nothing new. I pressed his swollen neck—the taut muscles pulled his face into a stark grimace—and a tremor of pain shot through Harvald's body as he coughed. When the coughing ceased, I felt along his square jaw and ran my fingers through his coarse, unkempt red beard, which contained flecks of spittle and what could only have been dried vomit.

As I worked, Gale returned with a pile of heavy towels made of the finest southern cotton. "Master Rune, my daughters found these ..." She held out the fine towels. "But"—she pulled them back before I could grab one and offered me a stack of tattered rags she had found under the finer towels—"surely you mean to use these."

"No, I do not. Those"—I nodded at the rags—"are for cleaning boots and floors. They're certainly not for my guests." Before she could protest, I snatched a towel and wiped away the layer of grime and filth from Harvald's torso.

"Before he came down with this sickness, did he get injured at all? An animal bite, a cut, a gash? It needn't have been great, only something deep enough to break the skin."

As I waited for her answer, I examined his eyes, which were also unremarkable apart from their brilliant emerald color. I pried his mouth open, too, and braced myself for the stench. Still, I found nothing remarkable apart from a few missing teeth. There was still no explanation for his suffering, but that was all too often the case with the sick.

"Aye, Master Rune. Nigh two weeks back, we walked alongside the wagons to lighten the horses' load, and my Harvald stepped upon a nail, which pierced his sole. He sat upon the cart and pulled the nail out without e'en a groan of pain. He was no e'en goin' to bandage his foot since it did no bleed, but I did make him wrap it. 'Twas deep, but when I had fixed him up, he kept on goin' as though 'twere nothin'.

"No more than six days passed, and his foot did pain him somethin' fierce. He grew feverish and took to sittin' on the driver's seat for the pain and weariness. He grew weaker and once did faint and fall headlon' to the road. By the grace of Andar, he missed the wheels and did no break his neck. You can imagine from there ..."

"Aye." His fall from the wagon explained the scrapes, cracked ribs, and bruises, but the nail wound concerned me most.

I unlaced his first boot, undid the winingas around his foot and calf, and looked for signs of a wound. Finding none, I moved to the other foot. This boot was already unlaced, and when I did little more than touch it, Harvald writhed. As I removed the boot from his swollen foot, the smell of necrosis filled my nostrils. Though I had smelled a faint odor of decay on him from the moment his sons had brought him in, I had paid it little mind—many sicknesses caused such smells without apparent cause—but now it demanded my attention.

I unwrapped the cloth that bound the wound but stopped when Harvald cried out. Upon the fabric were bits of skin that had torn away. I excused myself to fetch my hypocratheker's bag from a high shelf of the storeroom and larder. With surgical sheers in hand, I cut away the fabric.

Underneath, Harvald's foot was a swollen mass of red, purple, and black. The stench of sweat, decay, and pain were nearly unbearable, but I stilled myself, as I had been trained to do.

When Gale saw Harvald's foot, and when the smell filled her nostrils, the candleholder in her hand trembled. With her free hand, she made the Sign of the Two on her forehead and uttered a swift prayer. "Oh, the Two have mercy."

"Amen."

I ran my fingertips over the gangrenous foot, turning it toward the light. My night vision, though better than most men's because of what I was, still did not pick out finer details.

His skin burned, and the lightest touch elicited what surely would have been screams if Harvald could have opened his jaw. Despite the pain, I forged ahead and tried to focus while Gale muttered her prayers.

On the sole of his foot, a great abscess had formed, and angry, venous, red tendrils shot outward from the wound. The marks wound up to his ankle, like ivy climbing a wall, but stopped abruptly. Indeed, not only the tendrils but all the necrosis had stopped.

"That you bandaged his wound and left his foot wraps on so tightly may be the only reason your husband is still alive."

Gale made no sound or motion.

"I must work quickly now." I spoke more to myself than to Gale.

Unhesitatingly, I took the fabric sheers and finished prepping my patient. I cut along the outer seams of Harvald's linen trousers and soiled smallclothes so they would be easy to repair. Pulling the clothes from underneath him, I tossed them into a heap.

The light from the candle shifted, no longer shining upon me as Gale knelt at my side. She wrapped her arms around my knees again as a suppliant. "Oh, m'lord, do no shame yourself so." Tears poured down her cheeks. "What shame I brin' upon you, m'lord, that I let you tend like a servant upon my family. We soil your hands, your bed, and the air with our shamefulness and poverty." Her words became incoherent sobs and gasps.

I glanced at her husband's naked, filth-covered body. If she had known what I had seen in my life, what I had done and dreamed of doing, she would not speak thus, for I bore deep within a shame greater than that of having my hands dirtied with piss and shit.

"Dear woman, th—"

Freya's bright-eyed face poked through the doorway. She looked first to Gale then to me. "*Such grief. Shame ...*" The images Freya scented were of wolves mourning the loss of a pack member, of a lone-wolf wandering with his head down as a storm buffeted him. "*Death?*"

I scented the image of stormy skies on the horizon. "*Must work. Comfort her.*" This image was of the pack surrounding a wounded companion, of one wolf setting her head upon the wounded's chest.

Freya nudged Gale's cheek, and Gale hung upon the wolf instead of me. Freya licked her, and Gale burrowed her fingers into the wolf's thick winter coat. Freya leaned into the embrace and let the woman pour tears into her fur.

One of the young ladies also poked her head into the dim room. Hearing her steps, I rushed to cover her father's nakedness. It was a hypocratheker's responsibility to bear a patient's shame so that others would be unburdened of it. Therefore, our art was called *noble*.

"Ma, is—" The young lady wrinkled her nose.

"E'erythin' is all right, Erika. Please, go—"

"Ma, 'tis no all right. If you leave the little ones in the dark, fine, but do no hide the truth from me. Aros, Haldis, and Arve, too, know somethin' is wron'. You canna hide this from us, Mama."

Gale wiped her eyes on a handkerchief she pulled from her sleeve. "Your father is no well, Erika."

Erika embraced her mother. "'Tis obvious, Ma, but what has you so in tears?"

"He ... his ..." She choked. "M-Ma-Master Rune, p-please."

I folded my hands behind my back and sighed. I loathed this part of the job more than working with the ill and the dying.

"Your husband, your father, is suffering from a disease called tetanus. You might call it lock-jaw, or—"

"Lock-jaw?" Erika gasped. "The wild man's disease? How's that possible? Ne'er've we gone north of the village, least no so far as to where the wilds begin."

"Peace. You may also call it bone-break fever. It's not only a disease of the wilds."

Gale embraced her daughter, her sobbing renewed. "'T-tis a d-death sentence ..."

I worked to keep my voice level. "Only if it goes untreated. Now, your father's case has progressed quickly, but I'll do my best for him."

Gale released her daughter. "Master Rune, you must do whate'er you can."

"I will, dear woman." I paused to collect myself. "However, your husband also has a serious gangrene infection. Because of this and the terrible cold he's been exposed to, most of his foot is diseased. When I stabilize his fever and muscle spasms, I'm afraid I'll have to amputate."

Gale threw herself back upon her daughter. "Oh, I pray 'twill no be so."

"If I don't get the infection under control soon, it will spread. I'll be able to do little after that. Of course, if I can control the gangrene and tetanus both without taking his foot, I'll take the least drastic action. Still, you need to prepare yourself."

Erika looked over her weeping mother's shoulder. Her blue eyes were full of something I did not know. "What do you need from us?"

"A pitcher of cool water—there's a pump in the kitchen—and a cup from the mantel. I also need clean cloths—you can find them where you found the towels. I know night is some hours off, but you'll need to set a watch for your father. Likewise, make up a hearty stew or soup, something your father can drink. He desperately needs his strength. The kitchen is just apart from the washroom."

Erika nodded and pulled back from her mother. "Ma, Da needs us now."

"And give your mother some tea. In the storeroom—and I'm sorry about the mess in there; the wolves brought their quarry in before you arrived—there's a tea marked *solvans* on one of the shelves. It'll serve her well."

When the women left, I took a towel and cleaned Harvald as well as I could. I covered him again, wiped my hands clean, procured my scalpel, and set to work. I laid several towels at Harvald's feet and gently fit a few more under his injured foot. I ran the scalpel through a candle flame and made the first incision. It took little effort to pierce the taut skin, and though I had done similar operations, I had to hold back an involuntary gag. Few were able to numb themselves to the putrid smell of gangrenous flesh.

As I drained the wound, Harvald moaned more loudly than before but did not kick or pull away.

I prepared to bandage the wound when the door opened. Gale and her eldest sons brought in everything I had requested and set everything upon the bedside table or the high-backed dining chair they had also brought in. Their job done, Aros and Arve left while Freya and Gale remained.

Gale folded her hands as if in prayer, and though I believed she was about to drop to her knees again, she only bowed her head. "Master Rune, how is he?"

"Well, I've drained the abscess." I grabbed a scrap of linen and wiped blood and pus from my fingertips, throwing the soiled linen onto the growing pile at my feet. "That should help prevent the infection from spreading quite as fast and ease the pain."

"Thank the Two."

"Amen." I took a smaller towel, folded it, and dipped it into the bucket of frigid water they had brought. I placed the dripping cloth onto Harvald's forehead, brushing a few strands of straight auburn hair away. "Now we can tackle these other symptoms. If he goes on much longer in this state, even with the wound taken care of, he's going to have fits."

As I spoke, Gale soaked more of the small cotton cloths and handed them to me.

"Refresh these every half-hour, at minimum." I placed them across his neck, wrists, ankles, chest and, folding back the cloth laid across his lap, two on his groin. "Likewise, give him at least two—better three or four—glasses of cold water over the course of every hour. When the food is ready, you'll need to feed him. Don't fret if he soils the bed." I took a cup of water and lifted Harvald's head with my left hand. I touched the cup to his lips and poured the cold water down his throat. He drank greedily.

"When you give him water, be careful he doesn't aspir—choke. He must have his head kept up." I tipped the cup toward him once more and wiped away what dribbled down into his beard.

"Anythin' you say, Master Rune." Gale held out her hand. "If I may?" She took the cup and whispered into her husband's ear as she gave him another sip.

"You'll need to change the linens and bathe him often—he must stay clean, dry, and cool." I took the chair and motioned for her to sit. She did but continued to lean over Harvald. She stroked his long, undercut hair, and ran her gentle hand down his bearded cheek.

"I'll be back with some physic soon. Holler if you need anything at all."

Freya remained by Gale's side, and I scented, "*Care for her.*"

"*As I do for you.*"

RRR

Chapter IV

A good teacher is a treasure; an ingenious student,
rare; finding both together, a sign from the Two.
— From *On Learning and Teaching* by
the Divine Pædagogue

R

A fter years of solitude in my lodge, now converted into a bunkhouse, the buzz of activity disoriented me. Before the hearth were twelve pairs of boots, stockings, winingas, cloaks, and other clothes hung out to dry on a line my guests had rigged to hang across the length of the room. Puddles of wash and meltwater dripped upon the floor, and the pungent, earthy smell of wet wool filled the entire room, mingling with the sweeter aroma of the tea the older children sat drinking.

The four youngest boys—both sets of twins—Magnus and Grimm, and Troy and Eirik—ran wild in nothing but their smallclothes while their other clothes dried before the fire. Though their sisters lamented their rambunctious behavior, Raynor was overjoyed with it. Rarely did he find anyone as willing to play as these boys were, and he bounced around the room like a pup, his barking adding to the general disarray.

The little blonde girl, Yoanna, had been dressed in dry, clean clothes, and she played with a doll her elder brothers had fetched along with their family's possessions. Next to her was the basket-turned-cradle of her baby sister, Kari, whom

Gale had come out to nurse before returning to Harvald's side. The babe could not have been more than three months old, and it did not surprise me in the slightest to see Ada curled up nearby.

At first, Yoanna had yelled at Ada whenever she approached the cradle and, at the start, Ada had obeyed the little girl. The she-wolf's persistence had won out, however, when she crawled toward the cradle on her belly, rolled over before the scolding child, and let out a whine. Only then did Yoanna suffer the wolf to look in on the babe. She soon realized, too, that her acceptance of Ada's presence was its own reward. The she-wolf acted as Kari's surrogate mother, poking her coal-black muzzle into the cradle any time the babe so much as cooed.

It was an inexplicable injustice—one of many in this world—that Ada, who was not only fit to care for but also deeply desirous of having her own litter, had never had any pups. A mix of anger at the Two and sympathy for my friend overwhelmed me as I watched her care for this stranger's child. Though Ada persisted in her confidence that she would have her pups, Ragnar once confided in me how unfulfilled she felt without them.

Among Gale and Harvald's many other children was also Arve. He was the younger of the two eldest brothers and was a near replica of his father, from the undercut, braided auburn hair and green eyes to the bold angles of his beardless jaw, broad cheekbones, and strong nose. He sat by the fire in a linen nightshirt that stretched down to his ankles while he whittled away at a piece of firewood with a small knife. He handled the wood deftly, and though I couldn't tell what he was making, he clearly knew his craft. He engaged in lively conversation, occasionally yelling at his younger brothers for being careless around him, but he never stopped his work.

His two older sisters also made the most of the precious downtime they now had. Haldis, the younger of the two, tied her two golden braids back, rotated the clothes on the line, mopped up the puddles—which her brothers insisted on splashing in—fed the fire, and even swept the ash-covered hearth stones. She was a comely lass, with her mother's gently rounded, fair face, freckles, and golden hair, and her father's shining green eyes. Even the grime of travel could not mar her beauty.

Her elder sister, Erika, was also fair of face and skin—the Two had graced this entire family with stature and beauty—and she had her father's red hair and mother's sagacious blue eyes. Her voice was soft, yet it commanded attention, and she carried herself with grace. With her younger siblings, she showed a motherly side, and they came to her with any need, though they feared her scolding, too. Like her sister, she busied herself with many chores. She washed and mended garments and, with her sister by her side, she flitted in and out of the pantry and kitchen as a bee buzzed about its hive in spring.

Their tirelessness and drive revealed just what an old bachelor I was, and I grew red-faced as I considered their efforts. The young women washed my discarded clothes, too, including—to my great embarrassment—my smallclothes, which lay strewn near where I slept with my pack by the hearth. They likewise gathered—though to Ragnar's initial displeasure—the pile of blankets and assorted animal hides that served as our den. Such a long time had passed since I had washed these that I was lucky not to have fleas.

When the women carried off the great pile of linens and clothes to the washroom, the water cascading from the hand pump into the enormous metal tub echoed in the living room. Though the tub was quite large, the water stopped flowing shortly after it had begun. A moment later, Haldis appeared and asked how they were to heat the tub, which had no fuel compartment underneath.

It is disconcerting to have one's presumed humility proved false by innocently simple people. Aye, and it is even more disconcerting to realize how much pride one took in one's supposed humility. Yet, it was that exact dissonance that overwhelmed me—this young lady's honest question revealed just how much I still took my luxuries for granted. There was still so much I would need to forsake—greater things than my pipe—if I truly wished to fulfill my penance. When these guests were gone, I would need to reconsider my lifestyle once more.

But my self-chastisement had to wait.

I showed Haldis and Erika how, with the flip of a lever, the pump could draw water from the nearby hot spring. However, I left unexplained that the entire mechanism was of dwarven make, for few men had any contact with that elusive race, and I did not want my guests asking too many questions. It was bad enough these strangers knew I was a hypocratheker, let alone that they knew I existed at all.

As her children worked, Gale remained steadfast at her husband's bedside. Freya, too, faithfully comforted her as only the matronly wolf could. Though Gale said nothing about her companion, Freya scented messages about how welcome her presence was.

Ragnar, who sat at my side, sensed me relax as I worked on the remedy. *"Trust? Dangerous ..."* He looked up at me with hard, brown eyes, a lieutenant waiting to receive his superior's orders.

"Aye, caution. Less danger now, but still strangers. Remember, laws of hospitality."

"Vigilance." I could sense my friend's apprehension but was sure he would keep his cool. *"Alpha-pup ... he watches you."*

As I laid out my medical equipment, I glanced at Aros who, indeed, watched me from across the table. Whenever he saw me glance his way, he would dart his eyes away and fiddle with the hunting knife he held in his hands, picking at the dirt under his nails. Then he would set the knife down and run a hand across his youthful, patchy beard or the once-shaven sides of his head. He fidgeted with his platinum blond hair, which was bound in a thick, high-sitting ponytail.

I wondered again if there were something wrong with the lad. Maybe he was just overly shy, or ... maybe it was something else entirely that caused him to draw my attention so. But it did not do to dwell on such uncertainties. All I knew was he was not of my nature, and that was what mattered.

My secret and pack would remain safe.

Rather than make a fuss, I pulled flasks and phials of different sizes out of boxes filled with straw—some phials were full, others empty—and alongside these, I arrayed my instruments. From a small, hard-sided box, I even took a set of my finest brass scales which, when calibrated, were more accurate than a jeweler's—I had seen the effects of improper dosages and had no desire to cause this family any more grief.

Last, I took several wax-sealed clay jars that bore Orcish runes on their lids.

I puffed a few times on my pipe—I knew no better way to keep my focus while I worked—and drank from the mug of steaming mint tea that Haldis had served me with a coquettish smile. She had cast that smile my way a few times now.

She, too, was a curiosity to me. While there could be no accounting for a person's tastes, I was, by all appearances, twenty-five or thirty years her senior and had done nothing, said nothing, to make her so ... *flirtatious*. Yet, she batted her sparkling green eyes and pulled on her blonde braids every time she glanced at me.

Lost in thought, I pulled the top from a phial with undue strength, spilling fine powder across the table. I muttered a curse against my carelessness and wiped away the mess. Yet, almost at once, my thoughts went back to the young woman. I knew there was only one plausible explanation for her behavior—my curse. The thought filled me with both fear for the girl's safety and anger at myself.

After so much time in seclusion, after so many penances, even the lesser symptoms of my curse—the magnetic pull I had on some, and the unnatural longevity I supplied to those who lived with me—remained strong. I would have to do better. Aye, I would redouble my efforts and quell this evil inside me.

Meanwhile, I had to end this flirting. The only question was how to avoid drawing attention to the issue.

Frustrated and unfocused, I puffed away on my pipe, and it bit my tongue fiercely.

As the haze of aromatic smoke floated about my head, I checked the label on the nearest clay jar and peeled away the wax seal. I wrinkled my nose as the lid popped off, and Ragnar sneezed and shook his head, and his shaggy winter coat shook, too.

Into the mortar before me, I tipped out several greenish-yellow blossoms, each roughly the size of the top of my thumb, and sealed the jar, and thus the stench, up again. The relief was short-lived, for the moment I crushed the blossoms, the stench returned.

Across the table, Aros gagged. "By the Two Holies, what a stench."

I smirked. "It's not an accident that these are called *corpse blossoms*." I set down the pestle, which was covered in brownish-green residue, and sat up straight with hands folded on the table. "Lad …"

His green-gray eyes—they were nearly the same color as my own, though lacking the blue undertones I had inherited from my mother—met mine. He swallowed hard. "Aye, sir?"

I pulled out the chair on my left, turning its back to the fire. "Have a seat here, lad."

Aros looked around the room, as if I had spoken to somebody else. His posture, let alone his scent, betrayed his mistrust. His mistrust didn't bother me, though. I, too, had been mistrustful as a young man, anxious from—

A flash blinded me.

I jerked my head. The scent of brine assaulted my nostrils. The creaking of ship timbers filled my ears. I snorted to expel trapped salt water from my sinuses, but when I opened my eyes, I was still home.

Aros narrowed his eyes. Did he sense some unknown quality in me like I sensed in him, or did he simply dislike me?

"If it's all right, I—"

"Lad, I'm not *asking*." I flashed a weak smile. "Please, come sit here."

He narrowed his eyes even more but joined me. He turned the chair slightly so he did not face me directly and folded his arms as he looked at the ground.

"I've seen you looking over here, lad." I picked up the pestle and shot him a sideways glance. "So, I figured I'd invite you over."

"'Twas no much of an invitation ..."

"What was that, lad?"

The young man started. "Uh, I ... No, Master Rune, I was no watchin' you. Just ... just lookin' 'round, 'tis all." The boy uncrossed his arms and rubbed his hands together, bouncing his leg. I nearly wrinkled my nose at the sour scent of anxiety pouring off him.

"Ah, my mistake, then. I thought for a minute you might be interested in my work." I took a small phial and dropper, adding a few drops of red liquid to the mortar.

"Well, I ..." Aros looked up. "I suppose 'tis interestin' enough."

"Would you like to learn?"

The young man's slouch vanished, and the cloudiness in his eyes cleared. "Aye, I'd like that."

I offered the pestle to him but pulled back before he could grab it. "You sure, lad? If you'd rather go back to what you were doing—not looking over here, as it were—you're free to go."

Surprise filled his eyes. "Oh ..." He huffed and twitched slightly. "No, I'd really like to learn, sir."

"Oh, well, I'm glad I called you over then, even if I was wrong about you looking over here." I offered him the mortar and showed him the right technique.

"Aye, maybe I was lookin' o'er here a bit, just to see what you were workin' on for my da—my father, I mean."

"There's nothing wrong with calling your father *da*. You don't need to put on an affect with me."

The boy's face flushed. "Oh, all right. Sorry." He ground the herbs faster.

I grasped his wrist, and he jumped. "Too fast now. Slow down, and not so hard." Holding his wrist, I guided him to make regular, light strokes.

The boy's face grew even redder. "Sorry."

"All's well." I watched him for another moment. "You seem anxious about your father."

He paused, finding the right rhythm again before continuing. "'Course I am ... We did no e'en know if he was goin' to live through the night."

"Mmm ... Well, he's obviously a fighter."

The young man set the pestle down, closed his eyes, and nodded his head with a sigh.

I took the equipment and poured out the ground blossoms into another bowl before adding a new ingredient. "So, lad, tell me about him." I started to grind the ingredients before passing the mortar back.

"My da was—is a carpenter."

That would explain Arve's skill with the whittling knife, I thought. "It's a good trade. My father was a carpenter, too."

Aros cocked his head and raised an eyebrow. "Did your older brother take o'er the business?"

"No, I had no brothers or sisters." I returned the questioning look. "Why?"

"Well, you ... you're no a carpenter, so who took o'er your da's business for him?"

I lowered my eyes. "Well, nobody did, lad." It had been a long time since I had thought of my father. The memory of his death, of his mangled body, invaded my mind, but I pushed it away.

"Oh ... I guess I'm glad Arve will take up the job then. I just always imagined 'twould be me." The young man sighed. "My da, he always said I was too much in the books to be in his trade. He said I just did no have the knack for his job, no like my brother."

I glanced at Arve, who was now clearly crafting some instrument.

"He said, 'Aros, son, you're no like me in this. You'd make a good learned man or some such.' So, my brother is his apprentice, but I've still no apprenticeship, though I'm almost three years older than him." Aros' countenance fell. The pestle ground to a halt. His brow furrowed, and a frown crept onto his face. He exuded the scent of an alpha and beta vying for supremacy in a pack, of an omega watching his betters get first rights to the spoils of the hunt.

"I was like you, lad—not quite cut out for carpentry." I laughed. "I never had the mind for it. Too much free thinking, the ability to see beauty in your mind's eye and draw it out. Too much abstraction ..."

The boy continued to frown but looked at me with renewed interest. "But, did you no want to take your da's trade?"

"Oh, I certainly tried. When I was five or so, he started taking me to his workshop, showed me how to use different tools. He even gave me some simple tasks, but I never did them well. I didn't realize it at the time, but now I know why my father stayed late at the shop so often. He was fixing my mistakes, but he never grumbled about it.

"Eventually, he told me the same thing your father told you. 'Son, you're just not cut out for this.'"

Aros stared, mouth slightly agape.

"I ran home and cried in my mother's lap until Da ran into the house after me and took me into his arms. I blubbered into his tunic—it was so wet and covered in snot that he had to change—and said, 'I'm sorry, Da. I'm sorry I disappointed you. I'm sorry ... I'm sorry I'm a bad son.'

"I really thought I *was* a bad son. Now, that thought, of course, didn't come to me all of a sudden. From early on, my father never gave me difficult tasks, never trusted me with anything remotely complicated. Deep down, I knew what was coming."

Aros sniffed but kept silent, blinking back tears.

"But my father—my da—he looked at me and said, 'I'm not disappointed in you, son. I love you. I could never be disappointed in you.'" I trailed off, and a silence I could not immediately surmount lingered. I should have let the silence win out, as I was revealing far too much about myself, yet I could not help but speak about my father now that the thought of him filled my mind. Maybe the little boy in every man who admires his father never really dies ...

"Does your da tell you he loves you, lad?"

Aros sniffled and cleared his throat as he searched for his voice. "Uh ... Aye, 'course he does. He tells me all the time, like he does with all of us."

"Then don't ever think you've disappointed your da, lad."

"But Da ... he seemed so"—he sniffled again—"so upset when he told me ... I—"

"Lad, 'course your da was *upset* when he told you. What father wouldn't want their firstborn son to be their apprentice? But that doesn't mean he's upset with *you*. He might be sad, upset, but I'd bet my life he's not disappointed in you."

"But you did no hear him when he told me ..."

"Lad, the fact your da tells you he loves you is all the proof I need." I put a hand on the young man's shoulder. "Look at me, lad."

The lad looked up. A few tears trickled down his cheeks.

"I've met more men than I can count whose fathers never told them what your father tells you—that he loves you. I've met just as many who didn't believe their fathers when they did. Those men ... well, they spend their entire lives acting like fools, doing foolish, ungodly things because they want their fathers to be proud. Really, lad, I've met more men like that than men who have fathers like yours." I sat back and relit my pipe while Aros contemplated what I'd said.

"Thank you, sir."

I grunted with the pipe's bit in my mouth and gestured for him to pick up the pestle. We worked in silence for a little while; the air was thick enough with weighty conversation already. Eventually, however, I spoke up.

"So, you must be lettered, then, Aros, if your da thinks you'd be a good candidate for this trade?"

Aros smiled, a twinkle in his eyes. "Aye, sir, I am. Ma and Da say I can read e'en better than them. And"—he leaned in—"my brother does no read hardly t'all."

I smiled back. "Well, like your brother, I could barely read until I was in my twenties. My mother taught me some while I was growing up, and my father—he was Sviari—never learned to read Oserdeni at all." A frown replaced my smile. "But they were both taken from me when I was still young, so I never had much chance to finish my lessons."

I stared into the fire for a moment but broke off my gaze. "Anyway, if there's time, I'll show you my library upstairs." I pointed to the open loft above. "I might even have a few books I can part with."

The young man's jaw dropped. "Really?"

"Aye, even if you don't have a formal teacher, you can at least take the time to learn some basics. Though a lot of the technique has to be taught by someone else, you can still learn theory, formulæ, the uses for different herbs and plants, and other useful bits from books. That way, when you do find a teacher who'll take you on, you can start at a steady jog instead of a crawl."

The boy bobbed his head, trying unsuccessfully not to let his excitement show. "Still, I wish there'd been a regular apothecary or e'en a barber-surgeon in our town. There was one who'd come 'round e'ery two weeks or so. When she came, I'd always try 'n watch her work, but she ne'er wanted me as an apprentice. She said men have no the way with the sick."

I shrugged. "I won't say it's right, but hers is a common opinion. Women certainly have a certain caring touch—your mother and Erika are proof of that—and most of us wouldn't be alive if we only had fathers."

The boy frowned.

"But men tend to make the tough snap decisions easier. We're *less involved*, as they say. That's why you won't find many combat hypocrathekers who are women."

My vision faded, and I stood on an open plain.

Defensive palisades made of sharpened timbers stood all around. The bodies of men and horses, some still clinging to life, were impaled upon them. All around, shouts and clashing steel rang in my ears.

Here, dozens of bodies lay strewn across the battlefield, either impaled by spears and arrows or in various states of dismemberment. There, some lived and cried for their mothers or for the Two Holies to come and save them. Others screamed utter nonsense.

A gust of wind blew by me and rustled my white medic's cassock. I stood paralyzed, my bag of instruments hanging limply from my hand.

Someone called out to me, "What's the—"

A paw resting on my lap pulled me back to reality. Ragnar's brown eyes narrowed as he pressed upon my leg.

I breathed deep.

Aros spoke, "Master Rune, what's the ma—"

"I'm fine." I wiped the corners of my eyes with my thumb and forefinger and pinched the bridge of my nose. "Just, uh ... just caught up in thought." Sweat beaded on my forehead, but I wiped it away, sliding my hand across my brow as if to push back my hair. My hands trembled, so I put my loose brown hair into a tight bun to hide my nervousness.

"You sure, Master Rune? You're awful pale. Do you—"

"I'm fine," I spat, glaring at him.

The boy pulled away, and I sighed.

"I'm fine, lad, really …" I cleared my throat. "Why don't we get back to work?"

Aros slowly nodded.

"Let's see …" I took the pestle from him and crushed up the bits that remained too large. One of the bits was particularly tough, however, and when I ground it, pungent dust flew up. I wrinkled my nose, and the boy sneezed. His older siblings by the fire shot glances our way but returned to their work.

I patted him on the back and laughed. "If you want to be an apothecary, Aros, you'd better get used to unpleasant smells." I immediately thought of Harvald's gangrenous foot. "And nasty sights, too. Part of your job will be to keep your composure. People count on you to keep a level head."

My mind wandered again to some of the most haunting things I'd ever seen—baskets of amputated limbs, arrows that failed to kill lodged in eyes, men lain out on the ground, screaming while their bowels lay strewn for the crows to eat. The din of raging battle roared in my ears as my field of vision shrank, and cold sweat beaded on my forehead yet again. I growled. Blood filled the edges of my vision. I—

Somewhere in the distance, Ragnar growled.

"Master Rune?" Aros touched my shoulder.

"Sorry. I …" I was at a loss for words. I gripped the edge of the table, but nobody except Aros had noticed my slipup. My pack had also sensed my distress, and they watched me, tails twitching.

"Are you sure you're all right? You're no sick, too, are you?"

I waved off his concern. "I'm fine." I grabbed my pipe with a trembling hand and took a few drags before adding the ground-up corpse blossom into the mortar with the other ingredients. I focused on steadying my hands as I worked but still sprinkled a few drops of water onto the tabletop as I poured it from a phial and into the mortar.

"What're you doin' now?" Thankfully, the boy's attention had been piqued, even by this simple action.

My heart still raced. "What? With this?" I held up the little phial.

The boy nodded.

I rolled my eyes. "What does it look like? I'm adding water." I immediately regretted my words.

The young man flushed. "Oh, sorry. I h-hope I'm no bother." He rubbed his hands and cleared his throat rhythmically.

I rubbed my eyes. "Sorry, lad. I didn't mean to snap at you. I was caught up in thinking about …" I paused. I had already told him so much, so why not this? But no, the less they knew, the better. "About things that happened a long time back, things that upset me. I forgot what I was doing. That's why I snapped at you, lad. I'm sorry. You're no bother to me."

Aros stared at the floor and nodded.

"Look at me, lad."

The boy lifted his head just enough for me to see his face. "Truly, you're not a bother, and you've done nothing wrong." Before Aros could object, I kept on working as if nothing had happened.

"So"—I picked up my pipe—"let me show you a few more things. Consider yourself apprenticed out, at least until you go your way."

RRR

Chapter V

In my judgment, a hypocratheker ought to smoke a pipe, especially when decisions of vital importance must be made. The pipe, I say, gives something of a divine mind, one which rises above earthly limitations.

— From Roderick's *Rules and Guidance for the Novice Hypocratheker*

R

As the two of us worked as master and apprentice, Aros asked questions about everything laid before us. Some of the basics, like the pestle and mortar, the boy already knew, but he gawked at the more intricate equipment, like the scales and the herb storage jars, with their strange markings.

"Can you really read this, sir? These scribbles?" He gestured to the symbol on a jar lid.

"Aye, but they're not *scribbles*, lad, they're Orcish runes. I learned Orcish when I first took up my training, though I don't remember it quite as well as I once did."

The boy marveled at the runes. "What does this one say?"

I examined the lid. "*Asc'el.* We call it *abdoliter* or *corpse blossom.*"

Aros muttered the difficult orcish word under his breath, stumbling over the glottal stop. Then he asked, "But there's only one letter, so how's it such a lon' name?" He fingered the intricate symbol.

"Orcish doesn't have an alphabet like Oserdeni. So, technically speaking, this isn't a letter at all. Orcs use runes—symbols, if you will—which bear hidden meaning within. After all, that is what *rune* means—secret.

"Literally, this rune"—I took the container—"means *pungent-soft-body*, which describes the properties of corpse blossom."

Aros studied another jar. "Will I have to learn Orcish if I become an apothecary?"

I shook my head. "*Have to?* No. But I'd recommend it, even if others would say it's not worth it. The worst orc medicine men are better than our best hypocrathekers and apothecaries, and though some of their procedures and recipes are translated, they're often inaccurate.

"Sometimes, the recipes are less effective because of it; and other times, they're not effective at all. I once saw a text in a library with a marginal note saying several of the translated recipes had proven fatal, but it was because of a mistranslation."

"How long did it take you to learn Orcish?"

I scratched my bearded chin. "Well, I lived among the orcs for ... twenty years, maybe? But it took me five years just to learn how to speak and understand, and I never lost my accent. It took me another five years to learn enough runes to read anything worthwhile and, even then, I was continually learning new runes until I left that people."

Aros stared open-mouthed. "You *lived* with them? I always heard they're savages."

"Ha. Not even remotely. They have that reputation because they look brutish, and because, centuries ago, they waged brutal wars. Now, though, they're pacifists, at least the goodly number of them. There are a few who leave their homeland to become mercenaries and follow the old ways, and those orcs are truly fearsome." Joash, the kindly yet fearsome orc whom I had once served with as a mercenary, came to mind. "But the majority study medicine, healing, and what we would call *magic*."

Aros scoffed. "My da says magic is just jiggery-pokery. I mean, I know the Writings speak of magic, but I only believed 'twas a way to talk 'bout trickery."

When I did not nod my head or give any sign of agreement, the boy blushed and had a sheepish look.

"Uh, but you believe in magic, sir? I just mean, I've ne'er seen real magic, so …"

I smiled and patted Aros' shoulder. "You've not offended me, Aros." I withdrew my hand and ran it through my dark brown beard again. "As to your question, I absolutely believe in it, aye; but, believe you me, it's nothing to be envied or sought. The Writings are right to warn us away from it. Getting wrapped up with the spirits is a dark and dangerous thing …"

"Sir?"

"Mmm?" I wondered if the boy would ask me another question about my personal metaphysics.

"May I ask: how old are you? I mean, if you did no learn to read till you were in your twenties, and you spent twenty years with the orcs, you must've been …" The boy's eyes bounced as he counted invisible numbers. "I dunno … maybe forty when you left them? But you also said—"

"Don't rack your brain over it, lad. I'll just say I'm older than I look."

"Okay, sir. But you're older than fifty?"

I stroked one of the graying patches of hair by my ear. "That would be telling. I'll only say I'm older than you, boy. Now, let me show you a few more things."

I let Aros measure out the necessary ingredients for his father's tinctures, and I wrote down some basic recipes and formulæ for him.

"The orcs," I explained, "are adamant in their refusal to teach the young to read until they can recite the thousand most common recipes and herbal properties by heart. At first, I thought this was mere superstition, but as I lived among them, I quickly saw how weak my own memory was. Books are a luxury for the occasional slip of the mind, not a substitute for memory itself."

The boy took the list and mouthed the words. "Thank you, sir. I'll take these to heart."

I complimented the young man's zeal and sagacity, but when he continued to ask questions, I finally told him to hold his peace. "The keen eye and open ear," I said, quoting an orcish proverb, "will find answers to yet unasked questions."

Thus, we worked on in silence, and though it felt like many hours had passed, scarcely over an hour and a half had when I sealed up the last of the open jars and showed Aros how to disassemble the scales. He studied my every motion and tried his hand at removing certain pieces.

I clapped him on the back. "You've done well."

He rubbed the back of his head. "Ah, thanks, sir, for bein' willin' to teach me. It's an honor."

I packed away the remaining items. "Now we can put this physic to use."

As I closed the final box, Aros stuck his hand out. "Thanks 'gain, sir, for helpin' my da and all."

I wiped my hands clean of the oil from the protective cloths that covered the instruments and took his hand. The boy's handshake was limp.

"No, Aros, not like that."

The boy looked from his hand to me and back again.

"Weak handshakes, lad, go with weak hearts." I stuck out my hand again. "Try again." I kept my hand out. "Go on."

He grasped my hand firmly.

"You see? With intention and meaning." I broke my hand free. "All right, once more."

We rehearsed the act once more, but this time, the boy took the lead.

"Better, but keep thinking on it."

"Aye, sir, though I think I just do no have stron' hands like you." He wrung his hands.

"It's got nothing to do with physical strength, lad. A bull of a man can give a heartless handshake, and a man on his deathbed can shake a hand with all the might and heart of a king."

Aros nodded halfheartedly.

I slapped him on the shoulder again, smiled and, with everything packed away, sat down. I scratched Ragnar's ears before picking up my pipe and relighting it.

"You smoke, Aros?" I asked, my pipe between my teeth.

Aros shook his head. "No, sir. Da says I'm no old enough."

I cocked my head at him. "How old are you? Seventeen?"

"I'll be seventeen in two moons or so. Ma says I was born around the solstice."

"Hm, you were born around the same time I was." I puffed on my pipe. "Anyway, you're old enough in my home to smoke." I tamped down the pipe and wiped the stem on my tunic. "If you want to, of course." I held the pipe out to the young man.

He looked at the pipe, then at his siblings, then at me.

"Don't worry about them. I'm telling you it's all right ... *apprentice*." I smirked at him, and the young man snatched the pipe and put the bit in his mouth. He drew a great deal of smoke into his mouth before I could stop him. I winced.

Aros nearly threw the pipe as he coughed violently. Half-burned tobacco flew out of the bowl, and I caught the fine wooden pipe before it fell to the floor as I laughed at the young man's misfortune.

"You're not supposed to inhale it, boy." I slapped his back a few times.

He spluttered and rubbed his watering eyes. "N-now you tell me."

"I was just about to tell you this was a mild blend, too, but I'm guessing you won't believe me anymore." I repacked the pipe.

The young man caught his breath, occasionally sputtering. I passed him my mug of lukewarm tea, and he took a great swig.

"You actually enjoy that?" He gestured to the pipe.

"You probably don't like beer either, do you?"

He grimaced. "What's that supposed to mean?"

I shrugged. "Maybe you're still too young to enjoy a man's—"

The young man snatched the pipe. I let him have it and laughed at his red-faced, watery-eyed indignation. He took another toke, this time holding the smoke in his cheeks.

"You trying to store some up for winter, lad?"

The boy blew out the cloud of smoke. He glared but then laughed with me as we played through this age-old game of cat and mouse as master and apprentice. I puffed a few times myself, exaggeratedly puffing out my cheeks with smoke like he had done.

"Oy, I did no look so squirrelish as that."

"No, you looked even more so. If anyone else had seen—"

"Aros," a woman behind me said, "are you smokin'?"

The young man had just put the bit in his mouth when his mother saw him. He blanched and swallowed smoke again. Spittle flew in my face as he coughed.

All Aros' siblings, young and old, stopped and stared as Gale snatched the pipe.

"No"—Aros pounded his chest—"Mas-Master Rune gave me—"

"Enough." There was fire in her eyes, and she seemed to grow in stature as her face darkened. "Do no go blamin' our host. I've half a mind to take a belt and bend you over my knee right here."

Aros' face went from pale to crimson. "Ma, you—"

"Silence." She jabbed the pipe stem at him. "You're no old enough to smoke, and that is no my rule but your father's. If he were well, he *would* bare your bottom right here so you couldna sit for a week."

The young man looked at me pleadingly as his mother's invective continued.

"Gale, ma'am."

She turned on me, eyes still burning.

"I'm sorry. This is my fault. I—"

"Oh, Master Rune, no." The fire dimmed as she realized it was now I who spoke, and her normal grace returned to her face. "You do no need to stick your neck out for him. He knows his father forbids this." She waved the pipe at her son again, and the fire flared. "He's the one in the wron' here."

"No, truly, I am." I held out my hands in supplication. "I told him he was old enough to smoke in my house."

The heat of her wrath fell upon me now. "And, Master Rune, dear host, may I ask *why* you did that?"

Now it was my turn to swallow hard, and I wondered if she wouldn't bend me over her knee and switch my rear until I cried like a child. "I, uh … I thought he should get a reward for a job well done."

The young man added, "An *apprentice's* job well done, Ma."

She glared at him, and he withered.

I held out my hands again, nearly falling upon my knees. "As your boy says, ma'am. He told me how he wanted to learn pharmacy, or rather that you said he should, and so I told him I'd teach him while you were here."

The inferno in her eyes died down to a controlled blaze.

"And he did well. Truly, he did. So, I thought, seeing as he took this step …"

"You thought, seein' as he took this step, 'twas your place to make yourself his father?"

Aros jumped up. "No, Ma, 'tis—"

She spun her head back around, the fire roaring as she placed her hands on her hips. I swore she would soon breathe fire.

"One more word out of you, Aros Harvaldsson, and that threat 'bout switchin' your hide will no be a mere threat no more."

Terror radiated from the lad, while his siblings looked on with mind-numbing awe.

I had let her bear her wrath down on Aros long enough.

"Truly, I'm sorry, ma'am … I never intended … I should not have encouraged him to break your rules. Please, don't blame the boy."

Now the full heat of her wrath was upon me again, and I, too, withered. Suddenly, though, the blaze in her eyes died down. "You say, Master Rune, that he did the work of an apprentice?"

I merely nodded, afraid to speak.

"And that he did a fine job?"

Another nod.

She sighed deeply. "Aye, well, I'm willin' to o'erlook this, then." She turned to her son, who sank down reflexively. "For both of you."

The boy sat up a little, but fear still filled his eyes.

As if sensing his recovery, she looked indignantly at Aros once more. "But I'll no see him drinkin' or doin' anythin' which he knows is forbidden him."

Aros shook his head, eyes unable to grow any wider.

She presented the pipe to her son, who refused to touch it. "But, I suppose, if he has done a man's work … I think 'twould be fine for him to enjoy a man's pastime."

Aros slowly reached for the pipe.

"But"—she pulled it away, making Aros flinch—"as a gentleman should, he will know when he's had enough and ought to stop." She proffered the pipe once more, this time allowing her son to take it into his trembling hands.

She gave me a slight smile, though her seriousness was by no means diminished for it. "I'll say 'gain that I'm none too happy with you, dear host, for your way of encouragin' godless disobedience, contrary to Andar's law. Howe'er, I can o'erlook that for what you've given my boy." She smiled a bit more. "So, I thank you."

I nodded stiffly and bowed. "I am both ashamed to have disrespected you, and yet honored to have been your son's teacher."

Aros studied the pipe as if it were a great treasure. I would have to make sure he left with one when that time came ...

"He's quite bright. I pray he'll find a full-time tutor when you arrive in Ebria."

Aros had a glint of pride in his eyes.

"But, if you'd excuse us, ma'am, Harvald needs his physic."

R

"Hold the candle there, lad, and watch carefully. I'm going to do this all because of how delicate your father's condition is."

The boy nodded, holding the candle to cast more light on his father's covered feet.

He let out a great sigh that made the candle flicker. "'Tis true what my sister told us? My da might lose ... you know."

I met Aros' gaze. "Aye. Your father might lose part of his foot."

Tears welled up in the corners of Aros' eyes.

"Do you still want to do this? If you want to sit ou—"

"No." He rubbed his eyes with the back of his hand. "I have to be stron' for my family. If they see me ..." A few tears streamed down his face, but he looked away.

"It's all right, lad." I took his chin in my hand. "I know the thought of losing your father is hard, but I'll do everything I can to make him hale again." I took a strip of cloth I had laid out and handed it to Aros. "Now, wipe your eyes, take a deep breath."

The boy breathed deeply.

"You ready?"

Aros stood tall and nodded.

"All right. What you're about to see might shock you." I uncovered Harvald's foot. It was just as black as it had been earlier, though the swelling had decreased.

The boy gasped.

The bandages I had wrapped around Harvald's incision were bleeding through with yellow-red fluid, so I peeled them off and applied a tincture to a clean bandage. Harvald moaned in pain as the tincture touched his wounds.

The candlelight shifted sharply as Aros turned. "Master Rune, he—"

"It's all right, Aros." I tapped the young man's shin as I knelt. "The tincture just stings a bit. Now, turn that candle back this way." I took the second phial, stepping to Harvald's side, and applied the ointment to his bed sores.

"Now, this last one is the easiest." I unstopped another phial. "I'm just going to mix it in with some water." I offered him the phial and cup. "Why don't you do this, Aros?"

The young man took the cup and phial. "I just mix it up and give it to him?"

"Aye, just be sure to raise his head while he drinks."

He reached out to lift his father's head but stopped short, the cup shaking almost imperceptibly in his hand.

Though I wanted to intervene, I knew I could not—every young man had to come to terms with his father's mortality on his own.

After nearly a minute of silence, Aros took a deep breath, steadied his hands, and put the cup to his father's lips. When he was done, he took the corner of the sheet to wipe his father's face. "His skin is on fire ..."

I touched Harvald's forehead. "Well, it's good we're giving him this physic, then." I gestured for Aros to continue.

"And all these tinctures, they'll really help my da get well?" He stroked his father's red hair and kissed his forehead.

"Aye, somewhat." I took Harvald's wrist and found his pulse again. "I don't have some of the ingredients I need to make something for his tetanus specifically, though."

The boy shook his head. "So, where can we get what's missin'? If I have to march through the snow to that town, I will."

I patted Aros' arm. "As soon as the storm clears, I'll ride into town and see if Old Man Connor has what I need." I collected the remaining unused linens and supplies. "Until then, Aros, there's not much more we can do but pray and keep your father comfortable."

RRR

Chapter VI

Let them eat to their hearts' content, and let no man forbid them!

— The Festal Decree of the Oserdeni

Kings

R

B y winter's early sunset, the smell of bread and venison stew filled my home, and the table was set with the few wooden bowls and spoons I kept on the mantle. Though nobody remarked about the shortage of place settings, the looks of disappointment were hard to mistake. So, I snuck into the storeroom, obliged to remedy the situation.

From a strongbox hidden under the floorboards, I produced a set of fine porcelain bowls and cups. In the darkness, the porcelain glowed a faint orange-red, the color of dragon's fire. I set the stack of bowls and plates aside and took enough dwarven silver flatware for the family, too. While the dwarven work did not glow, it was impervious to tarnish and never required a shine.

I scooped up the porcelain and flatware into my arms to set the table.

The bowls no longer glowed in the bright light of the fire but appeared whiter than virgin snow, amplifying the firelight many times over. The spoons, too, amplified the light and reflected it upon the vaulted ceiling and walls in hypnotic fashion.

Erika rushed over as I laid the settings out. "Master Rune, please allow—" She marveled at the porcelain. "Oh my ... Master Rune, you need no use such lordly porcelain for—"

I waved away her concern. "Well, lass, it's either this, or we eat out of a shared pot all huddled 'round the fire."

"I ... We ..." She brushed my arm with her badly chapped hands as she took the bowls from me. "Master Rune, really, this is—"

"Oh, 'tis a real kin' and queen's bowl and spoon, Erika." Her younger sister, Yoanna, too, had sidled up to the table the moment Erika had said *lordly*. The child gripped the table's edge and squealed as she jumped up and down, her hair flying wildly. "Just like in the stories you tell. Do we—"

"Yoanna, I do no think we'll—"

"Erika"—now Haldis was by my side—"if our host, Master Rune"—she smiled at me, batted her green eyes, and patted my forearm—"wants us to use his fine porcelain settin', we should let him." She removed the wooden bowls from the table and turned her nose up at Erika.

Erika sighed and took the silverware from me. "But you must no set the table, sir. Allow me and Haldis to tend to this."

"Yet you are my guests. It would be wrong for me *not* to set the table with the best of what I have."

Haldis giggled. "See, Erika? He thinks 'tis right to set out all this fine porcelain." She smiled at me again.

I shuddered.

"We sure are thankful to you, Master Rune. If there's anythin' we can do for you ..." She curtsied after setting the wooden bowls back on the mantle.

Erika rolled her eyes and flicked her long braid back behind her shoulder. "Well, I'm sure our host has little use for help like us, Haldis."

Haldis folded her arms across her chest, turning up her nose. "Speak for yourself, Erika, but I'd be more than able to serve our host." She brushed against me. "If you'd like me to sew for you, Master Rune, or"—she took a loose lock of my dark brown hair—"trim your hair."

I sidestepped her. "Don't you like my hair?" I ran a hand through my thick locks and undid the loose bun to let all my hair fall to my shoulders. Not wanting to make my distaste for her advances too obvious, I joked, "I always considered it one of my few redeeming features."

The young lady blushed. "Oh no—I mean, aye, Master Rune, your hair is beautiful. I only mean e'en beautiful hair needs a trim now and 'gain." She gathered her golden hair all over her right shoulder with a little tug.

"I know what you meant, lass. I'm just giving you a hard time. Now, why don't we eat?"

"No"—Gale stood in the bedroom doorway with hands on her hips—"with such a fine service, Master Rune, we simply canna accept this." She stopped her eldest daughters with a look. "We're no fit to dine with—"

"Oh?" I crossed my arms. "I see no reason you're less fit than I am to—"

"Master Rune ..." Gale took the wooden bowls from the mantle and set them out again. "We—I know nothin' of who you are. You say you're no lord, nor do you e'en desire us to call you *master*. Yet, though you clearly try to hide your nature, you've lordly possessions. Whether you let us call you

71

lord or no, you're of a higher station, and we've no right to be treated by you as lords and ladies.

"Already, you've done more for us than we could've hoped. I truly believed my husband would soon die, and all I wished was for him to die in comfort and no on the road."

I opened my mouth to object, but she stopped me.

"No, Master Rune, let me finish. I know he may still die, if Andar so wills, but now we've hope, and that"—she gave all her children, but especially Haldis, a sharp look—"is more than enough for any of us. We must no allow ourselves to think we deserve this treatment by you, our better and most gracious host, for we're no but your servants." She set the last of the wooden bowls in their place. "'Twould be a dishonor for us to act as if we were your equals." Her eyes were full of adamant resolve, and none of her children spoke a word in rebuttal.

She had been all too close to the truth when she said I hid my true nature, and so I doubled down on my objection.

"Dear woman, I know of no reason I should be considered better than you. I, in all truth, am no lord, nor do I have servants that I should be a master to any. My father came from among the Sviari and was, like your husband, a carpenter. My mother, an Oserdeni who was nothing more than the daughter of an alderman. All I have, which you call lordly—and perhaps it seems so—has been earned during my lifetime.

"As the Two have been to me, so I am to you. Now, not another word against all this, for that would be the true dishonor. You dine with a man, not a king or lord."

I removed the wooden bowls yet again. "Now, let's set the table, pray, eat, have a moment of respite, and go to bed.

The day is spent, evening is upon us, and you've all spent too much time working."

R

Much of our early dinner conversation was left to the youngest children, who complained they would not be allowed to use the porcelain. "You'll break it," their mother and siblings argued. The complaints of the children turned to cheers, however, when I tossed a plate for Raynor to catch. The wolf leapt and caught the plate turned discus in his maw and returned it to me without a scratch. Much to my chagrin, the amazement of all nearly turned to chaos when the four youngest boys raised their dishes with a collective mind to toss them to the wolves. With an equally unified cry, Gale and the four eldest children all shouted. I, meanwhile, could only hide my laughter behind my hand.

When the children calmed down, they fought over how many cows their father would have gotten for even one *magic* bowl at the village market. Though the women shushed them, they finally gave up and so granted me another much-needed laugh. Indeed, if my guests knew what this dragon bone porcelain and dwarven silverware were, they would have found it just as humorous. One setting would have purchased and run an entire estate for years, even without revenues, and the entire twelve-piece set would have been enough to ransom a city.

When the young women dished out stew and hunks of bread to all, the conversation halted, too. They poured cut wine for Gale and me, and tea or water for themselves and their siblings. When the boys tried to eat before all had been served, however, their hands were swiftly slapped. Likewise, though the women served me first, I waited for the rest.

When all were served, I chanted, "All Father."

The clattering of spoons being set down resounded, and everyone sang the response, "Hear thy children as we pray."

That these strangers, despite the two centuries separating our births, were yet connected to me by the sacred—even if the sacred itself had recently lost much of its savor—was of great comfort.

When the resonant chanting ceased, I took a hunk of bread and my cup, raised them, and chanted, "On this earthly bread and cup, gifts of the Two, let your Spirit abide so we may have life unto the ages of ages." I set these down, brought my hands together to rest on the table, and I hung my head in silence to ponder the irony of the prayer's final petition. Did anyone understand the curse that is eternal life?

When a moment of silence had passed, the family intoned the close, "Bless we the All Father and the Two."

After the blessing, the only melody was of spoons clinking against porcelain. After not even five minutes passed, Aros and Arve sat with empty bowls. They glanced at me, at the pot, and at their mother, but they did not rise.

I had once been as they now were—hungry, tired, and without a clear future in sight—so I filled their bowls to the brim.

"You're welcome to whatever you want in my home, to have as much as you like."

Eirik pushed back from the table and strutted up to me. He stared up at me with a stew-smeared face, wolfish green eyes partly veiled by his red-blond bangs, and he held his bowl outstretched. "I'd like some more stew, tah' much, mister."

I ruffled the boy's curly mop and took his bowl.

The elder children and Gale opened their mouths to chastise the boy, and Eirik looked at them with a great scowl on his dirty face, his bottom lip hanging out.

Gale took the bowl from me and, with a deep bow and mumbled apology, filled it for her son.

"You must no ask *Master* Rune to serve you—'tis rude—and you must say *please*, no *'tah much*. He's our host, and you'll treat him with due respect, Eirik. Now, apologize to Master Rune for bein' rude."

"But Ma, I was no wantin' to be rude. Master Rune said 'twas—"

"Well, I'm tellin' you, you were rude, and do no talk back to me 'gain, or 'twill be a spankin' for you. Now apologize."

The boy hung his head. "I'm sorry for bein' rude to ya, Master Rune."

"It's all right, boy, but listen to your mother."

"Aye, Master Rune," he mumbled before putting a spoonful of stew in his mouth.

"I'm sorry for his rudeness, sir." Gale locked her swollen, bloodshot eyes with mine, but I could not meet them—they bore too much sorrow. "And I apologize for how much we're eatin' of your food, and for soilin' your good porcelain, and—"

I raised my hand. "It's no trouble."

Now it was she who turned her face away, and she silently sopped the last bit of stew from her bowl with a morsel of bread. Unlike her children, she did not serve herself again.

Her sudden show of pride surprised me. She had readily cast herself at my knees only hours before. Then again, everyone had their limit. Apparently, self-service was hers.

Instead of drawing more attention to her, I picked my two favorite pipes from the mantel, packed and lit one, and packed the other for my temporary apprentice. I passed him the pipe and leaned back in my chair with legs crossed as I blew smoke rings.

"You've all had a long journey, so please don't hesitate to eat your fill here while you can."

Gale did not budge. "You're most gracious, sir."

Haldis and Erika served themselves and their younger siblings, and Aros and Arve showed no qualms, either, about serving themselves many times over. Still, Gale feigned contentment.

As Erika stood by the pot, she looked at her mother. "Ma?"

"No, dear, thank you." She smiled unconvincingly. "I'm rather full."

Indeed, everyone had their limits. This was mine.

"Erika, fill her bowl again, please."

The young lady did not hesitate.

Gale opened her mouth, but I cut her off. "You need to eat, Gale ... ma'am."

Her frown accentuated the gauntness of her face.

I folded my hands and leaned forward. "I say this not as your host, but as someone who has traveled across this world several times over. That, and as someone trained in medicine, I also speak. You, of all people, as a mother of so many, should know the importance of a good meal."

She opened her mouth again, but I pressed on, "Moreover"—I lost my congenial tone—"as someone who has seen people die of exhaustion and malnourishment, which you are clearly experiencing, I urge you—no, I order you—to eat for your family's sake, if not your own."

She shut her mouth, waved her daughter ahead, and hung her head as she ate in silence.

After a few minutes of tense quietness, I spoke again to nobody in particular. "If you want, you could try giving Harvald some broth from the stew. He needs to keep his strength up, too."

Surprisingly, it was Gale who responded, "Aye, sir, he does. Thank you for thinkin' of him." More surprising still, she got up to fill another bowl not for her husband but herself. She filled it to the brim and took another morsel of bread.

"If I may, now that you're all fed and have had a chance to settle in, I'd like to know your story. I know nothing besides your names and that you hail from the west. I don't even know how you've found yourselves traveling in midwinter like this." I took a moment to puff on my pipe. "I don't wish to pry, of course, so tell me only what you wish, if it be anything at all."

The older children looked at one another and their mother. When no one spoke, Gale began.

"If you really wish to know, sir, I'll tell you what's right to tell." She sighed. " 'Twas the day the crier came that e'erythin' changed. We had all heard rumors of fightin' at Seagate, ships comin' from across the sea, but no one knew how bad 'twas till that day. Certainly, nobody expected we'd be fleein' a war in midwinter."

Erika cleared her throat. "Ma, maybe Haldis and I should tell this part. We were there."

Haldis hummed her agreement and twirled her long, blonde braids. "Aye, I 'spose we can start."

RRR

Chapter VII

*Sæterlaners are little more than sheepherders, and
they are expert in little else than that.*

— From the travelogue of a Capitolian

merchant

R

T he peal of a handbell rang through the market, and the
crowd grew silent.

"People of Compton," the herald rang out with a baritone
voice, "hear the decree sealed with a mighty hand and set forth
by King's Regent Athelstan, son of the late Regent, Governor
Wallace, and Lady Edris, who sits on the Emerald Throne in
Sea Gate, who rules also this Province of Sæterlan."

Though most in Compton would have ignored a herald's
calls—rarely did they bring news about anything but taxes
due—the sizeable crowd in the market stayed silent for this
herald's words. Now murmurs rippled through the gathered
crowd.

What news did the herald bring from Sea Gate? Would
this be the first official report of the war? Why else would the
herald have armed guards posted at the rostrum unless there
was danger? Until now, there had only been rumors from the
traders and the few refugees who passed through from farther
west, and these were mostly fantastical and
hysteric—inhuman monsters and dragons were said to be the
enemy.

The paraments hanging upon the podium and the squire's standard, both of which were emblazoned with an aquamarine sea serpent supporting the emerald throne on its undulating back, rustled in the breeze that rolled into the foothills from the mountains to the east.

The herald waited for the crowd to quiet down before continuing, "By the close of this month of Ninemoon, those not wishing to be conscripted into the king's armies, who march to war against the invading godless ones from across the Western Expanse, must vacate this Province of Sæterlan for their own safety." The herald took a deep breath. "Those unable to vacate these lands due to age or infirmity are urged to petition the priest of Compton who, as steward of the grace of Almighty Andar's mercies, will call upon the faithful to aid them."

The herald lowered his arms to stop his emerald tabard from blowing in the late summer wind but continued to read from his unfurled scroll. "Know that the Southern Pass into the Province of Gårlan is yet open to travel, but be ye warned that the armies of our king, His Majesty Eleutherios the Seventeenth, Custodian of the Most Holy Seat of Andar, now march against the heathen invaders by way of this pass. Those who would travel by means of it may be waylaid and subject to the requisitioning of provisions, whether of chattels or provender, and of manpower as deemed necessary by His Majesty's forces. Yet, the passage to the north, commonly called Sharptooth Pass, that leads to Nordlund, is open and, as yet, unvisited by soldiers. Thus, all those wishing to evacuate this province with greater ease upon their possessions are urged to travel by the northern roads."

The herald rolled up the parchment and raised it high. "This decree shall be posted in the market square of Compton forthwith. No excuse shall be accepted for ignorance thereof. Therefore, make clear to every neighbor and kinsman that this decree has been promulgated." He handed the parchment down to the young squire, whose clothes were also decked with the seal of the Emerald Throne, at his side.

Those gathered murmured anew as the herald finished. The words "six days," "winter," and "impossible" were easily discerned upon the lips of all.

The murmuring continued until a man in the crowd shouted, "You can tell Athelstan to take his decree and shove 'er up his arse. I did no spend all summer plantin' to leave come harvest."

A rumble of agreement reverberated, and another shouted, "You canna expect six days should be enough time for me to pack my entire family and gather the flocks from pasture. No, I tell you, I'll no be goin' nowhere."

A roar of agreement went up, and townsfolk hurled insults against Athelstan and the herald. Someone threw an apple from a nearby stall, striking the herald squarely on the jaw.

The herald, a short, pudgy man with great gray mustaches that flapped when he spoke, grew red in the face. "To assault the lord's herald"—his mustaches quivered—"is to assault the lord himself. Now, your lord is merciful, and so I order you all to disband, lest you be declared enemies allied with the invaders."

The guardsmen surrounding the herald, and even the squire, put their hands to their sword hilts.

The people quieted, and the raised hands holding apples and other foodstuffs fell at once. Yet, nobody disbanded.

"I will not tell you again," the little man, who now had a great red welt where the apple had struck him, yelled, "disband or be treated as traitors to the empire. There shall be no extensions given, so I suggest you make haste to prepare."

Erika and Haldis stood toward the back of the crowd, each carrying a basket of fresh produce on their arms. They looked at one another but did not speak. What had they just heard?

When the crowd slowly disbanded, the young women returned to the market stall, ready to finish their last purchase. Erika held out the ten coppers she had pulled from her pouch when the herald had begun, but the old woman who stood behind the booth stopped her.

"This'll cost you thrice that now, girly." The old woman's words whistled through gaps in her teeth.

Erika glared. "That's outrageous, ma'am. A moment ago, we agreed on ten for the two dozen of eggs."

The woman returned Erika's glare with an even nastier one. "That was 'fore I done hear the war's comin', and we be needin' ta move out in no a week's time, girly. What the crier done said means I needs be chargin' you war prices."

Haldis frowned, not understanding how this could be, but she remained silent to let her sister do the arguing. She watched as Erika rummaged into her coin purse and pulled out ten pence more. "I'll give you twenty and no a copper more. What you're doin' … 'tis extortion."

The old woman snatched the coins and filled the basket.

Erika stormed off, and Haldis followed close behind.

The market bristled with the frenetic movements of shopkeepers closing their stalls early or hurriedly selling goods with a din of raised voices arguing like Erika just had.

"Erika," Haldis said as she held up her skirt to catch up, "should we go to Da's shop and tell him, or should we go home and tell—"

"Garth." Before Haldis finished, Erika burst through the crowd. She flung her free arm around a brawny, flame-haired man who stood among a small group of older men. "Garth, did you hear the herald?"

Caught off guard, he stumbled. "Whoa ... By the Two ..." He mouthed an apology to the man he had jostled and righted himself.

"Eri, can you no see I'm busy talkin' 'bout just that?"

She lay her face against his chest and met his gaze. He smelled of charcoal and smoke, the scents of the forge, and had soot smeared upon his face. "Sorry, Garth." She looked at the gathered men; some glowered at her, others smirked or laughed behind raised hands.

Garth silenced them with an over-the-shoulder glare.

"What are you plannin', Garth?"

Garth returned her embrace with a peck on the cheek and ran a hand through her long hair. He put his face close to her ear. "We've no decided yet, Eri. Only give us men"—he gestured to those around him, some still annoyed at the presence of this young lady—"some time to talk."

Erika frowned but said nothing.

When Haldis finally caught up to her sister, she tried to wedge her way into the conspiratorial circle of men. "Another lassie, Garth? Soon nothin' will be decided if you keep lettin' every woman in town in on our plans."

"This is my fiancée"—he gestured at Erika—"and her sister. They're just sayin' hello is all." He looked at Erika and Haldis and jerked his head to the side for them to leave.

"Time's short, Garth," a man said, stroking his great, gray-flecked beard. "There's no time for pleasantries and romance. Beggin' your pardon, youn' lady." He tipped his head at Erika.

Another man, even older still, gestured in a circular motion. "Right, let's wrap this up, anyway. Gather as many of our folk as you can, and we'll all meet in the Sheep and Ram tonight after the temple bell rings the eighth. Then and there, we'll tell the council what must be done."

A rumble of agreement resounded in their midst, and the men departed, some glaring once more at Erika and Haldis with a shake of their heads.

Erika placed her hands on her hips. "I thought you said you had no yet decided what to do? What's this then 'bout *tellin' the council what must be done*, and what did that man mean by *our folk*? Are these men Separatists, Garth?"

Garth put his hands on his fiancée's shoulders, shook his head, and tried to hide an eye roll behind his half-closed lids. "No, Eri, 'tis nothin' like that. Tonight, in the pub, the town council is goin' to meet and discuss plans ... Us men, well, we're just plannin' to tell the council what we'd like to see happen."

She pushed Garth's arms from her shoulders. "And, what do you want to see happen?"

"Do no worry yourself 'bout that, Eri."

"Why? Because if we *lassies* get involved, nothin' would e'er happen 'round here?"

Garth rolled his eyes again. "Oh, c'mon, Eri ..."

"I deserve to know whate'er is goin' on as much as you do, Garth."

"Enough, Eri. Now go find your da and tell him 'bout the meetin' tonight, and tell him to brin' Aros. He's old enough to have a voice in the town's business now."

"Oh, so *he's* old enough, but I'm—"

"Agh, be quiet, Eri." His eyes filled with a fire that died as quickly as it had appeared. Erika had seen that flashfire before but never had it unnerved her as it did now.

Erika turned her back on Garth. "Come on, Haldis; let's go and find some stron' men to save us from this mess."

Garth spun her around. "Eri, you know 'tis no like that. I'm just … I just want to make sure we—the whole town—makes the best choice tonight." The fire in Garth's eyes began to smolder.

"We'll see …"

R

"So, there 'tis." Haldis twirled the tip of her braid between her fingers. "Then we went to my—our da's shop to tell him what we heard. But me and Erika, we did no stay lon'."

Arve cleared his throat. "I was there, though, after they left. Da … well, he was no happy."

R

"Thank you for lettin' me know, lassies." Harvald threw his block plane on the swarf-covered workbench and brushed his hands on his heavy brown leather apron. "Go tell your mother … tell her to prepare for the worst." He threw his toolbelt and apron on the table, and the tools rattled. "I've gotta do the same here."

"All right, Da."

"And send Aros o'er here. I'll need his help, too." Harvald ran a hand through his full beard and hung his head as he leaned against the workbench. "Two Holies ..."

Arve hung a tenon saw and clamp among the many other tools his father possessed. "Da, what's all this 'bout?"

"I dunno, boy. Right now"—he picked up a plaining scraper, studied it absently, and tossed it back on the workbench—"we gotta collect on these projects and pack e'erythin' else."

"But ... what they said 'bout the herald? Are we really—"

Harvald slapped the workbench, and sawdust flew. "No now, boy. I know as much as you. Right now, we've to work on gettin' these projects out and pack whate'er we can."

"But, what if they ...? What if Erika and Haldis are ...? I mean, could the war—"

"Enough!" Harvald slammed his fist upon the table, green eyes flaring. "No another word, boy."

His son jumped and bit his lower lip.

"I know only what you know." His eyes softened as he looked at his son, and he sighed. "Sorry, Arve. E'erythin' you're askin', I'm askin', too. The council meetin' tonight'll answer e'erythin', but looks like we're bein' sent away."

R

Arve shrugged. "That's all, I 'spose."

Aros sat tall. "I can tell you what happened at the meetin'. That is, if you want me to, Master Rune?"

I waved my hand, and the young man began straight away.

R

That evening, the common room of the Sheep and Ram, which was normally boisterous on any night, was fuller than it had ever been. The round tables scattered around the room were all full, some milled about, while others poked their heads in at the opened windows. Near the fireplace, which was normally surrounded by a few chairs and ottomans, was a solitary, long table with chairs only on one side. There sat the council of village elders—four men, no younger than fifty—and the town's priest, who was dressed in his customary black cassock and pileus. Though the priest was young, he commanded the townsfolk's respect.

The room filled with the haze of pipe smoke as everyone gathered, and the rumble of nearly two hundred voices filled the tavern, creating an unintelligible cacophony.

The eldest member of the council cleared his throat but choked on the smoke. Nobody heard him. He wiped his mouth with an age-spotted hand and said, "Let's begin." The old man's words were drowned in the sea of voices. He looked at the youngest of the four council members and nodded.

This man, a giant even by Sæterlan standards, slammed a fist on the table. "Oy, quite down, the lot o' ya! We've business to discuss, and here you are, like hens in the coop, spreading gods-da—" He looked to his left at the priest. "Er, sorry, Father." The councilman inclined his head toward the cleric, who waved off the offense. "As if you were spreadin' foolish nonsense," he finished.

There was a clattering of mugs being set down, and the men who stood held theirs still. A few even set their pipes on the tables or held them at rest.

The eldest councilman waved the smoke from before his face again and rose. "Thank you for bein' here tonight." He stroked his gray, wispy beard. "You've all read the notice in the market, I'm sure."

A ripple of acknowledgement surged through the crowd.

"Though nobody expected that this … war"—he spoke the word as if it were foreign—"'twould spread this far and so fast, here we are." He took his long beard between his thumb and forefinger and ran them down his beard. "'Tis deeply troublin' …"

An even louder murmur rumbled through the crowd.

"Aye, deeply troublin' to think we should be removed from our homes before harvest, and e'en as winter approaches. Then, if this were no troublin' enough, we're told, if we go by the safer route, we'd face havin' our sons conscripted or our stores ransacked by the very soldiers bein' sent to protect us."

Though the councilman spoke in a calm, level tone, the murmuring grew angrier. Foul curses rose above the other voices. Someone shouted, "Damn the kin' and his men. We're no goin' nowhere." An even louder, "hear, hear," echoed, and the approving thumps of feet, fists, and mugs resounded.

Another elder, only slightly grayer than the youngest, raised his arms.

The crowd quieted down.

"Watch what you say 'bout the Lord Kin'. This decree came from Athelstan, no the kin'—"

"Then damn Athelstan and his decree."

This outburst was met with greater approval.

The priest rolled his eyes and picked at the dirt under his nails, while the final elder, who rivaled the oldest one in decrepitude, stood shakily.

"Enough. As elders, we're sworn to obey 'n brin' 'bout the king's will, includin' the rightful decrees of his servants.

I'll tolerate no more of this rebellious talk." Despite his age, he spoke with a firm voice.

Half the men gathered in the room booed and hurled obscenities.

One of the men at a nearby table spoke up, "Since when've you been a loyalist to Athelstan, Krossbyr?" Though his words were sharp, his tone was less caustic than those gathered behind him. "You used to be amon' the first to say we should fight for better at the hands of—what'd you call him?—the *absentee regent* who refused to rise from his throne 'cause it might get cold, and he'd have to *warm 'er with his own arse.* I believe you also said the *whoreson* had no right to rule."

Krossbyr frowned, his long, white eyebrows drooping nearly to the level of the tip of his nose. "Aye, I've said many things, and I still do no like Athelstan, but—"

"Then tell 'em to shove his bloody decree."

The crowd burst into applause and shouts of acceptance.

Krossbyr waited for the crowd to settle while he shook his head at the man. "If you'd let me finish … E'en for a swine like Athelstan, his decree is as good as the king's own, and I've no quarrels with our kin', 'specially no if war is on the horizon."

This time, the crowd's murmur was lower and subdued, and the few heads that had not bobbed in agreement with the heckler now bobbed in agreement with Krossbyr.

"As a council, and in conference with our priest, we've decided—"

The crowd burst into an uproar.

"There's been no deliberations yet."

"Senile old bastards do no care what any of us have to say."

"Bugger Athel—"

R

Gale nearly jumped to her feet. "Aros! By the Two Holies, watch your language."

Aros opened his mouth, but his mother silenced him with a look.

"And I do no care if you're just sayin' what they did. I do no want filthy language comin' out of the mouths of my children."

"Fine ..."

R

"To the devils with Athelstan."

They also shouted many other coarse words not fit to be spoken in the presence of one's mother.

"Enough of this." The priest rose, shaking out his cassock. "Be silent, the whole lot of you. Let your elder finish and keep your tongues in check, lest you damn yourselves." The cleric's Capitolian accent was high-pitched, standing out against the musical accent of the Sæterlaners.

The crowd quieted, and Krossbyr nodded at the priest.

"We've decided 'tis best for all that we make our way by the north pass together. That is the decision of this council, and there shall be no discussion. The Lord Athelstan gave us no other option."

All were silent. Nobody, whether in favor or opposed, could believe what they had just heard. *No discussion?* That was *not* in keeping with custom. Maybe it accorded with law, but not custom ...

Someone snorted and cleared their throat, and a great blob of green mucus flew over the crowd to splatter onto the elders' table. "I hope y'all die in the mountains, you and your families, the whole lot o' ya."

A tankard smashed against the fireplace's mantle just above the elders, and potsherds rained upon the table.

The priest slammed both hands on the table. "Enough!" He straightened his pileus, which had slid forward onto his forehead. "For Holy Andar's sake, control yourselves. You shame the elders, whom you yourselves appointed, and bring disgrace to this village. If you cannot behave in a way becoming of men old enough to have the vote, then leave and see to your affairs as you like. We'll not stop you."

Nearly four score men pushed their way out of the inn. Aros and Harvald, who had been two of the last to enter the tavern before it was full, made way. One of the younger men pushed past Aros with a muttered curse. Aros caught only a glimpse of red hair that was quickly covered with a hood.

Aros nudged his father. "Da, was that—"

Harvald held up a hand to silence his boy and paid him no mind. "No now, Aros."

R

Aros sat back, nodded at me, and took a long drag on his pipe.

Gale cleared her throat. "Now, I'll tell you what I know."

R

Gale stared at her cooking utensils hanging from pegs near the hearth, one hand on her hip and another supporting her pregnant belly.

"But Ma, do you no think we should wait and see what the council decides?" Erika placed the crate of her mother's sewing near the door—it was full of unfinished clothes for the coming baby. The number of crates had not stopped growing from the moment the girls had brought back the herald's news. "They may decide we're no better off leavin', and all this'd—"

"Erika, dear"—Gale ran a hand through her blonde hair and sighed—"I know this is no what you want—"

"Do no speak to me like I'm still a wee girl, Ma. I'll be twenty in a moon, and I'm 'bout to marry." Erika gripped her white apron, leaving dirty palm prints on the fabric. "Surely if Aros is allowed to have a voice in all this at sixteen, then I damn well—"

Gale shook out her own apron and stamped her foot. "Watch your language, youn' lady. You may be a woman now, true, but for a few more moons, you're still under my care and your father's until he gives you to Garth to be his wife."

Erika lifted another crate of her family's possessions. "Ma, I know, but—"

"Let me finish."

Erika set the box down and folded her arms. She knew there was no point in trying to speak over her mother. Not even her father could do that.

"Now, Erika, dear"—Gale took her daughter's hands into her own—"I know you're worried this'll delay the weddin'—"

Erika threw her mother's hands down. "No, Ma, 'twill *ruin* the weddin'. You've seen the refugees come through, how e'en families get separated. If that can happen to folk who're already marri—" Tears trickled down her cheeks.

Gale embraced her daughter. "Those people—Andar have mercy on them—fled from burnin' villages. That's why they were separated, but we're leavin' together." She wiped a silent tear from her daughter's rosy cheeks. "I promise, your father and I'll do e'erythin' we can to stay near Garth and his family."

Erika sniffed, resting her head on her mother's shoulder. "I just canna stand the thought of losin' him, Ma."

"I know, Erika, and that's why 'tis best we prepare now, so we can leave when Garth and his family do … If we leave 'tall, of course."

"I hope we stay."

"None of us hope for anythin' else, Erika, but when—"

The front door burst open. Garth stood in the threshold, his cloak's hood pulled tight around his face. A chilly breeze blew in, and the fire in the hearth flickered. His cloak billowed as he rushed in.

At once, Erika released her mother and embraced her fiancé. "Garth"—she kissed him on the cheek—"what did the council—"

Garth threw his hands up, and Erika stumbled back with a grunt.

"That hurt, Garth."

He brushed her away. "They're damn fools, e'ery one of 'em. The Two take those cowards." The boxes and other goods the women had stacked by the door rattled as he tromped to the fireplace in his heavy boots. He leaned on the mantle with his forearms and grabbed his hair in his fists.

"Keep your voice down; the little ones are asleep in the next room." Gale flattened out her apron and stood erect. "And watch your language, youn' man. You're no in that tavern anymore. Now"—she spoke calmly—"tell us what happened. What did they decide?"

A piece of crockery that wobbled on the mantle's edge jumped as Garth slammed his fist against the mantelpiece. The piece teetered, fell, and exploded, potsherds skittering. "They decided to turn and run. The elders did no e'en entertain the idea of stayin'." He whirled around, eyes frenzied. "I canna believe …"

Erika had begun to collect broken pieces of pottery when her mother approached him. She held out her arms to him as if he were her own son. "Garth, nobody wants to leave, but we were no given much choice. The kin'—"

"Oh please, 'twas no the kin'." He jabbed a finger at Gale, who stepped back. " 'Tis that cowardly bastard, Athelstan. He's the one orderin' this, tryin' to get a hold of our land, no doubt. So, why should we listen to him? He taxes us, sets levies of e'ery kind, demands tribute, but when we've needed his help … when our crops failed or our flocks died, did he e'er answer us? No. Instead, he sits his ass—"

"Enough, Garth. I do no like you speakin' so." Erika let the potsherds she had collected fall. "Really, what's gotten into you, Garth? I knew you'd no like the idea of leavin'—you hinted as much—but now"—she stepped closer to him—"you sound like a—"

"Like a what, Erika? Like a Sæterlan Separatist?"

Erika stood tall and locked eyes with Garth. She thanked Andar she had been graced with stature like her mother. "Like a drunk old man who's been boozin' in the tavern."

Garth grew as red as his hair, and he clenched his fists.

Gale stepped closer. Her daughter had also been blessed with her mother's ability to control conversations, though now it seemed that ability was a curse.

"You should know better than to talk this way, Garth. Now stop speakin' like a fool and go home to help your family prepa—"

Garth raised an open hand, but Gale interposed herself between him and her daughter and slapped Garth. "Get out of my house, and do no dare come back unless you're ridin' in your mother and father's wagon."

Garth wiped the back of his hand across his split lip.

"And the first words out of your mouth better be, 'Forgive me, I was a fool.'"

Seeing the blood on the back of his hand, Garth cursed, "You bit—"

"If Harvald were here, boy"—she drew so near to him that their noses nearly touched—"you'd have much worse than a split lip if he'd seen what you almost did to his daughter. I'm of half a mind to tell him, too, and you'll be lucky if he does nothin' more than have your father tan your hide."

Garth turned heel and left.

Erika chased after him. "Garth, wait—"

The door slammed in her face.

"Ma, how could you speak to him that way? He was just upset, is—"

She grabbed Erika's arms. "That fool boy was goin' to strike you, Erika."

She broke free of her mother's hold. "He'd no have really—"

Gale held her arms wide to embrace her daughter. "Erika—"

R

95

"I've heard enough, I think." Erika rose from the table, taking her dishes with her. "I'm sorry, Master Rune, but please excuse me."

Gale started to rise. "Eri—"

I raised my hand, mouthing, "*It's all right.*"

Gale watched her daughter disappear into the washroom. "I'm sorry, Master Rune, for her rudeness. She's been upset e'er since Garth … since Harvald forbade them to be married when I told him."

"It's all right. No harm done. Wounds of the heart can be slow to heal, and sometimes all they need is a little solitude." As I spoke, thoughts of Mara filled my mind for the thousandth time.

I lay naked next to her in a forest clearing in the heat of summer as a young man. She had bits of brush and twigs in her beautiful, raven-black hair, and she lay with her back to me as I gave her my arm to lay her head upon. I pulled the bits of twigs and leaves from her hair as I savored her scent. She smelled of wild rose, even after a romp in the woods.

I rolled onto my back, and my she-wolf straddled my chest to cleanse me from my own signs of illicit passion, just as I had done for her. She leaned over me, and her cascading black hair became the canopy of night. Her lambent hazel eyes were the stars, and her breasts, the moon. I filled myself with their splendor, took hold of her, and made the infinite mystery of her night my personal possession.

And night covered me. She ran her hands through my wild hair, across my chest, and she grabbed any perceived impurity to tear at it with her nails, pulling, scratching, biting. This, she said, was to cleanse me of my sin.

Oh, how I once loved the penances she would inflict upon me. How I would relish her remedies for my wounds. We atoned for one another's sins, she would say, nullifying them by our overpowering, mutual lust.

When we made atonement, we sang ritual hymns with our impassioned cries. We poured out our sacred libations of sweat, blood, and more ... Aye, we offered the culminating sacrifice and died a little in one another's arms. There we lay on our bier, the grass of our trysting glade.

We rose from death to live as the dead and invited one another to sin anew. Then the stars went dark, a candle going out in the dead of night. She and I left our bodies to become something else, someth—

No. I pulled my mind back to the present. I would not think about that ... that godlessness, no matter how my flesh and mind longed for it. Already, I had come close to falling today. I would not be tempted further. Yet, I could not deny the overwhelming wave of sorrow that washed over my heart as I denied myself. This grief ... it was one which no amount of solitude had been able to heal. It was sorrow over sin, certainly, but also sorrow for the hole in my heart, which I did not know how to fill *without* sin, without her and what we were.

"Master Rune? Master Rune, are you well?"

I pulled at the open, swooping neckline of my tunic. My face burned. My heart raced. I wiped sweat from my brow with my bandaged hand, the bandage I had forgotten about, the bandage I wore because I had pierced myself through with that same passion.

"Aye, I'm fine. Just heartburn ..."

"Shall I continue?"

I nodded.

R

"Harvald?" Gale lay on her side with one hand on her belly. "You asleep?"

"No." He rolled over to face her, head resting on his hand. "I doubt anyone in the entire village is sleepin' tonight." He pulled the deer hide blankets up around his wife's bare shoulders. "I keep wonderin' if we've e'erythin' we need. Goin' through the supplies again and again in my mind. I just—"

Gale silenced him with a kiss. "We've e'erythin', Harvald. E'en if we do forget somethin', so lon' as we've the family, that's all we need."

He grunted. "And you're sure your cousins'll take us in? I mean, you've no seen them since—"

"Since I was a wee girl, aye. But we're still kin ..."

"I just wish we had more than custom and hope on our side."

She placed a hand on his bearded cheek. "Harvald, if you do no want us to go there, 'tis fine. I just do no think Burgia'll be far enough for us to get free of this mess. That and—"

"No, Gale"—he took her hand into his own—"I'm no sayin' we should stay in Burgia, though I hate to leave so many of the townsfolk behind there. What I worry is that the distance is so great. E'en if there're no problems on the road, we'll no get farther than Mittleham by first of Elevimon, and with the baby comin' so soon ... I know Congar and Eiver said they wanted to winter in Mittleham with their families, but if we must winter over, I do no want to do so in the north. The sprin' will come late, and only the Two know when the roads might open 'gain. If we do this, we must get past East

Laketon by the solstice, e'en if we must travel durin' the first weeks of winter."

She wrapped her arms around her husband, her head under his chin. "Then that'll be the way we go. Let us only pray for good weather and health."

ᚱ

"The next mornin', we left with the townsfolk who had agreed to obey the decree. There were, I think, five hundred or so among us, and of those, only five families kept movin' past Burgia."

"Well, you've made good time, and with a newborn, no less."

"Aye, though the Holy Ones seem content no to grant us either health or good weather."

"Yet, they've brought you safely to my home, so what they did not supply as you expected, they provided in their own way."

"Aye, you speak the truth, Master Rune. That my faith were stron' as yours …"

If only she knew how deeply my soul was troubled, she'd never say such a thing. No, if she knew, she never would've come under my roof. She'd have preferred to die in the cold …

I glanced at the clock—another piece of dwarven work—hanging on the wall. It was nearly six, the time for my evening prayers. "Dear guests, the hour is now late, and I would ask if there is anything else I can provide this evening. Please, only say the word. If not, I only ask a short time of silence when the clock strikes six so I may pray. Otherwise, my home is yours." I pushed back from the table and folded my hands on my chest.

Gale spoke without a moment's thought. "No, we've nothin' which—"

"Ma, may we ask Master Rune if we could run a few baths?"

Gale shot Haldis a baleful look, to which the young woman was oblivious.

Before Gale could speak, I replied, "Aye, of course you may. The large tub will serve you well for that."

Gale frowned at Haldis, who still did not notice, and said, "You are too kind, dear host, and forgive my daughter's interruption."

"I can draw a bath for the boys right away. Then I'll draw one for us, Ma. Just think how nice 'twill be to have hot water, and soap, and a real tub instead of a river." Haldis sighed and gazed up, as if into Heaven. "Then, of course, we'll draw one for the men. You should see the enormous tin bath—"

"Haldis, I think we can afford our host the benefit of the first bath. We can grant him the privacy of his own, too. This may be a bathhouse to us, but 'tis his home."

Haldis' fair cheeks flushed. "Oh, 'course, Master Rune. I should've—"

I laughed softly. "It's quite all right. I've spent enough time on the road and with enough caravans and soldiers to know what a luxury a hot bath is. I remember once, after three weeks in the dead of winter on the back roads without a single stop at a bathhouse, we finally reached the Seat and headed to a bathhouse first thing. There were eleven of us and only five tubs, but since no one wanted to wait, we bathed three to a tub. Except for Joash—he was a giant—who was barely able to fit in the tub alone."

Aros made a face. "Agh, the smell must've been enough to—"

Gale slammed her palm on the table. "Aros, mind your tongue." She clucked her tongue and sighed. "Master Ru—"

Arve and his younger brothers, who had followed Arve's lead in biting their tongues, burst into laughter. The youngest of the boys had the greatest time of it, pinching their noses and pretending to die as they sniffed the air.

When Gale saw the entire table in fits of laughter, even she had to hide her smile behind a hand.

"Aye." I laughed. "The poor bath attendant nearly passed out when we took off our boots. Oh, the Two have mercy, the stench was horrid. We ended up burning the clothes because the launderers refused to wash them, and none of us dared try what the professionals would not."

I leaned back with a sigh. "Anyway, my point is there's no need to fill the tub once more, though the thought is kind. Moreover, I'd prefer not to be first. I need to see to Harvald after my prayers."

Gale nodded curtly. "Aye, Master Rune, as you like. Thank you, too, for lettin' us have such fun at your expense."

"So long as you're laughing *with* me, all's well."

RRR

Chapter VIII

A hypocratheker must be ever mindful that outward scars often cover much deeper wounds.

— From the *Enchiridion*

R

W hile Haldis and Erika filled the tub after dinner, they herded their four youngest brothers, none of whom were happy about the prospect of a bath, into the washroom. Unlike the boys, when Raynor heard the water running, he raced to peer into the tub, into which only the two youngest boys, Troy and Eirik, had been placed before the older two escaped. The wolf leapt into the path of Magnus, who had been stripped to his smallclothes and weaved between furniture and under the table to avoid his sister, and Raynor lifted the boy off the ground by the hem of his braies. He dropped him at the feet of Haldis, who finished undressing him and put him into the tub. Erika, meanwhile, managed to catch Grimm unaided.

I laughed at the sight as I enjoyed my sweetest tobacco before my prayers. However, a loud splash and the screams turned laughter of those in the washroom interrupted my leisure.

I leaned against the doorframe and peered in. "Everything all right?" There was a great puddle of water, which flowed through the drain channel in the floor, and one bright, golden eye peered at me from over the edge of the tub. "Raynor, this isn't your bath."

The wolf immediately sank under the water as I rolled up my sleeves and plunged my arms in after him.

"Truly sorry, ladies." I fished about in the sudsy water for the hound.

The boys laughed hysterically all the while, and the women, whose clothes had been splashed, also giggled.

Haldis placed her hand on my bare arm and squeezed. "Oh, 'tis no problem, Master Rune."

I pulled my arm free.

"If it keeps the boys in the tub, Raynor can stay."

At once, Raynor popped his snout and eyes above the waterline. The boys all burst into another fit of laughter.

"He's a turtle," one shouted as another jumped onto Raynor's back.

Erika pulled the boys away. "Boys, be gentle now. The last thin' I need is for one of you to get hurt, or to hurt Master Rune's do—wolf."

"Are you sure you're all right with this?" I glared at Raynor, who winked at me.

"*Water. Swimming. Pups. Play,*" he replied.

"Behave, Raynor," I said aloud as I scented my own frustration.

"Oh, 'tis fine, Master Rune," Haldis said. "We'll e'en give him a bath, too, while we're at it."

"If he gives you any trouble, holler." I returned to my pipe and listened to the laughter of children and the occasional bark as I smoked.

R

When the clock struck the top of the hour, I knelt at my altar. Out of the corner of my eye, I saw Aros and Arve, who washed the dishes in a small tub by the fire, eyeing me. "If you wish to join me, you may. It's only the *vespertines*."

Aros and Arve took their places beside me, and I intoned the *incipit*. The antiphonal call and response of the "Divine *Hymnarium*," which culminated in the recitation of the "Symbol of the Holy Theophanic Mysteries" and with petitions for Harvald, filled the room.

Behind us, Ragnar and Ada sat and, to the surprise of the young men, howled along with our own chanting. Their voices and ours melded, and the whole of the cosmos coalesced into the song of wolf and man. In the chant, the immeasurable distance between the divine and creation closed. The distinctions between us vanished, and only one indissoluble unity that is known in hearing remained.

With his head cocked, Aros stared at the wolves. "Do they know what we're doin'? I just ... I guess I always believed in Luváli but ne'er thought wolves worshiped like we do. I always thought Luváli was ... different."

"Aye, they know what's going on when we pray. The wolves ... well, they also have their own way of worshiping Luváli and Andar, and I bet they think much the same of Andar as we do Luváli until they learn otherwise. One will find there's always more to any story than what we could possibly know."

"Do you think they've got souls, Master Rune? I mean, you speak like they're human."

"Oh no, they're definitely not human. They're very much their own, but why should that mean they have no souls? The orcs and dwarves have souls, don't they?"

"Aye, I suppose they do, but they're more like us. They think, and—"

"You don't believe wolves think?"

"N-no ... I think ... I mean, they just do no think like us. They do no feel like we do, right? They do no wonder 'bout the future, or ask 'bout the meanin' of the world, or love like we do, do they?"

The young man contemplated Ada and Ragnar, who were now huddled up by the fire as Ragnar rested his head upon his mate's neck. There was a thirst for knowledge about things beyond man's ken in this lad's eyes, and again I sensed something different in him, but what it was, I still did not know.

"Well, lad, they may not think about those things like we do, but they do understand hope and think about the world. Aye, and they most certainly do love."

"But they canna speak or show love like we can, so—"

"Lad, what is the essence of love? Is it the good feelings we have toward one another? Is it a desire? Or, is it something more?"

The young man's eyes were full of confusion and wonder, which were the same in his eyes.

"I don't claim to know the answer myself, lad, but I know wolves, for all the savagery of their appearances, and for their inability to express themselves as we do, often love more greatly than men."

The young man squinted and furrowed his brow. "I guess I ne'er've heard anythin' like that before, Master Rune. And the idea of wolves bein' able to love ... 'tis hard to believe, but you know them better than me."

"Aye, well, just think on it and ask Luváli to show you the truth."

"I'll do that, sir." He returned to help his brother finish the dishes but glanced back at me. "Thank you for lettin' us pray with you."

"My pleasure, lad. Now, finish all that up and relax a little. I'm going to check on your father."

R

Gale sat by her husband's side and, unsurprisingly, Freya lay nearby, ever the silent guardian and stay of those in need.

"How is he?"

Gale had changed the bandages, and the glistening light reflecting off Harvald's bare skin revealed that she had bathed him.

"He's doin' better, I think. His fever's gone down, though I do no think 'tis entirely broken."

I removed the wet cloth from his forehead and laid a hand upon him.

"His body is more relaxed. When I fed him, his jaw was no so stiff as earlier."

I checked the wounds on his chest and feet, which were doing as well as could be hoped. "Aye, he seems to be improving somewhat. He looks more at ease." I looked at Gale. "I assume you're on first watch tonight?"

"Aye, and I'll be stayin' in here for the night. I fear he'd wake up and panic if he did no have me by his side."

I nodded, wrapping up his foot anew. "All right. Though he looks fine now, he'll need another treatment tomorrow. Likewise, if the weather abates, I'll need to ride to Melbù. He might look better, but I haven't given him a proper treatment for tetanus yet. He's still at risk to have fits during the coming days."

"I pray the Two Holies would speed you, then."

"I pray so, too."

R

When the boys and Raynor finished their bath, the women and Yoanna took their turn. Following the pattern established by Raynor, Ada and Freya also joined the women. These two, however, were not nearly as wild as the pack's beta had been.

While the women bathed, the young men laid out bedrolls and helped put their brothers to bed before the hearth. Raynor again became the focal point of the children's attention, and they arranged themselves so he would be their communal pillow. Raynor, however, did not mind.

The young men told their brothers a story, each taking different roles. It was the story of Galad the Blind, who had been granted the gift of sight in battle. With this gift, he had fought for the oppressed, never asking for more than food and shelter in return. Wherever he would hear injustice, there he would draw his blade. Yet, when he would sheathe his sword, his sight would vanish, and he would become utterly blind so that all he knew was blood and death. It was only the love of the most beautiful woman of that age that had saved him from madness.

I had been told this story as a young boy, too—both my Sviari father and Oserdeni mother knew it, though each had their own version, and both would tell it to me to help me fall asleep. The orcs also told the story, but they called Galad "Gorak" and believed he was a half-orc. I had heard them tell it, too, when I had lived among them.

The orcs believed Gorak the Blind had become the patriarch of the orcish peace that prevailed for centuries. Because of this, Gorak quickly became the chief figure for all ancestor worship among the orcs, and they often called him simply "The Paragon." However, in my own studies, I had learned Gorak was, according to the earliest telling of the tale, an Andarasian. That part of the history, however, was for the missionaries to tell.

As I listened to the retelling of the classic tale, the boys nodded off one by one, with Raynor falling asleep last. Ragnar, however, stood vigilant.

"Raynor, good guardian. Pups for our pack? When?" Ragnar's head reached my hip bone, and I patted his neck gently. He scented loneliness, the scent of the lone wolf, and of hope's failure, the continual darkness of a moonless night when even the stars were veiled by clouds.

"Luváli provides," I replied, barely believing the thought myself. *"Patience."*

Ragnar's only reply was the scent of desperation and hollowness, the scent of a starving wolf who returned hungry from the hunt once more. Ragnar, the great pack leader, leaned his enormous frame into me. I wrapped an arm around my friend, and he sighed. *"Tired ... Patience spent."*

I patted his side and sank my fingers into his warm undercoat. *"Strength. Courage. Endurance."*

"Aye." The alpha's scent expressed a resignation to resolution, the scent of a warrior heading into a suicidal charge. I only wished I could muster that same persistence when desperation overcame me.

R

When the women emerged, their hair wrapped up in the plush towels I had welcomed them to use, they sat before the fire. Ada and Freya did likewise, their fur still damp and wild.

All three daughters had dressed in modestly cut, full-length nightgowns made of simple, unadorned linen that fell to their ankles. The fabric was clearly of quality, a sign of Harvald's ability to provide well for his own yet, at once, their simplicity hardly bespoke great riches.

The girls sat cross-legged on cushions a few feet from their sleeping brothers, each one combing out the other's hair. The occasional whisper or giggle was exchanged between them as they went through the motions of this well-practiced ritual. Ada and Freya lay nearby, grooming one another, too.

Gale, however, emerged dressed for a new day's work. She stood near the fire to comb out her waving locks and, compared to her daughters, who combed every strand, she seemed to care about her appearance as much as a soldier under siege. She then took the infant Kari, who had remained content to sleep most of the day in her improvised cradle, loosened the ties at the bosom of her tunic, and fed her baby. Though she did these things with tenderness, they were nonetheless hasty, and she returned to Harvald's room without so much as a word to anyone.

"Who's taking over for your mother next?" I asked.

Haldis, who had sat Yoanna in her lap while tending to her hair, looked over her shoulder. "I am. After me is Arve, then Aros, and Erika'll be last."

"Good. Your mother explained what you need to do?"

Arve rolled his eyes and huffed. "Aye, and more than once, too, as if we did no hear her the first time."

Erika shook her brush at him. "Do no speak 'bout Ma that way, 'specially no in front of Master Rune. Ma is only worried for Da, so show some sympathy."

Arve sighed and stared into the fire.

Fearing further confrontation, I changed the subject. "Ladies, the three of you may take the bedroom upstairs. The bed will be large enough for you all, and there's extra bedding in the trunk by the foot of the bed. If you want to light a fire, too, you may, though I've no supplies up there."

Yoanna squealed and bounced in her sister's lap. "Oh, Master Rune, will you really let us sleep in a kin' and queen's bed like the one Da is in?"

"Aye, lassie." I smiled at the little girl. "And you will sleep like a princess in it, I'm sure."

Yoanna beamed. The only thing keeping her from running up to bed that moment was Haldis' firm grasp upon her hair. With a gentle whisper in her little sister's ear to calm down, Haldis then turned to me.

"Aye, Master Rune, you do certainly make us all feel like princesses. That bath, too, was fit for a queen. I've no felt so good since we left home." She sighed. "But I suppose I should go draw a bath fit for a kin' now. If you're still wantin' a bath, that is."

Both Aros and Erika shook their heads. Aros, whose face I could see more clearly, rolled his eyes. "Quit your flirtin', Haldis. If Ma heard you speakin' that way—"

"Worse," Erika scoffed, "if Da heard you—"

"I'm no flirtin'; just bein' kind to our host."

Aros waved his hand at her. "Whate'er, Haldis. Just go fill the tub."

R

As the tub filled, so the room also filled with steam, and I pulled the shaving box I had not used in years from the linen cabinet and sharpened and stropped the blade. I set Aros and Arve down in turn upon a stool before a washbasin and looking glass near the tub. I lathered up the sides of their heads as well as Aros' face. It was easy work with Arve, who did not so much as twitch when I ran the straight razor across the fuzzy sides of his head.

Aros, on the other hand, was hardly so easy. He bounced his leg as I laid the razor to his temple, so I laid a heavy hand on his shoulder. When he ceased to fidget, I leaned in and whispered, "You've got to hold still, lad. I don't feel like doing sutures tonight." I patted his back.

Rather than bounce his leg, he ran his hands up and down his legs and cleared his throat compulsively.

"Just take a nice, deep breath."

He tensed as I dragged the razor across his temple and relaxed only when I lifted the razor.

I wiped the razor on the towel hanging from my shoulder. "Nervous about something, lad?"

Arve looked up from where he knelt, patting Ragnar, and huffed.

Aros straightened up and shook his head, but I knew the lie for what it was when I saw his face in the looking glass. I silently put my hand on his shoulder, giving it a pat and a squeeze. I smiled at the lad in the looking glass, and he returned it with a weak smile of his own.

"Right. Now I'll do your beard, so hold still." I made quick work of the patchy beard and wiped his face with the towel. "If you don't like getting a shave, you should just grow it out, lad."

He shook his head. "Da says I look better without it, least till I can grow it out."

"All right, lad, whatever you want." I slapped him on the back again. "Now let's wash up before the water gets cold."

I stowed the shaving kit and set a heavy cotton towel for each of us on our freshly laundered nightshirts and smallclothes, which sat folded on the small bench by the washroom door. I also handed both young men, who had already stripped off their tunics, a washcloth, bars of soap, and two small serum phials. As I did, Ragnar jumped into the tub with a splash, and a wave of sudsy water slopped over the edge of the tub, onto the geothermally heated tiles—yet another dwarven innovation—and trickled down the drain.

Aros was the first to open the phial, and I told him to apply some to his wind-whipped face. He hissed but then sighed as the serum worked. "That's great. Arve, you gotta try this."

Arve's reaction was even more pronounced than his brother's.

I took the empty phials from the lads and put them back. "I always keep this on hand in the winter."

We all stripped down then, and the boys raced to jump into the soapy water, which cascaded over the edge and down the heated tiles into the drain again. Their clothes fell in heaps where they had stood, but I wrapped my towel about my waist and gathered up our clothes into a neat pile. As I padded across the wet tile floor, I undid my hair and let it fall about my shoulders before I climbed in. The boys sat with their backs against the tub, both resting their necks and arms on the side, and I, too, sank down into the water. I settled in next to

Ragnar, who sat up to his muzzle in suds, and put a wet hand on my friend's furry head and let out a deep sigh.

As I washed, Aros and Arve stared at me, their eyes tracing the patchwork series of scars that webbed across my body. One web of scars ran from my shins up to my neckline and down my arms again. A similar web covered my entire back and flanks. Some scars stretched for several hand lengths without breaking, and a few only appeared to be broken up by thick hair that grew over my entire body. Others appeared small but were paired with other scars on the opposite side of my body—the entry and exit wounds of more arrows than I cared to remember—and one great starburst-shaped scar from a javelin covered my left breast. The longest scar, though, stretched from my right shin, curved around to the back of my thigh, and shot upward toward the opposite shoulder blade.

These puckered lines and great blotches of raised, discolored skin spotted my torso like a strange disease. Elsewhere, other great gouges and craters covered portions of my front and back, the greatest of which had nearly doubled the size of my navel. Thankfully, though, the only scar on my face was fairly small, stretching from above my right eyebrow, near to my nose, to just below the opposite eye.

Ragnar leaned into my side, and I welcomed his presence. He paid no mind to how I appeared. Wolves only cared if you hunted well and stayed in your place, while outer beauty meant little.

I put an arm around my friend, though he smelled—and they truly hate this comparison—like a wet dog, and I slid down until the water came to my chin. I let my head hang loosely over the edge, and my hair cascaded down the side of the tub as I stared at the exposed rafters of the ceiling. They desperately needed a dusting …

Eventually, the splashing caused by the young men's scrubbing died down, and I raised my head and created a great lather in Ragnar's fur. Yet, as I washed Ragnar, the two young men stared again. They were men who had seen something forbidden, something which, when seen, ever remains burned into the mind's eye, no matter how much the beholder wished to forget.

I focused on Ragnar's bath, but Arve broke my concentration.

"Master Rune, how'd you get so many scars?"

I heaved an involuntary sigh, and Aros splashed his brother.

"Arve, you canna just ask someone somethin' like that."

Arve gasped, chest rising sharply. "Oh, Master Rune, I'm sorry. Aros's right; I should ne'er've asked that. Really, I'm sorry. 'Tis only I've ne'er seen so—"

Aros splashed him again. "Shut up, Arve. You're only makin' things worse."

Arve pushed his brother. "Hey, do no splash me like—"

"Lads," I interrupted the incipient fight, "it's fine you ask. I know it's a bit of a shock to see so many scars." I hung my head back over the side of the tub again as I thought of how to get beyond this. "These"—I pointed to some scars near my neckline—"are mostly from when I was a mercenary and actively part of the Stateless."

Aros raised an eyebrow. "Hey, I've heard of the Stateless."

I immediately regretted my self-revelation.

"Were you really one of them? Do you have the, you know … the mark?"

Now it was Arve who splashed his brother. "Oh, so *you* can ask questions?"

I shot the boy a nasty glare. "Enough with the splashing, boy."

Arve blushed and sank down.

"Now … aye, I've got the tattoo." Knowing it was too late to hide it, I held up my right arm to show the faded red knot-work tattoo that encompassed my wrist. "It's pretty faded now. It used to be blood-red, and I wasn't allowed to cover it up except in battle."

"Wow, amazin' … I read 'bout the Stateless—the priest had this old history book he let me read—but I ne'er thought I'd meet one." Aros moved closer, tentatively stretching out a hand. "Can I …? May I touch the mark, Master Rune?"

I held out my wrist to him. "Aye, but it's just a tattoo."

Aros touched the tattoo with the tips of his fingers. "'Tis true what they say 'bout the mark?"

"And what is it *they* say, lad?"

"You know, that the mark glows and gives you power and such."

"I thought you didn't believe in magic, boy?"

"Well, I—"

"I'm joking, lad. The mark does give us certain rights and privileges, if that's what you mean. Otherwise, there's not much else to say." The latter point was a lie, of course—there was some spirit magic in the tattoo—but even I wished the lie were true.

"I always thought 'twas supposed to give you some kind of power. At least, that's what the book said."

"I'll leave it to your imagination, lad." I pulled my wrist back and leaned my elbow on the tub's edge.

Arve scratched his head. "What are the Stateless, Master Rune? I've ne'er heard of them."

Aros, who now sat next to Ragnar, spoke for me, "They're a group of elite soldiers, Arve. They've the right to go anywhere they choose, e'en into the Sviari Electorate and the Southern Cities. They basically hunt criminals the regular city watchmen canna deal with. Right, Master Rune?"

"More or less. The Stateless were founded hundreds of years ago by our king, the Sviari electors, the autarchs of the Southern Cities, and the elders of the Orcs. There were hundreds of us once ..." *And now we're all but gone.* "Anyway, our guild is empowered by the founding treaty to execute justice on certain crimes anywhere we go, and no king or ruler can command us, though they often ask our help. We often serve as peacekeepers during times of war."

"So, you've been to those places? To the Sviari Electorate and the South?" Arve sounded amazed.

I nodded.

"And you've captured all kinds of criminals and such? Have you e'er ... you know, killed—"

Aros splashed water at his brother again. "Arve, shut your mouth. You really think he'd tell you if he had? Ma'd have his head."

Arve stuck his tongue out. "Master Rune can decide if he wants to tell us."

I shifted uncomfortably. "Aye, well, not only do I not want to upset your mother a second time tonight, but there're some things I don't like to talk about. There's a lot of ... memories I'd rather forget."

Ragnar sensed my discomfort and leaned into me lazily.

"But I don't blame you for asking. When I was your age, I'm sure I would've."

I finished scrubbing Ragnar and scrubbed my own body after the conversation had died down. The young men did likewise, a film of dirt and oil coating the surface of the water near each of them.

Aros turned his back to his brother. "Get my back, Arve."

As the younger rinsed the older's back, Aros asked, "You want me to get your back, Master Rune? I do no think your wolf will be much help."

I patted Ragnar's side. "He's got you there, friend."

Ragnar narrowed his eyes.

"The truth hurts, Ragnar ... But, to your question, lad, aye." I turned my back to the young man, who splashed warm water to clear the suds.

"By the Two ..." The young man brushed his fingertips over the elvish seal, branded between my scourge marked shoulder blades. I tensed, and the young man pulled back. There was another sudden splash of warm water on my back. "Did you get this mark and these scars when you were with the Stateless, too? It looks like a—"

I put my back against the tub again. "No, I didn't." I took another deep breath. "I got them when I was a boy."

"*A boy?* Like me and Arve's age, or—"

"I got them when I was a slave."

Both young men gasped. "A slave? But slavery is outlaw—"

I thumped a fist on the side of the bath. "I know that." I wanted this conversation over with. "I was taken when I was a young man. The slaver who took me ..." His awful face, scarred and mottled, filled my vision. Even from beyond the grave, the gaze of that horrid red demon's eye in his skull pierced me. I shuddered. "He sold me in the far south to the elves. But—"

"You've seen the elves? What're they—"

I jabbed a finger at Aros, the demon in my own eyes rising. "Don't interrupt me, boy."

He pushed far from me. I knew what he saw in my eyes.

"The elves are nothing to marvel at. They were animals, beasts. No, worse than beasts—monsters—and if I could, I'd—"

Ragnar pressed his claws against my leg. I still had my finger pointed like a dagger at the boy.

"Sorry ... I didn't mean to snap at you."

I forced my eyes shut, breathing deeply as I put my arm around Ragnar, squeezing him tightly. "The elves were cruel." My voice was a whisper. "It's for the best most people never see them. They're the ones who gave me most of those scars on my back." The image of me strangling my elvish mistress as I lay with her filled my vision. The sweet rage and hatred flooded my veins anew. That same rage and hatred I had felt after all the years of being beaten and forced to ... to sleep with that monstrous woman.

Ragnar pressed his paw harder into my thigh and dug his claws in.

I shook my head. "Enough. I'd rather not think about that anymore. It was a long time ago ..."

"Master Rune ... I'm sorry. I did no ... I shouldna—"

I held up a hand, my eyes shut tight. "Aros"—I tried to keep my voice level—"please, enough. It's all right you asked, but enough now. Please ..."

Nobody spoke another word after that as we finished our baths. Ragnar rested his eyes upon me while I dressed, and he scented concern for me, the image of an alpha guarding a wounded packmate. I refused to acknowledge him. I would not be thought of as weak.

In the living room, the women had since climbed the spiral staircase to the second bedroom. I banked the coals in the fireplace and pushed the still smoldering logs apart so they'd burn out. The young men laid out their bedrolls in silence near their younger brothers, and Ragnar, Ada, and I curled up with one another in the pile of freshly laundered linens and furs by the hearth.

I curled up and shifted uncomfortably. The wolves all scented thoughts of shared warmth and of a clear, starry yet moonless sky in the middle of summer to comfort me. Yet, as I drifted off to sleep, the image of my old mistress' dead face, with its bulging, bloodshot eyes, returned to haunt me. It was with this image in my mind that I fell asleep.

R

I woke to the sound of rustling and the scraping of metal on stone. There was a shadowy figure hunched by the hearth. I rubbed my eyes, and the wolves stirred but did not wake.

"Who's that?"

"Ah, Master Rune, sorry to wake you."

As my vision adjusted, I saw Aros' shadowed face.

"I was cold and was goin' to light a little fire."

I crawled over to Aros and sat next to him as he dug up the banked coals. "I suppose it is a bit cold in here. You looked like you were pretty bundled up, though."

Aros threw some kindling onto the exposed coals. "Aye, well, I just get cold easy, I 'spose." He cleared his throat rhythmically.

"I can get you a heavier blanket, lad."

"No, sir, I'll be fine. You do no need to stay up with me. I'll go to bed in a little while." The room grew brighter as the incipient flames consumed the kindling.

"You sure you don't want that blanket, Aros?"

"Aye ... Really, sir, I'm fine." He clenched his hands on his knees before rubbing his palms on his legs.

"You seem nervous, lad."

He said nothing but stopped moving his hands across his legs, clenching them in tight fists instead.

"I can make you something to help you—"

"Sir, I'm sorry." He turned his face toward me, dropping his eyes to the floor.

I cocked my head. "What?"

"I'm sorry I asked you those questions ... 'bout your scars, and the elves, and bein' Stateless, and—"

I held up my hands. "Whoa, there's no need to be sorry, lad—I told you that already. I'm not mad at you or your brother for being curious."

"Sorry ..." He hugged his knees close to his chest and set his chin on them. "I just worry ... feel bad ..." The young man trailed off.

I put a hand on the young man's shoulder and gripped it. "It's all right, Aros. But, is that what's really causing you to lose sleep?"

Silence.

"Or is something else bothering you?"

The boy sniffed and wiped his nose with his hand, hiding his face in his knees. He began to shake. "I-it's—"

I embraced the young man like my dearest friend, Ulfric, had embraced me on the slaver's ship when I was first thrown into that abyssal hold. I had once been where this young man now was—anxious and frightened about the future. Anxious and frightened by the prospect of losing one of the most important people in any young man's life, by the thought of having to take his place. I held the young man close to my chest as if he were my own son, the son I had always wanted but never had.

"Easy, Aros. It's all right." His tears dampened my nightshirt. "I lost my father when I was a bit younger than Arve. He was killed ... murdered. I still miss him, so I'm going to do what I can to help your father." As I ran through the woods, the blurry images of trees rushing by filled my vision. My mother's shouts for me to run rang in my ears. The mob beat on our door, demanding my father come out. I forced my eyes shut and shook my head.

Aros breathed heavily. "Ma-Master Rune?"

"Just call me *Rune*. I'm nobody's master." I held the back of his head in one hand while I rested the other on his back.

"Wh-what's losin' your da like?"

I breathed deep. "It's one of the worst pains—I won't lie. Your heart will ache, and your mind won't comprehend it ... But, after a while, you'll rise up and keep moving on. It won't be easy—your heart will always ache—but you'll keep going because your family'll need you, because you know it'd make him proud you were strong, even though it hurt."

"Is my da ...? Is he go-goin' to die, Rune?"

"I'm doing everything in my power to make sure he doesn't. I'm not a god to make promises concerning life and death, but I can promise he won't leave this life easily while I'm taking care of him. But, right now, Aros, you have more reasons to hope than to despair, and your family needs you. So, save your tears for when you have reason to shed them."

The young man pulled away and wiped his eyes. "Thank you, sir. You've … You're too kind to us."

"Don't mention it. Now, get back to sleep, all right? You think you can do that, or do you need me to fix you something?"

"No, I'll be fine." The young man covered the fire with ash and re-banked the coals, still rubbing his eyes. I watched him crawl back into his bedroll as I crawled back in among the wolves.

As I curled back up with the pack, Freya popped her head out and scented, *"The pup? Great fear … sorrow …"*

"Fearful for alpha." The wolves, for all they understood about us, had a difficult time with our family structure. Mothers and fathers, while wolves recognized them, were less important than the alpha. Even to an adult wolf, his leader was his mother or father. *"Freya. Comfort him?"*

Her claws clacked against the floor as she trotted over. The young man grunted as Freya tried to crawl into his bedroll, and he laughed softly. "All right, all right. Come on."

After no more than two or so minutes, Freya scented, *"He sleeps."*

"Good." I, too, shut my eyes.

RRR

Chapter IX

*As the fool grows old, he will seek to be thought of
as a wiseman. As the wiseman grows old, he will let
himself be thought the fool.*

— From *Proverbs of the Hierodules*

ℝ

S omeone shook my shoulder, and I jolted awake.
　　"Master Rune, wake up. Please, wake up." Erika
stood over me, a covered candle in her hand.

I rubbed my eyes, and the wolves stirred. "Aye, lass,
what—" I yawned with a stretch. "What's the matter?"

"My da ... you must come quick. He's havin' fits like
you warned us 'bout. Please, hurry."

I ran to Harvald's side where Gale stood over him. He
shook violently, back arched, and white, foamy spittle poured
from the corners of his mouth. His eyes rolled back.

"Master Rune"—tears streamed down Gale's face—"oh,
by the Two, please help him."

"There's only so much I can do for him now. This
fit ... it'll pass." As I spoke, his back ceased arching, and his
thrashing became more violent. I rolled him onto his side.
"Erika, take hold of your father's legs and keep them in the
bed, but don't try to stop the shaking."

Harvald's skin burned again. "As soon as the sun rises,
I'll ride into town, even if the storm isn't finished. I have to
get the ingredients for the antitoxin. The sickness is

progressing too rapidly for the other medications to help much at this point."

As I fought to keep Harvald in the bed, there was a muffled snap and accompanying moan from Harvald. His arm twisted in a sudden, powerful spasm, and he vomited foul, brown bile upon himself and the bedclothes.

"By the Two, oh please, let this stop. Oh Andar, make this stop."

In answer to Gale's prayer, Harvald stopped shaking, and his muscles loosened. He stared out between heavy lids, and a low, continuous moan emanated from his mouth.

Gale took several rags from the bedside table and cleaned her husband's face. "Harvald." She laid a hand on his cheek. "Oh, Harvald, I'm so sorry."

"All right, lass," I said to Erika, who continued to hold her father's legs, "you can let go now." I gingerly released Harvald's broken arm and raised his back. "Put the pillows behind him in case he vomits again. I'm going to fix up his arm." I wiped my sweaty forehead with the back of my hand.

As I bound his arm, Harvald mumbled unintelligibly. He gradually became clearer, and when I rolled him onto his back again, he spoke lucidly. "G-Gale, th-that you?" He spoke as if choking on his words.

Gale knelt at the bedside, a hand on his forehead. "Aye, love, I'm here."

"W-w—" He burst into a fit of coughing.

"What, Harvald?" She took his hand into her own. "Harvald?"

"W-wa—"

"Water?" She snatched the cup and put it to his lips.

I leaned over my patient. "Harvald, my name is Rune Corinsson."

Harvald looked up at me, blinking in recognition. He opened his mouth to speak, but I put a finger to his lips.

"Be still." I placed my hand on his bearded cheek as if he were a child and ran my hand through his hair. "Be still ..."

He opened his mouth again and mumbled, but I put my finger back to his lips.

"Shh ... Don't speak, Harvald. Save your strength. You're in my home. Your family is here, too, and all are hale. You've got a sickness, but I'm working to get you the physic you need." I laid my hand back on his cheek. "Do you understand?"

Harvald looked up at me and blinked slowly.

"I want you to rest, Harvald. Close your eyes and go to sleep. Your wife and children will be here with you, all right?"

He shut his eyes.

"Good man."

Eyes still shut, he muttered again, "Water."

I took the cup from Gale's trembling hand, and Harvald tried to lift his head. I cupped the back of his head in my hand and raised it. "There, drink."

He drank until the cup was dry.

"Good. Now rest. Gale will be by your side."

She looked at me with tearful eyes and nodded.

I helped Gale into her chair. "If he has more fits, don't try to stop him; just roll him onto his side and keep him from falling. Give him even more water than before, keep him cool, and don't let him speak. I'm going to ready my horse, and I'll depart at first light."

"I'm goin' with you, Master Rune, and I'll no take *no* for an answer." Aros stood in the doorway.

Ʀ

The heavens were spotless, and though I wore a scarf over my face, the air burned my lungs. Clouds of steam poured forth from under the scarf, and ice formed in my beard.

Aros and I trudged across the snow-covered ground to the stable. "It'll be light in an hour. Let's hurry."

In the stable, we hung our covered candles, and the horses woke, some with a startled whinny.

"Sorry, there." I patted the horses as I walked to my own silver dapple. "We've need of your speed, Ela." I patted her neck, and she greeted me with a snort.

"All right, Aros. Help me feed them and break the ice in their water barrels. Then saddle up your surest horse and bring him around front."

The boy nodded with a grunt, and we laid out fresh feed.

While they ate, the two of us saddled our horses, Ela and Thunder. Ela was content to have the saddle on, undoubtedly sensing there was important work to be done. Thunder, Aros' dun, was less enthused, however, about the prospect of going out into the cold, and it took a handful of dried apple slices to coax him from his box.

As we led the horses around, Aros spoke, "Master Rune, sir?"

"Aye? What's on your mind, lad?"

"I wanted to … to thank you for last night, for talkin' to me 'bout … you know, your da and all. Still, I'm sorry for what I said … I can tell I upset you."

I tied up Ela's reins at the post by the front door. "You've got to stop apologizing so much, Aros, 'specially when someone tells you it's all right. Besides, I should be the one apologizing to you for barking at you the way I did. There's just so many memories, even after all these years, that're painful for me. I still have nightmares of the elves at times, about being ... abused by them."

Ela nudged me with her muzzle, and I touched my forehead to her own.

"I'm sorry, Master Rune. I canna imagine what you went through, but ... thank you for tellin' me what you did all the same. I'm sure it's no easy to live with those memories and all ..." Even in the dark, and even covered with a scarf, I saw how his eyes shimmered with sympathy.

"You're a fine young man, Aros. I'm sure your parents are proud of you."

The young man rubbed the back of his head with a laugh. "Ah, thanks."

I pulled down my scarf as we entered. "Let's grab some food for the road, lad, and coin for your father's medicine. Then we'll be off."

"I'll ask my ma for some coin, Master Rune, if you'd no mind packin' me—"

"Don't trouble your mother with that. I've more than enough coin."

"Are you sure, sir? I do no want to put you out."

"You're not. Now, fetch something for breakfast and lunch from the pantry. There's salt pork, bread, and fat back. And make sure you've got enough layers on, too. The last thing I need is to treat you for hypothermia."

R

We set out twenty minutes before first light and traveled in relative silence for the first half of the journey. After three hours of trudging through heavy snow, we stopped to stretch and relieve ourselves before journeying on. As the sun rose higher, so did our spirits.

Aros, who had been slumped in the saddle, unwilling even to speak more than monosyllables as the cold set into his bones, now sat upright.

Once I awoke fully, I lowered my scarf enough to sing an old traveler's song I had learned as a caravan guard. I sang a few stanzas of the tune, and Aros, though he was initially embarrassed to sing it, skillfully picked out the harmony.

R

O, at the end of this road wide,
Awaits me there my blushing bride.
She makes sure that our family's fed,
While I make sure she's warm in bed.

R

For her, my love, I'd give my soul,
If it would keep her body whole.
And thus I trek this world so wide,
E'en though it keeps me from her side.

R

Yet on the 'morrow I shall see,
Her smiling face gaze up at me,
As we make love upon our bed;
How well she keeps her husband fed!

R

We sang several other songs as we rode on to Melbù. Some tunes we both knew; others were new. Regardless of what we sang, the music took our minds off the ride. Between songs, Aros and I would exchange rhymes and riddles, at which the young man was exceptionally adept. After a particularly challenging riddle, I asked, "How'd you get so good with riddles, lad?"

"My brother and Da, we used to—" He choked. "We like to tell each other riddles when we bring Da's goods to market." The young man looked at me. "He was—*is*—a good carpenter, and I'm no just sayin' that. We've had people all the way from Sea Gate requestin' his work." He dropped his gaze. "Do you still think ... you know, that you'll have to take his foot?"

I pulled Ela closer to Thunder. "I'm not sure yet, Aros. When I last took a good look at his foot, there wasn't much improvement, though it certainly wasn't getting any worse either." I patted his shoulder. "But things can change. Besides, I'm more worried about getting the antitoxin for him. If he has more fits like he did last night, he could break more than just his arm."

"I just ... I dunno ..." The lad pulled his scarf up over the bridge of his nose. "Sorry, 'tis no your problem." He sniffed and rubbed his eyes. "And I know you said I should save my tears." He sat erect in the saddle and looked at me.

I nodded my approval, and we kept on.

ᚱ

At the outskirts of Melbù, the scent of wood smoke filled the air, and the distant temple bell rang out a dozen times with a clear though faint tone.

"We've made good time."

I guided us along the main road, the sole road, of the town, and the number of buildings—mostly small, wooden homes with thatched rooves, though a few had proper timber

129

or shingled roofs—increased as we drew nearer to where the temple stood.

"I'd like to be back on the road by the time the bell chimes thirteen."

"All right. But, why are you tellin' me when we must leave? Are we no goin' together to get what we need?"

I clucked Ela onward since she had started to slow her pace in these familiar environs. "No, lad, I want you to go to the general merchant—I'll show you the place—and place this order for me." I handed him a slip of paper from an inner pocket of my cloak. "I'll go to the apothecary and get what I need there. We'll meet at the public house and fetch the horses after we have a warm drink."

As we rode, I gestured to the general merchant's store—a showy, little, two-story thing with shutters over glass windows and a covered, raised porch—which was only a few hundred paces from the tavern and inn.

Beside the merchant's home, the public house was the only building with painted weatherboard siding, and it was there that we dismounted at the hitching post. We rang the large bell hanging by the watering trough to summon the grooms, and two young men, not much different in age than Aros, hurried out and took the horses away after I told them what I wanted for them. The young men nodded, and I tossed them each a silver penny to ensure the good care of Ela and Thunder.

I handed a small bag of coins to Aros, who weighed it in his gloved hand as he glanced at the list I had given him.

"Master Rune, there's no much on this list, but this bag of coins must be—"

"I want you to find something nice for your brothers and sisters and yourself, as well as for your mother and father. Whatever is left of the coin, buy some sweets to bring back."

The young man held the coin pouch out. "No, sir, I canna accept this. 'Tis too much. My ma ... she'd no be happy if I took this."

"Then you tell her I bought everything, and you tried to stop me." I pushed the coins back. "I've seen what happens when people have to abandon their homes—things get left behind and lost, or are traded away for more needful things."

The boy held the pouch, staring at it in shock. "But, sir ... there must be in here what Da makes in a moon's time, at least. Surely, you do no really mean for me to spend all—"

I closed Aros' hand around the bag. "Aye, lad, I do. Now, go on. When you're done, I'll meet you at the pub. Get yourself something to eat and drink there. I'll join you when I'm ready and pay the tab."

R

I pushed open the door to the apothecary, and a little bell rang to announce my entrance. The pungent scents of flowers; dried, assorted fungi; and something like vinegar hit my nose in a wave. Had I not expected it, I would have retched. The sources of the smells hung from the rafters, tied in bundles, or sat in jars; some with lids on, others with lids off.

As I gawked, a racket resounded in the back of the shop, the sound of crates being shoved across the wooden floor or of chair legs sliding.

"I'm coming. Don't be impatient now. Give an old man a moment—"

A woman's muffled shout rang out, to which the man replied, "Aye, dear, I'm helping a customer … No, a customer is here … A customer, I said!"

There was another indecipherable shout, but the old man ignored it. Instead, he came walking through a curtained doorway, clicking his walking stick while he shook his head. He muttered under his breath while he shook his head, and his long, droopy eyebrows waggled back and forth. I knew what his next words would be. *Sixty*—

"—two years of marriage and you'd think she'd understand that when a customer is here …" As he shuffled across the floor, he kept his eyes firmly set on the ground in front of him. Occasionally, he used his stick to push the edge of a box under a table so he would not trip over it. When he was only a few paces from me, he finally looked up. "Ah, Corinsson. It's been a while. Are you picking up some things for a visiting patient or just stopping by to say hello to an old man?" His eyes, though cloudy and partly covered with heavy bags of skin, were as keen as any young man's.

I laughed. "Both, I suppose, Connor." I took the old man's hand firmly in my own.

"Don't think I can't see through your flattery, child." He smacked his lips and wiped spittle from the corners of his mouth with the back of his spotty, wrinkled hand.

"It's only flattery if it's not sincere and true." I really did like Connor. He was a wise apothecary, and I had added many of his remedies to my books. "I actually came to see if you two were still going at it or if you'd finally torn each other to pieces."

Connor took his stick and struck me across the shin.

I rubbed my shin while leaning upon a tabletop. "Mercy's sake, Connor."

The old man laughed and shuffled away from me. He knew he was stronger than he appeared and enjoyed showing it.

"You should know better than to harangue me, boy-o, and not expect retribution." He began to put the lids on several open jars and to open sealed jars seemingly at random. "What does a fine apothecary like you need from a poor old man like Connor?"

"Some supplies. I've an unexpected patient." I followed slowly behind the old man as he bumbled about. "He's got tetanus and gangrene. The gangrene's been contained, though it's mighty wet, and I fear he'll lose the foot, but his tetanus is worsening. Relaxants have lost their effect at low dosage, and the physic I gave him for the fever didn't work well enough—he's started to have seizures."

The old man hummed deep in his throat. "That is troubling. Tetanus always was nasty, but coupled with wet gangrene ... Two Holies have mercy on the fellow."

"Amen. That's why I'm here, Connor. I need some ingredients for an antitoxin. Plus, I'd like to hear if you have any powerful remedies up your sleeve."

The old man kept on fiddling with different items, acting as if he had not heard me. After a moment, he spoke, "Well, I think you're doing what I would do—antitoxins—but if this gangrene really is wet ... you need to take that foot sooner than later. So long as that infection remains, his body'll never fight the tetanus well enough to best it. A war fought on too many fronts ..." He held out his hand. "So, let's see what old Connor can get you then."

I produced the list from my belt pouch, and he snatched it from me in a flash. "Aye, good, that's what I'd use ... Extract of ... fine, fine. *Enchiridion Artium Hypocrathekeris* by Janna Edricksdottir? A set of basic scales and weights? A pestle and mortar? Hour glasses ...?" The old man stopped and scowled at me. "What do you need this for? I thought you swore off taking an apprentice. Now, after all these years—after I held on to those blasted books for ages—you're taking one on?" He smirked at me. "Who's calling in a favor?"

"No one. He's not my apprentice. It's just ..." My stomach lurched. "I see potential in him, and his family—"

"Oh ho, so the young man's a charity case for you, then, Corinsson? Maybe a penance for your sin?"

I scowled. He should have known better than to mention that. "It's not—"

"No, you're right. I forget that the Two have gifted you with a heart of stone governed only by rationality. Ever the hypocratheker."

"I see potential in the lad and want him to have a good chance. Is that so hard to believe?" I folded my arms across my chest. "Why must it either be a case of pity or an emotional attachment that drives me to show kindness? I see potential and want it to flourish."

"This is purely professional, then, is it?"

"Aye. He's not my apprentice, and I'm not helping him out of pity, or because I'm attached." My stomach twisted again. "I've known the lad for a whole day and a half. I merely want him to succeed in the *Ars Nobilis*."

"If you say so, Corinsson, if you say so ..." He looked at the list again. "Give me until just before the thirteenth bell."

I nodded and left the shop. I *was* growing attached to the boy—I couldn't deny it—but that was a mistake. There was just so much of myself in him, and that made me both love him and fear for him. Still, I couldn't take him on as an apprentice, not as I was.

R

At the tavern, I found Aros at a long table in the dining room near the fire, where he smoked a new sea-stone pipe carved in the shape of a horse's head. The pub was quiet but cozy.

I sat down next to the young man, shrugging off my cloak and woolen outwear. "That's a fine pipe, lad. A good choice. Only be careful not to smash the thing—sea-stone is rather soft."

"Aye, but I canna keep the blasted thin' lit." He grumbled and tried lighting the bowl again.

I showed the boy how to pack and light it properly, and then I lit my own. We smoked together, warming up by the fire, and I ordered each of us a warm drink—mulled wine and fresh spiced cider. We spoke little at first, choosing to enjoy a little quiet before we took off again. Indeed, for quite some time, the only sound came from Aros' foot tapping an erratic rhythm, and from the barely audible rubbing of his free hand against his trouser leg.

I had met a few men and women over the years with nervous ticks, especially among battle-hardened soldiers. I, too, had my own nervous habits, though I had worked through many of them over the years. My quicksilver temper, sudden cold sweats, and flashbacks remained unconquered, however.

As we sat, I resisted asking the young man what was on his mind. All too often, former acquaintances and colleagues, even my dearest friend Ulfric, had asked me questions about what was bothering me, and great shame always filled me for being called out for my obvious distress. Only when my old mentor, an itinerant priest of Andar, had spoken with me after meditation and prayer did I find myself welcoming the questions. Only then, when I knew the question was asked in earnest love and out of a desire to do no more than listen, did I feel free to speak my mind. I often miss those conversations, even now ...

No, but even though I had grown close to this young man in so short a time, it would take much more than a few days to gain that kind of trust. He might wear his emotions on his sleeve, but that didn't mean he wanted to be called out on them. So, I smoked and drank my wine, pretending not to notice his nervous ticks.

When we had our fill and smoked what tobacco we desired, we paid our dues with the pub and stable.

"Has the thirteenth bell rung yet, boy?" I asked the stable hand who brought Ela.

"Not quite, good sir. Though, it must be mighty close."

I nodded my thanks, mounted Ela, and patted her neck as I waited for Aros to mount Thunder.

R

Warning Aros about the smells in the apothecary, we entered, and Aros gagged only a little.

At once, the old man drew near to peer at Aros from an uncomfortably close distance. "Ah, so you're the young apprentice of Corinsson? You must be something special for him to take you on. He's refused for the past decade to take on an apprentice, even when he was offered a healthy sum to take on some noble's bastard." Connor laughed to himself.

"Ah, well, I probably wouldn't have taken on a bastard either, especially not a royal one. They're not called *bastards* without reason."

Aros stood at my side, his body tense, unsure of how to answer or address the old man.

I merely smirked, mouthing, *"Don't worry about him,"* while Connor's back was turned.

"Well, Connor, we really do have to be off. The ride is slow with the heavy snow, and our sick man needs this medicine." I took a small bag of coins that I had counted out at the pub and threw them onto the counter. "That should be enough. Anything extra, and you can just put it on my tab."

As I grabbed the supplies, the old man raised his walking stick and threatened to slap my hand. "You have an apprentice, Corinsson; make him carry the load. Come now, boy ... What's your name, anyway?"

Aros stood, open-mouthed.

"You dumb, boy? I asked your name."

"A-A-Aros."

"Where'd you learn to speak, boy? Speak clearly and loudly so this old man can hear you."

Aros swallowed. "Aros, sir."

"Aros? Hmm, you sound like a westerner, singing your words." The old man shrugged. "Whatever the case ... well, Aros, come get these things like a good apprentice."

Aros stepped forward, and as he reached out, the old man grasped his wrist. Aros jumped but failed to break free of the man's iron grip.

"You listen to what your master tells you. He knows about a lot more than just pharmacy, boy ... Aros." The old man stared at Aros with cloudy, blue eyes. "He's more than he seems." He lowered his voice. "Much more than he seems ..."

I frowned. So much for doctor-patient confidences.

"Aros," I spoke in a low tone, "let's ride." I glared at Connor, who merely smiled back.

He followed us to the door. "I truly wish you all the best with your apprentice, Corinsson. He'll be a wonderful fit for you."

I never quite understood what Connor meant by those words, the last words I would ever hear him speak, for they were uncharacteristically sincere yet portentous in tone. Connor had always been a strange man.

℞℞℞

Chapter X

I am thy Father, Dear Son, and in this thy work, I am delighted, but of thee I am even more proud.
— Evangelium Andaris, Caput III

R

The early twilight overtook us as we returned, and the glow of the waning gibbous moon scarcely provided any light as it beamed through the heavy clouds. Only Ela's innate sense of direction and my keen eyes guided us through the encroaching darkness. When we arrived, we stabled the horses and brought our goods inside, where we wasted no time in preparing Harvald's medications.

The young women prepared us hot tea as we worked, and I inquired about Harvald's health. None of the children spoke at first, and only after hesitating did Erika tell me anything.

"He's no well, Master Rune."

I set my hand upon a jar lid and met her eyes.

"He had another fit, and his fever seems to be gettin' worse. He wakes up in a panic then falls into a fitful sleep. Our mother's still with him, though she may've fallen asleep again."

"Then there's no time to waste." I set up my equipment as Aros watched intently. "Lad, I'm going to work quickly. Learn what you can, but I cannot stop to answer questions."

While we worked, the young women put their siblings to bed before the fire. Even they had begun to succumb to the stress of their father's failing health, so they put up no fight when told to go to bed. Yoanna, like her brothers, went to bed, too, and her sisters followed closely behind. Even Arve went to sleep shortly after we had begun our work.

In an hour and a half, we had prepared four different remedies, including the antitoxin.

When we approached Harvald's bedside, Gale was asleep with her head on the bed. Freya, however, dutifully kept vigil.

Though we hardly made a sound, Gale woke with a start. "Master Rune, Aros …" She stifled a yawn. "I'm glad you've returned safe, thank Andar. Have you the physic? He's gotten worse since you left this mornin'—more fits and a worsenin' fever."

I nodded as I examined my patient. "Aye, we've purchased what I needed, and Erika told us of his troubles." I motioned for Aros to come and aid me in putting his father on his side. "I've made all the same remedies as before, only stronger." I applied the medications as I spoke and poured the last two phials into a cup of water. "This is the first dose of antitoxin. I'll give him two more doses during the night."

"And his foot, sir?"

The gangrene had neither worsened nor improved, yet Connor's and my judgment remained.

I shook my head. "I spoke to the apothecary in town and explained the situation. He thinks we should take the foot, and I agree."

Gale hung her head.

I put a hand on her shoulder. "His body can't fight both infections at once."

"When?" She looked at her husband and put her hand in his.

I gathered my supplies. "I'll see how he progresses through the night, but I'd like to do it early tomorrow, if possible."

"Aye, then 'twill be so."

R

As Aros and I dressed for bed, he asked, "Do you think he … my da will live, sir? Please, do no lie to me."

I pulled my long nightshirt on over my smallclothes and loosely tied up my hair. "Your father's generally healthy, and I've seen people come through worse."

Aros crawled into his bedroll and pulled the covers tightly around himself. "All right, sir. Goodnight."

I banked the coals in the hearth. "Aros?"

"Aye, sir?"

"I do think he'll make it."

"Thank you, sir."

I crawled among the sleeping wolves and shut my eyes.

"Sir?"

"Hmm?"

"I saw what else you had in the bag from the apothecary. The scale and all …"

I had forgotten all about it. "It's yours, lad."

"Are you sure you canna have me as your apprentice, sir?"

When he asked me this, I nearly pretended to have fallen asleep. I could not, however, bring myself to lie.

"Aros … I'd love to have you as my apprentice. You're a fine lad with a good head on your shoulders. You're fit to be anyone's apprentice." I breathed deeply. "I'm not fit, however, to be a teacher. I'm ..." I wanted so badly to tell him why, to speak the truth, but I could not. "There's things you don't know about me, things that would prevent me from being a good teacher."

The young man was silent for a moment. "Is it because you're Stateless? Or because you're too old?"

"No, Aros, it's neither of those things. I wish I could explain, but I can't. I'm sorry."

Another moment of silence.

"All right, sir. Goodnight."

"Goodnight, lad."

That night, it was I who lay sleepless. Only after I rose to give Harvald his second dose did fitful sleep finally come.

R

When it came time for the last dose, Haldis woke me.

"Master Rune"—she shook my shoulder—"it's—"

"I'm awake." I rolled onto my side, brushing a wolf's tail out of my face. I rubbed my eyes and stretched, rising to my feet. "It's time for the next dose?"

"Aye, sir." She bowed her head, her golden locks falling about her shoulders. "We've got the physic all prepared, too, like you asked."

I nodded and mumbled my thanks, brushing off wolf hair from my nightshirt. Then, as I slipped into my calfskin slippers, Haldis grabbed my forearm. She looked at me with a wide smile, her green eyes sparkling in the dim firelight.

"Thank you again, Master Rune." She drew near and, on tiptoes, kissed my bearded cheek.

This time, it was I who blushed. "Uh ... I ... er ... A simple *thanks* would have sufficed, lass." *Holy Andar, if this girl knew how old I was, what I was ...*

"Well, I felt like you deserved something special." She giggled, still holding my arm.

I came at once to my senses. I had to break the hold this unreal infatuation had on her.

"I'm older than your father, lass."

She blinked at me, face blank.

"I could be your grandfather, even."

She let go of my arm. The truth had broken the spell my nature had cast upon her.

"Well"—she pushed her hair back behind her before jerking it into a bunch over her right shoulder—"that is why I kissed your cheek as I did. 'Twas how I would kiss my gran-da when I was a wee girl." She yanked on her hair again. "You remind me of him, is all, Master Rune, sir."

"I see …" I gave a curt nod and slipped away, closing the door to the bedroom behind me to cut myself off from her.

The room was dark, with only one candle lit, as Gale slept in the bed next to her husband. In the dim light, I took my supplies from the bedside table and gave Harvald the last dose of antitoxin. When I laid my hand against his neck to check his pulse, he started.

"Wh-who …?"

"Harvald."

He looked at me through half-open eyelids.

"I'm Rune Corinsson. Do you remember me?"

He blinked a few times and opened his eyes more fully. He cleared his throat, and I took his cup of water and put it to his lips. Though the fever had weakened, he drank greedily. He attempted to raise his right hand but hissed as he moved the broken limb.

"Easy there. You've got a broken arm and ribs." I gently placed my hand on the splint to ensure he didn't try to raise it again.

He took a deep breath and groaned as he tried to adjust his position on the bed. He closed his eyes before opening them wide again. He blinked several times. I stood over him, and his eyes grew wider as he realized I was a stranger. Despite his shock, he merely stared up at me.

"Let me wake your wife." I leaned across the bed and touched Gale's shoulder. "Gale, Harvald is awake."

Immediately, she was at my side, took her husband's face in her hands, and kissed him. "Harvald, dearest, here I am." She brushed a few strands of hair from his face as she leaned over him. "You look much better, Harvald. Do you no think so, Master Rune?"

"Aye, the medications all seem to be working well." I stood next to Gale, my arms crossed. "How do you feel, Harvald?"

Harvald looked from his wife to me, eyes narrowing. "Who ...? Who are you?"

"His name is Rune Corinsson, Harvald. He's saved your life ... all our lives." She put one hand into his and placed her other hand on his cheek. "He's a surgeon."

Harvald shut his eyes, his expression turning into a grimace. "I ... What? I do no ..." He shook his head slowly.

I leaned in and put a hand on the man's shoulder. "Shh ... Be still, Harvald. All is well. Just tell me how you feel."

He took another deep breath, groaning and pulling his left hand free of his wife's grip to touch his ribs. "I ... I hurt. My foot ..."

Gale took his hand again. "I know, love."

She spoke softly to me, "Master Rune, what do you think ...?" She trailed off.

"About?"

She looked at her husband, at his foot, and then at me. "His foot, sir. He's improvin', no?"

I bowed my head, clasping my hands behind my back as my heart sank. "Aye, he's showing some general improvement, but he still needs several more rounds of antitoxin, and his foot *hasn't* improved."

"So, you think we still ...?"

"Aye, I do." I did my best to put some resolve in my voice, like I did when I had practiced medicine more regularly. "Do you want me to explain to him, or ...?"

"No, I will. 'Tis only right."

I nodded.

She knelt by the bedside. "Harvald."

He opened his hazy eyes.

"Harvald, I have to tell you somethin' important. I know you're tired and that you hurt, but you have to listen."

His eyes grew more alert.

"You're very sick, Harvald, and your foot ..." She sniffed. "Your foot has flesh-rot in the worst way, Harvald."

His eyes did not waver.

"That means we ... Master Rune ... needs to take—" She choked on a sob.

Harvald raised his left hand to touch his wife's arm.

"We've gotta take your foot."

He blinked slowly. "Whate'er must be." He looked at me, saying nothing, and closed his eyes. Gale put his hand at his side.

"When?" She looked at her husband even as she spoke to me.

"It'll be a few hours before the last dose takes effect, and I need to make a sedative, too, if we're going to do this." I stroked my beard. "And I don't want your children inside when it's time."

"As you say, Master Rune. 'Twill be as you say."

R

When all had woken, eaten, and gotten dressed, I prepared more medicines. Everyone, even the youngest children, recognized the urgency with which I worked, though only the eldest knew what I had to do. Aros sat by my side, helping me to prepare the simplest components, though he worked with unusual silence, apart from the tapping of his foot.

After two hours of preparation, I called for the four eldest children to return to Harvald's side with me. "I'd like you ladies to take the children out to play until I call you back. Bundle them up well, as it may be an hour or so before all is over, and under no circumstances are they to come inside while I'm working."

Erika and Haldis nodded solemnly.

"Gale, I'm sure you'll want to remain with me?"

She nodded.

"All right. Then I'd also ask you to make the decision if your boys can stay to help me, as well. I may need them to hold Harvald still while I work, but it's not my place to give that kind of permission."

"What would you recommend, sir? Are they old enough to see this?"

I hummed. "Well, Aros is. I've never seen an apprentice who was of age turned away. However"—I turned to Aros—"given that this is your father, lad, if you'd rather—"

"No, I need to be here"—his voice faltered—"for Da."

I gripped his shoulders. "You understand what this means? Your father may wake up, beg you to stop, scream and shout, threaten and curse. Can you do what I tell you even if he does? Even if he begs you to stop me?" I could not have him give up partway through the ordeal.

The young man stiffened, breathing deeply. "Aye, sir."

"All right. So long as your mother agrees."

Gale nodded. "But, what of Arve, sir? He's no of age yet."

I looked Arve up and down. "I can't make this call. I've seen teachers allow young men his age in, and I've seen those who refuse them. It's truly in your hands."

She thought for only a moment. "No, I do no want Arve here, then."

Arve grew red-faced. "But 'tis no fair, Ma. Why can Aros stay with Da, while I—"

Gale stood tall, crossed her arms, and thumped her foot on the floor. "Do no argue with me, Arve Harvaldsson. I've made up my mind. You're no old enough to see this kind of terrible thin'."

"Master Rune, tell her it's all right. Tell her I'm old enough to help. I can stay stron', e'en if—"

"Arve ..." I bent my knee and placed my hands on his shoulders, like I had with Aros. "I'm inclined to agree with your mother, lad."

"But I swear—"

I raised a finger. "Let me finish."

The young man shut his mouth and glared.

"Don't envy your brother, lad. What he'll see is nothing enviable, nothing glorious. There's no glory in blood and pain."

The young man still scowled.

"Lad, if you want to be a man now, then what I need from you more than anything else is to go out with your brothers and sisters. I need you to be strong and assure them everything is all right, though you know things are dire."

The young man's face softened a bit.

"Can you do that?"

"Aye, sir."

"Good man. Now, let's give your mother a moment alone with your father, and then each of you can speak your piece."

R

While I gathered my surgeon's kit, Erika gathered the younger children around.

"All right, I want e'eryone to get ready to go play 'cause Da needs his rest. When you're all dressed, you'll go say goodbye to Da and tell him you love him, then we'll go out."

Though the youngest needed some help to don their boots and woolens, they were happy to get out of the house.

When Gale left the room, she called for everyone to come see their father. Erika, as the eldest, went in first with her mother, but when it was time for Aros to go in next, he asked to go last.

I looked askance at the lad. "He may not be awake then, Aros. Are you sure you want to wait?"

He only nodded.

"All right. Haldis, you're next."

The remaining children went quickly, especially the youngest, who were told only to say, "I love you, Da." Then they all went out, followed by the wolves.

Gale waved at Aros from the bedroom door. "All right, Aros."

He stopped at the threshold. "Ma, I'd like to speak to Da alone."

She nodded, gesturing for her son to enter.

As he did, he turned to me. "Actually, Master Rune, would you come with me?"

I raised my eyebrows at him and shrugged at Gale. She nodded at me and gestured for me to pass.

Aros stood at his father's side and slipped his hand into his father's. "Da? You awake?"

Though I stood a few steps behind the young man, I saw Harvald's eyes open. "Aye. That you Aros?"

The boy sniffed loudly. "Aye, Da, 'tis." He wiped his eyes.

"Why those tears, son?"

"Da, I wanted to tell you Master Rune's been teachin' me. I'm his apprentice … least for now."

Harvald opened his eyes wide. "Good, Aros, good …" His eyes dropped a little, his energy spent.

"Da …" Aros knelt by the bedside. "Da, e'en though … though I'm no your apprentice, are you proud of me?"

Harvald shot his eyes open. He placed his good arm around his son's neck, pulling his son close. "'Course I am, son. Why would I no be proud of you?"

Aros sniffed again as he lay his head by his father's, and the glint of candlelight sparkled in the tears streaming down his face. "I always thought you were disappointed in me 'cause I'd no be a carpenter like you, Da. I thought I'd failed as a son."

"Look at me, son." Harvald's voice was full and deep.

His son raised his head and met his father's gaze.

"I could ne'er be disappointed in you." Harvald took his son's chin in his good hand. "I may no be happy that I do no get to teach you my trade, but that does no mean I'm disappointed in you. And you're no failure, Aros." He ran a hand through his son's hair. "I love you, son, and I'm proud of you." Harvald laid his head back, and Aros kissed his father's brow as he fell asleep.

"I love you, Da."

I smiled at him, and he smiled back.

"You ready?"

He nodded.

I summoned Gale, who brought in my surgeon's bag.

We lit additional candles in the room to cast out the gloom, and I laid out my tools—bone saw, scalpels, artery clamps, and belts—and sharpened them.

When I had everything prepared, I addressed Harvald in a firm voice, motioning for Gale and Aros to stand away. "Harvald, I'm Rune, your surgeon."

He did not stir. Nevertheless, I spoke on.

"I'm going to give you some physic. It will make sure you feel nothing. I'm going to place a cloth over your mouth and nose, and you'll fall into a deep sleep. When you wake, we'll be done."

I turned to Aros and Gale. "This"—I waved the phial I held in my hand—"will take a few minutes to work. You can't go near him while it does. If you breathe any of this, you won't be able to help me. He may moan and shake a bit as it works, but he's in no pain. When I take the cloth away from his face, I want you, Gale, to sit by his head and hold his shoulders. Aros, I want you to hold his legs while I work so he doesn't kick. Any questions?"

His wife glanced at him then at me. "Will he feel any pain?"

"Only when he wakes. He may groan while asleep, but he's fine. If he wakes up, which rarely happens, he may scream or shout, but once I've begun, I cannot stop. If that happens, put this"—I took a small leather scrap from the side table—"between his teeth and tell him to bite down."

"How often does that happen?" Gale asked as she took her son's hand.

I shrugged. "Maybe one in twenty surgeries, no matter how well prepared the sedative is." I took a cloth from the table and folded it. "Any last questions?"

They shook their heads.

"All right."

I took a deep breath, held it, and opened the stopper on the phial. I poured the contents onto the cloth and laid it over Harvald's mouth and nose before stepping back. "Now, we wait."

As we waited, Harvald groaned and sighed as I said he would. When enough time had passed, I took the cloth away and put Aros and Gale in their places.

"Once I start, I'll need only a few minutes, but while I work, I can't stop for anything."

Gale pressed down on her husband's shoulders and nodded.

I, likewise, looked at Aros, who stood next to where I knelt. As he held on to his father's thighs just above the knee, he signaled he was ready.

"Let's begin."

I took the heavy leather belt and tied it tightly below the knee. Picking up the scalpel I had laid aside, I ran it through the flame of a candle. I made my incisions down to the bone on the sides of Harvald's calf, and blood poured onto the piled linens I had placed under his leg. However, with the tourniquet in place, the blood did not flow for long.

I proceeded to cut several flaps of skin that would cover the stump of the limb. Harvald groaned, and his limbs twitched slightly. At the first groan, Gale panicked.

"Oh, by the Two, he's wakin' up."

All the while, I kept working.

"No, it's the sedative. You'll know if he wakes."

Satisfied with my incisions, I laid the scalpel aside and took the bone saw. "Maker, guide my hand."

I set the saw aside and cut the muscle on top of the shin, but my blade quickly met with bone. There was a grating and snapping sound as the saw ripped through the tibia before reaching the fibula.

Harvald's leg instinctively jerked, but Aros held it steady.

"I'm almost through," I promised.

When I had nearly finished cutting the bone, Harvald let out another louder groan. His body jerked suddenly, and he mumbled and groaned deep in his throat. At that moment, the saw cut through the remainder of the gangrenous limb, which I covered with a loose cloth and pushed away. I then clamped and sewed shut the arteries I had severed.

As I filed the jagged bones and stitched the torn muscles around the wound, Harvald kicked with the stump of his leg and broke free of my grip. It was then that he began to scream.

"Lay on him if you must!"

Aros threw himself upon his father's legs, and Gale put the leather bit in his mouth.

"Bite, Harvald. You must bite this."

He continued screaming, and Gale wrapped her arm around his head, forcing him to bite down.

"I'm sorry, Harvald, I'm sorry!" she cried.

With his thrashing and screams subdued, I finished smoothing the jagged bones. Harvald's jerking and cries increased, but I kept grinding the exposed bones. I sewed the loose flaps of muscle around the bone and left a small opening for fluid to drain. Finally, I wound several bandages around the newly formed stump and tied them off.

"Don't let go yet, lad." I took the belt tied around his leg and slowly loosened it, making sure the sudden blood flow wouldn't burst the stitches. When I was satisfied they were strong, I removed the belt and readied another dose of sedative. Holding my breath, I pulled Gale away and took the bit from Harvald's mouth. Ignoring his renewed screams and pleading, I applied the sedative long enough for him to cease crying and jerking. Only then did I throw the cloth aside. "We're done. That's it."

Gale knelt by Harvald's side and laid her head near his. She stroked his sweaty forehead and whispered comforting words into his ear as tears flowed down her face.

Next to me, Aros stared at the bloody cloths covering the severed foot.

"Don't look at that, Aros." I took his ashen face in my hands. "Lad, you need to sit. Come." I helped him to his feet. "Let's get you seated in the next room." I guided his wraith-like form into the sitting room and sat him before the fire. I packed and lit a pipe for him and put water on to boil. There was little better I could do for him than that.

"Wh ... What will happen to ... you know?" He stared into the fire as he spoke.

"Don't worry about it. Just sit and get your composure."

I steeped a cup of *solvans* tea for the young man and put the half-full cup into his trembling hands. I took his chin into my hand and held his gaze. "You'll be all right, really. I'm sorry you had to go through that, but you did well." I patted his cheek, only to realize that I had streaked his father's blood across his face. I rubbed away the blood with the edge of my tunic, but he didn't resist or even question what I was doing. He merely gazed into the inferno before him.

I let him alone, prepared another cup of tea, and returned to the bedroom. "Gale, ma'am ..."

She did not look away from Harvald but replied with a hum.

"Why don't you drink this and get some rest? Harvald won't wake for some time."

She held her husband's hand in her own and took the mug with scarcely a glance at me. "'Tis what you said the first time ..."

"I'm sorry, but he *will* be fine now, Gale. There's nothing to wake him this time." When she said nothing, I gathered my tools together and thoroughly cleaned them before bundling the severed limb up with the soiled linens. I carried them out into the cold.

The children and wolves chased one another through the deep snow nearby, none paying me any mind as I walked by with my grizzly burden. None had heard their father's screams.

Only Ragnar and Freya trotted up to me, the heavy scent of concern pouring forth from them. I told them all was finished, and Freya went to comfort Gale. Ragnar, meanwhile, followed at my heel, and when we had found a spot soft enough to dig up, we buried everything and returned to gather those outside.

Inside, all doffed their outwear and set it to dry. Aros quietly moved away from the fireplace to sit at the table. He set his chin on the table and stared through the bedroom's open door, and though I left the lad alone, I kept an eye on him. Meanwhile, I told everyone to keep quiet so their father could rest, and the youngest children played with the toys Aros had purchased for them in Melbù.

Arve and his older sisters, however, sat at the table with Aros and tried to coax him out of his melancholy. Aros insisted on remaining quiet about what he had seen, though, and I merely affirmed all had gone well.

"The next days will be painful for your father but, hopefully, uneventful. What he needs—what we all need now—is a little rest."

RRR

Chapter XI

My master was a volatile man. One moment, he could have tears in his eyes as he thought about the loss of a patient; the next, he was full of rage for some fault only he could see. Yet, he was my master, and I his apprentice; is a servant or student fit to criticize or instruct his master?

— From *Memoirs of an Apprentice*

R

T he next few days passed without incident as Harvald recovered. With several additional doses of antitoxin, his tetanus resolved, and liberal use of pain medication kept him comfortable. After the third day, Harvald asked to sit in the main room with his family, and though the youngest children had a difficult time understanding why their father's foot was gone, life for my guests returned to relative normality.

In the evenings, Arve took the duct flute he had finished carving and played for his family. His sisters and Gale would sing as they worked, while Harvald would rest near the fire with the stump of his foot raised. Haldis had ceased to flirt with me as she once had—whether because of my reproach or because of her parents' presence, I neither knew nor cared—and so my own anxiety also faded. Aros and I, meanwhile, sat and studied at the table, taking advantage of what time we had left together.

After a week in my home, however, everyone grew restless. Aros' mind, so ready to learn, grew tired. Arve had set his flute aside, no longer desiring to play, and his older sisters would argue with their younger siblings about which child's turn it was to play with certain toys. Haldis bickered with Erika that it was she who now vied for my attention—she was, indeed, more eager to wait on me than before—though I sensed in Erika nothing like the same bewitchment that had ensnared Haldis. Erika's eyes *were* full of something, some affection, but I could only assume it was pure gratitude. Ragnar and Ada increasingly roamed outside, and even Raynor started to avoid the youngest children by hunting with his packmates. Harvald and Gale, too, showed signs of stress. Harvald argued with his wife for doting on him, and she would retort that he had nearly died and that she would not take his foolish man-talk.

I, too, grew tired and anxious. While I could not have hoped for better guests, their petty squabbles had worn on my nerves, and my desire to escape grew. That anxious desire, which had faded away during the first days with my guests, had returned. The thought of the next Triduum's approach also unnerved me. They had to be gone by then if I wanted to keep them and my secret safe.

On the eighth day, as Harvald sat smoking with his leg up by the fire, he called for Aros to bring him to his room. Helping to support his father, the two returned to the bedroom. A moment later, Aros returned and spoke with his mother, who went into the room, too. Aros then approached.

"Sir?"

I smoked in the other chair by the fire and looked up.

"My da wants to speak with you."

"Oh, do—"

He shook his head. "I dunno 'bout what, sir."

I found Harvald sitting on the edge of the bed, draped in a blanket, with Gale at his side. As I entered, Gale rose, and Harvald faltered as he attempted to rise. I shut the door behind myself and approached in silence.

Gale folded her hands. "Master Rune, we'd—"

Harvald touched his wife's arm. "Let me, dear." He cleared his throat.

"Master Rune, Gale and I want to thank you. I owe you my life, but more, the life of my family." He cleared his throat again and gave a slight tug on his wife's arm. She let him put his arm around her shoulders and rose. "If we can repay you, sir, only say the word, and whate'er you desire, you shall have."

I shook my head and opened my mouth, but before I could utter a single syllable, Harvald interrupted, "And do no say we owe you nothin', Master Rune. We owe you a great deal, more than we could e'er repay."

I bowed my head and stroked my beard. "Harvald, sir. Gale, ma'am …"

The two stiffened.

"When I swore the oath of hospitality, I welcomed you as friends. It would be wrong for me to ask anything of you."

Gale looked at Harvald then back at me and opened her mouth, but I cut her off.

"But, if you insist, I will make some request of you."

Gale shut her mouth.

"However, I will do so only on the condition that you agree beforehand to honor it and make no further offers of payment."

Without a moment's hesitation, Gale replied, "Aye, Master Rune, whate'er you ask, we shall do."

Harvald nodded his approval of Gale's words.

"Then what I ask of you is that you pray for me."

Both Harvald and Gale motioned to object.

"You said that whatever I ask, you would do. Do not fight me on this, lest you insult me."

They snapped their mouths shut.

"I've seen your family's piety toward the Two, and the prayers of the pious are always heard by them. You shall pay me with prayer. That is all I desire. That is all I need."

Harvald bowed as low as he could. "As you say, sir."

Gale turned to her husband and opened her mouth, but Harvald silenced her with a glance.

"We'll always remember you in our prayers."

"My thanks ..."

Harvald eased himself back down with a heavy sigh.

"But, surely, you didn't ask me here for this alone?"

Gale shook her head. "No, and I do no wish to sound rude, sir, but—"

"Gale, ma'am"—I smiled with my hand outstretched—"you and your family have done nothing to be rude to me, and I know you won't start now."

Gale flashed a slight smile and bowed her head. "Aye, forgive me, sir. Anyway, we wanted to ask you ... to tell you we must be departin' soon."

"Of course. I'm not stopping you."

"No, Master Rune, we do no mean you'd stop us." She looked at Harvald, who slouched, his left elbow on his knee and his right arm slung across his bandaged chest. "We mean to ask you if 'twere safe for us to leave ... for Harvald."

Harvald sighed and pushed himself back upright. "I do no want to be the one to keep us. We must keep movin', whether I'm—"

"Harvald"—Gale put her hands on her hips—"I'll hear no such foolish talk. We did no stop here for—"

"And I'm the head of this house, and if I say—"

"Dear guests, please." I held up my hands. "I beg you not to argue."

Gale took her hands from her hips and folded them, bowing her head. "Forgive me."

"Forgive *us*," Harvald corrected, "for our ... my hard-headedness, my lord."

I waved my hand. "It's no matter. And again, please do not call me *lord*. Now, if I may give my thoughts as to your departure?"

"Aye, Master Rune, please speak on." Harvald tried to sit tall but groaned as he clutched at his chest, the broken ribs still paining him.

Gale took the blanket that had fallen from Harvald's shoulders and draped it over him anew.

"Normally, I'd try to dissuade someone in your state, Harvald, from traveling. However," I added, seeing Harvald slump lower as I spoke, "given how well you've taken to the treatments and how well your fo—leg is healing—"

Harvald raised his eyes.

"—I think it'd be safe for you to leave in another, let's say, five days?"

Harvald looked up in surprise and smiled at his wife, who shot me a nervous glance.

I acknowledged Gale with a curt nod. "Let me stress, however, that you are not fully healed."

"Ah, Master Rune, I'm hale as e'er, e'en without my foot." He barked out a laugh, but then hunched over, clutching his ribs.

"Except for your ribs, *and* arm, *and* fresh amputation. Likewise, most men who are hale don't sleep fourteen hours a day and need help to use the—"

Harvald thrust his good hand forward. "Aye, Master Rune, I get your point. No need to wound a man's pride more than necessary."

Gale huffed. "I say, speak on, Master Rune." She cast a baleful look at her husband, and he withered. "I'll no be responsible if you go and get yourself in deeper trouble, dear husband."

I cleared my throat. "Anyway, because you are—your body is still weak, I can't recommend hard travel. Half pace at most, and frequent stops to rest. In all truth, because the solstice is drawing near and the worst of winter is only beginning, I recommend wintering in the Seat."

"Master Rune, we'd ne'er be able to afford such a lon' delay, no in the Great City," Gale protested. "We're humble folk, sir."

"Which is why I'll send word ahead of you to a dear friend of mine, Ulfric, to welcome you."

Harvald spoke now, "Master Rune …"

The stench of shame poured from him, so I added, "This isn't charity, but the law of hospitality. Ulfric is a brother to me. He'll—"

"Master Rune"—Gale clasped her hands at her breast—"we simply canna take and give nothin'—"

"You can and you will, ma'am. Or, in your pride, do you refuse the laws of hospitality that Andar and Luváli themselves established? As the Holy One said, '*Receive thou the lowly. Begrudge not the wanderer or sojourner, for I am such as these. Yea, of the one who receives these I say, his hands are mine own.*'"

Gale stepped back with a quick curtsy, and Harvald wrapped his arm around her waist and said, "What could we say against the Two Holies and their word?" Harvald looked up at his wife, who closed her eyes. "'Twill be as you say."

"Good. In which case, Andar willing, let's assume you'll be leaving in five days. I'll go with you to Melbù and make sure you're well, put you up for the night at the inn, and see you off in the morning.

"Meanwhile, I want you to rest, Harvald, as you've been doing. While I think you can risk the travel, it is still a risk. When you're ready, we'll plan out your trip. I've gone up and down the highways from Melbù to the Seat more times than I can count, in rain and shine alike."

Harvald and Gale both began to speak, but Gale's voice won out.

"As you say, Master Rune. We thank you for your help in planning our travels."

R

My guests' final days crawled by. The planning of the family's travel route, and of alternate routes, took only a few hours and, apart from the need to pack the few possessions they had brought into my home, there was little for them to do to occupy themselves.

While the greatest difficulty for most was fighting boredom, my temporary apprentice had a different struggle. Though Aros studied with me for a little while, he quickly expressed a lack of desire to continue. He claimed he was anxious about leaving, so his mind wasn't on his studies. However, even a blind man would have seen how he shadowed my every move, head hung low. Still, I resolved to keep him at arm's length, for his sake and mine, and I pretended not to notice his melancholy.

This went on until the thirteenth day, which was the day set for the entire family's departure. Early that morning, before the sun began to rise, Aros, Arve, and I went to fetch the horses. I saddled Ela, too, so I could ride into Melbù, as I had promised.

After we loaded the carts with the family's possessions and a few books I gave Aros, and after all had made themselves comfortable in the wagons, we departed.

The weather, while still cold, was good for travel. The sun, when it rose high into the sky, cast out the winter flaw that otherwise sapped travelers of their energies, and the road itself was clear. Arve and Aros sat in the front seat of the lead covered wagon, which was loaded with the family's possessions. Harvald, whom Gale had refused to let hold the reins, sat with his wife in the front seat of the second wagon, while their remaining children sat in the back. I sat astride Ela, guiding her at the leisurely pace of the wagons, and I could sense my pack following just out of sight in the woods. I let Ela have a great deal of control over the pace and, of her own accord, she kept pace with Thunder, to whom she had taken a liking.

Because Thunder was hitched to the lead wagon, I had ample opportunity to make conversation with the two young men. I encouraged them to be watchful of their father and to keep his eagerness in check. While Arve relished the idea of having influence over his family's affairs, Aros only responded with grunts and monosyllables.

When we stopped for a short break, I tied Ela to the front wagon and loitered nearby until Arve came back from the nearby hedge.

"Lad, would you mind riding with your family for the remainder of the trip? I'd like to have a word with your brother, just master and apprentice."

Arve rolled his eyes at the mention of his brother. "Aye, I'll do that, sir. E'en listenin' to my sister gush 'bout you and how she'll miss you'll be better than bein' 'round him."

I laughed and rolled my eyes. There was no doubt Haldis was free of my curse's hold, but sometimes the effects could linger. "She's still going on about me?"

"You haven't noticed?" He rolled his eyes again, whether at my apparent obliviousness or at the thought of his sister's flirting, I did not know. "But she'll get over it."

He then glanced at his brother, who was removing the horses' feedbags, and shook his head. "Anyway, can you tell Aros to stop bein' so sour, sir? He says he ain't, but he is. He told me the other day, when we were muckin' out the stables, he hoped Ma and Da would make him stay here with you as your apprentice. He e'en asked them to suggest it to you, but they already knew you'd said no."

I had guessed as much but was glad for the confirmation.

"Well, I've a few things to discuss with him, and you needn't worry yourself about it."

Arve laughed. "I'm no worryin' 'bout anythin'; 'tis him who worries, shakin' his leg or rubbin' his hands raw. Just tell him to stop bein' moody. I mean, he's always moody, but the past days, he's been unbearable. Maybe you can stop him from bein' so sour." With that, Arve jumped into the rear wagon.

When Aros came back to the wagon and found me with the reins in hand, he glowered. As he climbed aboard, he held out his hands. "Let me drive, sir. That way, I'll be useful for somethin' 'round here."

I ignored the acerbic edge of his words and patted the seat next to me. "No, lad, you just have a seat, and let's talk."

His glare was daggers and flame. "Fine, but I doubt we've much to talk 'bout."

A call came from behind us. "We're ready when you are."

Without a moment's hesitation, I clucked and snapped the reins.

I whistled the same tune I had taught Aros when we had ridden to town nearly two weeks earlier, but the young man only tightened his cloak around himself. I let a moment pass in silence before speaking.

"You know, lad"—I kept my eyes forward—"I really—"

"You really what? Would like to have me as your apprentice? I know, so you've said. If you really wanted me, though—"

"I'll not have you speak to me that way, boy." Now my eyes were full of their own fire. "Don't think I won't stop this cart and tan your hide right here."

The young man locked eyes with me. "What do I care if you did? 'Twould be worth the trouble to show you how I really feel 'bout you and your empty excuses no to have me."

I undid the ring belt that held my wool kaftan closed and wrapped it around my fist, snapping the leather. "As long as I'm still with you as your host and your master, oh apprentice, you watch what you say, or"—I shook the belt at him—"I'll take back the things I bought for you, and I'll make sure you've no future apprenticeship with anyone."

The boy paled slightly but kept his gaze. However, he did not speak, at least not right away. When he did open his mouth, he looked away. "I'm sorry ... sir."

I quickly put my belt back on and stared ahead as I let out a deep sigh. "I'll be straight with you, Aros. I can't take you as an apprentice because I'm not a safe person to be around. If I took you on as my apprentice, I'd almost certainly hurt you, and I don't mean emotionally."

Aros looked at me askance with narrowed eyes. "But you said 'twas no because you're Stateless."

"And that was the truth, lad. There's something else, but I can't tell you what." I clutched the reins tighter. "I almost turned your family away when you came because I worried I might put you all in danger."

Aros opened his mouth again, but I stopped him.

"Don't ask again, lad. Please ..." Against my will, tears welled up in my eyes. "Don't ask." I wiped my eyes with the back of my gloved hand. "I'm sorry, lad."

The fire in the young man's eyes was completely extinguished. "You're serious 'bout this ... I know you'd no shed tears for no reason."

A long period of silence came between us until Aros hummed the tune I had taught him. I took up the melody, and thus we continued. After we sang for some time, Aros spoke again.

"I'm sorry I did no take your word seriously, sir."

"You won't be the first one I've had to let down, lad, and you won't be the last. I'm just glad you'll leave believing me rather than doubting or hating." I tried to smile but bit my lip to stop myself from shedding more tears. This was the true cost of my sin, and this was what I was bound to suffer—to cast off any hope of having anything like a human family all my own.

"I 'spose this is why you wanted my family to pray for you?" The young man's face was firmly set. After I had spoken to his parents, and after they had told their children of my wishes, Aros was even more fervent in his devotions than before.

"Aye, if I'm to have any hope, I need them."

"You'll have them, sir. As long as I'm alive, you'll have them." Though the cart's front seat wasn't spacious to begin with, the young man made it a point to embrace me. Without letting the reins go, I returned the embrace. Thereafter, the young man's melancholy and resentment vanished.

ᚱ

I gave the reins over to Aros when we arrived and told him to stable the horses. While he and his brother busied himself with that task, I went into the pub to pay for our night's stay. Unlike the last time I was here with Aros, when the young lady working the floor was a new face to me, the woman behind the bar this time was familiar.

"Ah, Corinsson, what brings you in from your hermitage? It's certainly not a feast day, and I don't think the priest was scheduled to be here."

I flashed a smile at Sigrid and sidled up to the bar. "It's good to see you, Siggy. I was in a little less than two weeks ago, too, but you must've been out."

She twirled her locks of graying blonde hair between her fingers as she stood behind the bar. "Ah, so maybe you've finally broken out of that shell of yours? Did you finally decide you didn't want to spend any more nights alone and wanted to take old Siggy up on her offer to marry?" She laughed, her bright face and her youthful energy shining through her aging appearance.

I laughed. This was the old game Siggy always played with me and the widowers in town.

"You came in right after the storm, yeah? I heard a rumor from Connor's wife you had passed through." She leaned over the bar, exposing her cleavage like a young woman flirting for a tip. Siggy, despite her graying hair, was still an attractive woman, and she knew it.

She batted her eyes at me. "So, what can I get you, Corinsson?" She pulled up an empty mug and set it before me.

"I'll need a warm bed for the night."

She smiled and winked.

"A single, not a double, mind you."

Siggy leaned back from the counter, placing one hand on her chest in mock offense.

"And my guests"—I nodded at the first members of the family as they entered—"will need beds, too."

As the stream of children entered, followed by Gale supporting Harvald, Siggy clicked her tongue, and her eyes widened as she counted. "Well, Corinsson, your heart may be cold to poor old Siggy's desire for companionship"—she winked at me again, and I rolled my eyes—"but you apparently can be quite the softy. Maybe I'm wrong, but are these refugees from the war out west? We've heard the rumors, 'course, but this is the first proof I've seen."

I hung my head and nodded. "Aye. They were told to abandon their homes before the battles arrived."

"Poor folks ..." She frowned. "Well, I'm surprised to see so many. Connor's wife only mentioned a young lad, but surely"—she nodded in the direction of the boys who were being corralled by their sisters—"those four little monsters can't be the ones I heard about."

"You're right on that. There are two more putting the horses up and bringing in some essentials."

The family seated themselves at the long table nearest the fireplace, and I caught a glance from Harvald and Gale.

"Now, though, if you could start a tab for them, I'll pay in the morning." I opened the pouch on my belt and drew out three gold sovereigns from my coin purse. "This should be a good start, though."

Siggy picked up the coins and slipped them ostentatiously into her bustier. "Just let me know how many rooms exactly you'll need, and I'll make sure they're made up just right."

"Aye, I'll do that. They'll be wanting baths, too—they've got a long ride ahead of them, and I doubt they'll have time for another proper wash."

Siggy took a small wax tablet from under the bar and smoothed out the surface with the angled edge of the stylus. In an undecipherable hand, she jotted down what I assumed was the tab. "Aye, we'll do that, Corinsson. It may be a little while, though. My help doesn't come in for a few more hours. Normally, this is the slower time of the day." She put the tablet down and made her way over to the family.

Still at the bar, I took the mug she had given me and held it under the spigot of the beer engine nearest me. After I had a few sips, and Arve and Aros came in with a crate each of personal items, I made my way over to the table as Siggy finished taking their orders. We passed one another, and I saluted her with mug in hand. She shook her head, eyes rolling as I took another sip and wiped foam from my beard.

As I was about to sit, Gale motioned for me to come forward. "Please, Master Rune, have a seat here by the fire." She pulled a single chair out from the head of the table. "Erika, Haldis, please come take Master Rune's cloak."

The young women rose, but I motioned for them to sit.

"I can hang my cloak, ma'am. All is well." I undid the brooch holding my cloak together and hung it on a peg by the fire, where I kicked off my boots, too.

Harvald, Aros, and I all took our pipes and lit them. Shortly after, Siggy came bearing drinks for all—milk and tea with honey for the children, mulled wine for Gale, and a mug of ale for Harvald. "Food will be out in a little while."

Erika held her cup to her lips and glanced at me over the edge of it. "Miss Sigrid speaks highly of you, Master Rune."

"Aye, she's rather fond of you," Haldis added. "She was happy to see you're well."

"Aye." I laughed. "Siggy and I go back a while. I took care of her husband when he died of consumption some years back. Her work is her companion now, though. She's fond of me only as a friend."

Erika and Haldis shot each other knowing glances and laughed. Erika shook her head and rolled her eyes.

"If you say so, sir, but I do no think you'd recognize a woman's love except she came right out and told you."

I waved the comment away with a laugh and took another sip.

As we waited for the food, the conversation turned toward the usual. Harvald, while tired and a bit sore, was well.

Though I encouraged him to retire early, he scoffed at the thought.

"And miss the chance to thank you as fully as you deserve by drinking to your health?" He raised his mug and shouted, "To Master Rune, long life and happiness! The Two guard you."

Everyone else raised their drinks and shouted in agreement, making the quiet common area come alive for a moment.

I blushed at his words. "Ah, that's enough. I'm not doing anything you wouldn't have done for me."

"Aye, but there's only one of you, sir, and twelve of us."

"I hardly think Kari needs to count, seeing as she needed little from anyone but her mother." The babe lay next to me in the same basket as the day the family had first arrived. "May I?" I gestured at the baby.

Gale waved me on. "Aye, of course, Master Rune. I'm sure you know how to hold a wee one?" She clasped her hands tightly at her breast.

I scooped up the babe. "It's been a while, but I've helped deliver a number, and I've ..." The bright, blue eyes of the baby stared up at me as she woke. "I've cared for others, too." I smiled at the babe and put my finger in her hand. Kari clenched it in a tight fist.

Among the Stateless, I had once been tasked with bringing several children, including a few infants and their mothers and nurses, across multiple hostile borders. Yet, for as many children as I had been around, I had never had my own to care for, not in any meaningful sense at least ...

I smiled down at the babe and rocked her gently in my arms. With her free hand, she took hold of my beard. "Do you think this is Ada looking in at you, Kari? I'm afraid my beard is nowhere near as soft or as friendly as her."

Kari pulled on my beard with all her infant might, and Gale grabbed the child.

"Sorry, Master Rune."

I stroked my beard, patting it back into shape. "Ah, she was only admiring, nothing more." I stroked the baby's face. "Isn't that right?" I spoke in a tiny voice, and Kari smiled and waved her arms.

I let my eyes linger on the faces of all gathered. It would be strange to return to an empty house again after so many days with company. Though I hated to admit it, I had enjoyed a break from the silence that otherwise consumed my days and nights. Indeed, I had been so continually occupied with my guests' presence that I had spent little time troubled by my passions.

My musing was cut short when the food was brought, and only then did the light conversation cease entirely as we filled our bellies. While we ate, I made arrangements for our rooms. Harvald and Gale would take the great suite—if anything in the tiny inn could be called *great*—their daughters, the lesser suite; and their sons, the standard rooms. I would take the single room. Though Gale protested that her entire family could well sleep in the common room on their bedrolls, I refused to listen.

Siggy, too, insisted on allowing me to have my way, though her reasons were motivated by more than mere hospitality. With the five rooms taken by us, and the only other single room taken by a merchant from the Seat, her inn was full in the dead of winter.

"Let your host treat you now. Corinsson here is right; you'll be needing a good night's rest before your big journey."

RRR

Chapter XII

The narrower and darker the valley through which one walks, the broader and brighter the coming plain. The deeper and fouler the pit into which one is cast, the higher and holier the heavens.

— Canticum Magnum, Pars XXIII

R

A fter our supper, baths were drawn for all, and Gale's protests at the cost were renewed. After the perfunctory objections, however, there was little else anyone desired to do beside bathe and retire. Even Harvald, who had scoffed at the idea of retiring early, turned in to his room on the second floor.

After his wife helped him to bed, she returned to gather her youngest children and put them to bed, as well. She put the younger twins in Aros' care, while the older twins, she put to bed with Arve. All retired without complaint, bidding me, their mother, and sisters a goodnight. Haldis and Yoanna likewise retired, and I was left alone with Erika and Gale in the common room, which had grown crowded as the night wore on.

Erika hugged her mother, who ascended to her room after asking me to come check Harvald's wounds one last time. Erika and I stood alone in the dining hall then; she by the stairs and I by the tables. She bowed toward me. "Thank you, sir, for all you've done for us, but 'specially for my da. You saved his life ... Without him, I dunno what we'd've done. Truly, we'll ne'er forget you."

She climbed the first step but stopped. After a moment's hesitation, she added, "And"—she looked up the stairs to see if anyone was coming—"I wanted to thank you for what you've done for Aros, givin' him books and teachin' him and all. He's always struggled to ... to find his place, but you've set him on a good path." She flashed a timid smile. Her eyes were bright and kind. "If I may be so darin' to say so, too; Miss Sigrid would make a good wife for you, and she'd be overjoyed to have you, sir. She's no just havin' fun with you ... And if, by some miracle, she gave you children, you'd be a good father." She began to climb the stairs.

Her words, so kind and sincere, heaped burning coals upon me. I flashed what I could only hope was a convincing smile. I found no words to speak.

Nearly at the top, she stopped again and looked down on me. Her eyes were speaking, but I could not comprehend. "The thought of you livin' alone, sir ... my heart breaks for you." Without another word, she finished climbing the stairs to join her sisters.

I, for my part, sat at the table with a heavy heart and downed what remained of my beer.

After a brief visit with Harvald to check his wounds, I bid him and his wife a goodnight and left them to what would be their last night of privacy for weeks. I returned to the common room and took several sheets of parchment, ink, and my quills from my pack, which sat where the boys had left it by the fire. I wrote a letter—the first one in a long while, I hated to admit—to Ulfric, who worked for the royal intelligence service in the Seat. After I apologized for my failure to write, I wasted little time in introducing my guests. I enjoined him to receive them as I had done and wrote a blank promissory note, urging him to draw on the perpetual stipend I received as Stateless to pay for their expenses. I knew, though, that he would rather use his own substantial wealth to foot whatever bill my guests accrued.

The other letter I wrote was to the guild of hypocrathekers, to which I still held a formal membership. I requested with yet another promissory note—though this one I limited to a maximum of five-thousand sovereigns—a prosthesis for Harvald. Though I signed the letter with both date and locale, and explained how Harvald would be arriving, I told the guild to contact Ulfric's estate to make the necessary appointments.

With the sealed letters in hand, I pulled up to the bar and ordered another pint, and one of the half-dozen serving girls, who now assisted Siggy, poured me one. Siggy passed by a minute later, a load of empty mugs in her hand, and I slid the letters across the bar top to her. As she filled the mugs, she snatched up the letters and stuck them in a small satchel she kept under the bar. "I'll have 'em to the dovecote on the morrow, Corinsson."

"Thanks, Siggy. I can always count on you." I drained my beer and set the mug on the counter. "Get me another pint, too, while you're at it."

Siggy slipped my mug under the tap and slid it back to me. I took a sip.

"You just gonna sit here, chatting up the help, Corinsson?"

I shrugged. "What else am I going to do? It's too early to hit the hay."

She filled the last mug she had carried over and winked at me. "Why don't you enjoy that beer over in the common room? It won't kill you to socialize, will it?"

I peered into the common room across the dining room and foyer. A haze of smoke flowed out, and the din of voices and laughter echoed.

I hadn't spent a night away—well, not in my own skin, anyway—from my home in years. The prospect of ... *socializing* with a bunch of strangers made my gut lurch.

"I don't know, Siggy. What am I gonna talk about with a bunch of loggers and farmers?"

Siggy, who had just taken up the load of full mugs again, set them down and leaned over the bar. "Corinsson, you nervous 'bout a little chitchat?" She patted my cheek and took up the mugs again. "Why don't you just play a few rounds of cards? Get out of your shell a little. Do it for ol' Siggy?" She winked at me and went her way.

I pushed away from the bar with my mug and meandered into the common room. Some forty men, a few of whom I recognized as former patients, milled about, smoking and drinking, but there were no women to be seen, apart from the serving girls, of course. A half-dozen sat or stood by the fireplace, engrossed in serious conversation, if all the gesticulating and shouting was any indication. A few others drank, smoked, or rolled dice or threw down cards at the tables set around the room.

The further I walked into the room, the quieter it became, and the more eyes I could feel upon me. Eventually, even the dice stopped rolling. I shrugged and took a sip of my beer. It wasn't too late for me to walk out.

I looked over my shoulder. Siggy leaned against the bar and winked at me. I took another sip and frowned at her, but she folded her arms across her chest.

I sighed and found a table playing cards. I was no longer one to gamble for high stakes, but what these people would have considered high stakes were anything but. Tonight, the game was Lucky Lady.

"Care if I join?" I asked as I pulled out the fourth chair.

"So long as you know how to pay and play." The dealer barely looked at me as he spoke. "Coin only."

I threw my coin pouch on the table. "Lucky Lady?"

The dealer grunted, not even looking up from the cards passing between his fingers as he shuffled.

"It's been a while, but I know how to play." I took out a few silver pennies and threw them into the pot. "Deal me in."

As I played a few rounds, winning as many as I lost, the din in the common room quickly returned, and everyone forgot my presence. I drank another two pints, and the room started spinning slowly as a few players came and went. Though I recognized none of them, one did recognize me.

"You're the fellow who lives out at the old lodge, ain't you?"

"Aye, it's been in my family for a time," I lied. "Decided I liked the peace and quiet of the north and settled here."

The man laughed. "Sure, but that's not what the rumors say."

I had heard the rumors, mostly from Siggy, who had told me the wildest ones. I was everything from a royal bastard of Eleutherius to a wizard who stole the organs of my "patients." Some of the more realistic and crueler ones I had learned on my own, since Siggy hadn't the heart to tell me those. Some said I was a murderer on the lam. Others, that I lured or kidnapped travelers' children and did all kinds of godless things to them. Others still, that I was a mad man. Then there were those who were too close to the truth for my own comfort.

I shrugged. "Aye, and what are they saying about me now? That I'm some royal they banished because I bedded the wife of Eleutherius himself?"

A fourth man at the table laughed, his cheeks flushed from more than just mirth. "If you had so much as looked at Her Majesty wrong, Eleutherius would be the least of your concerns. Her Majesty would have had you strung up and stuck like a pig before her husband even noticed anything was wrong." This man had a Capitolian accent—crisp, articulate, and surprisingly high, given the man's rotund figure.

"Besides, there is no way you are from the Seat." He gestured at me with his mug. "First, you are much too tall, and you have not our way of speech. No self-respecting Capitolian—not one that could have gotten close enough to the queen to besmirch her good name, anyway—would ever hide his heritage. We are too proud"—he smirked—"and rightfully so." He laid down his cards with a grin made even more cheeky when he twirled the points of his well waxed goatee and thin, curled mustache.

As he gathered the small pot, we all threw our cards down with a groan.

"So, you're from the Seat, then?" I threw in a few more coins for the next hand. "I should've guessed from the accent and"—I rubbed my first three fingers on my chin—"goatee."

The other two men at the table, who both had wild beards, chuckled.

In all my years, the goatee had been a staple of Capitolian fashion. While the length and exact shape had changed, the basic qualities had not, and the current trend was one I liked even less than usual.

"Aye, I am. And, unfortunately, I am stuck with you barbarians while I wait for news here." He finished his mug of ale and hailed a serving girl. "But at least you have good ale." When he saw the serving girl come by, he added, "And pretty women, too."

The young lady, who I had to admit was quite attractive with her blonde hair done up in ribbons, blushed. As she left with his mug and mine, he was swift to pinch her bottom, and she jumped.

The dealer glowered at him. "And you call us the barbarians." He shot a pitiful look at the waitress as she hurried away.

The Capitolian waved a hand with a little giggle. "Oh, as if you have never taken one of these pretty young things out back behind the stable to *ride your horse*." He mimed shaking a horse's reins and swayed from side to side in his seat.

My hackles rose.

The dealer glared. "Maybe when I was sixteen, I'd have joked about it. When I was a foolish eighteen-year-old, if I'd been a few too many cups in like you, maybe I'd have done it. But"—he pushed back his long, sandy blond hair from the side of his face to finger the gold ring in his right ear—"now that I'm married and a man, I act like one."

The man who had recognized me also fingered the ring in his right ear. "Aye, and most of us *barbarians* don't think Andar would take too kindly to dishonoring a young lady."

The Capitolian frowned and scoffed before throwing in two more silvers. "You northerners and your pieties. Andar was a man, too, and I wouldn't doubt if he pinched the—"

The second man snatched his bet from the pot and pushed himself away from the table. "Capitolian pig." He hacked and spat the lump of goldweed chew that he had under his lip upon the table.

The Capitolian looked at the spit then at the vacant seat, mouth agape. "You would just let him take his bet back like that? If I were home, I would have the city gua—"

"Well, you're not home, stranger. Now shut your trap, keep your hands to yourself, and play."

As cards were dealt, I tried to change the subject. "You mentioned you're waiting for news?" I frowned at the cards I was dealt.

"That I am." He smiled from ear to ear, obviously delighted to speak about himself. "I was on my way back home from a winter run to Burgia—the Burgians love their southern fire brandy, you know—and I heard troops were moving northward. Normally, I could not care less about something like that—bugger the whole soldiery, I say—but from the sounds of it, these troops are worse than brigands. If they so much as hear you have something of value, they requisition it." The Capitolian tapped the table to request another card. "Now, I just so happen to have struck a deal in Burgia to bring a few items back to the Seat, so when I heard about all this, I decided to lie low here until I either get word from a colleague about it, or those thugs pass through."

I swallowed hard and stared blankly until the dealer rapped on the table with his knuckles. "Your bid."

"Oh …" I folded without even seeing what the dealer had laid out.

The dealer grumbled, and the round finished with the dealer raking in the small pot.

"Are you sure about that?"

The dealer glared at me with a questioning look.

"Sorry, I mean about the soldiers coming north?" I nodded my head toward the Capitolian. "I heard about them heading west, but—"

"If you had listened"—the Capitolian upped the bid as the cards were dealt—"I said I was waiting to hear from an associate. Damn pigeons seem to be taking their bloody time, though … the Two strike them."

"I know what you said. I mean, how likely do you think it is?"

The trader rolled his eyes. "If that is what you meant, then say it so the first time." He tapped the table for another card. "But, to answer your question, I would hardly be surprised. Last I heard, the war was dragging on, and frontline supplies, especially manpower, are running thin."

I also tapped the table. "Sounds like more than just the war dragging on. Sounds like we're getting a sound thrashing if even manpower is running short." I took up my extra card and smiled—two queens was a hard hand to beat in Lucky Lady—and I prayed it was an omen. I put in two extra silver pennies.

"That may be, but I care little. Nothing the military does is worth my time. However"—he met my raise and threw down his cards—"I know it is you who will be getting a thrashing this round." The prince and princess.

"Dammit." I threw my two queens. *And damn this war, too.*

I rose, thanked the dealer, and he nodded curtly at me before shuffling the cards. I nodded at the Capitolian. "Thank you for the news."

I decided to confer with Siggy—barkeeps heard the best gossip—so I sat at the bar and chatted her up, but she said it was all news to her, too. "I wouldn't be surprised, though, if the rumors about Seagate being under siege were true—I've heard such from enough folks. If the port falls, we're in for a rough spell, for sure ..."

I ordered one more beer and stared into the foamy head. *What in the name of the Two is going on?* I cursed the fact I had ever asked Harvald's family how they had gotten to my house, cursed the fact I had taken such a liking to them, and cursed my conscience. It would be dishonorable—no, it would be sin—if I did nothing to help them avoid what was coming when I had the power to do so. It would be doubly so because I knew the price they had already paid to avoid this exact outcome. There was no escaping what had to be done.

I downed my drink. *For courage ...*

ᚱ

I looked over the banister of the shady balcony and at the bustling public common room below. Though everyone had noted my coming, nobody cared about my departure, and the room was exactly as before. Down the hallway, the din and pipe smoke lessened with every step, and by the time I stood at Harvald and Gale's door, it was nonexistent. I raised a fist to knock but hesitated. I wanted nothing more than to run ... to be anywhere else ... anyone else.

With a deep breath, I focused my mind and heart and rapped on their door. The sound reverberated through the hall, and I waited before knocking again. Still no one stirred.

I knocked louder, and there was a sharp, high-pitched wail as Kari woke. There was then a low rustling on the other side of the door, and Gale spoke, "If that's one of you boys, you go back to your room this moment and ask your brothers for whate'er you need."

Gale could be heard cooing to pacify her baby's cries, and when the child was calm, I spoke, "Gale, ma'am, it's Rune. I must speak with you."

Feet tramped to the door, but it did not open. "Oh, Master Rune, I'm sorry. I thought you were one of the boys come to—"

"Get to the point, Gale," Harvald rumbled, loud and deep.

"Master Rune, give us just a moment to look decent, and we'll let you right in." There was hurried tramping of feet, and Gale and Harvald murmured somewhere behind the door.

Not a minute passed when the door swung open. Gale appeared in the doorway, candlestick in hand. She wore a rumpled nightgown, and her wild, blonde hair hung loose about her face and shoulders. The baby's cradle sat near the foot of the four-poster bed where Harvald sat up, wearing a tunic backward with a sheet up to his waist.

Gale stood aside from the door with her arm held out wide. "Master Rune, please come in. Now, what is so wron' that you couldna wait till mornin'?"

Harvald blew a few loose strands of red hair from his sweaty face. "Aye, what couldna wait, indeed?" He crossed his good arm across his chest, taking hold of the broken one, which was hidden under his backward tunic. I could feel his eyes on me even in the dark.

"Harvald, do no be rude … And your tunic is on backward, dear."

Harvald looked down, shook his head, and scrambled to strip off the tunic. "I dunno why"—he threw it to the floor—"you made me put the bleedin' thin' on in the first place."

"Decency, Harvald."

"Decency, dear wife, is fine and all, but I dunno why Master Rune would expect to find us doin' anythin' but makin' lo—"

"Harvald Eiversson!" She thrust a finger in his direction, and a faint blush rose on her cheeks. "By the Two Holies, have you no shame?"

Harvald let out a hearty laugh, crossing his left arm behind his head as he lay back. "No, dear wife, none. Besides, I like when you get so steamed up."

Harvald looked at me and added, "Sorry, Master Rune, do no mind us, and I'm sorry to have snapped at you there." He waved me forward, and I took another step into the room. "Tell us what brings you."

I rubbed the back of my head and fidgeted with my loose ponytail. That I had come at an inopportune moment made me hesitate even more. "Ahem … I'm sorry to have bothered you and woken your baby. I've heard some news—a rumor, really—that troops are moving northward."

Gale stiffened, and even Harvald visibly shifted, his jocund attitude disappearing. He leaned forward.

"What do you mean, Master Rune? Are you sayin' we …" He started shaking, his right hand clenched in a fist.

Gale went to his side and tried to steady him, but he pushed her away.

"Did we do all this ...? Come all this way ... Did I ...?" He looked down at his foot. "All for nothin'?"

I rubbed my arms before pinching the bridge of my nose, eyes shut tight. "I ... I don't know, Har—"

"Like hell you dunno. I can—"

Gale tried to push Harvald back down to the bed. "Harvald, 'tis no his fault. Do no—"

"Be quiet." He slapped her hands away, and Kari wailed again, but Gale did not tend to her.

"You"—he jabbed a finger at me—"you say 'tis a rumor, but I can hear it in your voice that you know—"

"I don't know anything more than I've said, Harvald." It was my turn to cut him off.

He scoffed.

"I've heard this rumor, and I've heard other rumors on top of it that make me think it's likely true. That's all."

Harvald hung his head. "We should've stayed in Burgia with the others ..." He jerked his head and slapped his thigh. "Would you please go quiet that child?"

Gale started, pulled away from her husband, and took Kari from her crib.

I shook my head. "You wouldn't have been any better off there. When they arrived, they would've still taken your—"

"Ha, listen to you. They'd've taken what? Taken my foot? My sons? My dignity? As if you care, anyway. You've still got both feet on you. You've still got that lavish mansion you call your home. You've still got—"

"Enough, Harvald." Gale returned to Harvald's side with Kari at her breast. "None of this is his fault, and we should be happy he came to warn us of what was comin'. Maybe we can—"

"You saw the maps—there's no other roads, no other way to get to the Seat." He grunted, a vicious frown on his face. "Go say goodbye to your sons. A week from now, maybe two, and they'll be marchin' back west with—"

"Enough!" Gale spoke with such force that Kari began to cry once more. "I'll no hear you speakin' this way. We're goin' to get through this all together, all in one—" She glanced down at where Harvald's foot should have been.

Harvald caught her glance and barked a cruel laugh. "All in what? One piece?" He flung himself back upon the bed, still laughing. "Some joke the Two have played on us, eh? They take my home, my health, make my daughter lose her husband-to-be, and now they want to steal my sons to fight in some war? Damn the Two."

He spoke in rash anger the words I had wanted to say in the hours before these people had shown up on my doorstep so many days ago. Indeed, had he spoken them at that time, I would have likely said "amen," abandoned as I had felt by the Two. Something had changed since then, and his words now incensed me.

"Do not blaspheme in front of me." I drew up to the foot of the bed, fire in my eyes.

Harvald met my shadowed eyes but shrank back. I wondered what he saw in them. Was it righteous zeal for the Two? Or, in my fit of self-righteous anger, did he see the darkness that still lurked within me?

I took a steadying breath. "I'm sorry"—I took a great step back—"but do not fault the Holy Two."

Harvald said nothing, but the scents of anxiety, regret, and the underlying hint of sheer terror poured from him.

Gale held the crying babe, tears in her eyes. "What hope is there, though, Master Rune? I'll no see my sons taken off to war …"

Just then, there was a knock on the open door, and Erika stood in the doorway. "I heard Kari cryin' and all this shoutin'."

Behind me, Gale sniffed and spoke over Kari's shrieking, "E'erythin'—"

"E'erythin' is no all right, Gale." Harvald spoke with his chin on his chest, his voice a low rumble. "Erika, Master Rune brought us some … bad news."

Before he finished speaking, Erika put her hand to her mouth and ran to the bedside. "Da, are you no well? Has the sickness—"

"No, lass, I'm fine." He stroked Erika's cheek to calm her and, patted the bed, and she sat by him. "There are more soldiers comin', Erika. They're comin' northward."

"But … Did no the herald say if—" She shook her head. "How can they do this, Da? How can they—"

Harvald put his arm around her but said nothing.

"Will they take Aros? Arve?" she sobbed, wrapping her arms around her father. "They already took Garth; now will they take my brothers?" Tears streamed down her face, and her eyes pleaded silently with me as she looked from Harvald's face to mine.

Her pleading eyes filled me with the courage I sought. "I can protect your family …"

With tears still streaming down her face, she released her father and ran to fling her arms around my shoulders. "Thank you." She kissed my cheek. "I couldna take the thought of losin' anyone else." She pulled away and, standing nearly eye to eye with me, held my gaze.

I shuddered, unable to understand what I saw in them.

"I—" She choked on her words, but her blue eyes continued speaking, though I still did not understand. This was still not what I wanted, but her pleading eyes were the sign that this was the course I had to take.

I rolled up my right sleeve, raised my fist, and pointed at the faded red tattoo. "Do you know what this is?"

Gale held her candle close. " 'Tis a tattoo, sir." She gingerly touched the mark. "What does this …?" She did not bother finishing, and Erika also peered at the mark.

What neither of the women were willing to say, Harvald muttered, "What's a tattoo to do with anythin'?"

"Do you know of the Stateless?" I lowered my arm.

Erika and Gale shook their heads, and Harvald grunted, "They're a legend." Clearly, the boys had decided not to betray my secret.

"We," I began, "are a guild of sorts, though now much smaller than we once were. I am among the last … We are citizens of no kingdom yet of every kingdom. We take orders from no king or lord, but rather from ourselves, though kings and lords often employ us. We are free to go where we please, when we please, and those we travel with are granted the same right."

I let this settle in, and when they said nothing, I continued, "Though I long thought my days of service were over, I will pledge myself to your family. I will bring you safely to Ebria." I placed my right hand, balled into a fist, over my heart and inclined my head. "My sword is yours. My heart is yours. I am wholly yours until the task is complete, or until you release me. You need only accept." I kept my head inclined, fist upon my chest.

There was total silence, even from Kari. I could say nothing more until they accepted. Erika was the first to speak.

"Master Rune ..." She paused for a moment. "Of course—"

"We accept your pledge, Master Rune," Harvald butted in.

I raised my head and lowered my fist.

"We're in your debt e'en more than before. Now I owe you no only my life, but the lives of my sons."

Gale was crying softly as she looked at me. "Why has Andar sent you to us? Why has he favored us so?" I did not know how to respond, though I wondered the same thing, and so I stared ahead into oblivion, playing the part of soldier at attention once more.

Erika approached me, but I kept my eyes forward and unmoving. "Master Rune"—she took my rough hands into her own—"thank you." With her other hand, she touched my cheek and sent shivers down my spine. "I truly couldna bear to lose anyone else." She embraced me and lay her head upon my shoulder. She was gentle and unbewitched by my nature. When she looked up at me, I broke attention for but a moment, and my eyes drifted to meet hers. They were still speaking ...

I refused to look at the young woman again, staring just over her head. "I am at your service."

If she knew what I was, she would never have come so near to me. No, if any of them knew what I was—and I could only pray that our journey together would not reveal my secret—they'd never have rejoiced to have me with them.

O Holy Two, I prayed, *only keep me from doing them harm.*

RRR

Chapter XIII

The world is full of great delights, and it is good for a youth to see, hear, and taste many of them. This shall broaden his mind and open his eyes to many truths he would not have otherwise known. Yet, there is also a certain blessing to innocent provincialism, which cannot be recovered once it is lost. Indeed, we who know would do well to consider what we no longer possess and to remember the axiom minima maxima sunt.

— Introduction to *Encyclopædia Mundi Optima*

ꓤ

Before I turned in, I knocked on Aros' door. It had been a long day, so I was hardly surprised when no one answered. Nevertheless, I opened the door and whispered Aros' name.

A silhouetted figure stirred. There was a grunt and muffled, "Aye?" Aros sat on the edge of the bed, rubbing sleep-filled eyes. "Master Rune? That you?" With a hand, he stifled a yawn. "Somethin' the matter? Is Da—"

"He's all right, Aros, but I need you to ride with me at sunup back to my home. Looks like I'll be accompanying you to Ebria after all."

Aros' slouch vanished. "But, sir, I thought you said you couldna—"

"I know what I said, and I still mean it, but something's come up that's forced me to act against my wishes."

A child raised his head behind Aros.

"I'll tell you more in the morning, though, lad. For now, just get some rest."

The young man nodded, yawned, and fell back into bed.

I shut the door and, as I walked the few paces to my room, heavy footfalls rumbled down the hall. The Capitolian man muttered curses behind a hand that covered most of his face. As we passed, I saw the trickle of blood flowing down the merchant's chin. *Serves him right,* I thought before grabbing his shoulder. "Looks like you got into a bit of a scuffle there."

He pushed my hand away. "Do't touch 'e. You dahm savaches bwoke 'ay 'ose."

"*Bwoke 'ay 'ose?*"

"'Ugher off." He pulled a key from his pocket and was behind his door in a flash.

I sighed. I hated the hypocratheker's oath I had sworn to help those in need.

"I'm a hypocratheker. I'll—"

The lock clicked, and the door swung open. "I 'eew you wuh' no' like 'da west." He gestured for me to enter.

"Sit." I pointed to the wooden chair against the wall, and the man obeyed, crossing one leg over the other and setting his unoccupied hand upon his knee. With his beady eyes, he measured my every move, but he did nothing to resist when I moved his bloody hand away from his face.

I scowled at his crooked nose, which gushed blood the moment pressure was removed. "It's broken. I'll—"

"I did't 'eed a doc'or ta' te—"

"Oh, shut up." I jerked his nose. The grinding snap of bones fitting in place was followed by a high-pitched yelp. "Now get your ugly face washed up and keep your damn mouth shut. You're lucky all they did was break your nose. I'm too many drinks in to remove a boot from your ass." I straightened up and withdrew my hand.

The Capitolian opened his mouth, but I shot my hand back to his nose and squeezed.

"Say one more word"—I applied the slightest torque—"and not even the best surgeon in the Seat will be able to set your nose right."

The man squealed as I twisted, and tears welled up in his eyes. "Al'igh'. Please, le' 'ee—"

I wiped my hand on his blue linen tunic, turned heel, slammed the door, and waited in the hall. He didn't come out to cause more trouble. When the only sound was the soft sobbing of a man in deserved pain, I washed my hands in my room's washbasin, stripped down to my smallclothes, and crawled under the sheepskins. The moment my head hit the pillow, sleep overcame me.

ℝ

I slept little that night, my mind preoccupied with returning home simply to leave again. More than once, I woke with a start. I dreamed Harvald's family had either discovered my secret and betrayed me, or that I ... had betrayed them. Normally when my nightmares haunted me, I had my pack to comfort me—indeed, this was the first night I had spent in years outside their presence in my natural form—and their absence unsettled me further.

When I woke, I descended to the dining room, dressed in my outwear, ready to depart. The faintest glow came from a solitary candle standing at the side of a padded chair near the fireplace of the common room. In that chair, a hunched, shadowy figure wrung and rubbed his hands together. The form produced the soft, rhythmic sound of someone clearing their throat.

"Aros, I'm surprised you're up already."

The young man knocked his chair backward as he leapt to his feet. The clatter boomed in the empty room. He straightened his belt, brushed out the folds in his tunic, and pulled his long hair back securely as he spun around. "Who …? Oh, Master Rune." His shoulders visibly relaxed. "Aye, I'm up. I couldna sleep. No much, anyway."

I gestured for him to sit and joined him in the neighboring chair. "You feel up to riding so far today, then? If not, I'll have your brother come, and I can fix you something to help you—"

The young man slapped his palm against the arm of the chair. "No!" He paused. "I mean, no, sir, no need to do that. I'm"—he stifled a yawn with his hand—"fine."

I inclined my head toward the lad. "As you say, lad. I'll find us something to eat quick while you get the horses saddled."

Aros jumped to his feet and bundled himself while I walked through the kitchen door behind the bar. Only with Siggy could I get away with something like raiding the kitchen while the cook was away. The Two bless her.

R

The ride back to my home was uneventful, and once Aros woke a bit more, we chatted about many things. At first, Aros kept things professional. He would ask me to quiz him on formulæ he had learned, but the conversation quickly turned to plainer themes. The mind can only ponder science for so long before it longs for the unquantifiable, human things of life.

We shared riddles, sang, and eventually came around to Aros telling me about his family's journey with their fellow townsfolk. I had heard stories like his a hundred times before—axles broke, wagons got stuck in mud, fellow refugees got sick, some died, and others wished quite loudly that they themselves were among the dead. Yet, for all the troubles and tragedy—the griefs of travel, the road weariness, and all—what most occupied the young man's mind was the beautiful strangeness of the world.

After so many years, after so many griefs, and after a weariness not of roads but of the world … aye, after so much, I was captivated by this boy's own captivation. His awe at seeing a "grand city with walls, and ramparts, and all"—and I knew that this "city," Burgia, was anything but grand—reminded me of a time when I, too, had been filled with that same terrible awe and wonder at the world. Though the boy was hardly a weaver of tales, his retellings of what would have otherwise been utterly mundane—markets that stretched for blocks, of houses with terracotta roofs, and of paved roads—swept me up as I saw them through this young man's eyes.

What had changed in me that the same world that had once enthralled me had become so odious? Nothing had changed about what I was. I had been the same monster then as I still was now—maybe even more so—for I had not understand then how great a sin it was for me to be what I was. If my nature had not changed, then what? Had the world changed? Was it for better, or for worse, that I had so grown to hate the world in which I lived with its enticements to sin?

Only now, as I look back on that ride home, do I know what made me so weary. It was that I did not know—or rather, that I had forgotten—what the remedy was for my ennui, for my world weariness and self-loathing. Suffice it to say, as we rode, I saw things anew through this young man's eyes for the first time in a long time ... for a moment at least.

"Aye, lad, I remember seeing many of those same things myself."

"Maybe I'll be able to travel the world like you did, sir."

My smile fell. "Be careful what you wish for, lad. There are many things man can wonder at in the world, but many of which he was better off for never having seen, nor even having heard of."

"Like the ...?" He let his words die in the gentle winter wind. He stared ahead, grasping the reins with undue force.

"Like the elves? Was that what you were going to say?"

He swallowed hard. "I did no say anythin', sir."

"*Bah,* don't lie to me, boy. Not only are you not good at it, but it's unbecoming." I spat. "Now—"

"Aye, 'twas what I was goin' to say ... but I remembered you did no like to talk 'bout such things."

"I—"

"That's why I lied. I did no want to offend you, sir. But I ended up doin' so, anyway. I'm sorry."

"Oh, I know why you lied, lad. You're a conscientious enough fellow to remember what you aren't supposed to mention. Still, honesty is the wiser choice." I let him settle in the saddle. "But, to your question; aye, the elves would be one example of something better left unknown. And there are other dark things, too, about which rumors and innuendo are more   than   enough   for   any   sane   man.

Knowledge—Truth—may be powerful, but she is dangerous. She holds no allegiances to anyone but herself."

"I do no understand, sir."

"Lad, only make sure you count the cost before you seek after Truth, whether she be in the heavens or on earth. Every bit of knowledge, every truth uncovered, changes you, for better or for worse, in a great or small way, and you can never return to a state of unknowing and ignorance. Truth will always change you, but to what end and for what purpose is the question. Truth has no master that someone can tell her where she ought to lead a man; she leads him where she wills, whether he likes it or not, whether he wills it or not. Man cannot will Truth out of existence, though he may try, and only a fool believes all knowledge is desirable."

The boy blinked. "I'm sorry, sir, you've lost me."

I sighed, not out of exasperation, but because weariness was overcoming me again. "That's fine, lad, just humor an old man waxing philosophical. Old men like to be listened to, even if no one is paying heed. Still, one will find their ravings are often filled with more wisdom than even they themselves realize."

"As you say, sir."

"Good, lad. You learn quickly."

R

When we arrived, the pack emerged from the woods and joined us. Aros tidied up and prepared my home for a long absence, as I had instructed. In truth, the tasks were minimal, and few were truly necessary, but I wanted to gather my things in private.

While Aros worked below, I entered my study upstairs. My writing desk—cleared of contents except for a stoppered inkwell and a diary that I had never used—took up most of the space. The two exterior walls were lined with bookshelves, upon which books and parchments were crammed, and more books were piled against the balcony's railing.

I took a few volumes down from the shelves and set them on the desk. Then I grabbed a few rolled-up parchments that might come in handy. Most were additional books I would ultimately part with, handing them over to my temporary apprentice at our destination. A few others, however, were of much broader appeal. I grabbed a book of tales and legends, many of which were more truth than fiction, and a few prayer books. Finally, I took the unused diary in case the spark to write took hold of me while I traveled—I am now glad I did.

When I had what I wanted, I shuffled a few of the books on the back shelf and tripped the internal locks to open the door hidden behind the shelf. There was a *click*, and a puff of dust blew out of the hinges, which had not been moved in at least a decade. I pushed the shelf, and it swung inward.

The room measured roughly six cubits by four, the air was stale, and dust and cobwebs covered everything. Against the back wall was a large armoire containing my Stateless armor. Inside, my armor was arrayed on a stand, caked in a layer of oily dust. My two swords—one for combat, and a rapier for my dress outfit—and a simple short bow with a quiver of arrows hung on the doors. My uniforms and accoutrements were stashed in the drawers built into the armoire's floor.

My hands shook, and my knees grew weak as I touched the relics of my former life. My breathing quickened. Sweat beaded on my brow. A lump grew in my throat. I swallowed hard, and tears ran down my face.

ᚱ

The open field, upon which I stood, was bathed in the light of the moon and stars. I wrinkled my nose as the lingering stench of blood and decay filled my nostrils. Rumors said something stalked the battlefield by night. It was a demon, some said. Others, a rabid animal. Others still, that it was something in-between. It would feast on the corpses of dead soldiers, they said, or steal soldiers from their beds. Even warriors believed in boogeymen.

Though I had cared little about the battle—a Latian squabble between city-states like this impacted me little—when the joint missive and fat purses arrived, calling me to resolve this problem, I had set out. Something clearly had even the brass spooked.

When I arrived on the field before dusk, I picked up a faint whiff of the beast's scent. I knew it at once. I had fought one of these monsters before. It was a feral, and it took all my self-control not to fly into a rage right there.

As the moon rose, the scent unbearable, my blood surged in my veins. The memory of the Watcher—that mutant, half-transformed monstrosity of a feral I had killed a lifetime ago—enraged me, and I relished the prospect of slaying another.

The beast's red eyes glowed in the distance. It crawled on all fours, and its twisted silhouette slunk among the shadowy forms of the unclaimed corpses. Great claws protruded from sinewy paw-hands, and they raked the ground as the beast prowled. It stopped among the dead and scanned the field. Its glowing eyes locked on me. Like a spider closing in on its ensnared prey, the feral crawled closer. It rose upon two feet like a man and towered over me.

I drew my sword from my hip. The blade grated against the metal lip of the sheath and glowed a faint blue in the moonlight.

The monster's eyes glowed all the brighter the nearer it got.

I picked up an unexpected yet familiar scent. It was Mara ... No, not quite her, but like her. I pushed the thought from my mind and roared. This was the only thing I could do to stop transforming in rage.

The beast hunched over and stretched out its hideous half-human, half-wolven muzzle. It sniffed at me. It was only twenty paces away. With its fiery, unblinking eyes, it studied me and unleashed a roar from its misshapen maw that shook the earth itself.

The beast dropped to all fours, lunging to reach me in one great bound. I rolled, but its claws ripped through my chainmail hauberk and tore my arm open. Hot blood poured down my arm and dripped from my fingertips, but I paid it no mind. It would close by night's end.

I jumped to my feet and leapt backward as I put my sword between myself and the feral. We circled one another and, after but a moment of this game, I lunged. I swung my sword, and a glowing trail followed it, lighting up the night and revealing the beast's face. It was grotesque—patches of thick wolf's fur and human hair covered its face, while human skin showed through elsewhere. Its right eye had a human form, and the left was angled like a wolf's, but both glowed demonic red. Its muzzle protruded unevenly; the lower jaw was half-human and half-wolf. Its too-long tongue protruded from between its snarling lips.

I aimed to take one of the beast's limbs but failed to connect. The feral stood its ground, swiping at me with one clawed paw-hand and then another as I swung again. I threw myself off balance to avoid the counterattack and rolled away. The beast chuckled deep in its throat.

I circled, but the beast stood its ground. I drew a half-circle in the air with the tip of my sword. The beast watched my every move. No moment would be better than another ...

I feinted to the right. The beast's defensive swipe flew past. I swung my sword with a scream. The beast howled. Hot blood spurted across my face as I severed the clawed fingers from its right paw-hand.

It let out another earth-shaking roar and swiped many times in succession. With its remaining claws, it ripped more links from my mail and dug great gouges into my chest. I fell back, losing my sword in the tall grass.

I cursed and somersaulted backward as well as I could in full armor. I pulled the dagger from my boot and flung it at the feral. The dagger found its mark, burrowing into the beast's eye.

It flung itself at me, claws flailing, and I rolled aside again. The feral spun and flung its clawed hands in a berserker's rage to force me back. When it was far enough from me, it wrenched the dagger from its eye. At once, it lunged at me with undiminished rage.

I threw myself aside, arms outstretched to grope for my sword in the dark. I rolled about as the beast lashed at me again, nearly smashing my skull into the earth as it attempted to leap upon me.

My blade's faint glow caught my eye, and I groped for it in the grass. I grasped the pommel and rolled onto my back. The beast leapt. I raised my sword. The beast came down upon me with a howl.

Its howling became a sudden snarling gasp as my sword pierced its chest.

The beast crashed upon me. I gasped, the wind gushed from my lungs. The dull snap of cracking ribs filled my ears.

The great beast's head lay next to mine, its mutant lips pulled back in a demonic smile. It was still breathing, though shallowly.

I mustered all my strength to push it away, and I yanked my sword from the feral's chest, ready to finish the job. The beast, however, whined and spoke in a gravely tone. Blood poured from its muzzle and spurted. "F-F-Fa—"

It ceased speaking and filled my mind with scent-images, powerful and vivid.

Her scent overwhelmed me. The last memory I had of her, the memory of when I had broken away from her, came to my mind.

"You're a father, Rune," Mara had said. "Four sons, all feral."

The memory was cloudy and disjointed, induced by the already fading scent-images with which the feral flooded my mind.

This beast bombarded me with more of Mara's scents. These were not the scents of my lover, but of this beast's mother. It longed for her comfort ...

The beast scented hatred, which it directed entirely and unequivocally at me. "You left her," it scented. "You hurt Mother ..."

A shiver shot down my spine. I fell to my knees to touch the dying beast's face. It was too weak to so much as move its head.

All I could smell on it ... on my son, was hatred—hatred was its essence—and it harbored every bit of its rage to unleash it upon me. It had marked me as prey to be devoured.

I saw images of wolves ripping a deer limb from limb, eating it alive. The dying deer, in its last feeble attempt to survive, kicked out and struck one of its four attackers in the head. The attacking wolf dropped in a heap, but the other wolves kept on tearing.

"They come ..." it scented. This was the last image to flash through my mind as my son died.

I stroked my son's malformed face. Was this my firstborn? Was it the youngest of the litter? Did it matter? I buried my face into my son's gore-splattered chest and gripped at his fur. Tears flowed freely down my face.

I wept not only for my son who had lived a life of death, but I wept because I had brought monsters worse than myself into the world. I wept knowing there were still others.

I turned my face to the starry heavens and howled. My cry shook the ground, and I cursed the Moon and Stars that had made me what I was.

R

I stared at the two swords hanging on the armoire door. My blood boiled, and I tasted blood in my mouth—I had bitten my cheek to keep from crying out.

My eyes shifted back to their normal hue, and the points of my ears shrank away. I fell to my knees, clutching my chest. My heart raced.

Feet tramped behind me. "Master Rune"—Aros panted—"I h-heard you shout. Are you—"

"Ugh." I shook my head. "I … I, uh … tripped and hit my head. Give me a minute. I'll be fine." As I rose with Aros' help, I took the helmet form the mannequin in the armoire. "Too bad I wasn't wearing this, eh?"

The helmet was open-faced, and a long horsehair tail rose from the crown and flowed down the back. Like all my armor, it had red-gold knotwork trim that looked much like my tattoo. Unlike my tattoo, however, the trim on the helm intensified the low light in the room and glowed dimly. And, upon the brow of the helmet, the "Writ of the Stateless" was written in ornate, glowing script in Oserdeni, Sviaral, and Latian. *"Neither king nor council may impede this man's just sword."*

"This is your armor? 'Tis amazin' …" Aros ran his fingers across the smooth metal, fascination upon his face. "Does that glow no give you away at night, sir? How do they make it—"

"It's dwarven work—beyond man's ken. As for the glow, it doesn't reflect star and moonlight. So, unless you're already in someone's torchlight, you're fine." I raised the helm to place it upon my head, brushing the plume back. The helm, which I had once borne effortlessly, was now ponderous. It was only by force of will that I kept my neck and back from stooping.

I sighed, lifting the helm from my head again and putting it back upon the mannequin. "It's been a long time since I last wore this …"

I hesitantly disassembled the mannequin's limbs so I could don the hauberk. I slipped the gambeson over the top, finding it fit more loosely on me than I remembered. That was hardly surprising, though, as my lean frame once swelled with muscle.

I fixed the hardened leather pauldrons and breastplate upon the gambeson's arming clasps, and I pulled the armored leggings on over my pants before donning my heavy marching boots. Only then did I don the helmet and war belt, to which I fixed my longsword at my left hip. Last, I pulled on my greaves, the right covering slightly less of my wrist than the left, to leave the Stateless tattoo visible.

I struggled against the armor as it pulled me down, though I once had borne it all so easily, without a care. I had taken and spared life as I executed justice and vengeance upon my enemies. Now, though, the armor weighed not only upon my body but my mind. Could I truly resume this role without reverting to my old ways?

You've no choice. You gave your oath and are bound to fulfill it or die trying.

I took my ceremonial sword, a thin rapier, off the door, along with my bow and quiver before turning toward Aros. "Lad, take these down for me." I handed over the weapons. "I have a few more items here to gather, and then we can depart."

He stared at the weapons as if some sacred mystery had been revealed, and he held them close to his chest. "I'll guard them with my life."

I opened a drawer in the armoire and pulled out clothing and other accoutrements. "You're just going down the stairs, lad. I don't think you need stake your life on such a task as that."

"Uh … I mean, you can count on me."

"I know, lad. Now, off with you."

RRR

Chapter XIV

The Greenhorn: [Looks at the Grizzled Veteran, who rests a sheathed sword on his lap.] *"You still know how to use that thing, old man?"*

The Grizzled Veteran: [Rising to his feet with a groan, joints popping.] *"I may be old and rusty, like a blade long out of use, boy, but given a little oil and care ..."* [He attempts to draw it with a skillful flourish but fumbles it.] *"Shit ..."*

Greenhorn: [With a laugh.] *"Maybe you need more than just a little oil."*

Veteran: *"Shut your damn gob, you shite."* [He leans over with a groan to fetch the fallen sword.] *"Give me a chance to warm up, and I'll run circles around you."*

— *Comœdia Militis Senecti, Actus I*

R

We carried everything—books, armor, and more—out and loaded the horses. The only book I did not store among the others was the small, leather-bound *fastus lunaris*, which I kept in an inner pocket of my gambeson, along with a small bag of precious stones and coinage I had taken from a lockbox in the armoire. Before we left, I checked the tables of the *fastus*. Only twelve days remained until the Triduum.

I plotted our trip in my mind and figured where the Triduum would begin. We'd be cutting it close—too close, in my estimation—arriving at East Laketon on the first day of the Triduum. If we were one or, worse, two days late ...

No, that was not an option. We *had* to arrive at East Laketon on time.

I ruminated on this as we rode to Melbù and tried not to let the weight—literal and figurative—of my task weary me. I would be making many changes in the coming days, not least of which was getting my body back into fighting shape.

While I found my armor a burden, Ela—shining in all her own regalia, which had been locked in a chest under the stable floor—did not mind being put back to her old task. She was a proud creature, and though I could not communicate with her as I could with the wolves, she was clearly content to be my noble steed again. Though I hung my head low, she held hers high.

Then there was Aros. Though he had been ecstatic to see my armor, his enthusiasm waned as the lack of sleep caught up to him. More than once, he dozed in the saddle, but as he started to list to the side, he would catch himself and jolt upright. When he fell so far that Thunder whinnied at the sudden yanking on his reins, I stopped Ela with a "Whoa," and Thunder, too, obeyed my command.

I leapt from the saddle to untangle Aros. "I thought you said you'd be all right to ride, lad?"

The young man yawned, a great cloud of steam rising. "Aye, sir, I am. I just—"

"You *just* nothing. Help me get the bags off Ela and onto Thunder. You're riding with me." I began to loosen the straps on Ela's saddlebags at once.

"But I—"

I shot a sharp look at the boy. "That wasn't a request, boy."

Aros did not speak another word aloud, though he muttered under his breath.

We departed again, Aros sitting in front of me in the saddle. We spoke little after that, and it wasn't long before the young man fell asleep, leaning back against me with his head resting lazily upon my shoulder. When the young man's cloak fell open, he shivered, and I wrapped my own cloak around him and held him close. He leaned into the crook of my shoulder with a sleepy, "Thanks, Da."

His kind, albeit mistaken, words stung me, and the image of my feral son's bloody maw tormented me. I heard my son hiss my name, "Father," with bitter hatred in his heart, and tears filled my eyes. I had finally heard that name spoken in love, but it was a mistake. I wrestled against this bitterness for the rest of the journey but buried it deep within so the boy would never know.

At Siggy's tavern, I woke the boy, and he broke free of my cloak's embrace.

Wiping drool from his lips, he shot me an embarrassed glance over his shoulder but said nothing. I wondered if he remembered what he had said in his sleep.

I gave the horses to the grooms, who did not recognize me at first with all my armor. When I called, however, they rushed to fetch the horses, eager to receive another hefty tip.

When we had all my necessary possessions in arm, I spoke to Aros as we entered the inn, "Now you know your limits, eh, lad?"

"Aye, sir," Aros grumbled, loosening his cloak and hanging it from his shoulder. "Sorry to have troubled you."

"It's no trouble, Aros. Now you know your limits." I clapped the young man's shoulder.

Inside, Aros' family had spread throughout the common room. Harvald and Gale sat by the fire with a few other guests who had come early that day, and the youngest children sat playing at their parents' feet. Arve, Haldis, and Erika talked among themselves at a long dining table.

"Now go enjoy your evening and get yourself to bed at a decent time tonight, you hear."

The young man nodded and joined his siblings.

With every step I took toward the fire, my armor glowed brighter. Enveloped by the aura of light, it took little time for everyone in the common room to notice me, and while I was still some way off, the young boys ran and pestered me with incessant questions about everything I wore. Grim pulled upon the broad war belt, and Troy clung to my leg while standing on my boot to pull on my leather breastplate and the edges of my mail hauberk that protruded from underneath. Gale and Harvald's protests to leave me be went unheeded, so I entertained the boys by showing them my accoutrements.

My longsword—the words *Týpte Orthôs* etched in the glowing script of the Ancients on the flat of the blade—amazed them the most. Their heads spun as I demonstrated a few simple swings, the path of the arcing blade traced in light. Even the men in the common room marveled. I must have seemed a master swordsman, though I was horribly out of practice.

I sheathed the sword with a simple flourish, and a small round of applause broke out, and the sound of the young boys' jumping feet added to the din.

"Mas'er Rune"—Eirik reached on tiptoes for the hilt of my sword—"gimme that"—he paused, working the word out with great effort—"that *sward*."

One of the older boys pushed him. "It's *suh-ward*, Eirik, and Master Rune'll let *me* hold it first 'cause I'm oldest."

A fight broke out—the younger wrestling with the older—and each brother's twin joined in.

Gale jumped to her feet and bared bottoms, leaving the boys in tears as they all screamed their apologies and begged for mercy. She bowed deeply. "I'm so sorry, Master Rune."

"Boys will be boys," I laughed. "I'd be more surprised if they *weren't* interested in my sword and armor."

We spent what remained of the day with feet up by the fire, and the inn began to hum with activity as the night dragged on.

As we planned the next days' journey, nearly every patron approached me, the hermit from the outskirts, to inquire about my armor. When they heard I was a retired Stateless, many who had perpetuated rumors about me apologized profusely—never, they all claimed, had they intended to besmirch a knight and his honor but wanted only to have a bit of fun—and many rounds of mead and ale were sent our way. I drank four full tankards of the stuff and finally told the waitress to hold back anything more. The Stateless code forbade drunkenness, but even if it didn't, it was never pleasant to travel hungover.

Even Gale and Harvald, who pretended for a long while not to notice the aura surrounding me, eventually asked about my affects and the protocols of the Stateless. "Need we also follow any special rules, sir?" Gale asked.

"Aye," Harvald rumbled, "we do no want to dishonor you and your guild, sir."

Their only obligation, I explained, was to obey me if there was danger. Only when they acknowledge this, did I explain the ceremonies, duties, rights, and privileges of the Stateless. I told them how, every day, I would rise, arm myself, and carry out my training. Likewise, I would always—unless sleeping or bathing—be in uniform, and a weapon would never be out of arm's reach. While we traveled, I would make rounds, ensuring that all were accounted for.

We chatted for several hours, but I finally excused myself, as I would have to rise even earlier than my charges. Before I retired, however, I pulled up to the bar and asked for Siggy.

She sauntered out of the back room with a laugh. "Well, hello, handsome. Come to sweep a damsel off her feet, oh knight in shining armor?"

I laughed and shook my head. "No, Siggy, not quite."

"What's with the get-up, then? Truth be told, you do look mighty handsome in that." She ran a finger down my leather-clad arm. "And the glow … You really are in shining armor. So, who's the lucky damsel?" She leaned over the bar, resting her chin on one hand.

"Well, the *get-up* is the battledress of the Stateless, and—"

"Ha!" She slammed her fist on the bar. "I always knew you were a merc or soldier on the lam. My husband, the Two keep him—"

"Amen."

"—always thought you were some wealthy caravan doctor who simply wanted to retire. But you never did strike me as the type, Corinsson."

"Oh, and how did I strike you, Siggy?" I narrowed my eyes with a smirk.

"Well, Corinsson, do you want the truth? Or, do you want ol' Siggy to humor you?"

My eyes widened unconsciously. Such serious words rarely came out of Siggy's mouth. I wasn't sure how to respond.

"Well ... why not the truth?"

Siggy nodded and flashed a sincere smile. "I always thought you seemed like someone running from himself." She leaned in close so not even the closest patrons at the bar would hear, and she slipped a hand, calloused from years of work, into mine. "I never knew someone who visited the priest as much as you did. No, he didn't tell me, so wipe that look of shock off your face. C'mon; you didn't seriously think I wouldn't put your comings and goings and the priest's rounds together, did you?

"Anyway, I always figured you had been a soldier or some such, and your conscience got the better of you." She now leaned against the bar with both arms, her face mere inches from mine, and she moved even closer to my ear. "And that's what I always liked about you, Corinsson—you're an egg—tough on the outside, but a big softy on the inside." She laughed that same playful laugh. "So, how close was I?"

"Closer than I'd like ... I guess I shouldn't be surprised, though, that you kept track of my every move, should I, Siggy?"

"Ha, you know me too well." She pushed away from the bar. "Well, Corinsson, I have to get back into that kitchen before the place goes up in flames. Anything else I can do for you before you head out in the morning?"

"Aye." I loosened the coin pouch on my war belt. "I need to settle up. How much'll it be?"

Siggy pulled out the wax tablet that contained our tab, and I counted out as many sovereigns, silver pennies, and bronze bits as required. I threw in a few extra coins, too.

"Give this extra to the girls, will you?"

Siggy nodded kindly, slipping the extra coins away into her bustier, shaking her bosom ever so slightly to let the coins settle. I rolled my eyes, and she winked.

"You stay safe now, you hear, Corinsson? I don't want my future husband coming back stone-cold on a bier, though if you get a few rugged scars, I wouldn't complain."

"Already got plenty of those, Siggy."

Siggy fanned herself and pretended to swoon.

As she pushed open the door to the kitchen again, she stopped and called out, "Corinsson, one more thing …" She waved me over until we stood nearly face to face at the bar again. "My girls … well, you know, they hear things when they go around …"

I nodded solemnly, expecting to hear that the Capitolian was plotting his revenge.

"Well, they tell me that you should watch out for that lass you're traveling with. She has a mighty big heart for you." Without another word, she turned around.

"What? Haldis?" I called after her. "Nah, it's nothing more than a young girl's infatuation."

Siggy let out yet another laugh. "You really are oblivious to a woman's affections, aren't you, Corinsson?" Her words reached me just as the door swung shut behind her.

R

The next morning, I rose well before sunup and began my old regimen anew. I washed, squared my beard to regulation, and tied my hair back into a tight, low-hanging bun that would not get caught in my helm. I then donned my armor and began my training.

That first day served as a testament to how physically weak I had become after my years of solitude—only my daily chores of chopping wood and mucking the stable had kept me in shape at all—so I struggled to complete even the exercises a recruit was expected to perform.

The weakness brought on by my extended inertia became even clearer as I executed the combat forms in the confined space of my tiny room, and I found myself fumbling my sword on more than one occasion. *I'm a hundred years too old for this shit.*

I finished the twenty-five-minute novice's routine in forty-five.

Afterward, I wanted to do nothing more than lie still for the rest of the day. My muscles throbbed, my bones and back ached, and joints I forgot existed popped as I stretched and moved in ways that a body as old as mine ought not. Though I was practically immortal, that did not mean my body experienced no aging pains.

When I was done, I doffed my armor and every stitch of my sweat-soaked clothes to wash at the basin on the side table once more. I washed the sweat from my arms and body, and I splashed my face to wash the sweat from my eyes. I wet my hair and combed it back before tying it up again.

A reflection I scarcely recognized as my own stared back up from the water's surface. I fingered a scar that tore across my collarbone and ran a hand through the gray patches that streaked through my beard and dark brown braids, which pulled my hair back at the temples. I frowned at my appearance, and the already present wrinkles that creased my brow and the corners of my eyes grew more pronounced. As I stood back from the basin, my shoulders rolled forward from years of poor posture. I did not like the man I saw, but now was not the time for further self-chastisement.

As I donned my spare clothes and refixed the plating onto my gambeson, there was a knock at the door.

"Sir, are you awake?" It was Erika.

"Aye, come in."

The young woman poked her red head in at me and smiled. "We've a hot meal waitin' for you downstairs, and the horses are bein' readied. Should I send the boys to fetch your things?"

I fastened my belt and attached my sword. "If they're done with their meals and waiting to go, you can send them up. If not, I'll fetch everything myself." I had hoped my efforts to be ready before the others would not have been in vain ...

"Oh, they're done, sir. Aros came earlier to get you, thinkin' you were sleepin' still, but he saw you were trainin' and let you be."

At those words, I hurried down the stairs, muttering curses under my breath, and found everyone at the table. At the head of the table was a mug of tea, a packed pipe, and a bowl of porridge. It was hardly a *hot* meal anymore, though I could hardly complain. I wolfed down the food before pulling on my outwear and sticking the packed pipe into one of my pockets.

"I've kept us long enough. Let's be off."

In surprisingly ordered fashion, the entire family gathered their last remaining items and climbed aboard the wagons. Before Erika climbed aboard, however, she tapped my shoulder as I counted heads by the door.

I glanced at her.

"Sir, this mornin', I made everyone lunch with some food Miss Sigrid left us." She held out a bundle wrapped in cheesecloth. It was rather weighty for a light meal on the road. "I made you a little extra, too, when Aros said you were trainin' so hard this mornin'."

"Thank you." I pocketed the meal. "But you didn't have to do that for me, lass. I don't need—"

"You're doin' so much for us, 'tis the least I can do to make sure you're well-fed." The corners of her mouth turned up in a smile, though the rest of her face was veiled by her hood.

"Thank you, lass, but now, we must get a move on."

I mounted Ela and pulled alongside Aros and Arve in the lead cart. "I'm going to scout ahead. I'll be back in a half-hour." Before the boys could respond, I spurred Ela forward, and she took off south, down Melbù's sole road.

I quickly put Melbù behind me as I followed the road south, and as soon as I was out of the town, my pack rejoined me. The wolves easily kept up with the leisurely pace I set. They scented little among themselves, preferring to travel quietly, and though they weren't great conversationalists, I was happy to have them at my side again. Only Raynor was not content to keep silent and, every few minutes, the scent-images of squirrels and rabbits running for cover under thickets invaded my mind.

I was happy to find naught but a thin layer of snow on the road. The horses and wagons would have no trouble traversing it, thus speeding our journey. The heavens, too, were clear, and the sun shone brightly, though not warmly, as wind swept across the barren fields that stretched to the horizon on either side of the road. An occasional farmstead in the distance or a copse broke the monotony, and birds flew about the trees and chirped. Small thickets and hedges also rose on the edges of the road, though nothing was large enough to hide an ambusher.

Unlike the land north of the town, which was heavily wooded, the south was dull. This was grain country, some of the most fertile land in the known world, and I knew that, in a few moons' time, the winter wheat would be filling the fields. For the next several days, however, barren, snow-covered fields was all we would see until we turned south-west, toward East Laketon. There, the thick forests would return and stretch out until we approached the Seat, where endless fields and towns would stretch out again into the foothills where the Seat was nestled. These first days of monotony, then, would be the worst part of the journey, if everything went according to plan.

After thirty minutes of scouting ahead of the caravan, I turned about, unsurprised at my lack of findings. Shortly thereafter, I rejoined the caravan and made my rounds to confirm that all were present and accounted for. It was a dull job, to be certain, but it was my job, and it kept my mind from wandering the darker haunts it otherwise frequented.

RRR

Chapter XV

The Three Days of the Moon shall be sacred to you, for during this Triduum the Great Beast was revealed. Ye shall observe this solemnity with fasting and prayer for three nights, from the Antenoctem *to the* Posnoctem *of the full moon. On the second night, you shall hold a vigil, for this is the height of the Triduum. For three nights, you shall observe the fast. At the setting of the sun, you shall begin the fast each night, whether the moon traveled in the house of the sun, or if it is swathed in the glory of the stars I have set about it, which are like unto an ornament with which a woman magnifies her beauty. Whether the moon is out among the starry host, or whether it travels in the house of the sun, three shall be the nights of fasting from dusk to dawn.*

But whoever should profane this holy Triduum, he shall be as an unbeliever to you. You shall cast him out of your midst so he has no part with you. Yea, he shall be as one who serves the Great Beast who was slain, and as the master is, so, too, shall the slave be.

— From *Precepts of the All Father*

R

T he first night came quickly, and we settled near a small grove of trees overhanging the road. Between the two carts, the family hung heavy tarpaulins to make a low-lying tent. They cleared the ground as best they could of snow and ice, laid out a bit of stored kindling, and made a fire, from which the smoke rose through an opening in the tent's top. Once tea and light rations were served, the family laid out their bedrolls close together.

I stayed up, however, and did a short sweep of the area. I rechecked all the horses' hobbles and wheellocks and tied Ela near to her companion, Thunder. The night was clear, and this brought a deeper chill, but the air was still, and the horses were unbothered by the cold.

Behind the wagons, out of sight from the horses, I met my pack, and they relayed little to me besides their contentment to be reunited for the night.

We crawled into the tent, the fire nothing but embers now, and I rolled out my bedroll near the tent flap. I lay next to Arve at the end of the line, and Ragnar closed off the semicircle when he lay next to me. Ada and Freya curled up at the head of Kari's cradle near Gale's side, and Raynor crawled into the mass of the four youngest boys.

Before first light, Ragnar and I stepped into the crisp morning air. There, I donned my armor—chilled from sitting on the cold ground—and completed my training, passing through the sword forms to hone my dulled skills. I made my rounds as I had the night before and, after taking headcount, set tea on to boil over a rekindled fire and waited for the family to rise. When all awoke, I checked Harvald's wounds, which were healing nicely, and we dismantled our camp and set out with little fuss.

This was the routine into which we quickly fell and in which we continued uneventfully for the next eight days. Over that time, the scenery grew livelier as we turned southwest, toward East Laketon. The nearer we drew, the more abundant the forests and the denizens thereof became. Soon, there was not a field in sight, and we crossed many bridged rivers—some bridges were worthier of confidence than others—and forded many streams as we passed over hills and through valleys. From the heights of the steepest climbs, when the gaps between the trees and contours of the land allowed it, we even spied the Great Lake at the horizon's edge on clear days.

The nights, though cooler in such tree-shaded places, became more bearable since the wind could not reach us. Likewise, water was much more abundant, and we were able to lighten the load by emptying our water barrel. Even our dinners became more enjoyable, as the wolves would share the spoils of their hunts, whether of fish or game, with us all. The horses, too, grew more accustomed to the wolves' presence, and so the pack showed itself more openly.

The roads, apart from the occasional snowdrift, became even easier to traverse as we drew nearer to the great lumberyards that surrounded East Laketon. Everything was well for all of us, and I relaxed knowing we'd be in the city by nightfall on the first day of the Triduum. That was, until the axle broke.

"Whoa there!" Harvald jerked the reins mightily, and his family screamed in the wagon. The horses whinnied and stamped their feet as they stopped, the cart dragging behind them.

As I heard the commotion, I pulled Ela around and surveyed the broken wagon before pulling open the wagon's canvas. Though Kari wailed in Erika's arms, and the other young children cried and laughed in equal measure, everyone was all right.

Aros and Arve jumped from their wagon and ran to help. At Harvald's command, they helped him to the back of the wagon, where he crawled underneath to check the damage. All the while, Gale protested Harvald's exertions, incessantly reminding him to watch his arm and leg. I, too, urged Harvald to do nothing further.

"Anyone else here goin' to put a patch on?" He rose with his sons' help. "Gale?"

She crossed her arms with a huff.

"Master Rune?"

I shook my head. "I don't have that kind of skill, and I can't go out to fetch someone—my duty is with you all. But, if memory serves, you have an apprentice, no? An apprentice with two working arms is better than a master with one in a case like this, I would think."

Leaning against the wagon, Harvald furrowed his brow.

Arve looked to his father with bright eyes, Gale with fiery ones, and I with urgency.

"This will no be an easy task. E'en I wouldna be able to do more than patch this. I'm no cartwright."

"Please, Da, give me a chance. You can tell me what to do."

Gale placed a hand on Arve's shoulder. "What other choice is there, Harvald? You're no fool; you canna do anythin' like this without both hands. More than that, I'll no send Aros and Arve all the way to Laketon on their own. Let Arve have a go."

Harvald threw up his good arm. "Seein' as you'll no let me fix that axle up enough to get us goin' … all right, Arve, you get your chance, boy. Lads, get me somethin' to sit on, grab the tools, and let's get workin'."

After the first three hours passed with no significant progress, I had Aros and his family set camp and make a good meal. The wolves brought a brace of hares and squirrels, and the women set about skinning and dressing the meat. Meanwhile, I made my rounds with Ela and ruminated over my predicament.

The pack came alongside me as I rode, and they scented images of concern and compassion. Still, I feared I would not have the strength to resist the lunar lust of the Triduum. The prospect of undergoing so much pain filled me with dread.

I gripped the reins with white knuckles, and self-loathing filled my heart.

When I returned, I checked and rechecked the horses, wagons, and my charges. I checked on the progress of repairs every fifteen to twenty minutes, too, and Harvald's family asked me to sit and relax more than once. I always refused, however. I would not sit on the job.

So overzealous was I that, when I next went scouting, Aros suggested I give Ela a break and offered to walk with me. Though I was reticent to allow it, he eventually prevailed over me. He walked at my side like one of the wolves—silent—but eventually spoke.

"Sir?"

My only response was a grunt.

"You seem anxious, sir. Somethin' the matter? You've been pacin' 'bout, and you've been askin' my da 'bout their progress an awful lot. He does no wish to be rude, but I know he dislikes it. I can see it in his eyes. Maybe you should sit down and have some of that tea you keep makin' for us?" Aros' eyes were full of warmth, and they held the same sympathy my pack showed me.

"Aye, maybe I should. I suppose I'm a little worried. Anxious even … I dislike being out when the Triduum is approaching. Call me superstitious, but strange things tend to be afoot during the full moon."

"What kinds of strange things, Master Rune? You mean footpads, or … or somethin' else?"

The lad rubbed his gloved hands, so I put my hand on his shoulder.

"No, Aros, not highwaymen. Like I said, it's more superstition than anything real. You don't have anything to worry about."

"Oh, all right. Well, I'm glad 'tis nothin' serious. Still, you must—ought—to take a rest, sir. If you send the wolves with me, I could take one of your rounds."

"Mighty kind of you, lad, but there's really no need. I've already taken enough rounds, so I won't take another till after sundown. By that time, I think you'll already be sleeping."

We walked for a few more minutes before I turned us around.

R

For the rest of the afternoon, I sat with the family and rested with a cup of tea. I took a book of legends to entertain young and old alike, and I read to all until near sundown.

About that time, Arve entered the tent, a wide smile on his face, while Harvald wore a look of exasperation.

" 'Tis done," the young man said, guiding his father through the tent flap. "Da took a look and said 'twill hold."

Harvald gestured where he wanted to sit, and Arve helped him to his place. He stretched his good arm toward the fire and muttered, "'Twould've gone faster if I'd been the one working—"

"What was that, dear?" Gale glared at him.

He shrank down and pulled his cloak more tightly about himself. "Nothin'."

"I thought so. Now, let me fetch you both somethin' warm to drink." Gale busied herself with making a fresh pot of tea. "You did a fine job, I'm sure, Arve."

Harvald nodded. "Aye, he did. You've got the knack for this, lad. You'll get e'en better with time."

Arve puffed out his chest, crossed his arms, and stuck out his chin. "You hear that?" He looked at his three older siblings. "I've got a knack. 'Cause of me, we'll get to East Laketon."

Erika nudged Arve. "Aye, that's assumin' we do no break down tomorrow on the way."

He stuck his tongue out at her, and she leaned in to embrace him.

"Still, good job, Arve."

"Aye, thank you, Arve," Haldis added.

Aros sat beside me, saying nothing and looking into his cup of steaming tea. He took a long sip and remained silent.

I nudged him lightly, and he looked askance at me before turning his lowered gaze to Arve.

"Well done, brother."

While Arve recounted his work, we all ate our simple meal of porridge and skewered meat, and I invited everyone to pray the evening order. At the start of our journey, I had slipped away after dinner every evening to pray, but Aros had caught on and insisted I remain with them so we could pray together.

That night, I prayed silently for strength to undergo the trial the first of the Triduum would bring. Yet my heart still trembled, and the prayers that usually comforted me echoed vainly in my mind.

The wolves gathered round. They knew what I feared—passion, the call of ecstasy, and the painful self-mortification required of me.

When all had crawled into their bedrolls, I left the tent and gazed into the hazy sky. The moon, nearly full, bathed me in its light. My skin tingled in the glow. The hairs on the back of my neck stood erect. My heart pounded. Oh, how I wanted this—the transformation, the bliss, the power, the rage, the—

I ran blindly down the road and did not stop. The pack kept pace beside me.

When I had run many miles, I rushed into the thick woods. I threw myself down into the deep snow and screamed at the heavens with a voice I did not recognize as my own. The wolves surrounded me and unleashed their own howls of agony.

"*Resist,*" one scented.

"*Fight.*"

"*Howl.*"

The images they scented were too powerful and numerous. I could not sort them out, but they gave me something of strength to fight the unholy desires within. I feared it would not be enough …

I bellowed with another bestial roar. "Why must I suffer this? Why do I long for corruption?" I shouted at the heavens. "Oh Andar, oh Luváli, why have you cursed me with this unholy desire? I did not want this, I did not choose this, yet it fills my blood, my heart, my mind, my soul … You've made me a monster, an abomination you abhor, a monster you forbid me to be. Why? Why can I not be what I was born to be? Why must this be sin? Why do you make me suffer?"

My skin burned to release what I was, to revel in sin. I sobbed in the snow but raised my head to howl at the moon, which was a devil who shone with purest white light.

The wolves stayed by me, strengthening me as much as they could, loving me as much as wolves could love a man, yet I remained alone.

After a time—I do not know how long—I returned to the tent. All were asleep, the fire long dead. I slept away from everyone that night, hesitating to even let the wolves near me, for I feared what might overtake me. I feared what I was, what I might do.

R

That morning, the first of the Triduum, I carried out my training, ate with the family, and hurried us all on our way. That day, only the smallest children sat in the rear wagon, while the elder sisters sat, albeit uncomfortably, in the overpacked lead wagon.

After I finished my first round, I lost interest in continuing. Insatiable longing, growing stronger with every heartbeat, filled my heart and mind with demonic desires, away from which I could scarcely tear myself.

These feelings—the first signs of the Triduum's bewitching power—began shortly after sunup. My senses grew stronger. The heartbeat of every living thing within thirty paces pounded in my ears. I knew who was strong, who was weak. I smelled them—horse, human, wolf, male, female ... The sunlight blinded me, though it was never more than a slight bother in the prior days. Sweat beaded on my forehead and neck, and it trickled under my armor. My clothes grew damp.

By noon, I shook in the saddle. When we stopped for a quick meal, I fell from Ela, my legs unable to swing over the saddle cleanly. Thankfully, no one noticed, and I gripped my sword's pommel to hide how tremulous my hands were.

My attempts to hide my weakness and lunatic sickness were all for not. When Erika offered me some dried fruit, my stomach churned, and I retched in the snow at her feet. I collapsed to my knees and heaved up bile, as Aros, Gale, and Erika gathered at my side.

"I'm fine." I waved them away. "Sometimes when I travel, my stomach gets the better of me."

Gale stood over me, hands on her hips. "I do no think this is merely a traveler's sour stomach, sir. You're white as virgin snow."

Erika and Aros helped me to my feet, and I leaned heavily on the young man, my legs too weak to support my weight.

Erika took a handkerchief from her sleeve and wiped my brow and the corners of my mouth of spittle and vomit.

Aros grunted under my weight. "Sir, I think you should lie down in the wagon."

"I'll do no such thing. I have a job to do."

With a curt nod, I took a cup of cool water from Erika and rinsed my mouth. I spat the water at my feet and drank what was left.

She took the cup back. "Please, sir, we know you're lookin' out for us, but we'd all feel better if you were to get some rest."

I opened my mouth to protest.

"And I'll no take *no* for an answer." She pulled my cloak more tightly around me and lifted my helm to pull up my hood.

I sighed. "Fine, but I won't lie down on the job. I'll ride—"

Erika and Gale both stomped their feet. "You'll do no such thin'."

"You'll fall off that horse and break your neck." Erika sounded so much like her mother that I thought I was one of the young boys being chastised.

I threw up my hands. "Fine, I'll sit on the driver's bench, then."

Aros nodded and guided me to the wagon. "Aye, you can sit between me and Arve and catch some shuteye."

As the day progressed, I worsened rapidly. I shook violently, vomiting over the driver's seat, and I had to stop often. The first time, I ran into the bushes and barely managed to doff my armor. Afterward, I did not wear the armor-padded leggings, as I ought to have—some rules had to be bent now and then.

Finally, as the sun set, Arve wrapped his arm and cloak around me as Aros drove. Though we normally would have continued for another half-hour, Aros called for us to make camp. He halted the horses and, with his brother's help, took me from the cart.

At once, a crate was brought for me to sit on, and the wolves rushed to my side as everyone else made camp. Freya set her forepaws on my lap and rubbed her muzzle against my face. Ragnar sat calmly at my right with Ada on my left, my supporting pillars. Raynor ran into the woods and returned with a stick. He set it in my lap as a gift, and though the other wolves knew I did not enjoy sticks like they did, they all thought this was a kind gesture. It was something to take my mind off the pain.

When the tent was up, Aros and Arve helped me inside, uneasy as I was on my legs. When food was set over the fire, however, I bolted and retched even though my stomach was already empty.

Aros and Erika chased me. One held my hair back, while the other held my shoulders to stop me from collapsing in filth.

When I ceased, I mumbled, "Bring me to the cart. It's too hot in the tent." That was the truth, if not the whole truth. I wanted nothing more than to be alone, to suffer alone, to be away from the world, lest they should see and know the truth.

It took some convincing, but Aros and Erika finally let me crawl into the wagon alone.

"What I have may be catching. Only bring me my bedroll. I'll have Freya with me."

Aros brought my bedroll and laid it out, and he and Erika both helped me undress. Wearing only my smallclothes, they laid me down, and Erika set a damp cloth on my forehead before taking her leave.

Even stripped, my skin burned, and Freya, who lay close by, pulled my covers away. My vision swam as the fever worsened. Glowing, animalistic eyes stared at me from the darkness all around. Freya stood over me and licked my face, but—as she later revealed—I muttered curses and flailed at her, so she lay at my feet while the demons drew nigh.

Their voices called to me, waking me from fitful sleep. They taunted me. Some were cacodæmons that screamed with shrill voices. They demanded I give in to desire and sin. Others beckoned with sweeter voices. They pleaded with me to be what I was, to unchain it, and thus live. These voices were gentle and spoke thoughts of pleasure, of relief, of bliss, of release. They sang a siren song. Yet, no matter which voice spoke, the call was the same.

I would become my truer self in sin.

Thus I lay, sweating out the fever of desire. I shouted and screamed, cried and moaned, and begged for relief from the taunting and temptations that bewitched my heart. Freya drew near again, but I kept her away with threats of violence.

I wished to fall. The pain would cease. I would be free.

As I lay dying, ready to sin, to live my living death, there came to me an angel. The darkness that had so engulfed my heart, mind, and soul was transformed, transmogrified into an otherworldly light. This light, sudden and inexplicable, expelled the darkness with radiance.

"Mother," I cried, believing it was her shade—no, her angelic form—come to deliver my soul into the hand of her god, Andar, Luváli, and the All Father.

"Mother ..." I sighed as the angel's hand lighted upon my face. She extinguished the fire within my soul, and I slept.

When I woke the next morning, the angel was gone. There was no sign of her. I asked Freya if she had seen the angel, the great light, the burning fire that cooled my heart. The she-wolf looked at me in confusion and said she had not, though she was glad that I had not fallen away in the night.

RRR

Chapter XVI

It is claimed the practitioners of magic belong to either white or black schools of the craft, but the so-called school of white magic is merely a lighter shade of black. Every spirit requires blood; it is only the amount and kind that differs.

— From the anonymous pamphlet
Concerning So-Called White Magic

R

I opened my eyes the following morning to see Aros kneeling at my side. "Sir, are you well?"

I shivered, and Aros handed me my clothes.

"Aye." I slipped my tunic on, rubbing the welts on my side that I had gotten from falling off Ela. "I feel a bit better."

Aros knelt to help me as I struggled with my boots. "Do you want somethin' to eat, sir? Or, are you still—"

"Aye, I'll take something light." I had little desire to eat, but I needed to keep my strength. "Thanks, lad."

Inside the tent, the fire was lit, and as I took my seat, there was a resounding welcome. My pack had already made itself comfortable around the fire, and they also greeted me. Haldis came up to me with my folded cloak on her arm, knelt beside me with a smile, put it over my shoulders, and pinned it with a broach.

"Mornin', Master Rune. How're you feelin'?" Her voice was sweet, motherly even, but not flirtatious.

I shrugged the cloak around my shoulders. "Fine."

She sat behind me and combed out my hair. I nearly pulled away at the uncomfortable advance. However, I stopped when nobody rolled their eyes at her or chastised her for her flirtatiousness. Then I remembered how she, her other sisters, and her mother had all doted upon Harvald when he had been at his worst. Gale, too, was quick to hand me a cup of hot tea and a bite of bread, though I turned down anything more substantial. She, like Haldis, showed nothing but motherly compassion. Even little Yoanna was quick to fetch my gloves when she saw me rubbing my bare hands together, and she gave me a gentle hug after helping me to don them.

Only Erika remained aloof from these ministrations. Instead, she tended to her younger brothers and Kari, all of whom she bundled up well. Though she wasn't at my side, she yet glanced at me with great pity in her gentle smile and soft eyes. They were still full of that something I neither knew nor understood, but even more so now than before.

After we departed, the lunar sickness came over me, though not as severely as it had the day before. The angelic form returned to my mind, and her touch continued to be my stay. Knowing this mysterious guardian was with me made the thought of what I would inevitably become that night—the night of the full moon—bearable. It made the passion tolerable, for I knew the angel would abide, though I could not.

With our pace reduced to avoid another breakdown, the day dragged on, yet signs of East Laketon did appear. The roads were travel worn, paths branched off the main road with signposts marking the way to villages, and the smell of wood smoke would occasionally drift through the trees. The wolves made themselves scarce at these signs, knowing how dangerous things would become if their presence were discovered. Still, they stayed close enough to the road that I could sense them.

When there were scarcely three hours left before sundown, the forest came to a sudden end, and the rolling farmsteads of East Laketon appeared. These were covered with snow, and the only signs of life were the occasional cow or pig, or smoke rising from chimneys and venting holes in thatched farmstead roofs.

As we got closer still, the smells and sounds of the lakeside city filled the air—fish, smoke, and the cries of gulls. At these signs, I stopped our caravan to don my armor and mount Ela. Though the armor had grown lighter over the past days of travel as my body grew stronger, all the equipment weighed twice as much that day.

I rode twenty-five paces ahead of the wagons to intercept any guardsmen, and my diligence was rewarded. As we came into sight of the city's eastern gate, a young, clean-shaven guard—a stripe above a trainee—stopped me. Seeing the sword at my side, he tilted his halberd toward me and shouted for me to halt in a would-be command tone. I pulled back on Ela's reins, and the guard cautiously closed the distance. The tip of the outstretched halberd shook, and he darted his eyes back and forth between my hands and my sword. He could not have been older than Aros by more than two years, and I might well have been the first armed stranger he had encountered. That or the highwaymen who always followed on the heels of war had him spooked.

"State your name and business." He jabbed with the halberd's point and shifted his stance. The thin layer of muddy, half-melted snow squished under his feet.

"Rune Corinsson. I am of the Stateless."

The young man furrowed his brow, adjusting his grip on his weapon. "I didn't ask about your guild. I want to know your business." His command tone faltered, and he made another little jab with the halberd.

I sneered down at him from atop Ela. "My guild and my business are the same. I am under no obligation to tell you more."

The guardsman sank into a fighting stance. "I'll not—"

I sighed, my patience spent. "If you don't know who the Stateless are, boy, then get your sergeant to explain it. If he doesn't know, get your captain."

"I order you to dismount and drop your sword. Failure to identify yourself—"

I swung down from the saddle, lunged forward, nearly losing my balance on my weakened legs, but nevertheless found my target. I grasped the brandished weapon by the haft and twisted. The young guardsman fell with a curse.

I threw his weapon aside and crossed my arms as he gaped at me. "I said, go ask your sergeant about the Stateless, boy, or your captain. Now, get going before I put my boot up your arse for making me wait."

The young man scrambled backward in the mud, blanched, and gaped as he met my wild eyes.

I unfolded my arms, relaxed my stance, and reached out to help the young man up, but he slid away, mud coating nearly every inch of him.

I inched closer. "I'm not going to hurt you."

The young man pushed himself upright, nearly slipping back down in the slurry of snow, ice, and mud, and fled to the gate, leaving his halberd abandoned on the ground as he went.

I picked up the polearm and leaned it against Ela's saddle. No sense in letting a blade rust during a time of war. Then I signaled my charges to wait well behind me.

I huffed and crossed my arms. *We really are a dying breed, we Stateless.* Such was the way of all things—to wax and wane—and the days of my guild's glory were waning fast.

Scarcely more than ten minutes passed before a short but well-built man approached us from the city. The horsehair tail sticking out of his helmet marked him as captain of the guard, and at his sides were two guards in chainmail, their stern faces glaring out from their open-faced helms. Trailing shortly behind these three was the young guard, still covered in mud, face flushed in a mix of embarrassment and indignation. The captain laid his hand on his sword's pommel, and the guardsmen readied their halberds. They stopped just out of the range of my sword's reach, though the captain took one step further.

"I don't know who you think you are—"

I pulled my left gauntlet off as I approached the captain, who drew his sword. Before he or his vanguard could move, I flung the gauntlet, and it bounced off his iron breastplate with a clang. I raised my bare fist to the level of my eyes and—surprising even myself—drew upon the long dormant power within me.

In my depths, in a part of me I had forgotten existed, a spirit not my own stirred. The many scarred-over wounds in this dark heart of mine ached as the foreign spirit slithered over them. From within that dark heart, this spirit emerged from its long slumber and slipped out of a small tear in the fabric of my being that served as its home. Unlike the other spirits that dwelt within me long ago—spirits which had torn great rifts in my dark heart, rifts which were now scarred over—this spirit had not torn out a new dwelling. No, but it had taken over the abandoned dwelling of a once greater spirit, though it was no less an alien for that fact.

As it slunk from its reclaimed home, pulsating energy emanated and rippled in its wake. These ripples became waves that flooded my body, soul, and mind with exhilarating force—*magic*. The force melted the snow beneath my feet, and life from the earth—the life of grass and of creeping things that crept under the earth—rose through my body and radiated up and out to the spirit-woven tattoo. The tattoo warmed, but the vital heat from the earth—the life of the grass and creeping things under the earth—grew cold. The spirit hummed and thrummed as it fed for the first time in what seemed a millennium.

The tattoo glowed with brilliant, dancing fire—red, orange, yellow—and the captain and his men stood with mouths agape.

"Do you wish to stop me, Captain?" I cut off the flow of power, and the spirit hissed as it retreated to its darkness. The glow subsided as quickly as it had begun.

"My ... My lord." The captain sheathed his sword and clapped his fist against his breastplate. "When Bergstrom said you claimed to be Stateless, I didn't—"

"I could throw you in the stocks for the insult"—I glowered—"*Captain*."

"My lord, you must—"

I took a step closer, and the captain shrank back. "I *must* nothing, Captain, and if you interrupt me again, I *will* have you put in the stocks."

The accompanying guards inched backward with their captain.

"But I understand your incredulity. My guild's numbers have waned ..."

"Th-thank you, lord. O-of course the city is open to you and ... may I suppose these folks are with you?" He gestured at the wagons.

I nodded.

"You may all come and go as you please, then."

"You will inform your other guardsmen of our presence?"

The horsetail plume waved back and forth as he nodded. "Of course, and if anyone should be a bother in the city, tell them to take it up with Guard Captain Tromsson."

I ceased glowering at Tromsson, though I refused to show my approval beyond a laconic, "Good."

Tromsson leaned over, took my gauntlet from the snow, and handed it back to me, ostensibly bowing his head. I snatched it, and Tromsson backed away.

"Now, my lord, only let us know what we can do for you."

"We need a cartwright, stabler, and an inn. Otherwise, I hope we find no other occasion to meet face to face."

"Of course. I'll send Bergstrom to show you around."

ᚱ

After negotiating with the stabler to fetch our horses from the inn where we would be staying—the Lady of the Lake, it was called—our guide, Bergstrom, led us to the cartwright.

Bergstrom, whose armor was still caked with mud from our altercation, barely spoke. He exuded both indignation and embarrassment, and though my guild's pride would not allow me to apologize directly, I thought how I might make amends.

When I entered the cartwright's workshop, I was greeted by an unseen man barking orders about the wheel alignment of a small, single horse wagon. Another man grumbled and cursed as he crawled out from under the wagon.

I raised a hand in greeting as he rose, and he looked at me in surprise.

"If ya be looking fer wagon work"—he rubbed his greasy hands on his pants and wiped his sweaty brow with the back of his hand—"ya be out o' luck, stranger." His accent was southeastern, and the tone of every word was flat and stretched into a drawl. "All these damn strangers—er, from the Capitol, whence ya seem not to be, no?—be ordering and demanding every minute o' me time."

Was it the custom of all East Laketon's residents to be rude to their guests? It mattered little. What piqued my interest was who these other strangers from the Seat could be. I saved that question for later, though.

"How much to get ahead of these other strangers? Name your price." I drew a purse from my gambeson and shook out a handful of coins.

The cartwright rubbed his stubbly chin. "Bart, c'mere."

From behind the wagon, a disembodied voice responded, "I don't care how much coin this stranger has, Jared, we're not about to bugger the soldiery by putting them behind another." His accent marked him as a local.

"The soldiery?" I clenched my fist around the pile of coins as I spoke, and Jared frowned. "They're here?"

"Aye, they be here. Done been here near a week now, making many a demand o' us." He cleared his throat and spat on the dirt floor. "If I do see one o' them soldiers waving another royal decree in me face, I shan't countenance it. I be at the end o' me patience already, the Two help me." He made the sign of the Two. "I be truly sorry we can be no help to ya, stranger. If I had the final say, I'd take ya up fer all o' that silver ya do have in yer mitt."

Bergstrom, whom I had entirely forgotten, stepped forward. "You will take his offer, Jared."

"Oh, will I now? I did no realize they made ya alderman, wee Broady Bergstrom."

Rather than cower before Jared, the young guard jabbed a finger at him. "Unless you want to have problems with Captain Tromsson, I suggest you take up the Lord Corinsson on his offer."

"*Lord?* So, ya do be just another Capitolian, eh?"

This time, I cut in before Bergstrom. "I'm no lord, but I am Stateless, and I thus have more right than these soldiers to your services."

"And you can talk to Captain Tromsson if you don't like it," Bergstrom added.

The other man, Bart, walked around the cart. "I don't like it, and you can expect Tromsson to hear about it, too, if the soldiers come barking up my tree."

Jared waved his hand. "Let 'em, Bart, and they'll be dealing not only with Captain Tromsson but a Stateless."

Bart furrowed his brow. "Well, Stateless, let's see that coin, then."

R

As we left, I said, "You didn't need to stick your neck out for me."

"Were you going to throw them into the mud, too?" He looked at me askance, lips creased in a deep frown.

I cleared my throat. "Ah, well, I'm not usually in the habit of throwing anyone to the ground." I shifted uncomfortably, adjusting my armor. "I'm in a bit more of a rush than usual."

"You Stateless have one hell of a way of apologizing."

"It's not an apology, boy." I had grown soft in my old age. Refusing to apologize had once been an art at which I excelled. "Still, I'm not in the habit of putting myself at odds with the locals, so"—from my gambeson, I took the coin purse from which I paid Bart and Jared, tossing it at Bergstrom—"use this to get your things cleaned and buy a round for the guards. Use whatever's left to buy something nice for the girl whose hair you keep in that locket."

The young man nearly fumbled the coin purse. "How did you—" He put a hand over the locket under his tunic.

"Please, boy, I'm old, but not so old that I don't remember being ... what? Twenty? Why else would someone your age wear a locket and fiddle with it every five minutes?"

He weighed the purse in his hand and swiftly tucked it away. "Well, if this is how you Stateless apologize, I'll accept it."

As we walked, Bergstrom answered the questions I had about the soldiers the cartwrights had mentioned. They had shown up about a week before us and had spent their time requisitioning supplies and manpower. The city guard had been kept busy trying to keep order in the meantime. According to Bergstrom, between soldiers getting drunk in the taverns and threatening the honor of the city's young women, and the growing number of angry fathers and mothers whose sons had been stolen to serve in the army, the guard had their work cut out for them.

"The farther you stay away from the northwest side—that's the port side—of the city, the better. That's where they're encamped. And few of the soldiers want to go drinking on the southeast side where we're at."

"And the recruitments?"

"So long as your two young men on the cart there stay out of sight, they should be fine. The alderman made it clear nobody was to be *recruited* from behind closed doors, and though the king's writ supposedly gives them the right, they haven't pushed their luck."

"I see. And this inn you're taking us to?"

"Well on the south side, sir. It's owned by my fiancée's family, so if there's any problems, I'll know."

"Will it be safe for the women?"

"I wouldn't let them go out alone after sundown, but I doubt anyone will give them trouble during daytime."

R

By the time we arrived at The Lady of the Lake—a three-story, wood building, from the top floor of which the masts of the boats docked at the lakeside port were visible—the sun hovered over the horizon as Bergstrom ushered us inside. While it was hardly the finest inn I'd ever stayed in, it was likely one of the best in this town—spacious but not barren, busy yet clean, loud but not raucous, and smelling of fresh food, tobacco, and wood smoke rather than stale beer, sweat, and piss. It was the same inn I would have picked. Though my guild's pride still prohibited me from showing it, I was beginning to like Bergstrom.

Harvald's entire family was even more impressed by the accommodations. The older children and their parents all stared in silent wonder. The younger children gasped, pointed, and ran circles around their older family members. Though they had passed through at least one larger city on their journey, they likely spent that time under open skies, and even compared to my home, this building must have seemed a palace to them.

Bergstrom announced his arrival as we entered, and his voice echoed among the balconies and rafters high above.

A young, brown-haired woman, about the same age as Erika, poked her head through a wide, open doorway that led to one of several sitting rooms. She smiled and hurried into the taproom to embrace Bergstrom. He, in turn, kissed her cheek.

Erika crossed her arms and averted her eyes.

"What are you doing here, Broady? And, why are you so filthy?"

Bergstrom glanced at me. "I took a little tumble …" He held his fiancée's hands and turned to face us. "Anyway, this is Lord Corinsson of the Stateless, Anissa, and his charges with him. They're traveling through and need a place to stay that's far from the troops. Captain Tromsson ordered me to help them, so …"

Anissa looked past Bergstrom and bobbed her head as she counted us. "Well, I'll make sure my parents know you sent them. In the meantime"—she embraced and kissed Bergstrom once more before putting him behind herself—"I'm sure all of you would like to get settled in."

We gave curt introductions, and after I explained yet again that my title was not "Lord," Bergstrom bid us farewell to return to his post. I paid for five rooms, baths, and for the cost of board for the three days it would take to repair the wagon. I then gathered Harvald's family in a quiet corner of a sitting room.

"I'm sure you all have many questions about what happened back at the gate."

Harvald, Gale, and the eldest children all nodded.

"Now, I'm not sure what you heard or saw when I spoke with the captain of the guard, and I'm not sure whether you heard everything Bergstrom and I discussed or not."

Thankfully, nobody spoke.

"To sum up, we're here for three days. Though I can see it plainly in your faces that a city like this is something of a novelty, I warn you now—you are not safe here." I looked at Aros and Arve. "You two in particular, lads, are not safe. The king's army has camped just outside the north gate, which is the lakeside gate. Though Bergstrom told me they're forbidden from taking anybody who's indoors, that's not the case if you go out."

"But, sir," Gale said, "I thought you said we'd be safe since you're Stateless."

"Aye, and you should be safe for that very reason. However, it seems that men are forgetting the rights associated with my guild."

"Is that why you threw Bergstrom down to the mud?" Arve asked.

"Aye, Arve, and the captain of the guard scarcely believed me either."

"And that's why you did that … that trick or whate'er with your mark, then, right?"

Aros nudged his brother with his elbow. "Be quiet, Arve …"

Arve shot his brother a nasty look but said nothing further.

"Aye, 'tis, lad, but I'd rather you forget you saw that."

The young man nodded solemnly.

"To cut straight to the point—nobody, especially you two, Aros, Arve—are to leave the inn without escort by either myself or one of the city guard. Likewise, should any soldiers decide to show their faces here, stay as far from them as you can." I looked around the table. "Is that clear?"

All nodded with dour faces.

"Tonight, I must be away to scout out the surrounding area. I want to see the lay of the camp." My wards looked about nervously. "You'll be safe inside without me. Your rooms are paid, as are baths and your board, so make yourselves comfortable and rest well. I need to be off."

Without waiting, I turned heel toward the door. Chair legs scraped against the floor behind me, however, and I stopped. Aros had pushed away from the table and now stood a few paces behind me, rubbing his hands.

"Sir, may I come with you? I'd like to—"

"Out of the question."

"But—"

"I said *no*."

Aros started.

I was beginning to feel the moon's pull. I had to be away.

"Oh, all right then …" The young man cleared his throat compulsively and wrung his hands before stepping back.

"Another time, Aros. For now, get some rest." With those words, I departed.

RRR

Chapter XVII

The signs illumined by the full moon may be bright,
but nothing auspicious ever happens in that light.
— From *Maxims of the Astromancers*

R

A s I rushed out of the southern gate, the protective rays
of the sun had nearly vanished, and the moon, full and
bright, ascended. I heaved a breath. My blood boiled.

I dashed to the snowy tree line. There, my pack guided
me deep within the forest along a path they had scouted.

"Speed," I scented.

They quickened their pace until we arrived at a clearing,
whence they departed.

"Luváli guard you," Freya scented.

"No, Luváli guard you from me."

At once, I doffed my armor and every stitch of clothing
as Freya leapt into the thick brush. I was left alone as the sun's
rays vanished, and the moon took its irresistible hold on me.

Though the pain was excruciating, the ecstasy of
transformation, of becoming the beast, transcended all else.
To transform was to unleash the beastly god chained up
within. My human senses, memory, heart, and soul faded as
the beast broke free of its fleshly chains.

The monster tore me apart and fractured every part of me.
My bones shattered and reformed in one infinitely short but
excruciating moment, and my skin tore without spilling blood

as the beast emerged. My eyes glowed redder than the hellfire awaiting me, and my face contorted, stretched, and became entirely other. My ears grew. My teeth broke as fangs ripped through my gums. My mind and vision grew dark. The beast emerged into the all-encompassing moonlight that overshadowed me.

I assumed the form of Truth herself as my heart then perceived her.

R

When the sun crept above the horizon, its protective rays forced the monster to retreat. I awoke deep in the woods, far from where the beast had overcome me. I lay naked, curled up in the light snow under a thick canopy of fir boughs. Blood covered me from head to toe, and clumps of mud and brush matted down my hair to break up the carmine canvas upon my skin. I bore a deep wound in my side that had already scabbed over.

"No, no, no …" I glanced left and right—no deer or boar carcass was nearby, nor any signs thereof. I then tasted the familiar metallic tang of blood in my mouth, and my tongue discovered something—a small bit of my meal, perhaps?—stuck in my teeth. I picked the stray bit free, hoping it would be a clump of fur.

Between my thumb and forefinger was a scrap of bloody linen.

I convulsed and vomited up sour, bloody bile and more bits of linen, befouling the virgin snow. When my stomach was empty, I dry heaved and collapsed into my own vomit.

The wound in my side ached, and fresh blood poured forth, the scab broken open. I wished the wound had been larger. I could have ripped it open again and again until I bled out.

I should never have come. This would never have happened if I hadn't come. Whom had I harmed? Whom had I—I heaved again as I lay on my side—*eaten? A man? A woman? A child?* The hellish image of Harvald's family, their bodies mangled, their bones and limbs strewn, their lifeless eyes staring at me, invaded my mind.

I pushed myself to my knees and unleashed an agonized howl into the still starry heavens. There were no words to express what was in my heart.

My legs shook as I rose, and I hung my head. My wild brown locks, which were caked in mud and gore, covered my face.

Freya emerged from the bushes. "*Peace. He lives.*"

"What?" I said aloud.

"*He lives. Only wounded.*"

"*Bitten?*"

She scented nothing.

I shook my head, praying the bite would not bring my curse upon this stranger. "*How did he escape?*"

My friend limped as she drew nearer. Blood and forest debris matted her fur, and three great cuts stretched across her flank.

I crawled toward her and said, "Freya. Oh, by the Two, Freya, I'm sorry." I hovered my hand, covered in blood, gore, and vomit, over the marks my claws had raked through Freya's flesh.

"*Peace. I am well.*" She licked my face and rubbed her forehead against my temple. "*Be cleansed.*"

250

"*Unpardonable. Abomination. Sacrilege.*" My scent was putrid flesh, a carcass savaged and disemboweled, left to rot under the rays of the summer sun.

Freya's scent was of Luváli and Andar. Aye, the image of the Dead Gods was what I saw in her. Luváli, betrayed by his own pack, lay on the banks of a river that ran along the edge of a field to water golden grain. His blood flowed into the water from the wound in his side, which a huntsman's spear had inflicted. Andar, too, lay slain by his kin, his body abandoned in his father's vineyard, his blood nourishing the vines.

"*Be cleansed.*" Freya limped into the woods but looked back. "*Follow me.*" Her eyes spoke, but I could not understand.

She led me to a spring of living water, which gushed from the heart of the earth. Around the spring, grass, verdant and free of snow, grew thickly.

I kicked chunks of bloody snow and ice from the edge of the glade with my bare feet, but it melted quickly and left no trace. The only sign of my presence were the footprints leading to the water's edge.

I stared into the pool but refused to enter. My reflection rippled on the surface, and my bloody mien gazed back.

Freya came up behind me and nudged my thigh with her head. "*Be cleansed.*"

I sighed, hesitated, but finally stuck my foot into the steaming water. "Too hot," I shouted, yanking my foot from the spring.

Freya nudged me harder. "*Be cleansed.*"

My foot, though pink from the heat, was clean of blood and filth.

I took a deep breath and dove in. I barely touched the bottom before I shot to the surface. Water exploded upward as I emerged, screaming. I grabbed the edge. The water burned, but especially stung the wound in my side.

Freya licked my face and refused to let me out, and the prickling pain of the purifying heat eventually faded, and enjoyable warmth filled me.

I pushed off the rock wall and treaded water until I found a shallow spot. I washed away the last bits of blood and dirt as my pack lay in the verdant grass, watching.

I crawled from the living water and, with no towel at hand, shook myself dry. Only my footprints in the verdant grass remained when I returned to where I had begun. I donned my clothing and armor in silence, gazing into the heavens to watch the last star of night blink out of existence.

R

As I approached the city gate, ready to resume my duties, the guards saluted me. I returned the salute.

The nearest guard approached. "Sir."

"Aye?"

"There's been an incident at the inn."

R

I marched in with my hand upon my sword hilt, while Captain Tromsson and two other armed guards followed. Though there were many guests, the inn was silent except for the sound of weeping. Gathered around the common room's fireplace were Harvald and his family, though Aros and Arve were notably absent. Harvald held his sobbing wife, and Haldis sat cradling the infant Kari, who screeched ceaselessly. All the young children wept, too, and clutched the women's legs. Only Erika, who was the first to see us, did not weep, though her puffy eyes betrayed that she had been.

Seeing me, she rose, shoulders back, eyes blazing. She shook the children from her skirt and bore down upon me. Before I could open my mouth, she was upon me with a raised hand. She slapped me across the face and spat, "Monster."

The two guardsmen stepped forward to detain her, but I barred them. Erika's entire family looked up but said nothing.

"You animal. You—"

"Erika"—I grabbed her wrist as she prepared to strike again—"enough." My temper flared, the beast lurking just beneath the surface of my consciousness, and I nearly lifted her from the floor.

She struggled to free herself. "Let go of me, you monster." Her words stung more than her assault. "You beast, where were you? You were supposed to protect them, to protect us. You swore—"

"That's enough, Erika," Gale intervened, holding Erika by the shoulders.

"No, Mama. 'Tis his fault, all his fault." She began to sob. "He should've been here, but instead he was—"

"Scoutin', as is his duty, Erika."

"Ha! If only that were true. I know what he was doin'. He's a monster, and 'twas nothin' noble that he was—"

"You be quiet this moment, youn' lady. Do no insult Master Rune, nor suggest anythin' as unbecomin' as you were 'bout to do. He went out, as his job demanded. If anyone is to blame, 'tis those soldiers who took your brothers."

Erika closed her mouth, but her eyes pierced me more deeply than any words.

A fresh wave of guilt washed over me. *I shouldn't have indulged my flesh ...*

They'd all be dead, a second voice said.

I should've fought against it.

Aye, you should have ... a third whispered.

Captain Tromsson came to my side. "Sir? I told you they would confirm the story. Those soldiers came and took the lads."

I nodded, pushing the voices out of my head. "Aye, and it's time for us to take them back."

R

The army's camp stood along the sandy lakeshore just outside the north-west gate to Laketon. Tightly packed tents stood in neat rows across the westward stretching plain, where traveling merchants and city festivals would have set up. Poking above the pointed tops of the tents were Oserdeni banners—a field of white with the crimson Sign of the Two superimposed upon a golden sun. Soldiers marched in formation for morning drill, and sergeants called cadences and shouted at those who failed to keep pace—it was obvious how green many of these men were. Other men in full armor with weapons at the ready took positions around the perimeter of the camp at regular intervals since there was no palisade.

"Which way to the command tent is fastest?"

Tromsson gestured for me to follow and led our little group of four about a thousand paces to where two soldiers stood within arm's reach of one another. A particularly broad path ran between the tents and assorted chattels, and some way down the path, a large, striped, octagonal tent flew the flags of Oserden and of a minor baronet.

"That would be the baronet's headquarters."

As we drew nearer, two soldiers—undoubtedly the guards of the non-existent gate—placed their hands upon their sword hilts and brought their shields to the ready. "State your business."

Tromsson leaned toward me and whispered, "The colonel knows me. I'll handle this."

Tromsson puffed out his chest. "I have a grievance to bring to the lord baronet's attention." He strutted about like a cock courting a hen.

I covered my face with a gauntleted hand.

"The lord baronet *colonel* is in the middle of his morning debrief and will not have visitors."

"We will wait outside his tent, then."

The soldier rolled his eyes. "You can come back later. The baronet colonel will be busy all morning."

Captain Tromsson lifted his head high. "Unacceptable. The lord baronet colonel knows me. Perhaps if you send word to him that the captain of the guard and Statele—"

The other soldier rattled his shield. "Move away now, sir."

"I will do no such thing. The Stateless, about whom I sent word yesterday, wishes to—"

The second soldier drew his sword halfway from its sheath. "We'll not tell you again."

The captain looked over his shoulder at me and shrugged, and his two guardsmen moved nervously behind me, their armor rattling.

I shook my head. I could neither permit my status to be ignored without punishment any longer, nor could I abide my wards to remain out of my care. I lunged forward with a raised fist.

Before the soldier could raise his sword, I smashed his nose with my gauntleted fist, his open helm useless to stop the blow. He crumpled to the ground, blood pouring down his face. The other soldier reached for his sword, but I lashed out with my foot to bring him down. I leapt on top of him and landed two punches. Blood exploded from the man's nose and lips, spraying across his face as a tooth flew wide and buried itself in the churned-up snow and mud.

Satisfied both would live but not soon rise, I passed along the avenue of tents. I pushed my heavy woolen cloak behind my shoulder and drew my sword.

Tromsson and his entourage's armor rattled as they rushed to catch up. Others shouted all around me, but my blood pounded so loudly in my ears that I did not hear a thing.

At the tent's entrance, I struck another soldier upon the head with the pommel of my sword. There was a crack, and he fell with a groan as I swung around to parry the blow of another soldier. As our blades crossed, I pushed his sword aside with my own and threw him off balance. I pounced upon him and beat him about the face so he would not hinder me further.

Covered in blood, I pushed the tent flap aside. "Who's the colonel?"

A man dressed in officer's livery kicked over the round table covered with a map and figurines that stood in the middle of the tent. With cup-handled ropera drawn, he vaulted over the table and struck with surprising grace. With his swift fencing blade, he forced me back, but I dug my heels in and parried his blows. My blade whistled in the air as my assailant dodged my riposte, and he advanced with the graceful step of a duelist, putting me on the defensive again.

His luck ran short when I somersaulted to one side, and he stumbled forward and swung back around. He was not fast enough, and my blade connected with the man's hand. It sliced through the metal guard and nearly severed his thumb.

His sword fell to the soft earth with barely a thud, and he, too, fell to his knees, clutching his hand. His thumb hung by a scrap of skin.

I flicked the blood from my blade with a quick snap of my wrist. "Anyone else?"

Tromsson and his two men took up positions around me to ward off further blows. I, too, prepared myself to strike down more men.

As if in answer to my anticipation, the tent flap flew open, and half a dozen soldiers rushed in. I raised my sword to strike, but another softly dressed man at the head of the overturned table raised his hands.

"Enough."

Everyone froze at the sound of the man's sonorous voice, blades hanging in midair.

I refused to face the man, not wishing to take my eyes off my next targets.

"What is the meaning of all this, Tromsson? Tell me straight, or I will have you and your men cut down where you stand."

I scoffed, my lips pulled into a vicious snarl. My victims' blood dripped from my beard and the tip of my nose. "You must be the baronet colonel." My muscles twitched. I wanted an excuse to strike.

"Is this the kind of order you keep among your men, Captain?" The scent of this man's arrogance was thick. It would be a pleasure to cut him down.

"He's not my man, m'lord. He's the Stateless about whom I sent word yesterday at eventide."

"Men, put your swords away."

The group of soldiers in front of me hesitated, looking from one to another. I, too, expected a trap.

The duelist whined, "B-but, Colonel, sir, h-he has taken my finger." He stood up, cradling his wounded hand near his chest. Blood dribbled onto his raiment. "I will never—"

"Be quiet, Major Aleric."

The major stared, open-mouthed.

"Now, put your weapons away."

In slow motion, the soldiers followed their orders, and Captain Tromsson and his men sheathed their weapons, too.

I growled deep in my throat. *Idiots.* I lowered my sword from above my head, but I would be dead before I sheathed my weapon in the face of my enemies.

The baronet colonel waved a hand and let out a little, high-pitched giggle. He entered my line of vision, his hands clasped before him as he peered down his nose at me. "I am deeply sorry I did not take your report seriously, Captain Tromsson. I see that this Stateless"—he looked me up and down like something set out at auction—"is either an incredibly adept fake or the veritable article."

He stood next to one of his men and stroked his ratty, black goatee. "Ah ..." He leaned forward, cold eyes narrowed. "You do indeed have the mark, and the helm reads rightly. Here I was among the apparently incorrect majority in thinking your guild had faded into history." His voice, high-pitched and nasalized with the slightly lisping lilt that marked him as an aristocrat, made my skin crawl.

"You think I'm some animal for you to gawk at, you arrogant prick?"

The baronet colonel scoffed. "You dare call me the arrogant prick when you are the one who came barging into my morning—"

"I'm not beholden to your schedule, but you are to mine, you whoreson."

He took a great stride toward me, eyes burning. Mine burned with their own fire, too.

"How dare you insult my parentage? You are"—he looked me over once more—"what? Sviari? Perhaps with a tinge of Oserdeni blood? The swarthy skin ... the ever so slight hook to your nose, and the tilt of your animalistic eyes." He stuck his face so close to mine that I could have headbutted him. "Indeed, your mongrel Sviari bearing speaks volumes, Stateless."

My lips twisted in a vicious smile. "Well, you're right about me, m'lord. My father *was* Sviari and of even swarthier skin than I. But I must apologize to you; I only mistook you for an effeminate whoreson because only someone as stupid as a whore's son would prance about while treating a Stateless so."

He snarled. "How dare—"

"I could have you flogged for your blatant disregard for my status. Competent authority advised you of my presence. You have no excuse."

The baronet colonel scoffed. "I hardly call the captain of the city guard a *competent* authority." He glanced at Tromsson. "Still"—he withdrew and held his head high—"I have more important things to do than bicker with you. So"—he sat down upon a high-backed chair that had not been knocked over in the scuffle and crossed one leg upon the other—"what is it that you want, then, Stateless?"

"First, your name, so I can write to His Majesty and tell him what pricks his baronets are."

His face grew red. "Lord Baronet Colonel Amaril of the noble House of Dunstan."

"Well, that's a start." I smirked. "Second, and more on point, I want to know where the two young men you kidnapped last night are."

Amaril snorted. "I have not the slightest clue what you mean."

I closed what little distance there was between us and, being of mongrel, Sviari descent, towered over the Capitolian. "The two boys you took from The Lady of the Lake."

Amaril did not back down but calmly placed his hands, one on the other, upon his knee. He wrapped his well-manicured fingers around his knee. "I told you, I have no idea what you are talking about."

"Then find out who does."

R

When I assured Major Aleric he would not lose his finger—assuming his surgeon was worth his pay, anyway—and after the other injured soldiers had been taken to the infirmary, Amaril returned to the tent with three new faces quite literally in tow. Before me, clad in irons, stood a young, baby-faced lieutenant and two stripling privates barely older than Aros, one of whom had a bruised cheek and fat lip. All three looked about ready to piss themselves as they saw that I, the mythical Stateless they had undoubtedly been warned about, was real.

At my side, flanked by Captain Tromsson and his men, were Aros and Arve. Aros had a black eye, fat lip, bruises on his face, bloodied knuckles, and—per his own report—bandages covering the stripes from his flogging. Arve, who clung to his brother since both of his eyes were swollen shut from the bruises about his face, was in similar shape, though he had not been flogged. I pitied the two young men, their pain quite evident.

I addressed the three prisoners, "So, which of you three wants to explain what happened last night?"

Nobody dared breathe.

Amaril stood a distance behind his subordinates, his hands clasped behind him. "Speak, Lieutenant de Letenhove; they are your men."

Lieutenant de Letenhove glanced at the two privates next to him. "Uh …"

My eyes locked with his. "*Uh* is not an answer, Lieutenant."

He swallowed hard. "My men, they, uh …"

"Say *uh* one more time, Lieutenant, and I'll beat you like you beat my charges."

The lieutenant blanched, looked at the colonel, whose own gaze was, I admit, more terrifying than mine now. The lieutenant met my gaze again. "You see, sir, my men came to me. Private B-Barretsson had a black eye, and they told me some young boys had picked a fight with them in the tavern. I asked if they were old enough to, uh—"

I slapped the lieutenant, and he shuddered.

He sniffed and shook but continued, "To be conscripted, and they were, so …"

"*So,*" the colonel roared, "you ignored a standing order not to conscript anyone in of doors, is that it, Lieutenant?"

"I ... We ... I was going to arrest them and—"

Amaril waved a hand, ignoring the explanation. "What the hell were your men doing at that inn, anyway?"

The private without the black eye spoke up, "The other inns—"

The colonel was on top of the private at once. He grabbed the young man by the neck with one hand and backhanded him with the other. "Did I address you, Private Wesker?"

The private trembled in Amaril's grasp and shook his head as blood dribbled from his split lip.

"Speak up, Private."

"No, sir—Baronet Colonel, sir."

The colonel threw the private down and waved the lieutenant on.

The lieutenant glanced at Wesker. "The other inns, sir, were full and were charging more for their beer—you know, from shortages and all—so my men went farther south."

I directed myself to the privates, "All right, and who started the fight? Was it you, Private Barretsson?"

Private Barretsson looked up at me with his good eye and shook his head.

"Then who?" I glared at Private Wesker.

To my great surprise, it was Aros who replied, "'Twas me, Rune, sir." His words were garbled from the bruises on his cheeks and from his swollen lip.

I whipped my head around. "What?"

"I saw ..." He pointed at Barretsson. "He touched Haldis, so I punched him."

"Is that true, Aros? Arve, did you see this?"

The younger boy nodded, still clinging to his brother and hiding his face as Aros wrapped his arms around his younger brother.

I turned back to Private Barretsson. The corners of my mouth twisted into a toothy snarl and twitched. I clenched my fist at my side. "What did you do to her?" My voice was barely above a whisper. Now it was my gaze that was more terrifying.

The private glanced at his colonel and lieutenant in search of aid.

"Look at *me*, boy. They can't help you now." I grabbed the young man by the collar, lifting him with a trembling hand from the floor.

"Sh-sh-she looked at me and s-smiled, and I ... I thought—"

"Out with it, boy." I shook the young man and slapped him across the face. "What did you do?"

He began to sob. "I ... I t-touched her b-breast."

I threw the young man to the ground with a roar and bore down on Private Wesker. "And you? What did you do?" My spittle sprinkled the private's face, and foam covered the corners of my mouth.

Wesker's eyes rolled back in his head, the color drained from his face, and he collapsed.

I picked up his limp body and raised my hand to strike when Aros grabbed my hand.

"Stop, sir! Stop, please. He did no do anythin' untoward. He saw me strikin' his friend and came to help him."

My wrath turned upon Aros, but then his words sank in.

I dropped the unconscious private on the ground with a *thud*. "All right ..." I glared at Baronet Colonel Amaril and breathed out a great sigh. Even Amaril looked at me with a noticeable tinge of fear in his eyes.

"Are you satisfied, Stateless?"

"I am." I jabbed my finger at the unconscious private. "Flog him for helping to kidnap my charges. Five lashes. Otherwise, I find no fault in him." I looked at First Lieutenant de Letenhove, skipping Private Barretsson. "Demotion and a flogging for failing to obey orders and allowing my charges to come to harm. Ten lashes."

I rested my eyes upon Barretsson and passed judgment, "Hang him."

The young private, who had not yet gotten back to his feet, crawled and clung to my boots. Tears poured down his ashen face, and he covered my boots with snot and tears.

"Get him off me." I shook him off, unwilling to show pity toward this boy who was barely older than my charges.

Amaril nodded and summoned his guards, voice cool. Two guards passed through the tent flap and stood at attention.

"Take the simpering private out of the camp and hang him by the neck until he is dead." He waved his hand.

The guards took Barretsson and lifted him to his feet without a word. Second Lieutenant de Letenhove watched in mortified silence as the guards took his subordinate away.

Private Barretsson thrashed, his chains making a horrible racket. "No, please, no!" He fought with every ounce of his strength. "Please, have mercy. Oh, by the Holy Two, have mercy, please. I didn't do anything to her." His sobs became squeals as he approached the tent flap. "Please, you know I didn't do anything. By the Two, please, oh please." The guards struggled to keep him in their grasp, but they finally succeeded in wrestling him out of the tent.

As Barretsson fought for his life, Arve began to sob, and his elder brother gaped at me in horror.

"Please, he did no do anythin' else to her. She pushed him off, and he did no try anythin' else. Please, do no have him killed, sir."

I shut my eyes and hardened my heart to their pleas. "He would have raped your sister, violated her, if he could have. Is that what you want? For a rapist to walk free?"

"He did no rape her, sir. He only—"

"Silence!" A deep wrath against my two young charges rose within me for their mercy. "I have made my decision. The boy ... the private hangs."

Aros grabbed me and wept, his face a mass of bloody welts. "Please, sir, do no do this. Have mercy."

His dry blood rubbed off on my hands and arms, and I looked away and clenched my fist. However, the victim's tears and pleas broke my resolve, and I opened my fist and commanded, "Guards, belay that order."

They had just begun to cross the threshold of the tent and stopped there. Barretsson continued writhing on the ground even after I spoke.

"Give him twenty-nine lashes. That's one less than the maximum I can inflict for attempting to assault a woman's honor. Let him remember this as a sign of the mercy shown to him."

Barretsson broke free of the guards and threw himself upon the feet of his savior, Aros. "The Two bless you. Thank you, thank you."

The guards were upon him in a moment. They pulled on the manacles binding his hands and led him away with the other two prisoners.

"Captain Tromsson, bring the boys to the inn and post a guard. If any of Baronet Colonel Amaril's men come within ten paces of the door, kill them." I locked eyes with the baronet colonel, but he did not even flinch. I turned back to Tromsson. "I have some business to attend to elsewhere."

Captain Tromsson saluted. "As you like, sir. C'mon, lads; let's get you back to your family."

As Tromsson led the boys from the tent, Private Barretsson laughed and shouted his thanks and praise even as the guards hauled him away to be flogged.

RRR

Chapter XVIII

*Anyone who believes a man's crooked ways can be
made straight, that his sins can be covered, without
sacrifice is a fool who knows nothing of this world
or the next.*

— From *Præcepta Solonis Legiferi*

R

I pushed the sanctuary doors open, hoping not to interrupt
the midday rites, but as I did, I was nearly pulled off my
feet by those pulling the door open. It was an unsurprisingly
small crowd that departed—a few elderly men and women,
and a few dressed as day laborers. Most did not notice me,
though one older woman saw my armor and shook her head.

When the temple stood vacant, I passed through the
narrow *narthex* and paused at the rood screen that separated
the mundane world from the sacred *kátafuge* and the
thusiastérion within. The aroma of incense wafted out and
filled my nostrils, and my footsteps reverberated off the
plaster-covered ceiling. The candles that burned inside
painted votive glasses, which stood throughout the temple,
scattered rose- and emerald-tinted light. The light danced
upon the walls and illuminated the marble faces of the blessed
Archonodules.

These twenty-four holy men and wolves stood with their
attributes upon high plinths in niches along the walls. They
cast stern gazes over me, warning me not to cross the

threshold of their holy dwelling. They gestured, each in his own way, to the raised *thusiastérion* in the domed apsis, where statues of the Holy Two sat upon rainbow thrones.

I was paralyzed, unable to pass over.

I gazed upon the illuminated, gilded frieze upon the screen in search of solace. The scenes from the lives of the Two engraved into the great wooden relief were resplendent in the candlelight. I fixated upon them. I could not look away.

The battered bodies of the Dead Gods were white gold, and the blood that poured from their wounds was burnished bronze. The eyes of the Dead Gods were topaz. They accused me.

Veins of embedded, bloody brass branched into the surrounding abyssal darkness of glassy obsidian and polished black gold. The bodies of the Two alone provided light to the scenes, for the hideous black glass and gold, though polished, absorbed the light of the world.

Though the *anástasis*, glorious and bright, was centered upon the screen, I passed my eyes over it. I would only gaze upon the *apókrisis*, where a rainbow panoply of precious metals and stones bewitched me. Against all my force of will, my eyes filled with tears that fell in torrents. This was what I most feared ... that day of wrath, that terrible day.

I clung to the portal's beams, still unable to pass over into the sacred. Therein, an old priest snuffed candles. I dried my eyes.

"Father," I called.

The priest continued with his task. "You've missed the service, child. If you wish, you can come back—"

"No, Father, it's not that. I must make confession." I leaned heavily upon the portal, suddenly growing weak.

The priest doffed his vestments unceremoniously at the *thusiastérion* and threw them upon the sacred place. He muttered as he stretched his arms, his joints cracking. I grew indignant at the old priest for his carelessness in the holy place, the place I dared not enter, but I bit my tongue.

"Time for confession," he finally said, his raspy, high-pitched voice grating on my ears, "is also past, child."

How could he chant the Divine Liturgy with that voice?

"Father, I'm not from here, and I desperately need to speak—"

He waved a hand as he gathered his vestments in a heap. "Fine, fine, but you'll have to do so as I eat my lunch." The old man stepped on a dangling cincture and nearly fell headlong to the floor from the dais upon which the *thusiastérion* stood. "The Two damn this confounded ..."

I nearly shouted but remembered my station.

"You, child, come and help an old man. It's the least you can do for making me hear confession on odd hours."

I hesitated but passed over at the priest's behest.

He foisted his bundle of garments into my arms and waddled away, hands behind his back, muttering something else profane. "Come, child ..."

R

The priest's study was underwhelming. The shelves along the walls and the desk were bereft of the books, codices, and icons a holy man in a temple this size should have had. Whatever books were present were covered in a visible layer of dust. The room, too, was frigid without so much as a coal-fired stove to provide heat, and the only light came from a small window above the priest's desk.

The priest sat at his desk in the tenuous sunlight and pointed at a crate in the corner. "Just toss that in there."

I set the vestments in the only open chair left and folded them before laying them into the crate.

"Hurry up now, child. Just toss them in."

I rested my hands atop the pile of sacred garments. I did not wish to comply, but he groaned, and so I dropped the vestments in the crate.

I sat in the shadows, opposite the priest's desk, and I hung my head and clasped my hands.

"What did you say you wanted again?"

"To confess, Father. I've sinned and require penance."

"All right then, go on." He waved his hand as he rummaged under his desk. "Go on …"

"I've committed a serious sin—no, many sins, Father. I—"

The old priest thumped a demijohn of wine and a loaf of hard bread wrapped in a handkerchief onto his desk. He waved for me to continue as he unwrapped the bread and poured wine into a small tin cup he had also set down with a rattle.

"I nearly killed two men, Father, and harmed—"

The priest took the loaf and broke it. He raised it toward the heavens, blessed it, and gave thanks, "On this earthly bread, fruit of the earth, gift of the Two, nourished by blood, let your Spirit abide. May it give us life for this age and the age to come." He then took the cup. "Thus bless this cup, fruit of the vines, nourished of the great rivers and of blood, gift of Andar and Luváli, that we may rejoice and praise Thy name unto the ages of ages."

The old priest's interruptions wearied me, pious as this one might have been. Could he not see how great the sins I was confessing were?

He bit into the half-loaf and spoke with a full mouth, "Carry on, child."

"I nearly killed two men, Father—"

"Mmhmm." The priest nodded his head as he took a drink from his cup.

My cheeks flushed. "Father, I ... All this because I indulged my flesh's desires ... I'm—" I choked back tears, but I could not leave the confession incomplete. "A werewolf, Father."

The priest did not stop eating but raised an eyebrow. "All right, go on," he said, mouth full of bread.

"Because I surrendered to the Moon and Stars last night, I neglected my duties and attacked an innocent man. He might bear my curse, Father ... And I brought other innocents to harm because of my sin." Tears now freely flowed, but I would not hide my face.

The priest wiped his mouth with the back of his hand, belching behind a clenched fist. "That's all, child?"

I knocked my chair backward as I jumped up. I thumped clenched fists upon his desk. "Did you not hear me, Father? I nearly killed two men and hurt innocent people because I'm a monster, and that's all you can say? Have you no words of chastisement? No words to make me low so I'll not seek these things again? Do you not take sin seriously? Do you not hate it?"

The priest took another sip of wine and belched again. "Child, sit." He shoved the other half of his bread across the desk toward me. "You look hungry and sound hungrier still. Eat with me, then we'll continue."

I held the bread in contempt. "I should be fasting, Father—that's what the penitentials call for to atone for sin like mine."

"Make this the start of your penance, then, oh pious one. Eat with an old man."

"Then you must assign a penance and give me absolution."

"Aye, if you like. Now"—he poured wine from the demijohn into another cup he took from under the desk—"eat and drink a little, and you'll feel better. It's quite something what a little bread and wine can do for the heart."

I huffed but took a morsel. It was stale and tasted like dust, but I ate to appease the old fool. I sipped the water-cut wine to wash it down.

"Father"—my eyes watered again, but I sniffed and held back the tears—"now, please, give me the absolution and satisfactions." I raised my eyes to meet the priest's. His eyes were bright despite his age. With nascent tears in my eyes, the light shining through the window danced around the old man. I blinked, but the dancing aura remained.

"Fine, you have it, child."

"What?"

He sighed. "You have your absolution, child."

I shook my head. "Father, use the formula."

"Fine, fine …" He smacked his lips and scratched his bare chin. "Hm, aye … As a servant of the Holy Two"—he made the Sign of the Two over me—"thou art loosed. There, you happy now, child?"

I raised my head and dried my eyes, noting the aura around the priest had vanished. "Aye, Father."

"You know, those words only tell you what already is, child." He waved a hand with a grunt. "But it doesn't matter ... Is that all, child? May I finish my lunch in peace?"

"You have to give me a penance, Father."

He laughed. "You are a stickler, aren't you, child? All right, take this bread"—he pointed at the bread he had given me—"and some of this wine." He stuck his head under his desk again and pulled out a small wineskin that he filled with wine. "Careful, this flask doesn't seal well ... Anyway, go home, meditate whence these things came, and eat. If you're not better afterward, you're doing something wrong."

I contemplated my penance. "Isn't this a bit unorthodox, Father?" I wanted to throw the stale bread and leaky skin at the priest.

"The penance is mine to decide, not yours."

"As you say, Father." I snatched the penance and slammed the door as I left.

R

At The Lady of the Lake, none of my charges were in the common areas, and when I entered, Anissa told me everyone had gone to their rooms.

I climbed the stairs and placed my penance on the nightstand of my room. "Old fool ..."

Since I was in no hurry to undertake my penance, I checked on my charges, instead. People murmured behind the closed door to Arve and Aros' room, which was across the hall from mine, and the sound of a woman's scolding voice stood out. Unsure of exactly whose scolding I heard, I braced myself for another potential tirade from Erika as I entered.

The only people in the room, though, were Arve, Aros, Harvald, and Gale. Harvald sat silently in a chair in the corner of the room, arms across his chest. Arve lay asleep in bed, bandages covering his face. Aros sat on a three-legged stool, the broken flesh of his back exposed, and Gale was behind him, a bucket and rag at her feet, and a needle and thread in hand.

"You must hold still, Aros. I know stitches are—"

I cleared my throat. "I can take over, if you like."

Gale rose to her feet, as did Aros, who was holding a cloth damp with melted snow-water to his black eye.

"Master Rune, sir," Gale began, "we were no certain when you'd return, so I thought—"

"Master Rune, please, you must do the rest of these stitches," Aros pleaded.

Harvald huffed out a low laugh. "Ah, come now, Aros, your mother has given me stitches many times. She's no that bad. Maybe no great, but certainly—"

Gale whipped her head around, and Harvald sank into his chair.

"That's enough, Harvald. 'Tis hardly a time for jokin'."

I folded my arms across my armored chest. "I'm sorry to have kept you all waiting. Please, forgive me."

"'Tis nothin', Master Rune. 'Tis we who must be beggin' your pardon for how my daugh—how *we*—spoke to you when you came in from scoutin'."

"No"—I took the thread and needle from Gale—"Erika was right to be upset. I shouldn't have gone out last night."

"Nonsense. You were only doin' your duty. 'Tis no as if you were out boozin' somewhere."

My stomach lurched. "Aye, right, as you say. Still, is Erika around? I'd like to make things right with—"

"Her father sent her to her room for refusin' to apologize to you, sir, and I doubt she'll be in any mood to see you e'en now."

I nodded. "Well, perhaps tomorrow, then?"

Harvald sat up in his chair. "Aye, I think 'twould be best for e'eryone. Now, Gale, how's 'bout we let our barber-surgeon take care of these two, and we'll gather the wee ones from Haldis?"

ᚱ

Aros lay prone on the bed with a sheet pulled up just below his hips while I applied a thick salve I had made to his black eye and from the nape of his neck to his tailbone. His muscles visibly relaxed as the analgesic worked.

I wiped away the excess with a towel from the bedside table. "All right"—I took up the needle and horsehair thread and made the first suture—"do you feel anything?"

The boy mumbled a negative.

Several hundred stitches later, Aros' back—now crisscrossed with lashes—was as good as could be hoped.

I turned my back, and Aros made himself decent before I wrapped his torso with tincture-soaked linens. The whole time, the young man said nothing, and not even his vocal ticks expressed themselves.

When I tied off the bandages, I asked how he felt, and he merely grunted before crawling back under the covers next to his brother.

"Aros"—I stepped around the bed to Arve's side—"I'm sorry you had to go through that." I applied some of the salve to the sleeping brother's face and tucked him back in. "But now you've got some scars of your own for people to gawk at, eh?"

Still, the young man did not respond.

I set the salve down on the bedside table and pulled up a chair by Aros' side. The young man rolled over in bed to put his back to me.

"Aros ..." I set my hand on his shoulder. "Lad, I—"

"You were goin' to kill that soldier." He rolled back to face me. His eyes were cold steel. "Why?"

I hid my face behind a hand. "That's my job, Aros. I'm supposed to protect people and judge—"

"You're supposed to judge *fairly* ... How was puttin' him to death—"

I opened my hand to strike the young man but gripped my knee with my trembling hand, instead. My stomach churned. I hoped the lad hadn't noticed.

"Lad"—I put my hand on his shoulder ever so gently, and he tensed but did not pull away—"I was wrong. I was upset about ... that I'd failed you and your family. I ..." I sighed. "Aros, do you remember how I said I'm not safe to be around?"

The young man grunted.

"What you saw today ... that's just a glimpse of why I didn't want you—anyone—around me. That's why I wanted you to pray for me. My soul, Aros, is so ... dark." I hid my teary eyes. "I'm glad you and your brother were there, Aros, to stop me."

Aros rolled onto his back with a groan. "Me, too."

I gathered my things in silence but stopped in the doorway. "Aros, please, forgive me."

The young man raised his head. "Aye, sir, I forgive you." I was about to shut the door behind me when he called, "Sir?"

"Aye?"

"Must be lonely, bein' afraid to have anyone near you."

I bit my lip.

"You might be afraid to have me near you, afraid to have my family near you, but I, at least, am no afraid of you, to be 'round you, though I've seen ... how you can be."

"Thanks, Aros ..."

"I love you, Rune."

"Rest well, lad." Tears streamed down my face as I shut the door.

R

That night, I woke enveloped in a blackness not even my heightened senses could penetrate. There was no sound except faint murmuring all about me. It came from everywhere and nowhere.

I rose from my bed. It vanished.

Out of the darkness, blurry figures drew nigh, their outlines sharp yet fluid. The skeletal, decaying faces of the dead stared with lifeless eyes. The Watcher, the elven queen and her guards, the man whom I had maimed the previous night, his face rent nearly in two by claw marks, and a seemingly endless company of men and women—some in civilian clothing, others in full armor—all drew nigh. They were the shades of those whose blood I had shed. I recognized many, while others—those I had killed in the heat of inhuman passion—I did not.

The shades opened their mouths in a silent scream and pointed long, bony fingers. The thousand dead voices cried out with unmoving lips.

Blood ...

The Life is in the Blood.

Your blood.

I shut my eyes and covered my ears. I pulled my hair out by the roots. I could still see the bloody, decaying faces, and their bodies, bloody pulps, in my mind, as if my eyes were wide open. Their bony fingers accused, and their silent screams for blood echoed inside my head. Those whispering screams filled my heart and soul.

The Blood is the Life.

I drew my belt knife and cut my palm. The flowing blood glowed. The ghostly, decaying hands of the shades all dipped their accusing fingers in the blood. They hissed for it as they overwhelmed me. They smacked their desiccated lips as they touched their blood-covered fingers to them.

More Blood.

Maggoty tongues lapped my blood. I raised my hand and squeezed my fist to make it flow. Bright carmine drops, like flames, fell.

The shades raised their dead eyes to watch my life drip upon them. Yet their eyes remained dark even as they drank, extinguishing the light of my life. My lifeblood could not satisfy them.

More Life.

I screamed, but their whispers drowned out my cry.

I slit my other palm before dropping the knife into the abyss. I shed more blood, but they remained unsated. Their voices multiplied tenfold for every drop I shed.

A voice resounded behind me, "Do not look at them."

I whirled about, and a great light in the darkness blinded me. I fell to my knees and covered my eyes with bloody hands. "Father?" My voice echoed.

The shades shrank from the light with a hiss.

A great shining tree rose upon a hill, a taut rope woven from thorny vines hung from its boughs. At the rope's end was a noose, and in the noose hung my father's gruesome yet glorious body. He swayed in the windless breeze, his head listing to one side, tongue hanging out, eyes bulging. The noose was perverse, a fallen crown that dug into his flesh. Streams of radiant blood flowed down his arms and his bound hands, which were rough from years spent at the lathe.

Upon his fingertips, crimson drops, each a beam of light, formed. They rent the darkness asunder as they fell. The crash of every drop exploded in the darkness, deafening me.

"Do not look at them. Do not listen to them." He spoke with unmoving, dead lips. His naked body shined so brightly that I could not gaze upon it as it swayed in the windless breeze. When he looked at me, his eyes were full of life.

I shielded my eyes from his brightness—he was the first to die because of me—and I proffered my bleeding hands.

The whispering shades surged with me.

Blood ...

"No, Rune. Do not shed your blood. I have no need of it. I have blood enough."

"But ... but I killed you, Father. You died because of me ... I want you to live."

"I am alive, Rune."

"No, you're dead ... because of what I am. It's my fault."

The Life ...

"Not *because* of you, Rune ... Not *because* of you ..."
His voice did not terrify me as the shades'. "No love without
sacrifice. No worship without sacrifice ..."

"I don't understand, Father. Please ..." I proffered my
hands to my father's hanged body again.

The Life is in the Blood.

"Do not listen to them, son." My father's voice
reverberated through my bones, and I fell to my knees. "Take
my blood ... Not my own ... Take my blood, which is not my
blood." From my father's battered side, a new stream of blood
and water burst forth, a dazzling rainbow bolt that pierced the
blackness of this moonless night.

"No, Father, no ..."

The Blood ...

"I am not dead, Rune. Behold, the tree ..."

The tree from which my father hung was made of
bleeding vines. They glowed white like the sun. The roots of
the tree sank deep into the abyss. Far down, at the edge of my
vision, the roots drew upon a river of water and blood. The
river gushed from the free-flowing wounds of Luváli, once
dead but no longer.

Enraptured, I shot my gaze upward from the black abyss,
which was not dark, and investigated the darkness of the
heavens, which were not dark. The canopy of the great bloody
tree spread its branches, its vines of shimmering, pulsating
blood, toward the east and west. In the heavens, the wounds
of Andar, once dead but no longer, watered the tree with
blood.

A voice thundered from within the darkness above and
below. It came from everywhere and nowhere. The shades

screamed and slunk into the darkness. The world itself trembled.

"The Blood. The Blood is the Life."

My father rested his bulging eyes on me. They were full of something I did not understand. "Give them my blood ... not my blood ... no love without sacrifice ... no worship without sacrifice." The blood dripped upon the ground from my father's hanged but living body.

I cupped my hands and collected the blood. It burned my self-inflicted wounds. I howled.

The collected blood splashed to the ground. The shades flocked wherever it fell. They drank the hanged man's living blood, which was not his blood.

My hands, which the blood had burned, were whole again. I cupped my hands again to gather it. The pain was now bearable. I sprinkled the blood with my fingertips upon the horde of shades. They faded with a sigh.

Blood ...

Blood ...

Blood ...

The voices and faces of the restless dead blinked out of existence, one by one. Their accusing fingers and terrifying screams faded into oblivion. Only the dead-who-were-not-dead remained. The dead-who-were-not-dead and I ...

My father's hanged body loomed large over me. It swayed in the windless breeze and spoke once more, "No love without sacrifice ..."

R

I shot up, my bedclothes soaked with sweat, and fear filled my heart. My father was lost to me again. Nevertheless, I sought him. With my eyes shut for fear, I groped for the bloody tree from which he had hung. I groped about in self-made darkness, and my hands lighted upon something strange. As it rested in my palm, my eyes were opened and beheld precisely what I had sought.

RRR

Chapter XIX

*There are many who believe the Seat is a holy city,
the nexus of the divine and the mundane. These have
never spent a day with courtiers and bureaucrats on
the Seat's high hills. If they had, they'd know the
Holy City is where true religion goes to die.*

— From *Private Discourses of
Eleutherius the Mad*

R

It was a great relief to be back on the road again after our three days in East Laketon. During those days, nobody dared venture outside, save when Gale helped me fetch the cart and horses from the stabler, and even the prospect of mingling with strangers in the common rooms had terrified them. Erika had locked herself in her room and refused to let me make my amends, not even deigning to acknowledge me when I called. Harvald and Gale thus became not only overly apologetic to me, but they also punished their daughter by refusing to allow her to leave her room even to eat with the family. "If she refuses to see you, you bear no fault, sir. She can have her meals apart. I'll no have you made out as the villain," Harvald had said.

Aros and Arve, too, while not scornful of me like their eldest sister, were both still reeling from their experiences. Arve began to tremble whenever he saw me, though a gentle apology from me repaired that damage, and neither of the brothers dared to go down to the common room unless I was by their side.

Haldis and Yoanna, for their part, treated me like a knight from some chivalric tale when they heard the sanitized version of what I had done "for Haldis' honor." So enthralled by my exploits was Yoanna that she presented a handkerchief she had embroidered, with her mother's help, as a "token of her favor," and which I was obliged to take from "her ladyship" and keep with me. Thus, the only members of the family who treated me no differently, which was to say they were still enthralled by my apparel, were the youngest boys.

Back on the road, however, we all quickly returned to our old routines. I would make my rounds, care for my charges' and Freya's healing wounds and, at night, we would pitch our communal tent, eat, pray, and sleep. Under conditions such as those, it was hard to hold grudges and leave grievances unaired.

One evening, while the snow fell lightly, I patrolled the perimeter of the camp with Freya, who continued to limp. When I returned, Erika waited outside in the cold with only a cloak over her traveling clothes. My stomach clenched into a knot, but Freya nudged me and scented, "*Go. Make peace among the pack.*"

I patted Freya upon the head and raised an arm in greeting, trying to put on a friendly front. "Something the matter, lass?"

She wrapped her arms around herself to keep the cloak shut. "Aye." Her voice was cool, and I braced myself. "I need to speak with you, sir." She raised her chin and exhaled a puff of steam.

A cold sweat broke out under my helm and trickled down my back. "Oh, about what?"

Erika shook her head and grunted—or, was it a laugh? Her scent betrayed little, apart from resolve. "I think you know."

I hung my head, the weight of my helmet suddenly ponderous. "Aye, but before you say anything, I must—"

"No, sir, let me speak, please." She drew near. "I must apologize for ... how I've treated you the past days. I know—"

"No, Erika." Now it was my turn to step forward. "I'm the one who should apologize. You were right; I should've stayed at the inn, but I—"

Our words ran together, each of us eager to speak. "No, I should ne'er have said that 'bout you goin' out."

"It's all right, Erika. Really—"

"I was just so upset to see my brothers get taken—"

"There's no need to—"

"I took my anger out on you. You had your reasons." She reached for my hands, letting her cloak fall.

We both went for the fallen cloak, and our heads collided. My metal helmet protected me from the blow, but Erika fell back into the virgin snow. She cried out and shook her head as I knelt with her face in my hands. I brushed her red curls away from her brow and examined the fresh welt.

"By the Two, Erika. Are you—"

As I touched her forehead, she let out a laugh. "Aye, I'm fine." She grabbed her cloak and, with my help, rose. "Well, so much for apologies. Guess we're e'en now."

I helped her get her cloak around her shoulders, unable to help smiling. "Aye, I suppose we are, though you're the one who dropped the cloak to begin with, so ..."

She blushed as she met my gaze, still holding my hands in her own, her cloak draped loosely over her shoulders. "Aye, well, this do no count as—"

Gale emerged, her own cloak wrapped about her. "Erika, are you al—ehm. Am I interruptin' somethin'?"

Erika dropped her hands to her sides, and a sense of … *disappointment* filled my heart at the loss of her strangely familiar touch. "No, Ma, we … I was just—"

"Your daughter and I were simply making amends." My face grew warm as I looked from Gale to Erika and back again. "She dropped her cloak, and we bumped heads reaching for it. I was just helping her back to her feet, Gale, ma'am."

"I'm fine, Ma. 'Twas nothin' more than a bump."

"Aha, well, I'm glad to see you've made amends." Gale held the tent flap open and motioned for us to enter. "Now, why do you no get some rest?"

Erika hurried inside without another glance at me.

As I entered, a slight blush still on my face, Gale grabbed my arm. She locked eyes with me, and I opened my mouth to speak, but she cut me off. "Please"—her eyes were serious, freezing me in place—"take care of her."

I had no idea what she meant, and before I could ask, she let me go, turned her head, and entered the shady, makeshift tent without another word.

I stood at the entrance for another moment, dazed. Had I seen a smile on Gale's face?

R

Even with so many wounded in our party, we made incredible time as we journeyed southeast toward the Seat of Andar, the greatest city in all the world. The roads had been clear, the weather cooperative, and the spirits of all were high. Never had I traveled so well through winter, even on imperial roads, as I did on this journey. Even my heart, which had been so heavy, was lighter than it had been in a long while. Even when temptation drew near on some nights, I was able to resist. The angel and my father gave me strength, though they remained unseen.

Day by day, the countryside, with its farmsteads and villages smaller even than Melbù, faded and gave way to signs of urbanity—homes were built of wood and brick instead of sod blocks, and they had terracotta or tar-shingled roofs instead of thatch. At these signs, the morale rose even higher. Even I was pleasantly surprised at the increased recognition, albeit still with hints of skepticism, of my guild.

Every night, without fail, during the week of our journey, at least one of my charges would remark how they had never seen such a great city. Their amazement was made complete when we slept indoors every night with hot meals, baths, and featherbeds instead of paillasses thrown upon the ground. Indeed, my charges, young and old alike, were mesmerized by the new world they were entering. Never had they tasted the wine of the Southern Cities, nor heard the songs the pub entertainers played near the Seat. They were children in a fairytale land.

The only disappointment for my charges was my refusal to meander through the open markets of these villages and towns. While I kept my real reasons for forbidding them to myself—I did not need to scare anyone with stories of cutpurses and pickpockets—I assured them they would regret wasting time or coin in these forgettable places. Indeed, I swore an oath that there would be more than enough to marvel at in the Seat. Aye, more than they could see even in a lifetime. They did not, however, believe my oath until they laid their eyes upon that city.

While we were still some miles off, the ancient white marble walls shone brightly in the midday sun. They glowed with reflected light and stood so high upon the hilltops that only the spires of the palace and great temple rose above them. The towers of the walls, decked with pennants and royal banners, were beacons to the weary traveler, a bastion to those who dwelt within, and a terror to enemies.

The city itself sat nestled among a series of gradually rising hills, which stood well above the level western plain that we now traveled upon. Such was the lay of the land that all who entered had to ascend to the city's heights, while those who departed became lower for it.

The Great River, Luváli's River, flowed out from the great spring in the heart of the high temple's courtyard, which itself stood upon the highest hill. Though the river was narrow as it wound down through the city, it spread its banks some twelve furlongs across the plain, where many tributaries fed into it.

Upon it, dozens of ships—from row boats and five-man fishing trawlers to grain barges and many a knarr—plied the waters, laden with goods and flying the colors of Oserden and the Southern Cities alike. Some sailed to the many wharfs and riverfront docks along the banks, and others departed to make their way to the Great Lake or to the Southern Cities and the Salt Sea.

Galleys flying the colors of the Oserdeni army also plied the waters, and their oars cut through the deep river like knives as smaller boats hastened out of their wake. The sounds of captains calling orders, of cockswains beating their drums of war, and of shanties the oarsmen sang at the banks all rang out across the expanse. Cheerful and hearty, if not salty, were the songs, but would they sing thus when they had sailed across the Great Lake's depths? Would they sing thus once they had marched from West Laketon's port across the World Spine to fight in this trans-mountain war? Would they dare sing thus when they marched home bearing their fallen brothers-in-arms upon biers made of shields, like I once had? Nobody yet knew what awaited them, but the galleys were a harsh reminder of how our group had gotten to be where we now were.

My attention turned from the ships and their darkness back to the city. A sole cobblestone road wound its way down from the main western gate in serpentine fashion and branched off in every direction. It was the artery of the city and carried the lifeblood of the world upon it. Every road, it was said, led to the Seat.

As the elevation rose, I pulled off from the busy highway. Dozens passed by us in wagons, on horseback, and on foot as we stood motionless along the building-lined streets. For miles in any direction on this side of the river, there was scarcely a quarter-hide of open land. I dismissed any number of cloaked peddlers who came hawking their wares.

From the back of the lead wagon, where I had stowed my ceremonial clothes and regalia, I pulled out a standard, which I unfolded and attached to the short staff I had also packed away. This staff, I fixed upon Ela's saddle so the flag and its emblem were visible to all. Upon the lightly waving yellow banner was the mark of the Stateless—a shield overlaid with crossed arrow, axe, and sword, and an olive branch, which tied them together. The border of the banner was red knotwork, much like my tattoo. The silver, emerald, and scarlet threads glinted in the sunlight as the banner waved in the winter wind.

After I raised the standard, I made my way around the wagons and made my charges hand over any weapons they had, whether bow, knife, or sling.

Aros drew his belt knife from the sheath hanging horizontally across his lap. "Why can we no have our knives, sir? They were gifts from Da."

"Inside the *pomerium*—the sacred boundary around the Seat—only the Stateless and royal guard may have weapons, but when we leave, you'll get them back." I examined the knife, measuring the blade against my hand, and tucked it in my belt before taking Arve's knife. "The only exception to the rule"—I turned Arve's knife over and handed it back hilt first—"are those small enough to be called tools."

Aros glared at his brother, who re-sheathed his knife.

I took my own belt knife and gave it to Aros, its carved ivory handle glimmering in the sun. "That doesn't mean the city is safe, though. Evil always finds a way."

When we rode on, I had three knives, one sling, and my unstrung bow set among my belongings in the cart.

We soon came upon a great line of carts that stretched down from the city gates for several thousand paces, and an exasperated groan rose behind me as we slowed. I waved my hand and pulled alongside our carts, however, and directed them to travel up the center of the wide highway along a pathway of bright yellow bricks. On this path, we sped past the slow-moving line, the frustrated occupants of that slower lane muttering curses under their breath as we did.

The gate to the city was a colossal thing of ashlar stone some three-hundred-and-thirty cubits wide with three gated arches, each tall enough for a war engine to pass. At each gateway were lanes of travelers preparing to pass into the great city. Guards searched the possessions of everyone who entered for weapons and untaxed or otherwise forbidden goods. My charges and I, sacrosanct as we were under my banner, were exempt from these intrusive searches, and the guards spread word of my arrival among their fellow guardsmen so none would delay us further.

We rolled through the gates of the city and into the great marketplace of the Seat. The cries of animals, of vendors and buyers, of passersby, and the rattling of handcarts bouncing along the cobblestone paths deafened us, and there was no escaping the din. Even when we had escaped the main hub of the market, the streets were still surrounded on every side by multi-story homes and apartments, shops, stalls, and hundreds of people.

As I forced a way through the crowds atop Ela, many cursed and grumbled at me, asking why no guardsmen had made us stable our horses. Their looks of indignation turned to shock, embarrassment, and fear when they recognized my standard, and a few who had hurled the filthiest of curses hurled equally loud apologies and wishes for my long life and safety.

My charges, however, barely noticed these indiscretions. They were enraptured by the city, and even I had to try hard not to get caught up in this infinitely vast world with its sights, sounds, and smells.

The roads sloped gradually up the well-worked hill, and many side roads—some barely wide enough for men to walk two-by-two—turned off here and there, but we stayed on the main road. The higher we climbed, the finer our surroundings became. The crowds thinned, vendors no longer lined the streets, laundry no longer hung from lines strung between apartments high above, and a general calm prevailed.

Even higher still, palatial homes stood along the street, and high walls and wrought iron gates closed them off from the outside world. Open spaces, too, which would have been occupied with market stalls and men in the lower districts, were instead full of evergreens and the sound of birds chirping and fountains bubbling. In these upper districts, the smell of crisp, clean air replaced the miasma of chimney smoke, animals and their waste, and of the hundreds of unwashed bodies below.

The silence of my fascinated charges persisted until we arrived at the gate of what could only be called a palace, with its gardens, fountains, and stables near the top of the hill. Two burly guards, whose arms were as large as tree limbs, stood just inside the gate under a wooden awning. They smoked thick tobacco rolls, which were preferred in the Seat over pipes, and each had a wooden truncheon, which were not technically considered weapons, on their belts. The guard on the left took his truncheon and spun it dexterously from its leather strap, while the other addressed us.

"Who are you, and what business do you have here with the Lord Ulfric?" His words whistled through missing teeth. And, though the man did not sport a mustache and goatee like most Capitolian men, his voice was characteristically crisp, each syllable articulated well despite the missing teeth.

"Tell Lord Ulfric the refugees he was expecting have arrived."

The other guard threw his rolled tobacco to the ground and crushed it underfoot, a wisp of smoke rising. "We heard you were coming ..." He looked to his identical brother, both of whose long faces looked as if they had been smashed by a board a few times. The brother shrugged. "But not this early."

I peered down at them. "Aye, we're earlier than expected. The roads were good; the weather, kind."

The first guard folded his burly arms across his leather chest armor. "Well, I suppose you look the part ... Except maybe you, Stateless." He glanced at his brother, who shrugged, too. "I will fetch Lombardus. He can decide."

A few minutes later, a rotund, diminutive man, only slightly taller than Magnus and Grimm, flung open a servant's door beside the home's grand double doors of bronze. His cheeks grew cherry red from both the cold and the speed with which he crossed the immaculate courtyard's cobblestone path, and he held out his arms slightly, careful not to slip on the fresh dusting of icy snow. All the while, he fussed over his flat-topped hat, frock coat, wide pantaloons, spectacles, and the most well-waxed mustaches I had ever seen as he tried to keep them orderly. Aros and Arve both guffawed when they saw him, and I shot them a nasty look. There were enough things to marvel at in the Seat without getting on bad terms with Ulfric's staff.

At the gate, he waved his white-gloved hands at the remaining guard. "Shoo. Out of here. Go patrol the perimeter with your brother, you ogre."

The guard spat out his tobacco at the little man's feet and growled at him as he hung his truncheon upon his belt. The little man, completely unfazed, waved away the guard once more as he clicked his tongue. From somewhere inside his coat, he drew an impossibly massive key into his tiny hands.

"My lords and ladies"—he climbed onto a small step attached to the gate's frame—"please, do come inside." He unlocked the gate and jerked it open as he jumped down from the step with surprising grace. "My Lord Ulfric is expecting you, though I must admit"—his large face grew even redder still—"you are somewhat earlier than we anticipated." With a sweeping gesture, he led us down the path to Ulfric's home. Topiary forest animals, the most prominent being two wolves, stared down at us from either side of the frozen reflecting pool that bisected the path we were on. "Nevertheless, we will have your rooms ready in short order."

At the front steps, I dismounted and stretched. "We're finally here."

The children, who had surely been given a stern warning to behave, climbed from the wagon and stared in awe at everything around them. I, too, took in the sight of Ulfric's home, which seemed to have grown since the last time I had been there.

The majordomo's squeaky voice broke the awestruck silence as he waved his arms at Aros and Arve, who unloaded the cart. "Oh, young masters, do not trouble yourself. The servants will take your things inside as soon as you are comfortably in of doors. Only"—the majordomo stood on tiptoes to see farther into the overpacked cart—"tell me which things they should bring in."

Aros and Arve looked down at the steward and at one another.

Arve scratched his head. "Are you talkin' to us, sir?"

The majordomo gave a deep bow and clapped his gloved hands together. "Of course, young masters, of course."

Aros and Arve looked at each other, bit their lips to hold back laughter, and gestured to what they needed to have brought in.

The majordomo then addressed us, "If you please, lords and ladies, do make your way in, out of the cold. You'll find the sitting room quite comfortable until we have your rooms ready, I should hope." He climbed the marble stairs and pushed open the double doors. "Please, come in and relax. A servant will be around with refreshments shortly. Meanwhile, if you need anything at all, only ask for Majordomo Lombardus."

At these words, Harvald, who leaned heavily upon me, barked out a laugh. "Ha, ne'er've I been called *lord* in my life."

Lombardus stiffened and bowed his head toward Harvald. "I—"

Harvald hopped up the first step and laughed again. "But I could get used to it …"

RRR

Chapter XX

It is truly a good and pleasant thing for brothers to dwell in harmony.

— *Carmina, CXXXIII*

R

L ombardus led us into the vestibule and, at the ring of a bell mounted upon the wall, a serving girl emerged from a door hidden in the wooden paneling that ran along the wall. We all began to divest ourselves, scattering mud, snow, and ice about the rug covering the floor. Though Gale apologized for the mess, Lombardus assured her it was nothing to worry about, and he proceeded to help the other servant gather our cloaks and kaftans. The servant girl even brought Harvald a stool and helped him, much to his initial chagrin, to remove his cloak, kaftan, winingas, and boot. She even stooped to help the littlest children with their broaches and bootstraps. Then, as quickly as she had appeared, she vanished without a word through the same door with an impossibly large pile of garments.

With stockinged feet, we followed Lombardus into the foyer, in which the entire first floor of my lodge could have fit with ease. Four windows—the two on the east wall behind us were ten cubits high, and two shorter windows were on the west—lit the space, as did oil candles hanging upon the walls at regular intervals. The floor was made of exotic redwood planks, and an ornately woven Sviari rug, which was some seventy cubits deep and twenty-five cubits wide, covered it. The plush rug was cut to fit neatly around the grand staircase, which was made of a coveted, creamy-brown marble that came only from the island mines of the Triapolis to the far southwest. Upon the walls, from the edges of the vaulted ceiling two stories above, enormous tapestries hung down to the floor. They depicted scenes of nature, of the Moon and Stars, and of many wild animals, especially wolves.

Upon the north wall was a grand fireplace, before which stood several small side tables and four plush chairs. A fire blazed in the hearth, and it was here that Lombardus led us. At the ring of another bell, several more servants appeared seemingly out of nowhere, and Lombardus gave them hushed orders. Mere moments passed before several more high-backed, cushioned chairs were brought from another room for those of us who remained standing. A few minutes later, and three silver trays piled with biscuits, honey, butter, and jam of every imaginable flavor were set out for us. Lombardus personally poured everyone hot tea with an offer of cream and sugar, a delicacy for country-folk.

"My Lord Ulfric should be with you very soon." He set the teapot down upon one of the trays and bowed deeply. "If you should need anything, you need only ring." He gestured to the bell hanging by the fireplace and then departed.

As my charges ate their fill of the food set before them, they marveled at the foyer and its furnishings. Even the littlest children remained utterly silent as they sat on the floor at their parents' feet, stuffing biscuit after biscuit into their mouths. Even when the biscuits were gone, the children kept their peace.

I, however, had little peace. I tapped my heel anxiously, my armor rattling. It had been a decade—or was it two now?—since I had last seen my dear Ulfric, and on that last occasion, we had parted on less than friendly terms. It was only through a flurry of mutually apologetic letters that we had made amends, but I wondered if our personal grievances would not be borne out again. I prayed it would not be so …

"You old, mangy hound," a familiar voice called from behind me, and I snapped out of my anxious ponderings.

No sooner did I rise was I locked in a familiar embrace. Ulfric laid heavy hands upon my shoulders and pushed me back so he could look me over.

"By the blessed Moon and Stars, it has been so long, brother." He embraced me again, lifting me from the floor, his incredible size and strength exactly as I remembered. Unlike me, he had not lost his strength over the years.

I choked as he squeezed the air from my lungs. "By the Two, brother …" When he released me, I returned the embrace, and we patted one another on the back as we laughed. I placed my forehead against his own before kissing his bearded cheek, and I nearly wept for the overwhelming, anxious joy in my heart. I leaned in close to his ear as I hung upon my brother's shoulders and whispered, "I've missed you so, brother." We held one another but said nothing. We had been with each other since the day I had been thrown in that ship's dark hold as a boy, and so we needed no words to express our love. "But"—I finally pulled away, giving my brother a playful slap on the cheek and shoulder—"who are you to call me a mangy dog? You look like you only just rolled out of bed and haven't had a shave or haircut in a few moons."

Ulfric threw his head back and barked a laugh as he shook out his wild, light-brown mane. "And *you* smell like a horse, brother." He patted his untamed beard into shape and shrugged the loose-fitting robe he wore over nothing but a pair of silk trousers back onto his shoulders. From a golden chain around his neck, a brilliant crescent moon and wolf pendant—a pendant I, too, once wore—hung brazenly upon his bared, shaggy-haired chest. When I saw it, I shuddered involuntarily, and Ulfric raised a bushy eyebrow at me but spoke on as if he had not noticed. "But you have an excuse, brother ... Had I known you all were going to be here so soon—and with you, brother, in tow, as well—I'd have at least bothered to put on shoes." He wiggled his hairy toes, the fresh dirt under his nails making it clear where he had been the night before. "But enough. Why don't you introduce me to your guests over a hot meal?"

Ulfric popped a roll of tobacco from the inner fold of his robe into his mouth and lit it at the fireplace. With a trail of smoke and ash following him, Ulfric invited us with a wave to follow him to the private dining room in the south wing. It was cozy and warm, with the floor-to-ceiling drapes partly drawn to keep the heat in, and a dark walnut table stood already set for twelve. It amazed even me how quickly and efficiently Ulfric's staff were able to set out a full three-course meal on a moment's notice for a dozen people. Yet, such, I remembered, was the way of things near the summit of the Capitoline Hill, and the nearer one got to that summit, the more pronounced the decadence became—or, so I had heard. Ulfric's home was the highest I had ever ascended on the hill, at least for anything as intimate as dinner.

As we sat at table, my charges glanced from me to Ulfric, as if looking for a sign, and none, not even the littlest ones, so much as put their hands upon the table. Undoubtedly, they had heard in stories about the particular, mysterious rules for how one was supposed to act in the presence of this kind of company. Ulfric, however, ever the one to buck the norms of polite society, quickly put his new guests' minds at ease by drawing up an unused chair to use as a footrest.

"Relax, friends. I might live like a king, but Rune and I both come from humble beginnings, and I've never cared much for the show." Leaning back lazily with his bare feet up, he pulled a metal case of tobacco rolls from the folds of his robe and lit it. He then passed the case around the table.

"Well, I'm not sure what Rune has told you about me—"

My charges eyed one another, eyebrows raised, for I had told them nothing about Ulfric.

"—but I assure you everything he told you is a lie."

Everyone remained silent. He, however, laughed as he saw how they squirmed, and he regaled us all with what could only be called an abridged, sanitized, and self-aggrandizing telling of our friendship. On several occasions, between fits of laughter, I objected to Ulfric's shamelessly embellished recounting. Yet, no matter how I retold the accounts, they never sounded as good.

"Eventually, we went our own ways. Rune joined the Stateless, while I took up a post as a communications officer. That, in turn, led me to my current position, Chief Intelligence Officer of the Realm"—this was Ulfric's official title, but *spymaster* was more accurate—"which is not nearly as grand as it sounds." Here alone, at the end of his tale, Ulfric's truth was not as colorful as the actual truth, but the real truth of the matter was one neither of us wanted to revisit.

After Ulfric's servants set food before us, Ulfric immediately dug in. Nobody else, however, touched their food.

"Shall we pray?" Gale asked.

Ulfric looked up, a roast leg of chicken in hand, and he spoke with a full mouth, "If you so desire."

"Would you lead us, m'lord? 'Tis your home."

Ulfric shook his head. "I am not of your religion."

There was a tense silence. It was likely they had never met a non-Andarasian, so I broke the silence.

"Ulfric holds to a lunar cult."

Their looks of confusion remained, but I intoned the prayer without further explanation. The family mumbled the response.

The first few minutes of the meal were silent, but the mood quickly changed as we savored the fine meal. When the main course was finished, Harvald introduced his family and gave a brief recounting of their travels. Ulfric said little in reply, nodding as he sipped wine from a crystal glass. He, like I, had heard such stories before. Then, as we ate dessert—cocoa-dusted macaroons, neither of which Harvald's family had ever heard of—Ulfric invited his guests to make themselves at home.

"Feel free to explore my home and the city at your leisure, and my staff is at your service. As far as I'm concerned, if you're friends of Rune, you're friends of mine. Now, unless you have any questions for me, I'll have Lombardus show you to your rooms."

Ulfric rang the bell at the table, and Lombardus led everyone except me to their rooms.

"Master Rune, are you no comin'?" Harvald asked.

"I'd like to catch up with Ulfric. But you all should go and settle in."

As they left, I put up my own feet. "Got a smoke?"

Ulfric reached into his robe's inner pocket and procured another tobacco roll. "So"—he tossed it to me, and I caught it—"how's the pack?" He poured another glass of wine from the crystal decanter on the table. "I haven't seen Ragnar and Raynor since they were pups."

I blew out a great puff of smoke. "They're all doing well. Freya's well, Raynor's still a handful, and Ragnar has a mate, Ada, but they've got no pups."

"Could I see them?"

R

We entered the spy passage, hidden in the basement of Ulfric's home, and followed it for what must have been a league. The end of the hand-dug tunnel merged with an underground stream, which emerged from a cave in a small, wooded hollow among the hills. I had passed through this tunnel on a few occasions, and I had told my pack about it so they would know where to settle for the next months.

As we emerged, Raynor leapt from the bushes and across the stream to pounce upon Ulfric. Ulfric fell backward into the shallow stream, cracking the thin layer of ice, but before he could rise again, Raynor wrestled with him, nipping at his beard and hair. Ragnar also joined the fray, splashing about in the stream in an uncharacteristic show of playfulness.

Ulfric crawled from the stream, his boots and pants soaked through, but he did not stop the wolves from playing.

Instead, he grabbed hold of the wolves and rolled with them, digging his hands into their fur. He laughed, and the wolves barked, scenting their contentment to be reunited with this long-lost pack member, and after a few frenetic minutes, they settled.

Ulfric rose, and Ragnar scented his eagerness to introduce him to Ada, who lay with Freya at the entrance of a burrow the wolves had dug among the thick roots of a tree. Ulfric knelt to greet the she-wolves, petted Ada, who licked his face, and embraced Freya, who also barked, her tail beating the earth.

Though the early sunset was already upon us, we enjoyed one another's company for a few hours. Even Freya, despite the evident pain her wounded leg continued to cause her, did not stay back at the den. As a reunited pack, we hiked through the hills, and Ulfric and I reminisced and rekindled our friendship. We had been slaves together, run through jungles, forests, hillsides, and plains together, and had even gone to war together. We were family, the only family either of us had, apart from the wolves, and I never wanted our differences to come between us again. I feared, though, that spending so much time together, going through at least two full moons together, might leave us at one another's throats again.

We stopped in a hilltop clearing and sat to watch the moonrise. The wolves howled at the nearly full moon, and Ulfric turned to me. I was running my hand through my beard when Ulfric spoke.

"You're anxious, Rune."

I started. "Oh, no, I'm—"

Ulfric nudged me with an elbow and turned his face back to the sky. "I've known you for two centuries, Rune. I know what you look like when you're anxious. I know the scent, too."

I didn't want to tell him that *we* were what worried me. I didn't want to bring up our fight all those years ago. I didn't want to lose my brother again.

"What's going on with the war?"

"You sure *that's* what's bothering you?" He looked askance at me, but I said nothing. "Well, in any case, the war's not going well." He hunched forward and put his forearms upon his knees. "Seagate has been under siege for nigh on four months. The last reports I received—and not many get through—said supplies are running thin, morale is low, and we're facing the real possibility of losing the city." He heaved a sigh and wore a deep frown. He had never been much of a patriot, but he still took whatever he did seriously.

"Who are we even fighting? I've heard next to nothing."

"More like *what* are we fighting."

I cocked my head.

"Here we were, thinking we knew all the races in the world, and then these—well, we've taken to calling them *dragon people*—sail from across the sea … Their fighters are reckless, but their numbers are strong, and the more of their fighters that go down, the stronger their mages become."

I straightened my back. "They've got mages? What kind—"

Ulfric spat. "You know my thoughts on magic, Rune. I'm not as … *scrupulous* about it as you are. But even these things make me sick. I've not seen it myself, of course, but it's the foulest necromancy I've ever heard of. I've had reports saying they're summoning *demons* with the blood of the dead, whatever that means. I'm not sure I want to know."

I had read about such things a long time ago at the *Arcani* in the South, but it was lost magic, and not even the most adept among us had been willing to dig too deeply. It was one of those things better left unknown.

"And these *dragon people*, they're making headway east?"

Ulfric shrugged. "The reports aren't clear. We know they want Seagate, and a few scouting bands have been seen nearer to the World Spine, but they've not made any significant advances yet. There's been a few battles within twenty leagues of Seagate, but that's the most of it. As the winter has set in, their speed has diminished, but we've not been able to make up much ground because of it." Ulfric stood and started brushing snow from his cloak and trousers. "Things are only going to get worse, Rune. I wish I had more positive news for you, but I can only say that you might want to keep your sword sharp."

"I'm retired," I said, rising to my feet. "You know that, Ulfric."

He laughed and looked me over. "You don't look it, brother."

About an hour after the sun had set, we reemerged from the hilly woods with my pack and returned to Ulfric's estate. Our cloaks were covered with pine needles, and our boots were caked up to our calves in snow and mud, which we tracked through the tunnel and hallways of Ulfric's home. Ulfric led me up the grand staircase and showed me to my room in the south wing. At my door, we embraced one another again and wished each other a goodnight.

My room was opulent beyond even my imagining. A fire roared in the hearth, an empty tin bath sat in the corner, my baggage had been brought up and neatly packed into the armoire that stood against the wall, and a plush robe hung upon the armoire door.

I kicked off my boots and unfastened my cloak, setting them outside the door, and no sooner did my feet sink into the rug before the fire was there a knock at the door.

"Who's that?"

"My lord, may I come in?" It was Lombardus.

I gave my consent, and the door creaked open. Lombardus bowed stiffly and said, "I only wanted to make sure you had everything you needed for the night, Lord Corinsson. I was not sure when you and my Lord Ulfric would return, so I did not have the staff prepare a bath for you, but if you would like—"

"Thank you, Lombardus, but I'll be fine."

He bowed. "As you like, my lord. If you should need anything, please do not hesitate to ring. In the meantime, I will have your boots and cloak cleaned for you and returned by morning."

"Thank you. That'll be all."

Lombardus bowed again and departed.

I doffed my armor, cleaned it, and dressed for bed before I bowed myself before the fire and said my prayers. *Holy two*, I prayed, *let the past be well and truly behind Ulfric and me.* I signed myself, rose, and climbed into bed. I laid my head upon the plush pillows and soon fell into an easy sleep.

RRR

Chapter XXI

*Your greatest trouble is with yourself, and you are
your own source of trouble. You do not know what
you desire, and you are better at approving what is
salutary than attaining to it. Indeed, you see where
happiness lies, but you do not dare take it. Let me
tell you, then, what causes you such grief, for it
seems to me that you know neither yourself nor the
way you are to go.*

— From *Ad Lucilium, Epistula XXI*

R

I bolted upright in bed, the hair on my neck on edge, aware
of the terrifying scent of an unfamiliar beast just beyond
my door. Reflexively, I grabbed my sword, which leaned
against the nightstand, and jumped into a fighting stance,
sword pointed at the closed door. When the door did not burst
off its hinges, however, I hesitated. The beast was still there.
Why did it wait?

There was a knock at the door, and a familiar voice
called, "Sir?" Aros shuffled in, hunched over, and he had his
arms wrapped around his middle. He trembled before me as I
stood there, dumbfounded, in my nightshirt with my sword
poised to strike him down. The stench of the beast poured
from the lad.

I braced myself as he shuffled forward, but he was
oblivious to me. He moaned, "I do no feel—"

His legs buckled, and I rushed to the lad's side to catch him. I laid him in my bed, and when I knew he wasn't an immediate danger to himself or others, I informed his parents he was ill. Gale and Harvald wasted no time in tending to him where I had laid him. Then, my mind in chaos, I ran to Ulfric's room. I burst in to find him clothed in a heavy brown robe as he sat burning the midnight oil at a desk covered in papers, maps, and charts.

"The boy, he's one of us. How—"

Ulfric dropped his quill and snapped his head to stare at me. "Moon and Stars, Rune, what are you talking about?" He stood and tied his robe shut, under which he wore the same silk pants he had worn when we had arrived.

Words poured from my mouth in a torrent. "He's one of us, Ulfric. I … I never sensed this before in him. This must be his first transformation. What do—"

Ulfric grabbed my shoulders and slapped me lightly. "Calm down." He stared into my eyes. "Now, what the hell are you talking about?"

I struggled to find the words. "Aros, he came to my room and was … He's becoming one of us. He collapsed. His parents are with him now, but—"

Ulfric patted my shoulder. "All is well, Rune. Tomorrow is the first of the Sacred Solstice's Triduum, and now the Moon and Stars have finally aligned to change him. I'm sure if we check the charts, we'd find this same alignment last happened—how old's the boy? Sixteen? Seventeen years old? He's probably just feeling the lunar sickness a bit early as his body tries to prepare itself for what's coming."

"But, what do we do, Ulfric?"

My friend squinted his brown-gold eyes at me.

"Do we tell him, or—"

"Of course we tell him. We can't let him transform out in the open, can we?"

I shook my head.

Ulfric gripped my shoulders more tightly. "Why are you so worked up?"

I stared vacantly. "I just ... I don't have the heart to tell him."

"*Don't have the heart*, Rune? What do you think this is? You're not telling the lad he's got some disease, brother. You're telling him he's got great power. He's immortal. You and I both know people the world over who would kill to have the power we do, the power he now has."

I rested my hands on his wrists as he gripped my shoulders. "Ulfric ... you know I don't feel as you do about what we are."

"This is what was bothering you earlier, isn't it? I should've known ..." Ulfric pushed away from me, a deep frown upon his face. "After all these years, Rune, do you still persist in hating what we are?"

"Brother"—I approached him with my hands outstretched—"you know I can't live as you do anymore."

He scoffed and crossed his bare arms. "What? Are your precious Two afraid of you, brother, that they can't grant you this? Are they afraid to let you be what you are? Are they threatened you've obtained immortality and divine pleasures apart from them? Or, are they and their clerics so desperate to control you that they've called what you are sin, a sin for which they alone have a remedy? Tell me, brother, how you became foolish enough to follow a religion that condemns you for being what you are, for living according to your nature?"

Anger rose within my heart, but so did great pity. "Don't speak that way about my gods, brother. I don't speak so about yours."

He rolled his eyes. "Fine, but my question stands."

I swallowed, knowing this conversation would go the way it had all those years ago. "What we are ... what we desire to be isn't ..." I stopped to think of how to explain. "You call us *immortal*, brother, and if all you mean is that we cannot die a natural death, then fine. However, there's a difference between living and saying you cannot die. All we have is immortality, but after so many years, Ulfric, can you really tell me we have life?"

Ulfric's face contorted into a toothy snarl. "This is your answer, Rune? That we don't really have life as we are? You can't truly believe that." He looked away. "Can you not remember what you, too, once enjoyed alongside me? We used to glory in what we are. Moon and Stars, Rune, we used to revel in it, and the people worshiped us like gods across Latia and the Electorate. We had everything and everyone we wanted. No, but we had even more—ecstasies men can only dream of, and which gods alone enjoy! And I still do.

"But you ..." His eyes bore great fire in them. "But you've thrown that away, and what do you get for it? A life of self-loathing and loneliness? A life of fear, and regret, and pain? And all for what? To persist in the delusion that there is something more than this? Because what we are is devoid of life and love? But"—his eyes bore great sadness in them now—"you're the one who doesn't really live, Rune, because you leave what you are behind for what you *think* you might attain. But there is nothing more than this ... There is nothing more or better than what we are."

I held back tears of anger and of regret, but mostly of sorrow, for my brother's soul. "You're right, Ulfric."

He raised an eyebrow.

"I did once revel in what we are. I, too, felt that we ... I wasn't truly living without letting out the monster—"

"Don't call us monsters," he growled, baring his teeth.

"What am I supposed to call what comes out of us, Ulfric? Even you can't control what it does during the Triduum. Or, do you wish to take responsibility for the death you've wrought during those blind, raging passions under the Moon and Stars you worship? If so, then you're a monster who brings death in his wake, but if not, then that thing inside you—that *divine power* you love—is a monster that enslaves you. You cannot have it both ways."

He glared at me with brow furrowed and teeth bared but said nothing.

"But, aye, you're even right that I'm often lonely and plagued with regrets over what I am and what I've done. Aye, I often also feel pain as I wrestle with myself over what I feel, desire, even crave—call it whatever you want, Ulfric, if *desire* does not suit you—to be and feel.

"I'll even admit, brother, though it shames me, that I often think fondly on our times together. In my weaker moments, I wonder if I'm right not to live according to what I feel, and so fill the void within my heart. Some days, I want it so badly ...

"When I think back on our times, though, for all the pleasure—aye, even ecstasy—I'm reminded how I remained incomplete. I saw that, though I would live forever, I could not give life but only take it. Everything I ever made was more a monster than myself."

Ulfric spoke through gritted teeth, "What would satisfy you, then, Rune? Was our friendship and love insufficient? Was Mara's love nothing to you that you say you never really lived?"

I shook my head. "What does our friendship have to do with what we are, Ulfric? Could we not have been friends apart from our shared flaw? Could I not have still loved you without fits of passion intervening? Would what we gave to one another—our companionship, our brotherhood, our love, our promises—would these not have been grander if they hadn't been forced by our nature?

"As for Mara, whatever I felt—feel—for her ... the love I had for her—if it really was love and not merely a shared lust to revel in our nature—all we could beget—all anyone like us can ever beget—are monsters."

Ulfric's eyes made it clear he knew about my sons.

"When you've slain your sons, your sons of passion, brother, then you can talk to me about what kind of so-called life you have as you are. Then you might understand why I can't say I had true life and love."

He snarled, eyes glowing red. "I will not be like you, Rune ... I will not loathe my existence and hate what the Moon and Stars made me to be to follow the Dead Gods slavishly like you. When your precious Two live again, then you can tell me that you know what life really is."

The heat of my friend's anger burned against me, but I did not want to leave our relationship in this state. "Brother, I—"

"Get out." He waved a hand. "Go teach the boy to live in misery as you do."

I took a step closer and lay a hand on his shoulder. "Brother, ple—"

"I said, get out." He pushed my hand away and growled, "I have work to finish before the Holy Triduum."

R

When I returned, Aros still lay in my bed with his back against the headboard, a glass of water in his shaking hand. His mother sat by his side, stroking his forehead. As soon as I entered, though, she set her son's glass upon the nightstand, bowed her head at me, and opened her mouth, but I cut her off.

"Gale, ma'am, I'd like to speak with Aros alone, if that's all right?"

She narrowed her eyes and asked her son, "Aros, is that okay, or do you want me to stay?"

Aros shivered violently but nodded weakly and said, "I'm all right, Ma."

She nodded and departed as I took her place at the bedside.

Aros sank back into the bed. "Wh-what's wrong wi-with me?"

I bowed my head and sighed. I wished to be anywhere else, doing anything else.

"I don't know how to explain this to you, Aros"—I took the young man's trembling hand in my own and squeezed—"so I'm just going to come right out and tell you."

The young man swallowed hard and squeezed my hand back.

"Aros—" I choked. "You ... You're ..." I let go of his hand and covered my face to hide my tears. "You're a werewolf, Aros." I shuddered and sniffed. "As am I."

There was no comprehension in his eyes. "Wh-what?"

"I'm sorry, Aros ... I ..."

The young man shut his eyes firmly and shook his head. "What're you t-talkin' 'bout?"

How could I explain this? I must have sounded mad. Few, even if they believed the Sacred Writings, believed the fantastical things written therein.

"I know it's hard—"

The young man shot upright and grabbed me by the neck. As he choked me, the beast's glowing red eyes stared back at me with their enormous black pupils. An unnatural voice growled out of the young man's throat. "You lie." He dug his claws into my neck, and blood trickled.

I pried his hands away, barely overcoming his demonic grip. "Enough." I pushed Aros down into the bed, his claws flailing. "Enough, lad."

The fury subsided as quickly as it had erupted, and the young man grew limp. He sighed as his clawed fingers returned to normal. "Wh-what happened?" His eyes had returned to their normal steely green-gray.

Unsurprised by his amnesia, I spoke on, "Lad, what I told you was the truth. You're a werewolf."

The young man stared, still dazed.

"Do you understand?"

He shook his head slowly. "But werewolves ..."

I tensed, preparing to grapple with the beast again, but nothing happened.

"Werewolves, and everything else the Writings speak of, are real, lad."

"I dunno—"

This moment had to come, but I dreaded it all the same. "I'll prove it to you." I held up my right arm. My body tensed as the changes began. My flesh tore, tendons snapped and re-anchored as my bones grew out, and the old flesh disintegrated as it fell from my body. The pain was overwhelming, yet the flood of ecstasy converted the pain to pleasure. It intoxicated me. My heart raced as I focused my entire being on not giving in to the change entirely.

The boy gaped at my now transformed limb. What little color remained in his face faded, his pupils filled his irises, and he screamed silently.

I took a deep breath to level out my voice. "Do you see now what I am? What you, too, are becoming?"

Aros said nothing, even as my hand reverted to its natural form. Tears poured silently down his cheeks. He knew I spoke the truth. Indeed, he had probably known the truth about his nature for a while but had been unable to admit it. Who could deny the meaning of the dreams of bloodshed and moonlight that preceded the first transformation, even if they could not accept it?

The young man's teary eyes revealed the consequence of his struggles. No doubt, he had enjoyed what he had been in his dreams—I certainly had, though I had been younger when I had first transformed—but he was surely ashamed of those dreams. He longed to live according to his nature but, all at once, he could not accept it, except at the cost of his soul.

How does anyone ever come to accept their dreams are sin? How did one come to believe he bears sin in his heart, to believe sin is inseparably twisted up in his essence and yet not his essence? Though I had long ago come to believe these things, I never fully understood it, nor did I cease to wish that

I could believe something else entirely. Yet no man chooses his beliefs, but he is borne into them ...

I reached out to embrace Aros, but he nearly leapt away from me.

"I'm not going to hurt—"

"This must be a dream. This canna be real." He spoke with a surprisingly level tone.

My heart ached to see him so, and I wished to tell him he would soon wake from this nightmare.

I shook my head. "No, Aros, this is the truth. This is what we are."

Aros remained silent.

"I'm sorry ..."

In what first seemed to be another oncoming outburst, Aros flung his arms upward, as if to rage against Heaven. He then brought his arms to his chest and buried his face in them, pulling at his hair with his hands. He sat upon the bed in a tight ball, legs drawn up tight.

I crawled next to him and held him close, wrapping my arms around him as my father had done to me when I had learned what I was. I pulled his head under my chin and placed my cheek against his head. I wept silent, bitter tears over, for, and with the lad.

For a long while, neither of us spoke. What could I say to express what I knew the boy felt? What words could he speak to express his sorrow over this newly discovered truth? No words, no rational explanations, no matter how sincere or true, would ever remove the pains that came from being confronted with the truth of what we are.

We were what we were. Nothing would change that. Nothing would make it right. Nothing could take it away.

No, but only true compassion, compassion which knowingly, willfully dips its hands into the filth of our existence to embrace it, only compassion which allows itself to be soiled with our filth, only compassion which allows itself to be wounded by the one it wishes to console … Aye, only this compassion, this love, can really suffice to numb the pains and still the dark-twisted hearts of men.

So, I said nothing but wept with him who wept.

Eventually, Aros broke the silence. "I … I do no want this. Oh, by the Two, I do no want this …"

"I know, lad, I know …"

"P-pl-please, take this away."

"I … I can't … I can't take this away, Aros. This is what we are now."

The boy cried aloud, the sound of his voice muffled in his arms and in my chest. "How do you live knowin' the truth 'bout what you are?"

Though I had grappled with that same question for a lifetime, I had no reply. So, I let a lifetime's worth of silence linger in the air before I finally spoke, "When I was a boy and realized what I was, I lived because my father assured me all would be well. All would be well, he had said, because he loved me despite what I was, despite what he knew it would cost him."

I held my breath, unsure if I could continue, but I had to. "When he let the mob believe he, not I, was the monster … he provided for my life by his death, his sacrifice. Aye, and I survived—no, thrived—on his sacrifice for some years … but the harshness of the world slowly overcame me.

"The memory of my father, of his blood, of his love, and of his worship, which was—at least at that time—my worship ... All this became dim little by little as the power and thrill, the ecstasy and utter pleasure, of what I was overcame me. With none to pull me out again, with none to renew that sacrifice in my sight, to provide a remembrance ... I forgot and came to believe the darkness was light.

"In darkness, I lived a life of utter contentment and ease. The elves came to fear me. The people of the Southern Cities, where I had long ago taken up residence, the Sviari, and even the orcs to the east ... all of them worshiped me as a god in the flesh. Anything and anyone I wanted was mine. I was immortal and wielded magics no other could possess. Only my soul was powerful enough to wield such mighty spirits. I even believed I had found love with another who was as I ...

"No, never did I regret, not for a single day, what I was and how I lived. No pangs of conscience, no guilt. The world feared me, loved me, praised me, worshiped me. Most importantly, I lived true to myself, and this is the highest form of life, according to the world.

"Yet, after a lifetime of every delight, I was confronted by the abject meaninglessness of this life. I was confronted with the death ... the un-life I bore within. There was nothing that lasted, no meaning that endured. I was eternal amidst inconstancy and death. I was a lie.

"This trial forced me to recall my father's sacrifice. I realized his sacrifice, the remembrance of it, had not lost its savor of meaning when it reemerged from the depths of my mind. Darkness, death, and meaninglessness had not touched it.

"Once more, there was light in the darkness of my fading world. This memory became again a lamp shining upon my path on a moonless, starless night. This memory of sacrifice was once more my light.

"Before you met me, I had again forgotten the truth. I forgot not because the truth is weak, but because my scarred mind is. I forgot because I struggled with what I was—still am, in part—and I still struggle. Even fleeting pleasures seem so bright and grand to a soldier at war.

"Yet, when the pleasures fade, I'm inevitably filled with that old sense of meaninglessness anew. Hatred, in turn, lies close at hand to fill the void. But hatred cannot propel or drive anyone toward something greater. It only ever destroys.

"Of course, my wolves tried with all their might to break me out of my self-hatred and remind me of the truth. They often succeeded, preserving what little remained of my sanity, bringing me back from the brink of utter oblivion. To them, especially to Freya, who is obstinate in her love, I'm grateful. Yet, it was only when your family came—when *you* came, Aros—that my stubborn unwillingness to remember was truly confronted.

"When you came, Aros, and I saw so much of myself in you—and now I know why—I was forced to return to my father's memory. It was only when you told me that you loved me, in spite of me, that the truth came back to me in dreams of realities beyond comprehension. And, when you came in tonight, I realized in the waking world how badly I had needed to be reminded of the truth of my father's love, of my father's sacrifice.

"I knew, too, that I would have to explain to you what you were. Yet, I knew I could not guide you aright by saying, 'Hate yourself as I have done.' That is not the truth my father had left me. Rather, I set before you what my father set before me when I was confronted by the darkness I bore within. It is, in fact, what you said to me—gave to me—in spite of me in Laketon ... I love you, Aros."

Aros wrapped his arms tighter around me as he dug his fingers into the fabric of my shirt. He said nothing as he laid his head against my chest. His tears ceased flowing, his breathing steadied, and he no longer trembled as before. After several minutes of silence, his grip upon me loosened, and his breathing slowed. He fell asleep in my arms.

I lay him in my bed and brought the covers up to his chin. I sat with him for a few minutes to make sure he did not wake. When he did not, I let his parents know that he was asleep but said nothing else. Aros had to reveal this in his own time.

I returned to my room and checked on Aros one last time before I curled up before the fire with a spare blanket and fell asleep.

RRR

Chapter XXII

A troubled man with a mind full of shadows will recoil when a light shines upon his darkness, for in the light, he must acknowledge his darkness for what it is.

— From *Proverbs of the Hierodules*

R

T he three days of the Triduum that followed were the most difficult of my life. I found myself again fighting off the lunar sickness while at once trying to help Aros cope with the same. On more than one occasion during the daylight hours of those three days, I had to help Aros calm himself mid-transformation, and each time, I barely succeeded.

When the first night came upon us, Aros and I aided one another in our suffering. Together, we resisted the change.

At dawn on that second day of the Triduum, an envelope was slipped under our doorway without so much as a knock. Ulfric's private seal—a full moon surrounded by six stars—was stamped on the envelope. When I unfolded the paper, a small key fell into my hand. Though the letter said nothing, I knew what the key was for, and that night, I used it to take Aros through the tunnel.

The sun set, its protective light fading fast, and the moon rose. As we emerged, my pack nearly knocked me and Aros to the ground in a furious rush. They had caught the scent of a werewolf they did not know emerging. They quickly realized, though not without lingering confusion, that I was not in any danger at all.

I explained all that had happened as quickly as I could, and Aros attempted to scent a greeting, with only minimal comprehensibility—it took time for men to learn how to scent well. They returned the jumbled greeting heartily but swiftly departed to safety within the forest. We followed the creek deeper into the forest to keep ourselves, and others, free from harm.

Not far from the tunnel, Ulfric, who had—much to my surprise—adopted his much-despised native wolf-form, sauntered out of the brush and across the creek. His fur dripped with water and was matted down with forest debris of every kind, and in the time it took him to close the short distance between us, he shifted to his preferred human form.

Shamelessly naked, Ulfric stood before me and Aros, who trembled with anxious expectation. He shook his head vigorously, his long, shaggy hair flying wildly and flinging water and mud all around. Though Ulfric, who believed himself to be as human as any naturally born man, would have vehemently denied it, he remained instinctively the wolf he was born as deep within. He would never escape his nature, no matter how hard he tried.

He crossed his muddy, well-muscled arms over his broad chest, to which a great deal of debris still clung, entangled in thick, matted hair. His filthy mane hung wildly about his equally dirty face, obscuring his glowing eyes. I could sense in him the ecstasy of the hunt—it was an act of worship for him—and I did not doubt he had been engaged in such all day.

"Well, brother"—he looked me and Aros up and down—"or, should I say, *brothers*? While you spent the first holy day agonizing, I've been glorying in the worship of my precious Moon and Stars." He flung his head back to clear his wild hair from his face. He had a genuine smile upon his face. "Would I be correct to assume you've finally come to heed the call to worship on our highest holy day?"

"*Brother*"—I let the word linger on my tongue—"I'm truly glad you've decided to call me that again, despite—"

"Let's not mention that, brother. We have our disagreements, but you're here with me now, and for that, I'm glad."

I put a hand on Aros' shoulder and gripped it tightly as I replied to Ulfric. "We spent yesterday and today worshiping the Two, brother, and we're not here willingly."

The elation on Ulfric's face disappeared, and a toothy snarl began to appear.

"But I am glad we get to be together—"

His snarl vanished.

"—even if our reasons do not align."

A slight smile crept back onto his face as he looked up through the trees at the first stars of night. "Though I wish you were here for purer reasons, at least we can still be together. Now, let's enjoy the night." When he said that, he turned and knelt to drink from the creek, which was his way of giving us our privacy.

I looked at Aros. "Brother …"

With his bloodshot eyes, he looked into mine and opened his mouth, though no words came out.

"It's time. It will be as I said." I looked over my shoulder at Ulfric, who knelt, gazing into the heavens in prayer, and I whispered, "Don't be afraid, Aros. Don't be afraid of what will come." I hugged him. "I love you, brother." With that, I put some space between us, undressed, and sat down upon my clothes.

Shortly thereafter, Ulfric gave himself over to the beast and transformed before us. His red, demonic eyes stared at us both, but as soon as he smelled what we were, he turned and ran into the woods. We would join him soon enough, he knew.

Aros' screams broke the calm of the woods several minutes later as the sun's light finally disappeared and the moon's power took hold. After his transformation, I curled into a tight ball as my blood began to boil, but I resisted long enough to utter one last prayer for Aros and myself before the darkness within and without took hold of me, too.

ᚱ

When we awoke the next morning, Freya was at my side. She comforted me as I tried to rub dried blood from my face and hands, only to make a greater mess.

"*Deer,*" she scented plainly.

I nodded, relieved to know I could trust her appraisal of our night's revelry.

She scented for me to follow her, still limping from her old wound, and led me to where Aros lay in wolf form. He had creamy brown fur that was matted down with blood and gore, but the clear rise and fall of his chest told me he was well.

I knelt down and touched his shoulder. "Aros, wake up."

His eyes shot wide open as he jumped up onto all fours, and he lashed out to bite before stopping short when he realized it was me. He whimpered and howled before biting at his fur.

Freya came to him, nuzzled his head and licked his face as she scented calming thoughts. I also put my arms around him to stop him from biting his fur.

"Take a deep breath, lad. Focus on your body, and you'll change back."

Aros whimpered again but shut his eyes. After a few moments, he reverted back to his human form. His face, which had been smooth-shaven the night before, was now covered with a short, wild beard, and the shaved sides of his head had also grown fuzzy. He threw his arms around me and sobbed.

I embraced him and raised him to his feet. I took his face into my hands and patted his cheek. "You all right, lad?"

He said nothing but shook.

"It's a bit of a shock to take on wolf-skin for the first time, I know. I still don't like it myself—it's *unnatural*—but you did fine. Now, let's—"

I saw blood dripping from beneath Aros' hand, which he held to his side. I moved his hand and whistled when I saw the gashes. "Looks like one of us had to show you your place in the pack, brother." I tried to smile at him, but he did not so much as blink, and my smile faded. "It might sting for a little, but you'll heal quick enough—one of the few benefits to what we are." I took his arm and began to lead him back to where our clothes were. "Now, let's get cleaned up at the stream and go back inside before we catch cold."

R

On the third and final night of the Triduum, which was usually the least powerful of the three nights, Aros begged me to sedate him. I obliged him and spent the night in quiet prayer as I held vigil over the sleeping young man.

If there were any benefit to the predicament in which we had found ourselves—being trapped in a walled estate, inside a walled town—it was that our apparent illness gave us a guise with which to hide our condition. When I, too, felt the lunar sickness, I merely told Aros' family and Ulfric's staff that what Aros had was catching and that they must stay away from us. Only Erika and Gale refused to leave us be, and they frequently knocked on our door to check on us.

After his first Triduum was over, it took Aros two days more to recover from his experience of living death and so return to life among his family. Even then, he was not his old self. His nervous ticks became more pronounced and, at times, he would rise and leave the company of his family to sit alone, staring into nothingness. If anyone, myself included, tried to speak or sit with him, he would excuse himself and depart to his room or the home's library, where he would take a book and pretend to read.

His withdrawals from the living did not go unnoticed, and after only a few days, Gale and Harvald approached me privately.

Harvald sighed. "He's always been an anxious boy, that one, but ne'er so much that he wanted nothin' to do with his own flesh and blood. What do we do to talk some sense into the boy, sir?"

Gale sniffed but held back tears. "Has somethin' happened to him, sir, that he's like this? Has he told you anythin' he has no told us? We know you've grown close ..."

I shook my head and explained this was merely an effect of Aros' illness and of exhaustion from travel, but I assured them he would be all right. His parents, though unconvinced, did not question me further. I had considered telling them the truth, but that was Aros' place, not mine.

He longed to tell his family, too, but he feared what they would think of him. He revealed as much to me shortly after the Triduum when, one sleepless night, he had snuck into my room. He had laid a hand on my shoulder as I slept.

R

I rubbed my eyes and sat on the edge of the bed. "Aros? What's the matter? Can't sleep?"

He shook his head and muttered a soft, "no," but said nothing else.

I patted the bedside, and he sat, his head hung. He rubbed his hands together, and his throat-clearing tick rumbled.

"Do you want me to make you something, lad?"

He nodded, and I took my medicine bag from the armoire and set about preparing a tincture.

I had barely begun when Aros spoke, "Sir?"

I looked back at him and raised an eyebrow.

"I ... Would it ...? Could I ...?" He grew silent.

I put my tools down to sit at his side.

The lad bit his lip and bounced his heel against the floor.

I patted my brother's back. "What's on your mind, brother? And don't say nothing.*"*

Aros became completely still. "I ... Could I just stay with you tonight? I do no want to be alone ... I'm ... I'm afraid I'll ... you know."

I put my arms around Aros and kissed his forehead. "Of course you can, Aros. You're my brother; I'm here for you."

He returned my embrace and buried his face in my nightshirt. "I wish I could tell my parents, 'specially my da ..." Tears began to soak through my nightshirt, and the boy sniffled. "I dunno what they'd say, though ..."

"Hey"—I patted Aros' back as he leaned into me, and I took the hem of my nightshirt to wipe Aros' nose as I would have had he been my own child—"they're your parents, Aros. They'll always love you, even if you tell them."

"But I can't ... I'm not ready. I mean, what if they do no ..." He sobbed violently and shook. Great strands of snot dripped from his nose, onto my shoulder, and down my chest as it soaked through my shirt. "I'm sorry ..." He wiped his hand across his nose and streaked mucus across his nightshirt's sleeve.

I took the hem of my nightshirt again and made him blow his nose.

"I'm sorry, Rune. I'm a baby, I kn—"

"You're not, Aros." I wiped his nose one last time. "And don't worry about the shirt; the staff will launder it tomorrow, and I've got extras. Now look at me." I lifted his chin. "You're not a baby, Aros. You're dealing with something nobody could ever be ready for, no matter how old. And this is something that you shouldn't have to deal with alone.

"I wasn't much younger than you when I was in your shoes, lad, and I did exactly what you're doing right now. I crawled in bed with my ma and da, and Da just sat with me like I am with you—crying, snot, the whole ordeal. The only difference between you and me is that you're going to your brother instead of your father. All right?"

Aros took my sleeve and wiped his eyes. "Aye. You won't tell anyone, though, will you?"

" 'Course not. You'll tell your family when you're ready. Until then, you've always got my ear, brother. Now"—I gave

Aros one more squeeze—"you make yourself comfortable, and I'm going to change this shirt."

Aros crawled under the covers, and I changed my nightshirt, setting the soiled one outside. When I returned to my bed a minute later, Aros was already fast asleep. I stroked his hair, kissed his forehead, and tucked him in.

"Goodnight, son," I whispered.

This was just the first of many things he spoke to me about on the nights when he could not sleep for the nightmares that plagued him. Most nights, he just wanted someone to watch out for him, someone to help him share the load, and after a hug and assurance that everything would be all right, he would fall asleep at my side. Other nights, he got no rest, and I would sit with him by the fire, or he would lay at my side, tossing and turning. Sometimes, he would weep, and other nights, he would say nothing at all. Other nights still, he would vent his frustrations and anger, or he would ask me to comfort and calm him as his blood boiled. Whatever the case, I gladly undertook the many long nights, just as my father had undertaken them for me. Never did I grow weary of him, even when he kept me awake until near dawn.

R

During the hectic days of our two-and-a-half moon stay with Ulfric, there was little else of note that happened. The solstice, which marked Aros' seventeenth birthday, and new year's celebrations came and went after we had arrived, and the weather, too, worsened rapidly, as we had expected it would. Blizzards and ice storms rolled down from the mountains in the south and east in the first days of the new year, and we were all grateful we had arrived when we had.

On the nicer days, Harvald, Gale, and all their children frequented the city with the household servants when they went to take care of the estate's business. Though the servants were horrified at first that "such honorable guests of Lord Ulfric" would want to be seen in their company, they quickly learned Harvald's entire family was of the same station as they. Indeed, though the servants continually treated their master's guests with all due deference, friendships quickly formed between them all, even among the children.

Unlike his family, however, Aros refused every invitation to the city. Seeing his unending melancholy and how he sat alone with the shades drawn for hours on end, I eventually forced him to go out. I threatened to tie him up in the saddle and parade him around town—a Stateless regaling the people with a bounty—if he did not comply, and it was this threat to which Aros succumbed. Though he pretended to hate the first excursions, he shortly came to enjoy the city more than any of his family, and on some of those sleepless nights, he and I would even walk through the empty city streets together.

There was also, of course, Harvald's new foot. Less than two weeks after our arrival, Harvald was fitted by a specialist from the guild of hypocrathekers for a prosthesis. Three weeks—and a king's ransom in gold—later, Harvald walked on his own, with nothing but a cane, which he quickly put away, too. The limb, he had said to me as we sat by the fire, was beyond his wildest hopes. So excited over it was he, that he jumped to his feet, pulled me up out of my chair and into an embrace, his strong carpenter's arms crushing the air from my lungs.

Apart from these events, though, only the going away party Ulfric threw for us stands out in my mind. Ulfric, busy as he was handling the constant intelligence reports streaming in from the front lines, spent little time with any of us, and the time he did spend—with me, in particular—was always laden with unspoken tension. Yet, he was by no means a bad host, nor even hostile to me. Indeed, he showed his hospitality most greatly by putting on an ostentatious masquerade—the likes of which exceeded what Harvald's family could have ever dreamed up—in their honor. So greatly did Ulfric play up his plans for us that even Aros, who then suffered from the effects of his second Triduum at the Seat, could not hold back his excitement.

Thus, the entire family passed all their remaining days in the Seat, preparing for the ball. At Ulfric's ungrudging expense, all were tended to by the most elite tailors, hairdressers, and instructors of dance and etiquette that one could hire in the city. Even during the exceedingly dull lessons on etiquette, there was never a word of complaint from even the youngest children. I, too—though I refused to take advantage of Ulfric's largess, apart from the dancing lessons, which I had hoped would cure me of my two left feet—looked forward to the festivities, even if I could not dress up in any other costume than my Stateless dress uniform.

On the night of the masquerade, Ulfric's home was filled to bursting with the best the Seat could offer. Even the nobles, whom I typically avoided at any cost, became pleasant company once the wine and liquor flowed freely. Moreover, despite being among the company of wealthy nobles, nobody was as well-dressed as my charges.

Harvald and Gale dressed as the prince and princess of swords, while their daughters dressed as the princesses of the three remaining suits. Arve and Aros dressed as the knaves of wands and coins respectively, and the youngest boys, for whom Ulfric had hired an entire menagerie and cast of jesters, went as knights errant, each with a pony to serve as their steed. Finally, Ulfric, much to my and Aros' amusement, went dressed as a black sheep.

Everyone danced the night away into morning. Even then, the festivities did not stop. The servants drew heavy curtains over every window and helped our flight from reality to go on for many hours more. While the older guests at the party—Harvald, Gale, and myself included—eventually left the ballroom floor in the north wing in favor of quieter conversations over glasses of wine and spirits in the foyer, the youngest guests danced ceaselessly. The young nobles chased after Ulfric's guests of honor like prizes to be won, all desiring to dance—albeit unawares—with commoners, for they seemed to be the noblest of all.

When the final dance was called and the last of the wine was poured, the young noble dancers vied for the hands of the guests of honor. Aros and Arve took the hands of two beautiful young ladies, and Haldis, the hand of a handsome young gentleman, with whom she had spent the entire night. Only Erika refused the hands of all her suitors—and there were many—and stood alone. As the overture began, she made her way from the ballroom and came toward us as we sat in the foyer. Assuming she was simply too tired for one last dance, Ulfric pulled a chair out for the young lady, but she declined this offer, as well.

She stood before me—her auburn hair, I can still remember, was done up in ostentatious ribbons and braids, and adorned with pearl studded clips—and extended her white-gloved hand. She looked at me with sparkling blue eyes, made even more prominent by the makeup she wore. "May I have this dance, Master Rune?"

Taken aback by the request, I shot a glance at her parents.

Harvald, half-falling out of a divan, was fast asleep, but Gale, who sat next to her dozing husband, nodded, a slight but sincere smile on her face.

I rose and took Erika's arm, and we danced together for the first and last time that night. As the music rose to a crescendo, Siggy's words of warning came back to my mind. My heart raced, and it was only my Stateless training that prevented me from betraying the panic that overwhelmed me as Erika's beautiful eyes stared into mine from behind her mask. They had never ceased speaking words I could not understand and were full of that same something I did not know.

RRR

Chapter XXIII

And behold, it came to pass in those days, when the king had passed judgment upon his son, that he rose from his throne of judgment and ascended to his chamber. And he threw himself upon his bed and wept bitterly, his soul vexed, and he cried out, "Oh my son, my son, would that I, and not thou, were dead." Thus he cried, for he had sentenced his son and his usurpers to death.

And the king did not eat but the bread of tears for seven days, and he rent his garments and threw ashes upon his head, for he had his son slain. But, on the eighth day, he rose from his bed, and, no longer weeping, he dressed himself in fine clothing and anointed his own head. And he descended from his chamber and sat upon his throne and took his rod and staff so that he might be king and judge over his people in peace once more.

— From *History of the Holy Kings*

ℛ

W hen we departed three days later, a deep somberness hung over all. Gifts and promises to write were exchanged between the entire family and those with whom friendships had been formed. In Haldis' case, even a kiss was received from a lower ranking noble boy who had visited for hours every day following the masquerade. Even Ulfric and I, though we had continually felt the acute tension between us, gave one another a tearful embrace at the city's east gate and promised not to let our disagreements divide us. Yet, for all the pleasures of the Seat and the sadness of departing, the desire to arrive at our destination was undiminished.

We journeyed on as before, though even faster still, as the army's press gangs had already moved well west of the Great River. The worst of winter had passed, and spring drew nearer every day. Even when we were far enough from the Seat again that the roads ceased to be paved, we continued making great headway. The one complaint from all, myself included, was that trail rations failed to satisfy like our former accommodation had. Still, the fact these arrangements would soon end kept all, even Aros, contented.

There was only one burden we all carried unabated, and I finally decided to address it as we sat around the fire.

"I want to tell you my plans ..."

Everyone looked up from their cups of tea and bowls of watery soup.

"When we arrive in Ebria, I plan only to stay for a week to resupply. Then I need to return home. You need a chance to return to having a normal life without me around."

My frankness left them speechless but, unsurprisingly, Gale spoke first.

"Will you no stay with us only a short while longer, Rune, sir? I know my family would be happy to have you for as lo—"

"Gale, ma'am, I'm sure you and yours would return all the hospitality I showed you ten times over, but ... I really need to return. It'll be nearly the start of summer when I return, and I need to maintain the land and my home."

Harvald frowned. "Surely, someone of your means could hire a caretaker for all that land, sir … if you do no mind me sayin' so."

I shook my head. "True enough. However, I'm weary of the road, and my duties weigh heavily upon me. I hope—"

"Please, sir," Aros said, his sudden outburst surprising everyone, "do no leave us, no so soon, anyway. Would you no—"

I held up a hand. "Peace, lad. I was also going to say I've reconsidered taking an apprentice. If your mother and fath—"

"Ma, Da, please tell Master Rune you'll let me—"

Gale set her bowl down with a clatter and shook a finger at her son. "Do no interrupt, Aros." She then looked at her husband, who met her gaze. After a moment, he nodded. "As I was 'bout to say"—she put her hands on her hips as she sat—"an apprentice shouldna be so quick to step upon the words of"—she smiled with tears in her eyes—"of his master."

Aros leapt and wrapped his arms around his mother's and father's necks, kissing their cheeks, pouring forth a continual stream of thanks. His parents returned the affections, and when they released one another, Aros flung his arms around me, too.

"Thank you, sir, thank you."

I patted the young man on the back, and when her brother sat down, Haldis smiled a polite but bittersweet smile at us.

"We sure will miss both of you when you're gone, Aros, Master Rune. Maybe you'll come out to visit us now and then?"

We nodded solemnly.

Next to her, Erika sat with her hand over her mouth. "S-sir, will you no ... no need to take some time to let our brother—"

Aros scoffed. "I do no need any more time than a week, Erika. If I must stay up all night every night to help get everyone settled in, I will." He looked at me. "You need no worry 'bout me slowin' us—"

I glared at Aros, who had already been reprimanded for interrupting once. He fell silent, and his sister was now clearly wiping tears from her face. She looked at me but could not speak.

"Erika ..." I glanced at Gale for support, and she looked at me with downcast eyes. Nevertheless, she nodded for me to go on. "I ... I truly cannot stay any longer. If I delay ..." I did not bother to finish my sentence but looked at the young lady with as much pity as I could muster.

She walked away from us until she was just beyond the range of the firelight, but I could nonetheless see her gazing into the twilit sky. After a moment, Haldis and Gale rose to comfort her, and I took the opportunity to excuse myself and make my rounds alone.

Thereafter, all but Erika were able to come to terms with my upcoming departure. Whenever she would look at me, she would become teary-eyed, though she shed no tears in my presence. Still, I did not change my plans, and when we had traveled for roughly two weeks, I thought of how best to handle the upcoming Triduum. While I loathed to delay our journey any longer with lengthy stops, I knew this would likely be the only way to keep everyone safe from Aros and myself on those dark nights of the full moon. Aros, too, had expressed a desire to stop and rest. His constant struggle had worn on him.

Two nights before the Triduum began, I declared my desire to stop in the upcoming town of Woadbury for the duration of the Triduum. While smaller even than East Laketon had been, Woadbury was the last fortified town on our journey, apart from Ebria itself, but it was still sufficiently large to allow us to rest and resupply. When I suggested this, Harvald protested, believing I had suggested this for his sake, but I explained it was for my own health that I wished to stop for so many days. This was only partially true, as I knew I could have handled this Triduum—at least the day before and after the full moon—on the road. Although the lunar lusts had not ceased or even been less acute since my experience in East Laketon, I no longer felt quite the same need to satisfy them either. Rather, my request to rest was for Aros' sake, though I allowed the shame of weakness to fall strictly on my shoulders.

When we arrived the next day, we lodged for four nights in Woadbury, which was in the southeast of Oserden. The city guard, which was not nearly as on edge as that of East Laketon, welcomed me with great pomp, assuring me they would not infringe upon my rights.

The Triduum came and went, and Aros and I feigned some shared infection again while absconding on the full moon to transform in the far reaches of the countryside. On the fourth morning, we packed and left at first light, and Aros slept off what remained of his lunar sickness next to his brother on the driver's bench.

The ease of our earlier journey from the Seat did not continue, however. The second day back on the road, I received strange messages from my pack. Other packs had passed along rumors of some plague or pestilence following in our wake after we had left the Seat. These rumors—garbled and confused as rumors always were—made little sense to my pack, and even less to me.

I could think of no explanation other than that the presence of three werewolves—sometimes wolves describe werewolves as bearing disease—near the Seat had not gone unnoticed by other packs. My estimation, however, was only half correct—news of our werewolf trio had, indeed, reached many wolves. What I had not guessed was that news of our presence had swiftly reached the unfriendly ears of a feral pack, too. It was this plague of ferals that had been following in our wake, and they had, for some unknown reason, marked Aros and I as their targets. This truth was only realized in hindsight ...

It happened in an instant. We stopped on the roadside, deep within the heart of the western woods of Oserden to the north of Ebria, where the trees had started budding, to make camp. There, the ferals' ragged, rumbling roar resounded. At once, my hair stood on end. Aros shook. The horses whinnied and stamped their hooves as Harvald and Arve tried to calm them. The smallest children cried, filled with an instinctual terror, and nobody could resist shuddering.

My wolves gathered and scanned in every direction for danger—a feral never howled except to begin a hunt.

As Aros shook violently, I pushed him up against the nearest cart so he was at my back. I prayed he would not transform, bewitched by the demonic call of those unholy monsters.

As I prayed, my vision narrowed, and my veins burned with adrenaline. I shouted for the family to huddle together with their backs to the wagons, as the ferals would target the strongest first.

Crouching, I drew my sword fluidly and held it poised to strike. My pack prepared itself to strike with me. I watched and listened for any sign of impending assault, but when I saw the glowing red eyes within the thicket ahead of me, it was too late.

The feral stood taller than any natural man, and it sprung with demonic might into the air, clawed paw-hands stretched wide to strike. The perpetually half-transformed monstrosity, which was stronger than even a fully transformed, full-blooded werewolf, landed in front of me. It shook the ground and emitted a bone-rattling roar as spittle flew from its maw. It held its arms akimbo, claws ostensibly spread.

Screams from Harvald's entire family filled the air, but this monster's bellowing voice drowned them out.

"F-F-Fath-h-er ... Brother-slayer. W-we f-f-found you."

My heart sank as the stuttering words roared out of the beast's half-formed muzzle.

"My son ..." My sword dipped not but a fraction of an inch.

The beast saw my hesitation, anticipated it even, and swiped at me with claws sharper than steel. Freya, however, saw me falter, too, and lunged forward, springing off her wounded leg. She barely sank her teeth into the beast's arm when, without so much as flinching, it swatted her away with the opposite paw-hand. Freya's blood and fur splattered across the dirt path and the nearby wolves.

The she-wolf yelped as the beast flung her against a tree in one swift motion. She collapsed with a shrill whine. Her sons, however, leapt upon the monster and tore at its flesh with a fury I had never witnessed from them. Ada's fury surpassed theirs by far, however, and she tore chunk after chunk of flesh from the monster's body, dancing gracefully to dodge the monster's swiping claws.

Time moved slowly. The seconds of battle felt like hours. The beast failed to throw off his new attackers, and though it struck at them with the tips of its claws, the wolves did not let up. I, for my part, only knew my pack was under attack, as were the charges I had sworn to protect, so I shook off the hesitation that had nearly cost me my life. I raised my blade and scented for my wolves to pull the beast to its knees. With every ounce of strength, I swung my blade in a crescent arc and screamed with primal fury.

Only the trail of light the blade emitted was visible as it cut through the air. It was that of a shooting star burning its way across the sky as it crashed to earth. The brilliant trail sped on, and the blade cut through the top half of the feral's head. Gore and a fountain of blood exploded across my face as the blade and I screamed in unison. With an impossibly greater speed, I swung the sword back around to sever what remained of the beast's head from its shoulders.

The monster's headless corpse fell to the ground in a twitching heap as the wolves continued tearing at the body until they realized it had died.

Aros was curled up on the ground, attempting to hide a half-transformed arm under his body as he, too, screamed in rage and agony. Before I could help the lad, though, the second feral roared.

It soared over the covered wagon. This time, the horses bolted, and even Ela, who had carried me through many dangers, was overcome by the terror. As the wheels rolled, I barely managed to pull Aros away from them before they dragged him away.

The earth shook as the feral landed near where its packmate and brother had fallen. It opened its maw and screamed, its demonic eyes piercing me with their hellish gaze. It said nothing, scented nothing.

My blood surged as I swung at the beast. It dodged my blow and slashed at me, knocking my blade from my hand. The blade flew long and landed in the ditch.

The monster swung at me again, and I barely managed to roll aside in time to avoid the blow. I howled as my blood boiled and, in a heartbeat, I was in the throes of transformation, unable to contain my rage any longer. My armor's straps burst, plates clattered to the ground, and my clothing was torn to shreds. I stood level with the beast now and roared with as much ferocity as I could muster. I would destroy this monster.

Though a non-lunar transformation afforded me more control, the instinct to kill was overwhelming. I lunged on all fours, swiping claws blindly, but my feral son intercepted me and matched me blow for blow. Not even the wolves dared intervene as we tore into one another with tooth and claw. And, after not but a few blows, our claws and fur dripped with the other's blood as well as our own.

As we fought, I made no headway in the battle. I gained no ground against my son and, already tired—short as my first duel had been—the feral surged. I fell backward, the feral on top of me, and I knew then I would die.

The beast opened its maw to clamp its fangs upon my throat and tear it out, and I tried vainly to fight as death stared me in the face. Blood—surely my own—splashed across my face.

A clawed hand burst from the feral's chest, and the monster's ribs exploded outward like a bloody flower in bloom. Clutched in this clawed hand was the beast's still-beating heart, and when the hand withdrew, the feral collapsed upon me.

My son's ferocious head landed next to mine, eyes wide open in death, and blood poured from its maw. Above me, my truer son, Aros, held the beast's heart in his claws.

The heart slipped to the ground, and Aros contemplated me with glowing eyes. He howled and collapsed as he shifted to his human form. I, too, reverted and lay naked and crushed under the beast. My pack came cautiously toward the monster and dragged its corpse away.

I crawled to Aros' unconscious frame but found him unharmed, so I rushed to Freya's side. Her breath came out in gasps, and blood dripped from her muzzle and nose, and even more gurgled and spluttered from the gaping wound in her side. I pulled at my disheveled hair as I knelt over my friend's mangled body. She was beyond earthly help.

I threw myself down next to her and buried my hands and face in her matted, bloody fur. I could only weep.

Freya, ever my comforter and companion, scented hazy images of memories from long ago.

"Freya, I'm sorry. If I hadn't hurt you before ... if I hadn't faltered now ... if I hadn't—"

She whined and scented the image of an alpha wolf consoling a pup who had botched a hunt and the image of a she-wolf protecting her pups from a rival pack.

I could say nothing in response. The weight of my guilt strangled my voice and thoughts.

My dear friend scented a vague image—a warm, comfortable den, and a man and wolf huddled together.

"*Is this us?*" I scented. "*Or—*"

Before I finished, she breathed her last.

I threw my head back and unleashed a bestial, agonized scream that shook the earth. My pack surrounded Freya with me and howled dolefully toward Heaven. When I had emptied my lungs, I filled them once more and shouted again into the heavens before collapsing onto my friend's still warm body.

I was oblivious to the cold of the early evening, which chilled my naked body to the bone. I was oblivious to the calls of my wards and the scents of my pack. I was dead to the world.

I carried Freya into the winter-dead woods that were coming back to life again. I bore her deep within until I found a rapidly flowing stream. There, I laid her. It was the custom of wolves to leave their companions' bodies for the earth to consume, but it was nevertheless considered a particularly blessed death if one died near living water. Thus, I laid her there and let her blood flow into the stream to be whisked away. This was the greatest honor I could show my friend in death.

In that moment, I felt no happiness to have laid her in an honorable place, though. I felt naught but sorrow. I closed my eyes, buried my face in her fur, and wept the bitterest tears I had shed since my mother and father had died. They were the bitterest tears in this lifetime's worth of years.

When my eyes could pour forth no more, though my soul continued to weep, I embraced her once more and kissed her head. Her blood covered me from head to toe, covering my scars and the gore from my slaughtered children of sin.

I stroked her head one final time and closed her eyes in final slumber. "Luváli take you, dearest friend."

RRR

Chapter XXIV

Concerning what I have said up till now, let me make but one addendum: There is one magic, and one alone, that is truly divine. It is as much empowered by blood as any black magic, but it is mightier and pure, and the punishment for trifling with this magic is rightly most severe. About this magic, however, there are few who are qualified to speak, and I do not dare number myself among them.

— From the anonymous pamphlet
Concerning So-Called White Magic

R

I returned to where her life had ended, and though the chill of the quickly falling night should have made me shake and shiver, something of her warmth remained with me.

Upon the road lay the corpses of my sons, eviscerated, mangled, bloody. Huddled together amid the ruins of my sin was Harvald's family, all of whom stood over Aros, whose nakedness was covered by his blood-stained cloak.

Harvald and Gale waved their hands and jabbed their fingers at one another, their son, and toward the forest where I had gone. I could not, however, understand anything they said over the shrill cries of the youngest children, especially Kari, who screamed incessantly. Haldis and Arve both stared in dumbfounded horror at the surrounding carnage.

Of all the family, only Erika noticed my return, and she followed my every step with her soft blue eyes. Of all her family, she alone was unfazed. Of all her family, only her eyes bore no anger toward me nor terror at the horrors they had beheld. No, but they contained that strange something, that powerful impetus or desire beyond feeling or emotion, which was directed only at me. However, I still did not know what it was. Indeed, I feared it.

When I felt her eyes upon me, when I felt the weight of that ... *something*, and of her knowingness, I fled. I covered my nakedness with bloody hands and ran headlong down the road. But her eyes continued to transfix me.

Only when I was out of sight did I start to shiver, the cold ravaging my body. I stopped running and drifted along the road like a shade, unsure where I was going. I eventually came upon our caravan, which had come to a halt in the road, none the worse from our misadventure.

I scented calming thoughts, hoping the horses would understand something of what I meant. Thankfully, none of the horses bolted, though this was more likely due to Ela having planted herself firmly in the middle of the road. She had always been a reliable one.

I found my ceremonial clothes—the only other clothes I had that I could wear—in the back of the wagon and donned them. The spotless, finely cut fabric turned red as it absorbed the blood—my own, my sons', my friend's—that covered me. Only the ceremonial blade did I leave behind among my possessions. I wanted no more blood on my hands.

Now dressed, I turned the caravan around and coaxed the horses forward. Sure they would keep going the short distance back without a driver, I checked Ela.

Her saddle was still secure, and the war horse's demeanor was calm. For her, it was as if nothing at all had happened. I could have ridden her anywhere.

I gripped the saddle horn, put a foot in the stirrup, but did not mount. I did not know where to go, whether back or onward, whether to face rejection from these people or to return to self-hatred alone. The question was not which was better—that would imply there was a choice I believed was good—but which was more needful.

I sighed, heaving myself into the saddle. I had made up my mind.

Ela arched her back and nickered as I slouched in the saddle.

"I'm not sure I can do this with my head held high, Ela."

She threw her head back, shaking her mane with a snort. She trotted without any signal on my part, her head still held high, as we returned to the place where we had begun.

She stopped some twenty paces from the bloody battlefield, and I dismounted and closed the gap between Harvald's family and myself on foot. I stopped at the place where my sons of sin lay. What remained of their mangled corpses—too gruesome even for me to countenance—lay on either side of the road and strewn about the road itself. They formed a kind of bloody chasm between my charges and me, a chasm which was, from my perspective, so fathomless it would never be surmounted or escaped. But I wasn't there to escape. I was there to tell these people, who were being pulled down into it, to let me sink and so save themselves.

From the carmine darkness all around, I spoke, "You must release me from my vow if I am to leave you, if you are to be free of me." The wind blew over me, bearing the cold of the coming night.

Nobody replied. All but Erika stared into the bloody black abyss before them, looking at me with ... hatred, horror, disgust. I was no stranger to odious gazes, but I had always borne up under them, shrugging them off. This collective stare, however, weighed upon and broke me. I sank deeper still into my abyss.

Finally, Harvald stepped forward. "Think 'twill be so simple, do you? Think you can have us speak some words and 'twill be over for you, you monster?"

An icy arrow pierced my gut. My whole body bowed forward in pain.

"To the devils with that, and to the devils with you, too." Harvald spat upon the ground. "But no, I'll no release you so easily from your vow. I want answers."

I could not meet his piercing gaze. "And you shall have them."

"You're damn right I will." He spat again.

Nobody else dared to look at me as Harvald inveighed against me. Nobody except Erika.

"First, you tell me what the devils you are"—he paused to spit yet again—"and what these things that call you *father* are." He dropped his gaze to where Aros sat, a prisoner at the feet of his captor, still wrapped in his gory cloak and trembling. "And, more important, you'll tell ..." He sniffed and wiped what I was certain was a tear from his eyes. "You'll tell me what you did to my boy." Harvald now wiped visible tears from his eyes, but he stopped as he jerked his head up to glare at me with blazing fire in his eyes. "Damn you, you'll tell me why. Why you've stolen him from us ... from me.

Because that is why you came 'tall, ain't it? You wanted my boy."

I hung my head and said nothing.

"Tell me!"

I lifted my eyes from the abyss, stiffened my back, and confessed the whole truth. "You know what I am, Harvald. You said it yourself. I'm a monster. I'm a werewolf. I have always been one. And these ..." I forced myself to look upon the decapitated and disemboweled bodies of my sons as I stretched out my arms over the whole bloody expanse. "These are the sons of my sin. They are ferals, born from the sin of two werewolves. They were once four, then three, now one ... I have borne the weight of their existence, the weight of their sins, and the greater weight of slaying them, my sons. Aye, and I'll bear that guilt once more."

I let my hands fall by my sides and locked eyes with Harvald. "So, know, Harvald, that I would never rob you of your son. I could never inflict that misery on another. He is yours even now, not mine."

Harvald clenched his fists. "He's as much my son now as a devil because of what you've done to him."

Aros threw his hands up to clench at his wild hair and keened. His cloak fell from his shoulders, exposing his blood-covered arms and torso.

My heart broke for the lad, but I held back from running to embrace him.

"No, Harvald, he is still your son. I've done nothing to him. I've not taken him from you."

Aros' sobs echoed across the abyss.

"And he's no monster, Harvald, but he'll become one if you refuse him, if you hate him for what he is instead of loving him despite it."

Harvald glanced down at his firstborn son, whom he had once loved, and paused. He put out a hand from under his cloak to touch the boy but stopped short, turning back to me. "Then what ...? How ...?"

I entered deeper into the abyss. "He bears a curse—you've seen it, Harvald, so don't ask me *what*—and all here, your son and I included, would agree it's an awful curse." I cast a pitiful glance at Aros then at his family, who all stared at me with fearful eyes. "But it is a curse he bears not by his own choice, nor by any man's choice. It doesn't make what he is right—that it's all against his will—but you must see how troubled he is by it. Now you know why he hid from you all those weeks in the Seat." I took another ponderous step, crushing the blood of my sin underfoot.

"And I could explain the mechanism—the way the planets, moon, and stars crossed—that caused the curse to be, but would it matter? I could even tell you, if I wanted, the moment, the exact degree of arc of every star between your zenith and the horizon, when you begot your son and when he was born, but would it matter?" Another step.

Harvald shook his head. "Why should that no matter? Should we no have a right to know the fault in our stars?"

I shook my head. "If knowing would change anything, I would tell you. But your son isn't some *thing* you made, Harvald. He's not some object that, when you know the flaw in it, you can undo it and build it all anew. Neither you, nor I, nor anyone, can undo what happened all those years ago—by the Two, how I wish there were some way—and no amount of time will end it, except by some miracle. No, but knowing *how* merely tells us with certainty what now is."

I took yet another step forward, and Harvald puffed out his chest.

He huffed, arms crossed. "Then at least tell me why. Tell me what all this serves." He looked down at Aros once more. "Then I'll let you go ..."

I stopped again. "*Why?* You want to know *why*?" I nearly laughed. "Am I a god, Harvald, to turn tragedy into joy by giving evil meaning and purpose? To transmogrify evil, the cruelty of the world, and of the Moon and Stars, into something good like an alchemist with his stones? That's what you want, isn't it? For me to say, 'At least it will lead to something meaningful? At least it will serve some purpose?'"

I paused to let him respond. He did not.

"But no, I can't tell you *why*. I don't know the answer. I wish I did ... I've spent my whole life trying to answer this question, yet I've still no conclusion. No, even after lifetimes of searching ...

"I don't know what purpose this curse serves, if any at all. If I'm honest, at times, I don't think there's any real meaning to any of it. I would be remiss to find any reason or purpose in all the damage"—I took in the sight of the eviscerated bodies of my sons—"and evil I've caused because of what I am."

Harvald sucked in a great breath, puffing out his chest once more in defiance. Before he spoke, though, I added, "No, but I don't deny there is an answer. The Two know, and maybe, one day, they'll reveal it. But now, the best you can do is to love your son despite all that he is, despite the burden he bears, the burden which he needs you to bear with him. The best you can do is to love, even when everything else is meaningless. It won't obliterate the vanity and futility of the evil you all now face, but it will at least cast some light into the darkness. It will, at least, provide some meaning where there once was none. Love bears its own meaning within itself."

I now stood not more than ten paces from Harvald, and a sudden courage filled my heart. "Now"—I spotted my longsword in the ditch, fetched it, and tossed the dimly glowing blade with the words *Týpte Orthôs* etched into it at Harvald's feet—"either love your son despite what he is or, if you can't, then love him by doing the merciful thing while he's still repentant."

Harvald took the blade.

Aros made no sound, even as the scratching of the blade against the gravel filled the air. The boy merely raised his blood-streaked face to mine. He knew the choice I laid before his father was the only one I could allow. The lad knew I would not let him suffer the hatred of his father.

Gale attempted to snatch the sword. "Harvald, he's our son. You canna—"

Harvald held her back and spoke with an unwavering voice. He raised the sword high above his head. The tip of the blade hung ponderously above his boy to pierce him with a swift, merciful blow. "This is my decision—"

I stared into Aros' eyes and scented the image of an alpha tending to his newborn pups. The boy closed his eyes and nodded, his face serene.

"—and I've made it." Harvald thrust the blade downward with incredible strength. It plunged down, piercing its target squarely. The blade grated and screamed as it plunged through and into the earth.

Aros saw the wavering blade sunken into the road. The lad raised his eyes, and I smiled back at him. Before Aros could rise, however, Harvald lifted his boy by his shoulders, wrapped his son in his own clean cloak, and embraced him.

Aros leaned into his father's embrace, resting his head, which was all that could be seen emerging from under his father's cloak, on Harvald's shoulder. Harvald held his son tighter still to shield his son's vision from the carnage, and he wept. Only then did Gale and the others embrace Aros, too.

I watched the family from my abyss of sin and felt a bittersweet joy. The boy would stand a chance in the world now, whether he remained with me or not. But I feared for the boy and his family. I knew firsthand what happened to the families of monsters like me.

A tinge of jealousy also arose in my heart. Was it a sin to feel this? It had been so long since I had felt that kind of fatherly embrace, and the prospect of departing to return to solitude left me hollow. *But that is your lot, your penance, for the choices you have made,* a voice whispered.

That is the cost of your salvation, another whispered.

As those voices whispered to me, my father's voice rose above them. *Do not listen to them, son. Behold ...*

"Rune."

I started as Harvald barked my name for what had likely been the third or fourth time. His entire family now stood behind him again, all watching me as I stared into space.

I fixed my gaze on Harvald, who continued to hold his boy. There was no malice in his voice when he spoke my name, nor was there any hatred in his eyes as he looked at me.

"I release you from your vow. You can retu—"

"No, Da!" Aros and Erika both shouted with one mind.

Aros pushed back from his father ever so slightly. "Please, do no—"

"You must no send him away, Da," Erika cried, running up from behind to grab her father's arm.

I understood nothing else as their cries blended in protest.

"Enough, the both of you." He frowned at his two eldest children. "This is his wish, and I told him I would grant him—"

"Please, Da, you canna do this." Erika pulled upon her father's arm. "Why would you send him aw—"

Harvald's glare silenced his daughter, but his irritation was quickly replaced by a sorrowful frown. "'Tis no I who wants this, Erika, lass. 'Tis Ru—"

At once, Erika broke away from her father and ran toward me with arms wide. She threw herself at me, nearly knocking me flat. Great tears poured from her eyes, and she buried her face into the folds of my dress shirt. Her tears flowed down my arms and pierced the fabric of my bloodied clothes to wash over my skin. "Oh, please, Rune, do no leave us."

I gaped at the young woman, utterly perplexed. I could neither push her away nor return her embrace, for she had so tightly wrapped her arms around me.

"Erika—"

"Please, do no leave us. Do no leave my brother, or ... me."

I could not allow this. It had to end here.

"Erika ..." *Did she not understand what she had just witnessed?* "Don't you understand what I am?"

Rather than let go of me, she embraced me even more tightly, if such were even possible. " 'Course I do," she whispered into my ear. "That night before we arrived at East Laketon, when I sat by you throughout the night, you said things … You started"—she stumbled over the words, as if unable to fathom the depths of my darkness—"to change."

Her words stung me, but before I could explain, she went on.

"But you cried out. You wept, begged for help … I put my hand upon your face, and you stopped siezin'. You were at peace again." She let go and ceased to whisper her secret knowledge. Her eyes shone not with the dark light of the moon but with sunlight.

I averted my gaze, terrified by the steadfastness of her own.

"Then you know why I can't stay in Ebria." I pushed her away, but her grip was indomitable. "You know why I have to leave as soon as I can."

"But … but I love you, Rune. Can you no see that? Did you no understand the things I said and did these past weeks and months? Did you no see how I looked at you?"

I shook my head and cringed back into the abyss. "You don't love me, Erika. You feel what you feel because my nature ensnares people, like it did your sister before I broke that off, too. If not that, then you love what I did for you. You love an idea, an imaginary form of what you think I am. Even if your love were true"—I turned my face away—"I couldn't let you love me, not while I am what I am."

She spun me and placed her hands upon my bloody cheeks. "You're wron', Rune." She blushed but regained her composure. "W-when I first met you, I did no think much of your kindness—the kindness of men often turns to wrath. Nor did I, at least at first, love you for your looks—I saw how tortured your body is—though now I can see beyond your scars.

"Nor did I love you 'cause of your loyalty, for I saw how e'en your best efforts could fail. When you left that night in East Laketon ... when they took my brothers ... I wanted to hate you for what you did, for what happened to my brothers. But I couldna stop lovin' you. That is why I wouldna speak to you for so lon'. I did no understand what I felt for you. I ..." Her cheeks grew red again, and she became silent. She slipped a gloved hand into mine. "So, no, Rune, I do no love some ideal, and I do no love you for somethin' other than what you are, scars 'n all. But I do love you ... There's no explainin' nor stoppin' it. After I was around you, I fell in love for no other reason than that you were there."

She stroked my bearded cheek with her other hand, completely undisturbed by the blood and gore stuck in my beard. "If you do no wish to believe my love, if 'tall seems too good to be true, then 'tis what 'tis, but my love is still true. If you want to reject me because you believe yourself unlovable, fine, but I'll continue to love you, anyway. Aye, I may go on and marry another man—I may love him, too, in the way a wife is to love her husband—but you're the one I want."

I held her hand against my cheek. "I can't give you a normal life, Erika. People like me, we can't ... I'll never ..." I lowered her hand. "I can't promise I'll stop being as I am, that I'll get better. I can only promise, at least in this moment, that I don't desire to be what I am. I know that isn't much of a promise at all—"

She put a finger to my lips. "And again, though I hope, and deep in my heart know, you'll one day be different, better, more … somehow … I love you e'en so."

"And if I … if I cease to love you? If I hurt you, being as I am?"

"If you cease to love me, I'll no force you to remain. You'd no be my slave, Rune. And if you hurt me … what is there that love canna heal? But if you persist in hatin' me, if you feel no sorrow for hurtin' me, then you're simply sayin' you do no desire to be loved any longer, and we'll go our ways. Though, no 'cause I ceased to love, but because you ceased to want me."

Great sorrow weighed upon me as she spoke, for she was a fool to me.

"Don't you understand what you're giving up by loving me? Don't you understand what the cost to you will be? To your family?"

"There is no love without sacrifice, Rune."

My knees grew weak at those words, and I fell into her expectant arms, leaning my head upon her shoulder. "You are too great for me."

She raised me up, and we held one another.

"If I love you, Erika, it will only be what you have poured into me. That is all I can give. That is all I have. But I will give it, for it is life."

She took my hand, and we returned to her family—my family—together.

On both sides of the road were the carcasses of my former life, and though there was yet one more son, it did not bother me to know it.

Before anyone spoke to me, Erika took a small skin of water from the ground and, pouring it into her hand, she washed my gore-covered face. She poured the water upon my hands and washed them clean, too. Only then did she present me to her family as family.

Seeing me with their daughter, how our hands were entwined, Gale and Harvald smiled at me, then at Erika, and then at one another.

Before I could explain, Harvald laughed. "Ha! Well, 'tis 'bout time you realized she was pinin' for you, Rune! I suppose you'll be reconsiderin' your plans to go back to your little town now, eh? I'll no see her taken away from me so swiftly as a week and some days from now."

"Aye," Gale said, "we're glad to see you're no as blind as we all feared, Rune."

R

That night, after we traveled out of the sight of the battle and settled anew, there was surprisingly little discussion about what Aros and I were. Even when I took a moment to explain what the effects of living with us would be—the inevitable secret keeping, the extended lives, the Triduum's pull, and all—nobody batted an eye. Everyone, even the youngest, acknowledged it. They expressed whatever bewilderment they felt, but they all confirmed their unwavering love for us. Harvald had spoken for them all when he had received his son. Indeed, what Aros and I had both feared—that we would either be hated and treated with disgust and contempt or, as I had feared, that we would be looked on with awe—never came to be. There was only love, the same kind of love Erika was full of to overflowing.

RRR

Chapter XXV

Blessed is he that finds a wife; more blessed still is he that finds a wife who willingly bears his faults for love's sake.

— From a hierodule's commentary on
the *Canticum*

R

We journeyed on the next morning, sorrowful over having lost one of our own but rejoicing all the while that she yet lived on, and not in our hearts alone. Aros, likewise, though he battled still against his innate anxieties, for which there was no earthly cure, found great solace in his father. I, too, found solace in them, but especially in Erika and her love. I racked my brain for the last days of our journey to find a rational explanation for it, but there was none. Though I had often found comfort in understanding, I found greater comfort still in knowing her love was beyond comprehension. It was of her heart and soul.

Every night on the road, we discussed our wedding. Though, if truth be told, our discussions were more like monologues. To these monologues, which assumed, albeit rightly, that my finances were as limitless as I had led everyone to believe, Harvald had encouraged me to say one thing, "Aye, love," at regular intervals. For that wise counsel, I am indebted to him even now.

The day we arrived in Ebria was joyous for all, but most especially for me. That day was less the end of a troubled journey, and more the start of something new. At once, Erika and I set our wedding plans in place at the temple, and we prepared to have our home built on the shore of a quiet lake near to the city. At Erika's insistence, we invited the young nobleman, whom Haldis never ceased to speak of fondly, and I, for my part, invited Ulfric.

His reply read:

> *Brother,*
>
> *I'm sorry to hear of your encounter with your sons but am glad you, at least, came out alive. Freya, however, will be sorely missed. I know how much she meant to you. Still, I'm glad you found a new companion.*
>
> *My staff also sends their congratulations. I think they had a bet going to see how long it would take for this news to arrive. Even I could see how she loved you. Anyway, aye, I'll be there. My business was going to take me south, anyway.*
>
> *Yours,*
>
> *U.*

I could not help but laugh. Everyone, it seemed, even down to the hired hands, had seen what I had not. People often say love is blind, but it was I who had been blind to love.

Meanwhile, as Erika organized the wedding with Gale and Haldis, Aros and I were quick to establish a practice serving Ebria's poorer citizens. We charged them nothing—what need for money did I have?—and I paid Aros out of my own wealth. Thus, Aros continued in his studies, and I doubt any apprentice had ever seen such an array of ailments in so short a time as Aros did.

More joyous still, on the day of our arrival, Ragnar told me Ada had conceived. The scent-images my pack exchanged were too potent and profound to describe in human words. Nevertheless, I will try. They were images of light itself come alive, of hopes that had once gone dark becoming bright once more. No more did the pack mourn Freya, for she had helped to bring this miracle to pass.

When I asked Ada about her litter, she replied there were seven inside her—four girls and three boys—and each was already mightier than she could have hoped. Each would be under my protection, I promised, and her firstborn daughter would be called "Freya" by men. She welcomed this but asked how Freya would be called among wolves. Though this was rightfully Ragnar's decision, he, too, deferred to me.

Her wolf-name would be Red-Flower-Blossoming-in-Barren-Land-through-which-Streams-of-Water-Flow. The Red Flower, I scented, was she who dropped her seeds in the stream, which bore them into a river that went to the sea. Wherever the stream, river, and sea stretched, more red flowers grew. It was, Ragnar and Ada replied, the perfect name.

After this, time went too swiftly to recount. The next thing I truly remember with any clarity was when I stood in the temple, a blindfold over my eyes. Though I could not see her, I sensed Erika by my side, a veil over her eyes, too. The priest took a string so soft and fine that it felt like nothing upon our skin. With it, he bound our wrists, our arms, and our bodies. He asked us what we saw, and we replied, "Nothing, Father."

He asked us what we felt upon our skin, and again we replied, "Nothing, Father."

He asked if we knew what it was with which he bound us, or whence it came. We replied in all sincerity, "No, Father."

He finally asked if we could free ourselves from the bond. Though Erika and I both struggled to break the fine cord, we could not. Thus, we replied, "We cannot, Father."

"Such is love, dear children. You may not see it. You may not always feel it. You may not know whence it comes or from what it is made. Yet, when it binds you, you cannot break free, nor can you be without it. Indeed"—he lifted my blindfold and Erika's veil—"in marriage, love binds two utterly disparate beings, beings as different as darkness"—this priest, who had heard my confession after our arrival in Ebria, looked at me—"is from light. Aye, in marriage, though something ends, something greater begins."

R

As Erika and I walked hand-in-hand into the banquet hall of Ebria's greatest inn, the crowd of guests—Harvald and his family, Gale's cousins and their families, Ulfric, and as many of the townsfolk as desired to come—erupted into a great cheer. We took the traditional place at the head table, looked out over the crowd, and waited for the priest to come forward for the blessing. When the *amen* resounded throughout the hall, a sudden murmur rippled from the back toward the front and, as if all shared one mind, a whoop, holler, and unintelligible shout resounded.

I pulled my bride close with a sense of urgency that surprised even me, and I pressed my lips to hers. The crowd grew even louder as she returned my embrace, wrapping her arms around my shoulders to return the kiss with a ferocity that surpassed even my own.

When we finally released one another, the wine bearers wended their ways through the crowd until everyone had a cup overflowing.

Erika placed her hand on the table near her cup, and I placed my hand upon hers.

A hush fell over the crowd. Every eye was upon us as I stroked my bride's hand, took her cup, lifted it to her lips, and gave her to drink no more than a sip. I set her cup down and placed my hand near my cup, and she then did the same for me.

The wine bearer brought forth a large, empty goblet and great pitcher of water, which he set on the table between our cups.

Erika took her cup, and I, my own. We poured our cups into the one, saying in unison, "No longer two, but one." We each placed a hand upon the one cup and raised it to our lips.

Over the brim, I locked eyes with my wife, and she returned the gaze. I tipped the cup ever so slightly, and she drank of it as I said, "This cup is my love for you, and it will never run dry."

She then tipped the cup toward me, and I drank as she said, "And this cup is my love for you. 'Twill ne'er run dry."

Setting the cup down together, I took the pitcher of water and cut the wine so the cup was full again to the brim. Never would the cup, no matter how thinly the wine was cut, be truly emptied of the wine that had been mixed from our two cups. Never would the cup go dry that night.

By the night's end, the face of every guest, of my bride, and even my own, was flushed. Many of the men had stripped off their jerkins and now danced in long-sleeved under-tunics or were entirely bare-chested. Most of the women, even those who normally would have cried scandal, had hiked up their skirts and pinned them in place, bearing ankles and calves as they danced throughout the inn's hall. Every guest had kicked off their shoes and boots and, some, their stockings, to dance with as much freedom as possible.

Even my bride and I did the same when our first dance concluded and the band struck up a wild tune. Without a second thought, Erika kicked her shoes to one side and held up her skirts to spin with a great flourish in front of me before holding out a hand toward me as an invitation.

I did the same, flinging my high boots, and eventually dress tunic, aside. I placed one hand in hers and another around her waist, and we danced the length of the hall—the dance lessons before the masquerade had paid off. Our hearts beat in time to the frenetic beat, and the world became a dizzying blur as we whirled around the room.

Sweat poured down my face and soaked my under-shirt through, and my hair hung about my face wildly, my neat ponytail undone. Under any other circumstance, I would have been embarrassed to be seen in such disarray, but tonight, this was not a sign of disorder but of love.

Guests drunker than I joked that, if I had danced any harder, there would be no sweat to break in the sheets, and though those words would have been repugnant to me on any other night—spoken as they were in front of my bride—tonight, I could only take them as a strange kind of well-wishing. Even my wife and mother-in-law could not contain their laughter when they looked at me and saw the wild grin on my face.

The band played the traditional last dance, a tune called "Drink Thy Fill of Love," and my Erika put her head upon my shoulder and whispered the ancient words, "Kiss me with the kisses of thy mouth, for thy love is better than wine."

I whispered in return, "Behold, thou art fair, my love."

"Aye, and our bed shall be green."

I embraced her more tightly still and obliged her request. There we remained as the world danced on around us.

When the final song faded, we returned to our seats. Our unified drinking cup, which had been filled so many times over that only water could be tasted and seen, was now filled anew with the best wine of the night.

When all who remained with us through the evening had returned to their seats, Harvald came forward, a cup in hand. "Honored guests, let us raise our glasses to this couple. May their cup be ever full." Harvald thrust his glass high, and wine sloshed over the edges to splash onto the floor.

Everyone in the hall did likewise, shouting, "Hear, hear."

As they drank their last, Erika and I lifted our cup once more. Our eyes met, and I tipped the cup toward her, and she toward me. We each drank a small sip and set the cup back on the table.

Before I could lift my bride into my arms, she leapt into them. Though I was nearly thrown off my feet, I caught her and carried her away. As I did, the entire hall burst one final time into applause and cheers.

R

As I carried my bride across the threshold, I gazed down at her, and she at me. I wondered, as I drew near to our turned-down marriage bed, if she could hear my heart racing, if she could sense how nervous and afraid I was of the change that was soon to come about between us. She, however, hardly looked nervous at all.

When I laid her upon the bed, I collapsed beside her. She smiled at me, and I smiled, too, though I must have looked somewhat dazed.

"What?" She giggled.

"Uh ... Well, do you ...? I mean, if you want ..." Never had I been so tongue-tied when I wanted to bed a woman as I was on that night. It was as if I were a boy again. My face grew so red that there was no doubt she had noticed. "You aren't tired, are you?"

Erika rolled her eyes and laughed softly before wrapping her arms around me. "No. Are you?"

I swallowed hard and shook my head.

"Good." She rose and stepped away, her back toward me. She pulled her long, loose locks of hair over her shoulder. "So, come and help me out of this dress, dear husband."

Enraptured by her voice, I placed my hands upon her hips, and she set her hands upon them, too. As she leaned back into me, I placed my cheek against her own. Her hair covered me as I kissed her shoulder and inhaled her scent—almonds, milk, honey.

I slipped my hands down and rested them upon her thighs. I inhaled deeply again as I savored the scent and taste of her skin. She sighed and leaned her head back against my shoulder, exposing her entire neck to me. The wolf in me knew there was no greater sign of trust. Except, perhaps, one ...

I moved deftly as I unlaced the ornate, white, leather girdle she wore around her waist. As it fell, I untied the laces of her dress. Over every new bit of smooth, life-giving flesh,

I allowed my calloused hands to wander freely. Every curve, every mark, every little groove and rise, I traced them upon the canvas of my mind. With every new inch of skin, she would remind me in a whisper or a sigh how much she loved me.

With the last tie undone, I freed her from her lacey chrysalis with tender care. The most beautiful sight I had ever seen emerged.

In a fit of passion, I embraced her and bit her neck all too harshly. Realizing, though, what I had done, I lavished kisses upon the tiny wound. "Forgive me."

She replied that even my missteps were nothing to her.

Absolved, I eagerly freed her from the last stitch, but she did not face me until I prompted her.

She was a rose, unblemished and untouched by sinful hands, and full of sublime beauty too rich for human words.

Blinded and unable to take in any more of her brightness, I shut my eyes, and my lips found hers.

There we stood, embracing one another, savoring the taste of one another's kisses. This embrace … it wasn't all claws and teeth as things had been with Mara. That had not been love but only passion.

As I dreamed of those dark, former days, I wept.

Erika wiped away my tears. "Rune?" She placed her hands on my hips, pulling me close.

I sniffed but then smiled as I beheld her beautiful face. "I thought of how dark my world once was … often still is …" I broke our gaze, but she gently guided me to set my eyes on hers again. "But you …" I stroked her cheek. "You're bright."

She raised her hand to touch my cheek and ran her fingers through my beard.

"I thought of how long it had been since I had loved … been loved by anyone … It had been so long that I had nearly forgotten what love was at all. All I knew was passion, pain, and lust, but—"

She silenced me with a kiss and brought my head to rest on her shoulder. She, too, rested her head upon mine, and we swayed back and forth in a dance all our own.

I listened to her heartbeat and breath, and I guarded those sounds away in my memory for all time.

After a few quiet moments, I gazed upon her face. Her delicate cheeks and perfectly rounded nose, her smile, freckles, and dimples … I stored these images away. I gently traced out her neckline and collarbone with my finger.

As I lavished kisses upon her, the beast inside me howled. I nearly cried out, but Erika placed her arms around my neck. She ran her hands through my long, sweat-damp hair and leaned forward to lavish my head with kisses. Her love subdued the beast, and it left me for a time.

I placed my hands upon her hips and pulled her close. She, in turn, took the corners of my undertunic and crooked it over my head. But I grabbed her hands and lowered them. I thought of how perfect she was—how flawless, undefiled, and holy—and of how I was flawed, broken by the scars of so much sin. I grasped her wrists in my hands to stop her from undressing me, though I knew at once I held her too tightly. She did not cry out or struggle.

It was my second misstep that night, but she did not chasten me.

I released her, and my face fell in shame. I hunched over, covering my face with one hand as I wrapped the other around my chest.

She touched my arm, but I resisted her promptings at first. Her persistence won out, though I kept my eyes lowered. The splendor of her beauty made me shudder.

"I don't want you to see me. I'm ashamed. You are flawless ... I ... I am defiled. Please"—I fell to my knees before my queen—"do not look at me."

She lifted me to my feet. "I knew 'bout every one of your scars before I married you. Why would they now frighten me, Rune?"

"It's not you they will frighten, but me. Your beauty ... it will destroy me."

She kissed me with great force, and I nearly fell back. "Oh, Rune, e'en if my beauty destroys you, do you believe my love would no rebuild you?"

"Please, don't look at my scars."

She pulled me close and whispered another ancient word, "Thou art all fair, my love; there shall be no spot in thee."

At those words, my fear faded. In a moment, she stripped me of my tunic. I stood before my lover, naked and unashamed, as she swept her eyes over me. She breathed in the scent of my hair and neck with a sigh—wood smoke and pine. She, too, tasted and even bit my shoulders. She touched the first scar upon my back.

A memory invaded my mind with demonic force. I was taken away from my marriage chamber and transported back to the chamber of the elven queen.

I stood shackled to the floor at the foot of her bed where she lay and, with a wave of her hand, her guard stripped me. She appraised me with her monstrous eyes and filled herself with the sight of my flesh.

With another gesture from that monster, the guard struck me with a whip. I cried. She, however, moaned with ecstasy and crawled from the bed to stand before me. She ran her fingers across my body, coating them in the blood of my wounds before dragging each of her long, bony fingers across her tongue.

Having tasted my blood, she threw herself back onto her bed and thrashed. She moaned and writhed in ecstasy.

I shivered as she motioned for me to join her. I refused. She screamed and compelled me with demonic magic empowered by my blood.

Her acrid smell filled my nose. Her nails and teeth ripped into my bare flesh, my back and shoulders, and tore through me. Her crooked heart beat in my ear as she forced me upon herself ...

But the queen, my true queen, was now before me, and I stood before her naked, trembling, tears streaming. I shook as she touched the scar, and I pulled away from her caress. I could not speak nor explain. I did not want to relive the memory again in retelling it. I wanted only to hide; a wounded, lone wolf without a pack to care for it.

Erika placed her hands in mine, which trembled for fear, sorrow, and pain. She kissed me and whispered. The sound sent a new shiver down my spine. "I will heal your wounds."

I clenched my hands, which intertwined with hers. She released them and turned me. She placed her fingers on the same scar. I stiffened.

A wave of pain rippled through me, the same as before.

She traced the scar with her fingers, and the pain faded at once. With her lips, she touched the puckered skin. She healed the wounds upon my soul. She did this to every scar, from my shoulders to my feet.

I had been anxious at the outset, but now, only the bliss of purity remained. She had destroyed me with her love, but she was so swift to rebuild me I did not even know I had died.

Now we embrace one another in silence. We say nothing, do nothing. We rest in each other. When we pull apart, our eyes meet.

I swallow hard, like a young, inexperienced man—no, not like *an inexperienced man, for I* am *truly such a man once more.*

My mouth goes dry. Erika, too, shows her first signs of trepidation.

Holding her hands, I open my mouth, but no words come. They aren't necessary.

Erika blushes and nods. I, too, blush, but no longer from the wine. Now I blush for the joy within.

I lay her down upon our bed and crawl next to her. We embrace one another, sighing and whispering endless words from deep within our secret hearts. They are words spoken in a language only two-become-one can understand. Aye, they understand, for husband and wife no longer have two hearts, but one. Indeed, the words which flow from there are understood only by the other, who is no longer other at all. The secret, hidden heart, then, ceases to be secret. Everything of mine is hers, and hers, mine. Her beauty is mine, and my ugliness her own, but she takes this unfair yet glorious exchange upon herself willingly ... knowingly.

In this infinite moment, it is not our senses, nor our hands, nor our lips, nor any part of our bodies that know the other. Rather, as we lie entangled, our two realities—no, our essences—merge, coalescing on a cosmic, divine level. We are one in body and soul ... Nay, we are something more, for to say body and soul is to make distinctions, but there is no distinction between us anymore.

There are no words for this union among men, though there is a rune—the signs for *rune* and *heart* bound inseparably together. This secret, this mystery, is a heavenly thing no man can utter, what it means to be united by love.

R

I do not remember if we slept or not. I remember only the ecstasy. Aye, and the only way I knew the night had come and gone was because the cock crowed, and because sunlight streamed in from a gap in the curtains.

Erika and I lay upon the bed, still entangled. My fingers were in her curling, auburn hair as she lay her head upon my chest, around which she wrapped her arms to run her fingers across my back. She smiled up at me, and I showered her head with kisses.

With my face buried in her lush hair, I inhaled deeply and whispered, "Good morning."

She put her hand on my cheek and pulled me in close for a passionate kiss. "Good mornin' "—she paused, as if practicing what she was about to say—"dear husband."

My heart leapt at those words. It was true and not a dream.

"I love you, dear wife."

She wrapped her arms more tightly around my chest. "And I, you, dear husband." She closed her eyes as if about to fall asleep but said, "Shall we go down and see 'bout breakfast?"

I smiled wryly at her. "I'm hungry only for you."

She laughed so hard that she snorted, which made me laugh in turn. She gave me a playful shove before wrestling me down upon the bed.

"Men!" She sat on my chest, knees on my arms. "My mother warned me the night before last that you men only have your minds on two things—food and sex."

I laughed, unable to deny the truth of what she said. "Well, good wife, will you feed your husband, then? Or, must I starve to death this morning, though a banquet is so close at hand?" I lifted her off me and rolled with her across the bed.

We both laughed, wrestling and vying for supremacy. Eventually, our struggle was ended by a truce signed by our kisses and the same sweet lovers' words.

When we had taken our fill of love, we rose, stood at the washbasin, and washed one another in silence. What was there to say anymore between the two of us who had only one heart now?

R

When we entered the hall together, there was a round of cheering and applause from the guests who had remained through the night. We waved and sat down with Erika's family, and the crowd quieted down.

As I sat, Ulfric came up from behind me and placed a hand upon my shoulder. "Brother, I'm surprised to see you out of bed at all."

I laughed and pushed him away, and he sat down opposite me.

Though some of Erika's family had eaten already, she, Ulfric, and I ate from a platter of honey cakes and fruit that lay before us. Erika and I ate more than our fair share, though

Erika did so much more decorously than I, and nobody dared to interrupt us as we feasted.

Only when Erika and I put the last bites of food into our mouths did Harvald finally break the silence. "Worked up quite an appetite, eh?"

Aros choked on pipe smoke and sputtered violently, Arve spat tea across the table, and Haldis covered her mouth with a gasp. Erika and I both choked on the final bites of cake, Ulfric slapped the table with a hearty laugh, and Gale gasped, slamming a fist upon the table.

"Harvald Eiversson"—her face was red both with anger and embarrassment—"for the love of the Two. Surely, the wine is no still gone to your head, so need you be so shameless?"

Though he normally withered under her gaze, that morning, he only grew bolder. "Oh, come, Gale; you must remember how much you and I—but especially you—did eat the mornin' after our weddin' night."

Against her husband's allegations, Gale gave a sharp reply. But precisely what she said, and how he responded, was all thoroughly gone from my memory. All I can remember about the rest of that day is that Erika ever remained beside me. Indeed, there is little I remember at all from before that time.

RRR

Epilogue

ᚱ

I set the quill in the inkwell and wiped my hands with the ink-stained cloth upon my writing desk. The little journal I had taken from my home all those months ago was now full.

I pushed away from the desk and picked up Freya as she slept in my lap with her head upon my forearm. The pup did not stir as I laid her with Ada, who suckled her six remaining pups before the fire. Ragnar lay next to his mate and scented his contentment as I caressed him and Ada.

Raynor also lay nearby, and he cocked his head at me. *"Play?"*

"No," I replied aloud, "it's time for bed."

Raynor rushed to jump upon the bed, settling down squarely in the middle. He dug a burrow in the furs, and his single golden eye was soon all that showed.

Erika laughed behind me. "'Twill be nice when we've a bigger bed." She wrapped her arms around me from behind and lay her head on my shoulder.

The single-room hunting cabin Erika and I rented until our home was finished was scarcely big enough for two adults, let alone a pack of wolves, but we made do. Thankfully, Harvald and Arve had made good progress in these first weeks of spring at preparing the timbers for our home. With the help of additional hired hands, they would finish in no time.

I swung Erika around and embraced her. "Aye, it will."

"Did you finish your journal?"

"Mmhmm."

"Good." She kissed me. "No more late nights for you, then?"

"Only once a month …" I replied with mock seriousness. The first Tridua in Ebria had passed without incident—Aros' transformations and mine went unnoticed—and I no longer dreaded the thought of the full moon like before.

She smiled at me, her blue eyes heralding her love. "Right. Well, the next Triduum's a few days off still, so why do we no get to bed on time for once?"

I returned her smile, and she pulled me away, toward our bed.

RRR

About the Author

R

Gino C. R. Marchetti, II was born and raised in Minnesota, *dontcha know*. However, his studies have taken him across the country and around the world—Minnesota, Nevada, Indiana, Argentina, and Vatican City are all places he has called home at one time or another. Currently, however, Mr. Marchetti's feet are firmly planted in Fort Wayne, Indiana. There he serves as a Ph.D. graduate assistant, studying historical theology, specifically the development of mystical theology in the early modern period. He has two cats, Freja and Astrid, who excel at stepping on keyboards and knocking pens on the floor.

RRR